Vancouver 04.09

TURING'S DELIRIUM

for Susan: this novel about the end of the old order and the beginning of a new one

Edmundo

BOOKS BY EDMUNDO PAZ SOLDÁN

NOVELS

Turing's Delirium
The Matter of Desire
Sueños digitales
Río Fugitivo
Alrededor de la torre
Días de papel

SHORT STORIES

Amores imperfectos
Desapariciones
Las mascaras de la nada
Simulacros

ANTHOLOGY

Se habla español: Voces latinas en USA/Spanish Is Spoken Here
(edited with Alberto Fuguet)

CRITICAL WORKS

Alcides Arguedas y la narrativa de la nación enferma/Latin American Literature and Mass Media
(edited with Debra Castillo)

EDMUNDO PAZ SOLDÁN

TURING'S DELIRIUM

Translated by Lisa Carter

A Mariner Book
Houghton Mifflin Company
Boston • New York

First Mariner Books edition 2007

Visit our Web site: www.houghtonmifflinbooks.com.

Library of Congress Cataloging-in-Publication Data
Paz Soldán, Edmundo, date.
[Delirio de Turing. English]
Turing's delirium / Edmundo Paz Soldán ; translated by Lisa Carter.
p. cm.
ISBN-13: 978-0-618-54139-3
ISBN-10: 0-618-54139-X
I. Carter, Lisa. II. Title.
PQ7820.P39D4513 2006
863'.64—dc22 2005024726

ISBN-13: 978-0-618-87259-6 (pbk.)
ISBN-10: 0-618-87259-0 (pbk.)

Book design by Melissa Lotfy

Printed in the United States of America

MP 10 9 8 7 6 5 4 3 2 1

To Tammy and Gabriel,
this time stolen from you,
now finally returned

To my brother Marcelo,
who only knows how to give

Inútil observar que el mejor volumen de los muchos hexágonos que administro se titula *Trueno peinado,* y otro *El calambre de yeso* y otro *Axaxaxas mlö.* Esas proposiciones, a primera vista incoherentes, sin duda son capaces de una justificación criptográfica o alegórica; esa justificación es verbal y, *ex hypothesi,* ya figura en la Biblioteca. No puedo combinar unos caracteres *dhcmrlchtdj* que la divina Biblioteca no haya previsto y que en alguna de sus lenguas secretas no encierren un terrible sentido. Nadie puede articular una sílaba que no esté llena de ternuras y temores; que no sea en alguno de esos lenguajes el nombre poderoso de un dios.

— JORGE LUIS BORGES, *La Biblioteca de Babel*

The king hath note of all that they intend,
By interception which they dream not of.

— WILLIAM SHAKESPEARE, *Henry V*

All information looks like noise until you break the code.

— NEAL STEPHENSON, *Snow Crash*

PART I

chapter 1

As soon as you turn your back on the uncertain sunrise and enter your office building, you cease to be Miguel Sáenz, the civil servant discernible behind the wrinkled gray suit, round, wire-rimmed glasses, and fearful gaze, and become Turing, decipherer of secrets, relentless pursuer of encoded messages, the pride of the Black Chamber.

You insert your electronic ID card into a slot. You are prompted for your password and type *ruth1*. The metal door opens and the world you unknowingly dreamed of as a child awaits you. Slowly, with measured steps, you enter a vaulted glass enclosure. Two policemen greet you formally. They see the color of your card—green, meaning Beyond Top Secret—without looking at it. It was all so much easier during Albert's time, when there were only two colors, yellow (Secret) and green. Then that smug Ramírez-Graham arrived (you had once called him "Mr. Ramírez" and he had corrected you: "Ramírez-Graham, please"), and card colors soon began to multiply. In less than a year, red (Top Secret), white (Not at All Secret), blue (Ultra), and orange (Ultra Priority) cards appeared. The color of your card indicates which parts of the building you have access to. Ramírez-Graham has the only purple card in existence, Ultra High Priority. In theory, there is only one area in the seven-story building for which the purple card is required: the Archive of Archives, a small section in the heart of the archives. Such proliferation is laughable. But you are not laughing;

you are still offended that some of your colleagues have Ultra and Ultra Priority cards and can go where you cannot.

"Always so early, Mr. Sáenz."

"For as long as the old body holds out, captain."

The policemen know who you are; they have heard the stories about you. They don't understand what you do or how you do it, but still they respect you. Or perhaps they respect you *because* they don't understand what you do or how you do it.

You walk next to the wall where the great emblem of the Black Chamber hangs. It is a resplendent aluminum disk encircling a man bent over a desk, trying to decipher a message, and a condor holding a ribbon in its claws that bears the motto "Logic and Intuition" in Morse code. True, both are needed to penetrate the crypt of secret codes, but they aren't used in equal proportions. For you, at least, intuition is what lights the way, but the hard work is done by reason.

They don't understand what you do or how you do it, but still they respect you. What you do? Is it correct still to speak in the present tense? Your glory days, you have to admit, begin to fade in the expanse of time. For example, December 6, 1974, when you detected a cell of leftists who used phrases from Che Guevara's diary to encode messages; or September 17, 1976, when you were able to warn President Montenegro that an insurrection was brewing in the Cochabamba and Santa Cruz regiments; or December 25, 1981, when you deciphered messages from the Chilean government to its chargé d'affaires regarding water that was being diverted from a river along the border. There are many, many more, but since then your successes have been sporadic. Ramírez-Graham reassigned you, and although at first it seemed that your new job was a promotion, it actually distanced you from the action. As head of the Black Chamber's general archives, you have become a cryptanalyst who no longer analyzes codes.

Your steps echo down the hallway. You rub your hands together, trying to warm them. The country's return to democracy in the early 1980s didn't end the work that was done in this building, but it did minimize it. At first messages between unionists were intercepted, and then later on between drug traffickers, careless people who spoke on easily traceable radio frequencies and didn't even bother to code their messages. The 1990s brought sporadic work listening to opposition politicians on bugged telephones.

You were happy when Montenegro returned to power through democratic means; you thought that everything would change under his rule and your work would again become urgent. What a disappointment. There was no significant threat to national security as there had been during his dictatorship. You were forced to admit that times had changed. Even worse, during the last stretch of Montenegro's administration, the vice president, a charismatic technocrat — pardon the contradiction — with wide eyes and dimpled cheeks, had decided to reorganize the Black Chamber and turn it into the focal point of the fight against cyberterrorism. "This will pose one of the key challenges to the twenty-first century," he had said when he came to announce his initiative. "We must be prepared for what is to come." Immediately thereafter the vice president introduced Ramírez-Graham, the new director of the Black Chamber: "One of our countrymen who has succeeded abroad, a man who has left a promising career in the north to come and serve his country." A round of applause. He had annoyed you from the very start: the impeccable black suit, the well-polished loafers and neat haircut — he looked like some sleek businessman. Then he had opened his mouth and the bad impression only worsened. True, he might have had slightly darker skin than most, and somewhat Andean features, but he spoke Spanish with an American accent. It certainly didn't help when you discovered that he wasn't even born in Bolivia but was from Arlington, Virginia.

You search the walls for a sign of salvation. Around you are only silent structures, muted by the vigilance of a supervisor who believed it prudent that employees of the Black Chamber not be distracted. Aside from the aluminum emblem at the entrance, there are no signs or notices, no noise that might distract you in the endless search for the text that resides behind all texts. But you can find messages even on immaculate walls. It's simply a matter of looking for them. Your glasses are dirty — fingerprints, coffee stains — and the frame is twisted. There is a slight pain in your left eye caused by the lens bending at the wrong angle. For weeks you've been intending to make an appointment with the ophthalmologist.

Ramírez-Graham has been director of the Black Chamber for almost a year. He has fired a number of your colleagues and replaced them with young computer experts. Since you obviously don't fit in with his plans for a generational change, why haven't you been fired? You put yourself in his shoes: you can't be fired. After all, you are a living archive, a repository of information regarding the profession. When you go, a whole millennium of knowledge will go with you, an entire encyclopedia of codes. Your colleagues who haven't yet turned thirty don't come to ask you practical questions. Rather, they come to hear your stories: of Étienne Bazeries, the French cryptanalyst who in the nineteenth century spent three years trying to decipher Louis XIV's code (so full of twists and turns that it took more than two centuries to decode it), or of Marian Rejewski, the Polish cryptanalyst who helped to defeat Enigma in World War II. There are so many stories, and you know them all. Your new colleagues use software to decipher codes and see you as a relic from times when the profession was not fully mechanized. The world has changed since Enigma, but being historically out of sync is nothing new in Río Fugitivo.

You pause in front of the Bletchley Room, where slim computers use complex mathematical processes to understand coded messages and fail more often than not. Years are needed to decode a single phrase. With the development of public key cryptography, and particularly with the appearance of the RSA asymmetric system in 1977, a message can now be coded using such high values that all of the computers in the world working to decipher it would take more than the age of the universe to find a solution. The ultimate irony is that with computers at their service, cryptographers have won the battle against cryptanalysts, and people like you, who don't depend on computers that much, can still be useful.

Your younger colleagues are adept at computer science and useless before the power of the computer itself. Their work is more modern than yours (at least according to the movies, obsessed as they are with showing young programmers in front of a computer monitor), but it's still no use—they are just as out of date as you are. Deciphering codes in general has become a useless task. But someone has to do it: the Black Chamber has to maintain the pretense that it is still useful to the government, that power is not as vulnerable as it really is to the attacks of a conspiracy handled by means of secret codes.

The room is empty and silent. When you began work here, the computers were enormous, noisy, metallic cupboards sprouting cables. Machines have become smaller and quieter, increasingly aseptic (in the Babbage Room there is still an ancient Cray supercomputer, a donation from the U.S. government). At one time you felt you were less than those who worked tirelessly on algorithms in the Bletchley Room. You even tried to learn from them, to move from your old office to this one, which was more in keeping with the times. But you couldn't—you didn't last long. You liked mathematics, but not enough to dedicate the best hours of your life to it. For you, mathematics was about functionality, not passion. Luckily, most conspirators in Bolivia aren't that good and don't know how to do more than the basics on computers either.

You continue on your way, putting your hands into your coat pockets. A pencil, a pen, and a few coins. An image of your daughter, Flavia, comes to mind, and you are filled with tenderness. Before leaving, you went into her room to kiss her goodbye on the forehead. Duanne 2019, the heroine Flavia had created for some of her Web surfing, stared out at you from the screen saver on one of two monitors sitting on her desk, covered in photos of famous hackers (Kevin Mitnick, Ehud Tannenbaum). Or crackers, as she would insist. "You have to learn to differentiate them, Dad. Crackers abuse technology for illegal purposes." "So why is your site called AllHacker and not AllCracker?" "Good question. It's because only people in the know make the distinction. And if my site was called AllCracker, it wouldn't get even one percent of the hits it gets now." Hackers, crackers: it's all the same to you. But shouldn't you try to use the Spanish term and call them *piratas informáticos*? You prefer that term, even though it sounds strange.

English had come first and become the norm. People sent attachments, not *archivos adjuntos,* e-mails, not *correos electrónicos.* In Spain they call the screen saver *salvapantallas;* in truth it sounds ridiculous. Still, you shouldn't give up; it is worth going against the grain. The survival of Spanish as a language of the twenty-first century is at stake. *Piratas informáticos, piratas informáticos . . .*

Flavia was snoring lightly and you stood looking at her under the glow of the lamp on the bedside table. Her damp, tangled, chestnut-colored hair fell over her face with its full lips. Her nightshirt had twisted and her left breast was bared, the nipple pink and erect. Embarrassed, you covered her up. When had your mischievous, ponytailed little girl become a disturbing young woman of seventeen? When had you stopped paying attention? What had you been doing while she grew up? Computers had fascinated her ever since she was a child, and she had learned to program by the time she was thirteen. Her Web site provided information about the little-known hacker subculture. How many hours a day did she spend in front of her IBM clones? In most respects she had left adolescence behind. Luckily, she was not at all interested in the young men who had begun to flock to the house, attracted by her distant, languid beauty.

The Vigenère Room is empty. The hands of the clock on the wall read 6:25 A.M. Ramírez-Graham hadn't been thorough enough and had left mechanical clocks in the building. Surely he would soon replace them with red numbers in quartz, analogue with digital. Such useless modernization. Seconds more or seconds less, precise or imprecise, time will continue to flow on and in the end have its way with us.

The building at this hour is still chilly. It doesn't matter: you like to be the first to arrive at work. You learned that from Albert, your boss for over twenty-five years. Continuing on with the tradition is your homage to the man who did more for cryptanalysis in Río Fugitivo than anyone else. Albert is now confined to a medicinal-smelling room in a house on Avenida de las Acacias, delirious, his mind unable to respond. He is proof that it's not good to overload the brain with work: short circuits are the order of the day. You like to walk down the empty hallways, to see the desks in the cubicles piled high with paper. In the still air your eyes rest on file folders and ghostly machines with the disdainful arrogance of a benevolent god, of someone who will do his work because some unknown First Cause has ordained it and it's not wise to defy destiny.

You press the elevator button and enter that metallic universe where the strangest thoughts have always occurred to you. Will the elevator malfunction and plunge you to your death? You are heading to the basement, to the archives, to the ends of the earth, to a death chamber that only you inhabit. It is even colder down there. Suspended in the air by thick cables, you move without moving, in peace.

There is something special about this elevator. Its green walls, simple efficiency — a solid nucleus of stable movement. What would you do without it? What would people do without them? Otis, six passengers, 1000 pounds. You stare at the name. You spell it out: O-T-I-S. Backwards: S-I-T-O. It is a message striving to break free, and it is destined only for you. I-O-T-S. *I'm Obliged To Say.* Who's obliged to say what?

The general archives are in the basement. You are the link between the present and the past. You hang your jacket on a broken coat rack. You take your glasses off, clean the lenses with a dirty handkerchief, and put them back on. You pop a piece of spearmint gum into your mouth, the first of many. Never chewed for more than two minutes, they are thrown out as soon as the first flavor is gone.

You feel the need to urinate. That sense of having to go immediately has been with you since adolescence. It's one of the worst manifestations of your anxiety, the way in which your body compensates for your apparent immunity to emotions. All of your underwear is stained the color of burned grass. You suffer from it even more now that you work in the basement; the architect never thought to put a bathroom on this floor. Perhaps he assumed that whoever would work in the archives could take the elevator or stairs up to the bathrooms on the ground floor — a normal human being, someone who might go once or twice a day and not be bothered. But what about someone who is incontinent? How insensitive.

You open the bottom drawer of your desk and take out a plastic cup with a smiling Road Runner on it. You head to a corner of the room, your back to the archives. You lower your zipper and urinate into the cup: six, seven, eight amber drops. That's why you don't like to go to the bathroom; the result is usually incompatible with the sense of urgency. It's better to accumulate drops in the cup and then casually pass by the bathroom to dispose of your fragrant treasure at lunchtime.

You put the cup back in the drawer.

The pile of papers on your desk seduces you; bringing order to chaos, partially winning the battle against it, and being ready for the next onslaught is a game that lasts for days and months and years. Cryptanalysts' desks tend to be impeccable, with papers stacked on either side, pens and reference books lined up one next to the other, the computer monitor standing guard, the keyboard on the shelf hidden beneath the desk. It is the reflection of a pristine mind that does its work with great dedication to logic.

You turn on the computer and check your e-mail at both the public and the private address. You spit your gum out, put another piece in your mouth, and all of a sudden at your private address you find an e-mail consisting of a single line:

RZWIJWJWDTZWMFSIXFWJXYFNSJIBNYMGOTTI

You notice the sequence FWJ XYFNSJI. Frequency analysis won't take more than a few minutes. Each letter has its own personality, and even though it seems to be out of place, it is betrayed, whispers, speaks, shouts, tells its story, misses its place on earth — paper. Who could have sent you this message? From where? You don't recognize the address. That's strange — only about ten people know your private e-mail. Someone has managed to get past the Black Chamber's firewalls and is teasing your heart with a crude message.

All messages from within the Black Chamber come encrypted to your private address and your computer deciphers them automatically. Perhaps something in the program failed. You hit a couple of keys to try to decode the message. No luck. It isn't encrypted using the Black Chamber's software, which confirms your suspicions: the message was sent by someone unknown.

It is a taunt. For now, you had better do what you do best: frequency analysis. The *j* has to be a vowel: *a? e? o?* Common sense tells you it's an *e.*

You soon know: it is a simple code ciphered by substitution, a variation that, according to Suetonius, was used by the emperor Julius Caesar. Each letter has been moved five spaces to the right, so that the *j* is really an *e,* the *g* is a *b,* and so on. XYFNSJI spells *stained.*

MURDERERYOURHANDSARESTAINEDWITHBLOOD

Who's the murderer? You? Why are your hands stained?

chapter 2

BLACK STORM CLOUDS on the horizon threaten rain. Flavia says goodbye to her classmates and gets on the blue bus that will take her home. A black leather bag with books and magazines; in her pocket a silver Nokia, which she checks impatiently every other minute. It's one o'clock and she's hungry.

There is hardly any room on the bus. She grasps a metal pole and squeezes between a fat, bald man staring at his cell phone —someone else who's obsessed with Playground—and a mustached woman. There is the smell of cheap perfume and sweat. The driver has chosen to entertain himself with blaring tropical tunes. She should listen to music on her Nokia, create her own sound barrier against the noise that is bombarding her, but she hasn't downloaded anything new lately and she's not interested in the songs that are in memory. Maybe she should log on to Playground. No, better not. A screen larger than the one on her cell phone is better for Playground.

Uncomfortable, she lifts her eyes and reads the ads above the windows: cybercafés, cheap Internet connections, lawyers. It becomes increasingly difficult to rest your eyes on blank space, where no one is offering anything. The world is overrun with people and things; you have to look within or project yourself onto some virtual reality in order to escape.

"Fares, bus fares," intones the collector, a shy, snotty-nosed kid, as he makes his way through the bus. It's so old-fashioned. Elsewhere you simply have to slide a card through a slot in order to pay your fare, or a code entered on a cell phone will take care of it.

Flavia hands the collector her coins. Children shouldn't be allowed to work. What stories could be read in his eyes? Life on the outskirts of the city, five siblings, his mom working at the market, his dad a street vendor. Chicken soup his only meal each day. Progress was evident in Río Fugitivo, but it was simply an island in the middle of a country that was very much behind the times.

School had been her escape when she was a girl. Now it bores her. Information issues forth so slowly from her teachers' mouths. Her girlfriends gossip about parties and pimple-faced boys who press themselves against the girls' bodies when they dance, about nights that go beyond what is allowed and wind up in public parks or motels. She is looking forward to being in front of her computer and updating AllHacker. Thanks to her contacts, she has the exclusive on the suspicious deaths of two hackers a few weeks ago and is covering everything that happens concerning the Resistance. Newspapers such as *El Posmo* and *La Razón* use AllHacker to inform their readers about the Resistance but hardly ever cite it as their source.

The city slips past the windows, a brief trip through a landscape that is being torn down and rebuilt every day, one that does not know how to stay still. A thin woman in pink running shoes walking her Pekingese. Two men surreptitiously holding hands. A police officer taking a bribe from a taxi driver. A drunk sprawled on a bench. A construction gang in yellow hardhats tearing up a sidewalk in order to lay fiberoptic cables: work that will begin again as soon as it is finished, because during installation another, even more powerful cable will have been invented. Walls are covered in Coalition Party posters that call for protests against a government *co-opted by the interests of multinational corporations.* Globalization is blamed for everything these days. Now you can declare your patriotism by blowing up a McDonald's. No wonder the fast-food chain wants out of the country.

As the bus draws closer to the suburbs in the western part of the city, there is more space and it is easier to breathe. Flavia sits down next to an old woman reading *Vanidades* (the title of an article: "Jackie Kennedy Onassis—Forever on the Cover of Magazines"). Flavia has the urge to tell the woman that all heroines are somewhere else. Passive consumerism is passé; it's important to create your own role models now, ones so private that sometimes no one else even knows them.

She watches the e-mails, video messages, and short-text messages pile up on her Nokia. She quickly reads a few. Most are just the usual junk. But every so often she receives something of real value, so she tries to scan them all. Last week some stranger sent her an e-mail suggesting that Nelson Vivas and Freddy Padilla, the two hackers who died suspiciously, had belonged to the Resistance. The sensational part was the suggestion that the person responsible for their deaths was Kandinsky, the leader of the Resistance. Why? Because Kandinsky was a megalomaniac who did not allow dissent, and Vivas and Padilla had dared question the way the Resistance was being run. Flavia does not usually publish news from unreliable sources; however, this exclusive, if true, was both tempting and explosive. She managed to publish it in a piece that, while not directly accusing Kandinsky, at least suggested the possibility that his group was involved. Predictably, she received several insulting and threatening e-mails in response. In the hacker community, Kandinsky was idolized for his cyberhacktivism, for the way he attacked government and multinational corporation Web sites as a form of protest against their policies. Flavia admired Kandinsky, but she knew that she had to remain objective when reporting on him.

Vivas and Padilla had worked on the Web version of *El Posmo*. They were both murdered on the same weekend. Vivas was stabbed early Saturday morning as he left the *El Posmo* building, and on Sunday night Padilla was shot in the back of the head at the front door to his house. The media had reported the two murders as separate incidents united only by chance. Apparently neither one had any known problems or enemies; there were not enough clues even for speculation. That both had belonged to the Resistance, according to the e-mail, was interesting to Flavia, since it suggested that their connection went beyond mere chance.

She puts on her earphones and looks for the news on the screen of her cell phone. Lana Nova, her favorite broadcaster, comes on. The virtual woman has her black hair in a ponytail, which accentuates her Asian features. Through the earphones Flavia can hear Lana's synthesized, enveloping voice, one that can move you simply by reporting on the weather. No wonder teenagers have taken to watching the news and papering their rooms in posters of Lana.

For the second consecutive day there have been enormous protests against the hike in electricity rates. GlobaLux, the Italian-American consortium that won the bid to take over the power company in Río Fugitivo just a year ago, defends its actions by saying that the crisis has left it no alternative. It says the rate hike will allow it to finance construction of a new power plant. The Coalition is calling for a general blockade of streets and highways on Thursday. The protests in Río Fugitivo have spread to other cities. There have been violent confrontations between industrial workers, students, and police in La Paz and Cochabamba. A pylon was blown up in Sucre. Business owners in Santa Cruz are calling for community protests. Opposition politicians and indigenous leaders are demanding Montenegro's resignation, saying the months remaining of his term in office will be enough to destroy the country. It is early November. There will be an election in June of next year and a new president in August.

She hears nothing about the Resistance that she hasn't already reported, and not a word about Vivas and Padilla. Luckily, her competition is in rough shape.

She turns off her Nokia. Now that the bus has emptied she spots him. Sitting at the back, leaning against a knife-slashed seat, she sees the same guy she saw yesterday. About her age, maybe? Eighteen. Tall, curly hair, bushy eyebrows, earphones, and a yellow MP3 player in his hands. What music is he listening to to escape from the bus driver's tropical beat? The news? A soccer match in Italy or Argentina?

Suddenly a pair of eyes pin her to her seat, just as had happened yesterday. She tends to ignore men, but there is something in the way he looks at her that is unsettling. She passes a hand over her hair, making sure it is stylishly unkempt. Her dreadlocks are tousled as if she has just woken up. She moistens her lips with her tongue. Oh, how ridiculous she must look in the school uniform that the nuns continue to insist on: the blue, knee-length skirt, white shirt, blue vest, and, horror of horrors, the tricolor tie that is a designer's nightmare. Is she really any less interested in boys than her friends?

As she gets off the bus it starts to drizzle, the rain lightly tickling her face. She forces herself to keep her back to the bus, a small victory over the young man she pictures with his face pressed against the glass, ready to savor the moment when Flavia will turn around to look at him one last time.

A garbage can swarming with blue-green flies is in the bus shelter. An emaciated dog growls listlessly at anyone who passes by. Flavia thinks about Clancy, her blind Doberman, wandering through the house, running into walls as he anxiously awaits her arrival. The neighbors complain about his howling early in the morning; her mom has suggested that it might be time to put the old dog down.

She has five blocks to go before reaching her neighborhood. The streets are quiet and Flavia likes to feel as if she owns them, walking down the middle of the potholed asphalt, equidistant from the sidewalks flanked by dusty loquat trees. She walks, then jumps along an imaginary hopscotch, wonders what her dad must be doing right now at work, and discovers — annoyed, embarrassed — that she is not alone.

"From alpha to omega, from zero to infinity," comes a husky voice that is too old for the body of a young man. "A game with multiple theological and metaphysical connotations."

When had he gotten off the bus? She hasn't heard him walking behind her. For a moment she feels afraid. She is four blocks from her protective refuge, the gated community where two measly policemen guard the entrance.

"No connotations are necessary to have fun playing hopscotch," she says, affecting the most disinterested expression she can muster.

"You might like to remain on the surface of things, take them as they come," the young man says, "but it's not possible. Everything means something else, and that something might be what transcends — the mandala we're all searching for."

The drizzle is no longer gentle; the rain is now soaking and bothersome. Flavia continues on her way. She wants to run home but has to pretend to be calm. You never know. And, she has to admit, it's a strange fear, one that urges her to run from and yet stay near this stranger.

"I'm Rafael. You're Flavia, aren't you? Don't ask me how I know. Other names? Other identities? It's impossible not to have them. I have at least eight on the Net."

"Let's just leave it at that right now."

"No big deal. I'll find them out soon enough."

She walks without looking at him, feeling as if his presence is a threat. Now it is Rafael who keeps quiet, and she feels obliged to talk.

"You know which school I go to, but I don't know where you go."

"I left school a long time ago, 'just Flavia.' If you're interested, one day I'll show you what I do for a living. It has to do with information."

"You're a reporter?"

"No. There are those who'll pay a lot to obtain privileged information, and there are those who have to go to great lengths to get that information. At some point all of this might be useful to you. But first, just Flavia, you have to be very careful. Sometimes you're not. Sometimes you report news without being sure about it. And that makes some people angry. It's not a good idea to make light of dangerous subjects."

Flavia stops and looks at him. Is he a hacker? Which one? From the Resistance? A Rat? Or both? Is he threatening her? He is as nervous as she is; his lower lip is trembling, and his gaze does not seem as firm as it did on the bus. The rain on his curly hair, on his face, has made him lose his composure. He looks like a man with an important secret, weighed down by it. She is not afraid of hackers or of the Resistance either, even though he is dangerous if he's a Rat. It is a Rat's job to inform, and they have grown in number over the past few years; the continuous scandals that surround them, their threat to a citizen's privacy, have displaced them, made them illegal. Some are hackers in order to get information, while others prefer more traditional ways—rummaging through the trash, paying servants, or bribing colleagues.

"I should go," Flavia says. "But there's always tomorrow. I hope at some point you can be a little clearer."

"There isn't always tomorrow."

"You're being fatalistic."

"I am a fatalist."

Rafael shakes her hand and says goodbye. Flavia watches him walk away until he is out of sight in the pouring rain. Then she turns and runs home.

chapter 3

My name is Albert. My name is not Albert.

I was born . . . Not. Very. Long. Ago.

I was never born . . . I have no memory of a beginning. I am something that happens. That is always happening . . . That will always happen.

I. Am. An. Emaciated. Grimy. Man . . . Gray. Eyes . . . Gray. Beard . . . Singularly. Vague. Features . . . I. Express. Myself. With. Untutored. And. Uncorrected. Fluency. In. Several. Languages . . . French. English. German. Spanish. Portuguese from Macao.

I am connected to several wires that allow me to live. Through the window I watch the day pass by on the avenue. Jacarandas in the window box as well as on the sidewalks . . . No wonder . . . The avenue is named . . . de las Acacias.

Where are the acacias? Good question.

In the distance. The mountains. Of Río Fugitivo. Ocher-colored. Not like other mountains. That I remember. From a village. In a valley. Bluish mountains. Markets. Medieval towers. The ruins of fortifications. A river. I don't remember which village it is . . . But the image is there . . . There's a boy. Who runs and runs.

It's not me. I can't be me . . . I have no childhood. I never have.

I can speak and sometimes do. I prefer not to. Pronouncing just a few words takes all my energy. Which can lead to thoughts about my fragility. About my possible demise. But that's not how it is. It never is. There's no death for me.

I am an electric ant. Connected to the earth. And yet more

Spirit than anyone . . . I am the Spirit of Cryptanalysis. Of Cryptography. Or are they the same?

My ears are ringing. And there are voices in the room . . . Saying . . . That . . . I . . . Need . . . This. Isolation . . . This. Peace . . . It's very good. For. Collecting. Your. Thoughts. Peace. There must be a path. That they follow. Somehow. Thought. Must become. Thought . . . Somehow. The mixed-up. Associations between ideas. Must have some hidden logic. So that the image of a nun. Is followed by that of a piano. And all of that leads us. To decide whether or not to spare the lives . . . Of our fellow men.

Delirious logic.

Responsible for my actions. For everything that led me to this bed.

There were feelings. There was intuition. But reason. Made the final decisions.

I'd like to know how it happened. To help this silence.

But the footsteps never stop echoing. I hear them. They resound in here. In this amplifier that is my head . . . They wait for my words. They wait. And wait.

My name is Albert. My name is not Albert.

I. Am. A. Mechanical. Ant.

As. I. Recall . . . My. Work. Began . . . In the year 1900 B.C. I was the one who wrote strange hieroglyphics. Instead of the usual ones. On the tomb of Khnumhotep II. I wrote them on the last twenty columns . . . Of the two hundred twenty that were inscribed. It wasn't a secret code. That was fully developed . . . But it was. The first intentional. Transformation . . . Of writing . . . At least . . . Of the texts that are known.

Ah. Exhaustion. I was so many others. Impossible to list them all.

Markets. Medieval towers. The ruins of fortifications.

The year 480 B.C. . . . At that time I was called Demaratus. I was Greek and lived in the Persian city of Susa. And I was witness to the plans that Xerxes had for invading Sparta. Five years to prepare a military force capable of destroying the insolence of Athens and Sparta. I decided to scrape the wax off some wooden tablets. To write of Xerxes' plan on the tablets . . . And then cover them in wax again. The tablets were sent to Sparta. And Xerxes' guards did not intercept them . . . There, a woman named Gorgo. Daughter of Cleomenes. Wife of Leonidas. Guessed that the tablets contained a message. And she had the wax scraped off. Thus Xerxes lost the element of surprise . . . The Greeks began to arm themselves. When the Greeks and Persians confronted one another. On September 27. Near the Bay of Salamis . . . Xerxes thought he had won. He thought he had surrounded the Greeks. When in reality he had fallen into the trap they had set for him.

As Demaratus, I invented stenography, which is nothing other than the art of hiding a message . . . My. Name. Is. Also. Histiaeus . . . Ruler of Miletus. To encourage Aristagoras to reveal himself to the Persian king Darius . . . I had the head of a messenger shaved. I wrote a message on his head. I waited until his hair had grown. And I sent him to find Aristagoras . . . The messenger entered Persian territory easily . . . He arrived where Aristagoras was . . . Had them shave his head. And Aristagoras was able to read my message.

Stenography. I. Am. A. Mechanical. Ant. I hear voices . . .

I am also the inventor of cryptology. The art of hiding the meaning of a message. I am the one who sent a message to the Spartan general Lisandro . . . Lisandro was far from Sparta. Supported by his new allies. The Persians . . . When a messenger arrived looking for him. The messenger had no message. He had only been ordered to find Lisandro. Who saw him . . . And knew what. It was about. He ordered the messenger to hand over his wide leather belt. And found . . . Printed all along the circumference of the belt. A sequence of random letters . . . He carefully wrapped the belt in a descending spiral around a long wooden pole . . . As he wrapped it. The letters formed phrases that told him that his Persian ally. Planned to betray him and take over Sparta in his absence . . . Thanks to the message. Lisandro returned in time and destroyed his former ally.

My right leg hurts. Such . . . A . . . Long . . . Time . . . In. Bed. My back. I won't ever get up again. Yes, I might . . . My lungs are destroyed. So many cigarettes . . . Sometimes I urinate without realizing it. The nurse comes to change me. It's humiliating to defecate

. . . When the nurse isn't here. She's almost never here. I have to call the guard using a bell. The smell of my skin is the smell of age. Scabs fall like flakes to the floor. At times my headache is unbearable . . .

So many days and nights wasted battling with messages. It was obvious I wouldn't escape unscathed. Everything has a price.

Something happened inside my head. I search for that lost world.

I want to know how it is I thought what I thought.

I need a Universal Turing Machine.

A Universal Albert Machine.

Albert. Demaratus. Histiaeus. I shed names like a snake sheds its skin. Stories. Identities. Nothing human is alien to me. Nothing inhuman is alien to me . . .

I traverse centuries and influence history. Without me. Wars. History would have been different . . . I'm a parasite on the body of men. I'm a parasite on the body of history.

I'm thirsty. My throat is dry and cracking. My eyes are closed. I can't open them. They're open, but I don't see anything . . . I see without seeing . . . And smell. I smell everything. This stuffy room. Smelling of urine. Of vomit. Of medicine. People who come and go. Old women. Men. Uniforms. Faces I don't recognize. Turing's face . . .

I'm the one who gave him that name. Of course the real Turing. Was me at one time. But that's another story. What's important now is that I was a CIA agent. I had been given that body after World War II . . . I was sent by my government to advise the Bolivian intelligence service. I arrived one rainy, foggy day in 1974. I fainted at the airport in La Paz. The altitude . . . I had had just enough time to admire the snowy mountains. That were visible. Outside the dirty, broken windows. Of the terminal . . .

I spent one day in bed and then the interior minister met me. Times were different. Montenegro was dictator. Now the Home Office secretary is called the minister of the interior. We began a pleasant friendship. Anyone who is no one in another country can be someone here. And before coming here I was no one in the north . . . Just another agent . . . After having been many people in other places and at other times . . . I was more than someone here. Not just a consultant . . . Someone who held a lot of power.

That's why I was sad. When. After. A. Year. I received the order to return . . . To the United States. I didn't want to go back to being no one . . . I liked the country and wanted to stay. I had found my north in the south. So I convinced the military they needed to create an organization that specialized in intercepting and decoding messages from the opposition. And Chile. The Black Chamber.

Montenegro was obsessed with Chile. He wanted to be the one who would return the sea to his country. I laughed. But I told him yes. Certainly. Of course. Whatever you say. And from the shadows he put me in charge of the Black Chamber. I quit the CIA. This country is very good to foreigners. A German led their army in the Chaco War.

Medieval towers.

Faces. Pass in front of me. They sit down. They wait. They wait for me . . . Their gestures are codes. Their clothing is a code. Everything is a code . . . Everything is secret writing. Everything is written by an absent God . . . Or a hemiplegic . . . Or a stupid demiurge . . . An incontinent demiurge . . .

We don't know how the message began. We know. That. He. Is. Having. A. Hard. Time. Finishing it . . . And continues to write sentences. Pages. Notebooks. Books. Libraries. Universes.

Someone comes in and wants to touch me. They don't . . .

I'm here and I'm not here. Better if I'm not.

Or are they the same?

chapter 4

IN HIS OFFICE on the top floor of the Black Chamber, Ramírez-Graham reviews the files that Baez has just brought him. He is drinking his third coffee of the morning. Not as hot as he wanted it, but they can't get anything right in this fucking country. The last few weeks he has had stomach problems. The doctor told him that it might be gastritis or the start of an ulcer and that he should avoid alcohol, spicy food, and coffee for two months. He paid attention to the doctor for ten exasperating days — the exact length of time a doctor's orders should be followed. Then he remembered his father, who had had emphysema and continued to smoke, saying that everyone had to die of something and that there was no use in denying yourself the pleasures of life. He died a year later. What a senseless death, Ramírez-Graham had thought; if only his dad had taken better care of himself, he might have lived for five more years. But now that he is about to turn thirty-five, he is starting to understand his dad a little better. In the last two years the top of his nightstand has filled with medications and his life with prohibitions.

Various mathematical formulas float on the computer monitor. In an aquarium with blue-green water, four angelfish swim in circles, magnetized by their own boredom. A Nokia cell phone rests on the desk.

Behind him, in a glass case protected by an antitheft system, is a rusted Enigma machine. The first time he saw it, the cover reminded Ramírez-Graham of those typewriters that date back a few generations. But in truth the device was a typewriter that was tired of its humble purpose of transferring men's words onto paper and was willing to carry out a much more advanced role by means of its rotors and cables. No one knows where Albert got it; there are only a few left in the world, in museums and in the hands of private collectors — they understandably go for an exorbitant sum. With Enigma, the Nazis had managed to mechanize the sending of secret messages and, thanks in part to their impenetrable system of communication, had achieved a great advantage in the war for a few years. Luckily, a group of Polish cryptanalysts was undaunted by the complexity of Enigma; luckily, there was Alan Turing.

Albert brought the machine to the office on his first day of work at the Black Chamber. He took it home each night for the first few weeks, until the case was built. Behind his back, Albert's employees called him Enigma and spread rumors about his unknown past. In their eyes, the device was irrefutable proof that he was a Nazi refugee. The government was lying when it said he was a CIA consultant. After all, his Spanish, with its *r* that became a guttural *g* and a *w* that sounded like a *v*, was German-accented, not American. Albert never bothered to contradict the rumors.

Ramírez-Graham is intrigued by his predecessor. He feels that all of his actions are measured against the bar that was set by the creator of the Black Chamber. He wonders how much truth there is to what he hears about the man, but he has resisted the temptation to go and see Albert on his deathbed. Perhaps the image of his decrepit body would destroy the invincible aura that people have built around him. But no. Ramírez-Graham would rather study history first. He will go down to the Archive of Archives and review the documents that set out how the Black Chamber was built and what it was that Albert actually did.

He is exhausted, isn't sleeping well. Sometimes, a few hours after he finally nods off, he will wake up with the image of Kandinsky in mind, and then it is impossible to fall back asleep. Supersonic sleeps at the foot of the bed with his metallic hum. Ramírez-Graham has gotten used to the noise — although at first he had to stop himself from throwing the dog out the window or shutting him up by piercing his heart with a screwdriver.

The image he has of Kandinsky is his own, because there are no photos of him. Surely, though, Kandinsky is pale and malnourished from countless hours locked in his room in front of a computer monitor and is incapable of having an adult conversation with a woman.

Will this be the end of Ramírez-Graham? The president is not at all pleased with the way he is handling the case and wants answers immediately. The vice president is trying to buy time and defends him, but he could withdraw his support at any moment — after all, he is a politician.

Ramírez-Graham scribbles numbers and algorithmic formulas on the edge of the papers he is reviewing, a thankless labyrinth of codes. He thought that some underlying structure might emerge, the forgotten fingerprint that would allow the criminal to be caught, but studying the various crime scenes is getting him nowhere. Those kids in the Resistance are professional when it comes to their work. Kandinsky has surrounded himself with capable people. The ironies of fate: a year ago Ramírez-Graham arrived in Río Fugitivo with the arrogance of his past as a National Security Agency expert who was too good for the job as savior of Bolivia's Black Chamber, and now a Third World hacker has him in checkmate.

It's not the fault of the codes, but his own. He never should have accepted a bureaucratic job that would remove him from daily practice with the theory of numbers, with the algorithms of cryptology.

Ramírez-Graham's dad, an immigrant from the rural highlands outside Cochabamba, had married a woman from Kansas who taught math at a public school. He had established himself in Arlington by managing a Latin American restaurant and hadn't even bothered to register his son's birth with the Bolivian consulate. Six weeks after Ramírez-Graham was born, the Social Security card that made him part of the great American family had arrived in the mail. It had been so difficult for his dad to obtain residency that he was amazed when his son, simply for having been born on American soil, was considered a citizen of that country.

Ramírez-Graham learned Spanish at home and spoke it very well, except for his somewhat deficient use of the subjunctive and his pronunciation of *l* and *r*—undeniably English-speaking traits. Growing up, he had visited Bolivia several times; he loved the social life there, the multitude of relatives, and the never-ending fiestas. It was perfect for vacations, but he never would have thought of living there. Never. Not until he met the vice president at a reception at the Bolivian embassy in Washington, given in honor of the community's distinguished young Bolivians. Ramírez-Graham had been invited because of his notable work as an expert on cryptographic security systems for the NSA. His work was supposedly secret and had remained so for the first few years, until a new boss, who wanted to improve relations with the media and make the NSA more transparent, made certain things public. Unsurprisingly, it was a resounding failure—the NSA was so secret that the funding it received annually was hidden within the nation's general budget.

At the reception, the vice president had come straight out and asked Ramírez-Graham if he would be interested in taking charge of the Black Chamber. He had to stifle his laughter. The Black Chamber was the name given to European intelligence agencies two or three centuries ago. The name spoke of a desire for modernity but perhaps indiscreetly revealed how backward the Bolivians were. However, he was surprised by the offer. Without knowing anything about the Black Chamber's annual budget or its equipment, but suspecting that they were infinitely inferior to the NSA's, he asked himself whether it was better to be a little fish in a big pond or a big fish in a little pond.

The vice president explained what the Black Chamber was.

"It was created for the challenges of national security during the seventies and has now become obsolete. President Montenegro, who gave the order for its creation, has come to realize that and has put me in charge of making it useful in this new century. In my opinion, one of the main challenges to national security is cybercrime. Sí, incluso en Bolivia, mark my words. Because I say these things, people think I'm ultra-modern, when the truth is that in Bolivia one has to face problems that are premodern, modern, and even postmodern. Both the government and private industry increasingly depend on computers. Los aeropuertos, los bancos, el sistema telefónico, you name it. We don't really believe in these things and consequently not even one tenth of a percent is spent on computer security. It will be our downfall."

Ramírez-Graham was seduced by the vice president's words. All of a sudden he saw himself assuming a post that was vital to the interests of a nation.

"Make me an offer I can't refuse," he found himself saying, without entirely having digested the consequences of his reply.

The vice president made him an offer that, while not spectacular, was tempting.

"But I'm not even Bolivian," Ramírez-Graham said. "I suppose a government institution should be run by Bolivians."

"I can make you a Bolivian in the blink of an eye."

Ten days later, when his new passport, ID card, and birth certificate from Cochabamba arrived by courier at the door, he was stunned at the confidence with which things were done in his second homeland. That very same day the vice president phoned. Ramírez-Graham simply could not say no.

He drinks his coffee and remembers his first few days in charge of the Black Chamber—how he cursed his decision when he discovered a reality that was much more precarious than he had imagined. Unknowing, he had brought Mathematica on his laptop, thinking he would have time to program. Impossible. It was frustrating to want to sit down and work with his numbers and not be able to.

As for Río Fugitivo ... What would Svetlana have said? He missed her. There was a photo of her on his desk—curly black hair, prominent cheekbones intensely rouged, lips that seemed to depart from their natural position, preparing at once for a sullen frown or a passionate kiss. Not a day went by when he didn't e-mail her, not a week when he didn't phone her, but she never answered. They had been dating for ten months when one day she told him she was pregnant. His mouth hung open, his eyebrows arched, and he spoke the words he would later regret: he wasn't ready to have children. Svetlana stormed out of the apartment. The next day when he phoned her sister's house, he learned that she was in the hospital and had lost the baby. Her sister told him that it wasn't his fault; Svetlana had been distracted while driving after she left the apartment and had collided with a taxi. Still, Ramírez-Graham couldn't help feeling guilty, a feeling that only grew when she wouldn't see him at the hospital or later at her sister's house. It was during that time that he received the vice president's offer. He thought perhaps it would be best to stay and try to win Svetlana back, but his pride prevented him from doing so. He accepted a two-year contract at the Black Chamber.

He watches the soporific movements of the angelfish in the aquarium. Back and forth, ebb and flow. At times he thinks that the reason he left the NSA was his impotence at the direction things were taking. The agency, one of the American government's central organizations during the cold war, was drowning in irrelevance, plagued by both budget cuts and new data-encoding systems that were practically invincible. The NSA continued to intercept messages from all over the world, at an average of two million per hour, but it was increasingly difficult to decode them. This shouldn't really have bothered Ramírez-Graham, since after all, he was in charge of developing security systems and at that time cryptographers were far ahead of cryptanalysts. But it did worry him—a great deal. The NSA's loss of prestige resulted in his own loss of prestige. Perhaps accepting the vice president's offer had been a way to feel relevant again, in order to return to the NSA with renewed energy. He hadn't even been in Bolivia for a year and everything had worsened. In the days prior to the attack on the World Trade Center, the NSA had intercepted a variety of disturbing messages from Al Qaeda that had mentioned the proximity of an attack of unimaginable proportions. Those messages, however, had not been deciphered or translated in time. That was not uncommon; it was simply that the consequences had never been as dire as they were on September 11, 2001.

What would Svetlana be doing right now? She was so slim; he liked to kiss her rib cage. He recalled her overwhelming collection of shoes, her compulsion for catalogue and online shopping, and then her surprise at the Victoria's Secret and J. Crew packages that UPS left at the entrance to the building. The way she took over the bed as she slept, leaving him so little room that he could move neither left nor right. He misses the apartment they shared on Twenty-seventh Street in Georgetown, less than ten minutes from Dupont Circle. He misses Svetlana's cats, which would curl up on his legs when he lay on the soft orange futon to watch television. What is he doing in this far-off country with its strange customs, so different from his place of birth? His dad had gone to great lengths to instill love and respect for his culture and Latin American roots. He had succeeded. Ramírez-Graham followed the recurring mishaps in Bolivian history with genuine interest, but living in Bolivia was a different matter.

He was on the verge of leaving only a few days after he arrived. Albert, the creator of the Black Chamber, had done a remarkable job on a meager budget. Nevertheless, it was so very different from Crypto City, as the immense complex of NSA buildings in Fort Meade was known. The computers were over five years old; their memory and speed were out of place in this new century. The communication systems were extremely limited, as were the systems for monitoring conversations and deciphering codes. There was not even any software for machine translations from Quechua and Aymara into Spanish, in a country where the majority spoke one of those two languages. Was it that indigenous people never conspired? Perhaps one could plot only in Spanish? And there was just one old Cray supercomputer . . . He had come from a high-tech world and wasn't prepared to use low-tech systems. The only reason he stayed was that the vice president had promised a budget sufficient to upgrade the Black Chamber's hardware and software.

The monitor goes black for a few seconds, then comes back on. Power surges have been occurring frequently these days. To hell with GlobaLux. Blockades are now being announced, as if that will produce electricity. To hell with this country.

He approaches the window. He had finally started to feel comfortable after four months of work. He had to admit that he liked the power, the instant access to the vice president, who came to Río Fugitivo often. Ramírez-Graham did all he could not to go to La Paz, since he reacted poorly to the altitude. Several new computers had been installed, and he had hired capable young people. Veterans like Turing had been relocated. He could understand why Albert had surrounded himself with linguists and not computer science experts: sophisticated equipment wasn't needed to decipher the majority of codes that were intercepted by the Black Chamber. "Technological advances over the past few years have made the NSA's message-deciphering systems obsolete," an expert had pronounced. "In order to become useful again, the agency has to resort to the three *b*'s: bribery, blackmail, and burglary." There was no such problem at the Black Chamber, since the majority of those who ciphered messages here did not use all of the technological advances at their disposal. However, trained as he was to be prepared for the unexpected, Ramírez-Graham had decided to continue with the vice president's plans for modernization. It had been the right decision. In this instance, Kandinsky and the Resistance were the unexpected.

There is a knock at the door. It is Baez, one of his most trusted employees. He appears shaken.

"I don't know how this could have happened, boss. Our security systems are the best in the country, but a virus has gotten through. It's devouring our files."

Ramírez-Graham pounds the table forcefully. No need to ask who's responsible. Sons of bitches. Will this be the end of him?

chapter 5

JUDGE CARDONA GAZES OUT at the plaza from the balcony of his room at the Palace Hotel. He is seated on a metal chair with a crumpled *Time* magazine in his hand, swatting at the flies that buzz around the remains of his lunch: potatoes, a piece of lettuce, a slice of tomato swimming in its own juice. The city's dusty air penetrates his nostrils, making him sneeze. The midday sun shines on him from the waist down; his bearded face is protected by the shade, his lips pursed, his gaze flitting here and there. He has loosened his belt and taken off his shoes. He has drunk two bottles of Paceña beer but isn't ready for the third—at least not yet. From behind him, through the open door leading into the room, comes the sound of the television. The Palace Hotel is located in the Enclave, on a corner of the plaza. The architecture is neoclassical, dating from the late nineteenth century. It had been the home of one of Río Fugitivo's most traditional families. There is a large patio with fig trees and treillage, a fountain adorned with swans in the center, around which Cardona can picture men in hats and corseted ladies coquettishly laughing and exchanging glances as the afternoon passes languidly by. The open-air concert at the city bandstand in the plaza had been visible from the balconies; people strolled, unlike now, when hustle and bustle reigns, unlike thirty years ago, when violence ruled.

Such a long time has passed. He shouldn't have come back. But time's sudden fury has done the trick, yes. A hinge that creaks from a space that could materialize in the blink of an eye. Like an injured god who opens and closes his eyes, not knowing why, until realization suddenly dawns.

Cardona's skin is covered in wine-colored spots. They dot his cheeks, partially hidden by his new beard. He can remember the exact date when the first spot appeared, on his right cheek: he was nineteen years old, in his second year of university, and had spent all night preparing for an oral exam. How odd, a lawyer who stuttered in public, whose blood raced when he had to speak in front of a class or a courtroom. Then the second spot appeared. And the third. A body as spotted as a lizard in the desert or a toad in toxic water. The spots are of all shapes and sizes, like scattered maps of islands and countries and continents. They don't hurt. They are just there, as a reminder: he touches them, strokes them, toys with them. Doctors have recommended every kind of cream and ointment, that he stay out of the sun, avoid spicy foods. Nothing has worked. He has come to accept them — they are part of him, they are who he is. He has also come to understand how distracting they are to those who speak to him: court clerks, fellow lawyers, clients, enemies. On his forehead, his nose, his neck, like a worn-out metaphor. He can live with those who stare at him on the street, especially children, who know nothing of tact, of hiding what they think and feel. If the intense sun of Río Fugitivo were to burn these marks right off him, make them disappear, and he were to see himself in a mirror and not recognize himself, perhaps he would fall dead to the floor, or he might continue to live, but as a ghost, the uninhabited inhabitant of a body.

He looks at his pocket watch. It's almost time. The cover of the magazine has something about genomes and an inset about the ongoing challenges of democracy in Latin America. He lets it fall to the floor. An article about attempts by a judge in Argentina to extradite Montenegro had interested him. Judge Garzón had set a precedent with his petition for Pinochet's extradition. Now countless lawyers want to be as heroic. But there are different ways of exacting justice, and following legal procedures is the most useless of them all. That a confused believer in the law as he once was has come to accept that truth lends credence to the fact that one day a child with a pig's tail will be born in this dark land.

He gets up and walks into the room. The bed is still unmade, white sheets and a blue bedspread piled on one side; he has only recently woken up from a dream in which he was a child running behind Mirtha, his cousin, on her bicycle. Mirtha appears in so many dreams, like a restless being who will not accept eternal peace. She has many disguises: behind the face of a bald university professor, wearing the glasses of a paralyzed neighbor, or with the puzzled freshness of adolescence. They are dreams that at times become nightmares — such a thin line separates calm from panic. Like an earthquake that shakes us until we fall unconscious, crevasses that open out of nowhere to swallow us up, and we have no idea where the epicenter is. But he knows — just his luck.

He shaves, nicking the skin above his upper lip. That face is his face, the years continue to ravage it, and it's already starting to leave this place. He's so old. No. He looks so old. And yet wouldn't it be perfect to see one's face not in a mirror but on a wall, a ceiling: an image that reverberates throughout the world and comes back to you before leaving. Kleenex on the cut. Aftershave lotion that stings the skin. He uses mint mouthwash, determined to get rid of his viscous, alcohol-smelling breath. Hairspray. Cologne that smells like lemons. He puts on his black suit, the one made for him by the same tailor who makes Montenegro's suits — their only remaining commonality. Promiscuous tailor, given to politicians of all stripes. He puts on a white shirt and a blue tie. He needs to project a feeling of authority, a moral presence.

He turns off the television. He is tempted to watch *The Exclusive* on his Samsung. Or Lana Nova? There are more breaking stories on the Web than there are on the TV news. *The Exclusive* is his favorite because of its sobriety in an overhyped media. Lana Nova lacks depth; she is the ideal journalist for the MTV generation — so diaphanous that she literally does not exist. But in truth he cannot deny the power of her sexuality, which at times leads him to search for her on the Internet when sleep eludes him. He knows she will be there any time of the day or night, with her broad smile and belligerent breasts, reporting on some Palestinian suicide bomber in a Jerusalem shopping center. Lana's presence is incongruous with the news but at the same time makes the daily excess of tragedies tolerable. He wants to watch Lana, decides to watch *The Exclusive,* which is announcing new confrontations in Chapare. Campesinos from the federation of coca growers, urged by their leader, have decided to resist the government's attempts, backed by the Americans, to eradicate coca. The Aymara leader of the coca growers is beginning to acquire national stature, espousing an anti-imperialist discourse that is managing to reorganize the left, after decades of wandering in the desert, and give it a reason for being. Would he be a candidate in the next presidential election? If he is, Cardona muses, he won't get very far; he lacks support in the cities. Hackers belonging to a group self-appointed the Resistance are interfering with government sites. The country continues in its cyclical, drowning convulsions. Montenegro, as so often before, is teetering on the edge. Diverse sectors are calling for his resignation. He has achieved the impossible: people who were once so diametrically opposed that they would spit at one another if they crossed paths on the street have come together to reject him. Cardona tells everyone that there are only seven months until the election and that he prefers to spend his time amassing files so that on the first day that Montenegro returns to civilian life, a trial for the bloody acts of his dictatorship will await him. A new trial, one that will not fail as the first one did, one that will benefit from the errors and naiveté of the first, because the Argentine judge's attempt at extradition won't be successful. A new trial is being prepared in silence, Cardona tells people, even though the opposite is true. He has to go about it carefully, because one wrong step will prevent him from carrying out his plan. Death is always circling, and conspiracies lurk where you least expect them. A single misstep or negligent act could end it all without its ever beginning. No one is the savior of one's country, but it needs him, Mirtha needs him, politics is personal, politics is local. He exists and is memory in the face of so much forgetting. Someone has to remember, even someone fallible, despicable in his own right, capable of deals worthy of regret, and oh yes there are those, conscience, memory, disgust, such disgust. He turns off *The Exclusive.*

He was fifteen years old and Mirtha was twenty. She lived three blocks away and would sometimes come to visit him, wearing cork platform shoes, bell-bottom jeans, and a yellow headband that contrasted with her long black braids. She was always in a good mood and knew that Cardona, who would do his homework in his room, was shy, and she would jokingly say *Hurry and grow up, I'll wait for you.* He could remember those very words from the time he was ten years old, when she, in the space of a few months, had ceased being a little tomboy who called herself Mirtho and become a flirty teen who did not need makeup or provocative clothing to be noticed. One day Cardona realized that he had grown up and was taking Mirtha's playful words seriously. And he fell in love.

His sister noticed his delirium. She told him he was wasting his time: Mirtha was his cousin, his flesh and blood. The argument did not dissuade him. His sister tried another tack: Mirtha was a hippie, a commie, she had late-night parties at her house, where they sang and played the guitar, and those who attended were probably like Mirtha, ex-university students who hated President Montenegro and were plotting against him. It was no use. The fever of love consumed him. He would watch her coming and going from the second-floor window that looked out onto the street, his face hidden behind the semitransparent white curtains. He dreamed that Mirtha would tell him that he had finally grown up enough. But apart from fleeting white-toothed smiles, she had nothing more for him.

One Sunday she disappeared. His sister told him that the rumors were true; Mirtha belonged to a Marxist-Leninist party and had gone into hiding. There were a few painful months when he did not hear anything about her. Then one morning his aunt and uncle, Mirtha's parents, rang the bell and chokingly asked Cardona's parents for help. They had received a call from the morgue and had been asked to come identify a body. They did not think they had the strength; perhaps Cardona's parents would accompany them. His parents did not have the heart, nor did his sister. Cardona said he would go. And he did. He entered the morgue — crying family members at the entrance, the walls cracked, the lighting dim. A doctor led him to a large cement table on which several bodies were piled and pulled back the sheet. Cardona saw her bruised face, her slashed breasts, her headband, and closed his eyes.

He believes that love died for him at that very instant. And he wonders why he took so long to seek justice, to atone in some way for that senseless death. Because he had been seventeen years old and knew that however left or commie she might have been, she did not deserve to die like that. Later he heard that the group Mirtha had belonged to was conspiring with young military men to overthrow Montenegro. Idealists. Admirable.

On the nightstand is the file Cardona has put together over the past few weeks about Ruth Sáenz. He saw her at a history conference at the state university in La Paz. He had gone to hear her speak, wanting to meet her. She had worked at the Black Chamber during Montenegro's dictatorship, somewhere around 1975, and her husband still worked there. Turing. Ah, that name: shuffled off to a dishonorable retirement, now in charge of the Black Chamber's archives because it isn't in their interests to fire him, but at one time the right-hand man of Albert, the legendary cryptanalyst who was in charge of the Black Chamber's operations during the most difficult years of the dictatorship.

Cardona suspected that in 1976, either Albert or Turing had deciphered the code that the group of conspirators to which Mirtha belonged had established for their top-secret communications. Young army officials, allied with a group of civilians, were planning to overthrow Montenegro. Over a period of two days, all of the conspirators, one by one, were killed.

The years had not been able to erase Cardona's trip to the morgue to identify Mirtha's body, found in a garbage dump under a bridge. Signs of torture on her back, her breasts, her face. Mirtha, who had taken him by the hand to the matinee to watch cartoons. Mirtha, who never wore makeup and tamed her unruly black hair in two long pigtails, who organized parties where guitars were played and songs were sung until the wee hours. Mirtha, who admired Allende, read Che's diary and Martha Harnecker, and sang songs that spoke of a new dawn for the people.

Cardona does not remember a thing about Ruth's speech, which was too technical, plagued with the arcane language of cryptology. He approached her afterward to introduce himself. She was a mature woman with a dull face, no makeup, short, unpainted nails, and a shy gaze, wearing a black, asexual dress like a kindergarten teacher's, fake pearl earrings her only adornment. She greeted him as if she knew him, surprising in her effusiveness.

"I can't understand what a judge is doing among historians," she said as the few attendees were leaving the room, which was adorned with oil portraits of wrinkled patricians.

"The law and history go hand in hand," he said. "Now more than ever before."

"So why did honest judges at one time agree to work for dictators?"

"So why did honest historians do the very same thing?"

"The historians were young and inexperienced, and quickly corrected their mistake."

"The husbands of historians did not."

"And the young people really weren't so young and had enough experience to say no."

The lights in the room were gradually being turned off. It was time to leave. They continued talking in the semidarkness, set phrases that hid the communication that was taking place in silence. When saying goodbye, Cardona gave her his card. He was not at all surprised to receive her call the next morning from the airport. Her voice betrayed her nervousness. He pictured her constantly looking left and right, hesitant, uncomfortable, gripping a napkin in her long-fingered, restless, evasive hands. She wished to speak with him, but not in La Paz. Would he consider visiting her in Río Fugitivo? Cardona hesitated. He told her he would think about it. She was about to hang up when he agreed to see her there in a couple of weeks. It was an opportunity he could not afford to miss.

He opens the file. He knows what he will ask her, has it all organized. The trick is to appear natural, as if everything were happening spontaneously. He has even prepared a few alternatives in case there is some sort of roadblock, as tends to happen — a witness decides not to testify and holds his tongue just when everything is ready. There won't be any obstacles. She seems very open to talking; he simply has to act the part of a friend who listens and consoles.

What could be leading her to take this step, to jump into the abyss, to surrender to the precipice? He shouldn't ask himself that. Despite everything, she is the enemy; he is not interested in understanding her. What he wants is to record her confession, the phrases that will incriminate Turing. By putting dictators on trial, lawyers have concentrated on bringing the visible heads of power to justice — the military who gave the orders, the paramilitary and soldiers who pulled the trigger. They have ignored the whole infrastructure that sustains and allows a dictatorship to exist, the bureaucrats whose hands are not stained with blood but who, by participating in the government, in some sense facilitated the crimes. They have overlooked those who, hiding behind their offices at the Black Chamber, deciphered the codes or interfered with the secret radio signals that led to some subversive source, politicians in hiding who came to their deaths, idealistic university students who disappeared without knowing how they had been found. Cardona isn't really interested in discovering the names of those who had tortured Mirtha, mere pawns in a great war. He is more concerned with beheading those who, by means of their silent work, allowed the torture and death to occur. His goal is to get to Turing and Albert, and through them to Montenegro.

He heads to the adjoining living room and places the mini-recorder in a vase, hidden from Ruth's view. She will know that she is being taped, but if the device is out of sight she won't be intimidated and, he hopes, will talk freely. Two glasses of water are on the table. He straightens an impressionist painting of a cockfight. One of the cocks is blind, with rivulets of blood streaming from his eyes. Extricate the pus and rise above so much mediocrity, transcend such corruption, hands that are stained, consciences that are bought. It's all so easy, the past doesn't exist, it is erased in one fell swoop when it isn't really past, it's alive, it pulses each second and we pretend to ignore it, circus acrobats, lost in our splendid promise, human failure, a half-open window onto the room of the self.

There is a knock at the door. He lifts his gaze toward a spider that is hanging from the ceiling in the middle of the room, rubs his sweaty hands together, lowers his gaze, and walks to open the door for Ruth.

chapter 6

NICOLÁS TESLA SCHOOL was located near the main plaza in Río Fugitivo, in a sprawling, decrepit house that dated back to colonial times. The rooms on either side of the rectangular patio — now a futsal and basketball court — had been turned into classrooms crowded with students. The walls were covered in political and scatological graffiti.

He was fifteen years old and did not remember anything about Oruro, where he had been born. He was four when the government closed the mines and his dad became one more of the "displaced" who had to look for work. His mother's cousin in Quillacollo had helped them for the first few years. Then came Río Fugitivo. His dad was tempted to go to Chaparc, to plant coca as so many other ex-miners had, but a friend of the cousin's had offered them a house in tenure, cheap, in Río; his dad had some savings, and so that is where they ended up. A mechanic, his dad repaired cars and bicycles. At least they had enough to eat.

He was the best student in the class and especially quick at mathematics. When the teacher put complex exercises on the board, he would often correct him without a trace of ridicule or arrogance, as if knowing more than everyone else were part of the natural order of things. He had been chastised for going forward in the lessons, for studying on his own ahead of the class. It had been that way since the first grade, when, thanks to a neighbor who had also taught him how to play soccer, he arrived at school already knowing his multiplication tables. He was generous with his homework:

classmates would line up to copy from him before the bell rang. He was a tall boy of few words, and this attracted the girls, as did his sparkling coffee-colored eyes. He had lost his baby fat, become an awkward adolescent, and had a long, thin neck upon which his head seemed to turn independently of the rest of his body.

Tesla was a state school. He wished it had a computer lab like the one at San Ignacio, a block from his house, near a park dotted with graceful jacaranda trees. The San Ignacio students would come to his house so his dad could fix their bicycle tires or put air in their soccer balls. They would joke around, speak disdainfully about girls, and have money in their wallets. Behind the door, through a cracked window, he watched these well-dressed boys, who would sometimes drive to school, insolent in their belief that the world belonged to them. He hated it that his dad had to serve them.

He had also gone with his mom to wash clothes or clean immense houses with porcelain-adorned living rooms and backyard pools. He will never forget the house of a particular doctor: the children's bright rooms, the Macintosh computer, posters on the walls of Maradona, Nirvana, and Xuxa. It was from the "good classmate" awards on the walls that he discovered that the children went to San Ignacio. He did not want to divide the world so simply, but he was hardly a child anymore and was beginning to learn about injustice.

He used to play pool with his friends, until one afternoon he passed a video arcade and curiosity propelled him inside. The sounds of explosions, the intense, flickering colors . . . There he spent the few coins that he earned by occasionally helping his dad. He was extremely adept at pinball and Super Mario. He was obsessive; entire afternoons would go by as he tried to beat a record.

But the money disappeared quickly. What was he to do? One sunny morning when he had skipped school, he approached the entrance to San Ignacio. A Brasilia was parked outside with the window half open. He turned his head left and right; he was alone. He reached his hand in through the window, opened the door, and found a twenty-dollar bill in a compartment next to the gearshift.

That was his first robbery. There would be others. At first his victims were San Ignacio students. Later he expanded his area of operations. When he went with his mom to the houses she cleaned, it was easy to slip away from her and put anything that might be worth a few pesos at the pawn shop into his pockets: earrings, a ring, a fine ceramic ashtray that he hoped the owners wouldn't even miss.

He earned a reputation at the video arcade as the pinball king. When asked what his name was, he told them it was Kandinsky. He had liked the name ever since he saw a poster for an exhibit at one of the houses his mother cleaned. It was a sonorous name, there was rhythm and harmony in the combination of vowels and consonants; it was a name he liked to repeat as he walked the streets of Río Fugitivo alone, the first and third syllables explosive, the second a bridge that is stressed, the tone rising.

Soon he switched to the Internet cafés that began to pop up all over the city. For the equivalent of fifty cents he could play on the computer for an hour, war and strategy games in which he would compete with other players in the same café, or others on computers in the same city or in other cities, even on other continents. He soon learned the stratagems that made him a fearsome opponent. He was quick with his hands, and his mind was quicker still. He seemed, on a certain level, to understand the games or, more accurately, to understand the programmers who made the games. Asheron's Call was his specialty. The hours would fly by and he continued to miss classes, lost in the medieval scenery of fantasy.

At the Internet café he frequented most regularly, near Suicide Bridge, he was admired by several teenagers. One of them, older than he, called himself Phiber Outkast: freckled, full lips, well dressed, never without his Ray-Bans. One night Phiber Outkast was waiting for him at the café door and walked home with him in silence. As they neared his house, under the glow of a streetlight in the small square, Phiber said that his ability shouldn't be wasted on games. He said that a lot of money was to be made on the Internet.

Kandinsky looked at him without saying a word. Insects buzzed around the streetlight. He asked Phiber to explain. Exactly that, said Phiber Outkast. A lot of money can be made on the Web. It's a question of focusing your knowledge appropriately. If he wanted to develop his talent, he could take classes at the same computer institute that Phiber attended.

Kandinsky would have liked to resist temptation. By this time he was seventeen years old, in his last year of high school. Shouldn't he graduate first?

He thought of his dad's clothes, always stained with grease. Years had passed and he still hadn't gotten ahead. He would inflate soccer balls and repair tires for the rest of his life. He would take refuge in his house, light a few candles to the Virgin of Urkupiña — there was an altar with a plaster effigy of her in the kitchen — crossing his fingers that his luck would improve. He would be content with the victories of San José, soccer triumphs that were seen as necessary, just redemptions.

Kandinsky's mom would continue to work for a pittance at homes so big they were obscene. In such a poor country, there were those who lived as if they were Americans. Or like the vision they had of life in the United States: the land of plenty, of glorious materialism.

Esteban, his younger brother, no longer went to school. Instead, he helped his dad repair tires and sometimes went to the Boulevard, where he would earn a few pesos watching over cars parked outside an empanada shop.

At home the cold seeped in through the broken windows each night.

"Let's talk tomorrow," Kandinsky said under the streetlight. Phiber Outkast sighed, relieved. He knew what that meant.

Located in the Enclave, the institute was a shabby three-story building that at one time housed the *El Posmo* newspaper offices (when it was called *Tiempos Modernos*); there were cracks in the walls and rubble on the stairs. You had to be one of the first to arrive in order to get one of the few computers, all assembled locally. In an atmosphere like that, Kandinsky learned more from his classmates than from his teachers: several computer languages, a little about programming, dozens of tricks for Microsoft software and online games. His classes, paid for by Phiber Outkast, were at night; he always went home as soon as they ended.

His classmates were hackers who specialized in minor jobs—free phone service for a month, access to an Internet porn site, illegal copies of software, the occasional credit card scam. They would tell him their secrets freely and then look at him suspiciously when he showed them, without trying, that he knew more than they did. It didn't matter. He wasn't interested in making friends; he had decided to leave the institute at the end of the semester. His final project consisted of a program to acquire the passwords to private accounts on the Net illegally. He justified it by writing in his final essay that the flow of information on the Internet should be free and there shouldn't be any secrets. Passwords infringed on this free flow of information and should therefore be attacked. The director called him into his office and, returning his work, said, "This is not an institute for hackers, young man." They expelled him the next day. Phiber Outkast didn't need to console him; Kandinsky was elated.

Phiber and Kandinsky's first mission was to access private computers and steal the owners' passwords. They did this from an Internet café where a friend of Phiber's worked. The friend was paid a few pesos to let them work in peace on a computer in the farthest corner of the room. At first Phiber gave the instructions: he knew a bit about programming. Kandinsky would follow and improve on them, playing with them, twisting them, taking them to their breaking point, as if the equations on the screen were made of pliable metal.

With his first stolen password, Kandinsky went through the records of some unknown individual like a thief in another man's house, roaming through the rooms in search of objects to steal. Emotion overcame him; on the surface, he had to remain calm.

He would never go back to stealing from cars and houses, putting himself in physical danger. He much preferred to key in the correct characters that pulse on the screen, to steal from a distance, to obtain access through a rented computer and appropriate the numbers that make up a life: credit cards, bank accounts, insurance. Numbers, numbers everywhere, violated with impunity.

Phiber Outkast slapped him on the back and told him that before he knew it, he would be one of the best hackers around. Kandinsky liked the sound of that mysterious word, *hacker*. It lent him an air of danger, intelligence, transgression. Hackers abuse technology, find uses in artifacts for which they were not intended. Hackers enter territory that is forbidden by law and, once there, laugh at power. It was, perhaps, a metaphor for his life.

One afternoon he arrived home to find his dad at the door, brandishing a letter from the high school. Too many absences had led to his being expelled. His dad was furious. Hadn't he been the best student? And now he wasn't even going to graduate from high school? What had he been doing?

Kandinsky was at a loss for the words that would excuse him.

His mom was in the kitchen chopping onions, and he avoided her gaze. He couldn't bear the look of disappointment welling up in her eyes.

He entered the room he shared with his brother. Esteban was reading a book that he had borrowed from the municipal library: a biography of the man who was the leader of the Workers' Union for forty years. He was a bright kid and liked to read. Would he one day have the chance to go back to school? Unlikely. Would he have to continue helping his parents? Most probably.

Why continue with the charade? Kandinsky's parents had seen him as their only hope for a dignified retirement. Perhaps the best thing would be to run away . . .

Kandinsky fled the house in silence, accompanied by his father's shouts and his mother's sobs. He crossed the park, stirring up the pigeons, passing a boisterous group of San Ignacio students seated on a bench in front of the school. Soon the house, the school, the park, were behind him.

chapter 7

LIKE SO MANY OTHER NIGHTS at the end of a long day, you cross Bacon Street in your gold Corolla and immediately think of William David Friedman, the American cryptanalyst who was convinced that Shakespeare's work contained secret phrases and anagrams that referred to the true author, Francis Bacon. Friedman was the man who had deciphered Purple, the complicated Japanese code from World War II. *It's no coincidence that Bacon Street is on my way,* you think, and without noticing you nearly run a red light at an intersection four blocks from the El Dorado.

The streets converge in utter darkness. Every now and then a window lights up in a building like a flickering eye or a taxi with a blinking sign crosses a street with a fearsome rattle. A shortage of electricity has plagued Río Fugitivo for some time now. The city has grown in a disorderly fashion; no one thought to plan a power plant that could keep up with demand. GlobaLux had arrived to fix the problem but had quickly made itself extremely unpopular: blackouts with no prior warning, continual surges, and, in spite of all that, a shocking rate hike. It is the first time that both the working class and those who are better off have come together in protest. Would the electricity shortage trigger Montenegro's demise? How ironic, after having weathered much more ferocious storms and so close to the end of his mandate.

You pop a piece of gum into your mouth. Spearmint Chiclets. Luckily, there are only four more blocks until you can finally relax. Naked and protected by the night, a glass of whiskey in a dusky room, the television on, wishing that time would slow down, that the clock would stand still. Carla, Carla, Carla. There will be shadows on the walls, shadows that mingle yet fail to find one another.

It's not the first time and it won't be the last, you murmur, stepping on the accelerator. You wish you could stop thinking from time to time, let your mind go blank, avoid the overlapping thoughts that are always with you. To thrill with pure sensation, to let yourself be lulled by the nothingness of the day, to leave the exhausting analogies, the frantic associations of ideas, the obsessive readings of a reality reverberating with the echoes of another reality. *Everything in moderation* was what you wanted your motto to be; you have now resigned yourself to the fact that your thoughts are not in moderation.

Carla, Carla, Carla. Who would have imagined?

You park in the lot next to the building. Four cars: a quiet night. You spit your gum out. A billboard has been hung on a molding wall at the back of the lot: *Built Ford Tough.* An anagram in the last word: *Ought.* An ominous sign: imprisoned within those five letters is the word *go.* Ever since you were a child, you have felt that the world speaks to you, always, everywhere. That sensation has intensified in the past few months, to the point that you cannot read a sign or a word without thinking of it as a code, as a secret writing that needs to be deciphered. The front page of a newspaper can make you dizzy with the sheer volume of messages shrieking your name, asking you to free them from their precarious packaging. Most people think literally and assume that *Built Ford Tough* means *Built Ford Tough.* You suffer from the opposite and spend entire nights awake, mourning the loss of the literal.

Under a red neon light, the receptionist is playing blackjack on the computer, the screen showing a closeup of his hand. The blackjack table is in a casino in the virtual city of Playground. All of Río Fugitivo is addicted to Playground, where thousands waste countless hours making millionaires of the three young men who bought the rights to it for Bolivia. You are one of the few who are immune to the virus. Nonetheless, and despite Ruth's protests, you still finance the unhealthy number of hours that Flavia spends glued to the screen. She said she was going to stop, that she was tired of all the advertising, and yet she can't help logging on one more time, just once more . . .

The receptionist greets you with a mere nod of his head, as if it is an effort to lift his eyelids and move the muscles in his neck. With a click of the mouse, the cards on the screen — stolen hearts, kings in decline — give way to a calendar. He hands you a gold metal key numbered 492. Four. Nine. Two. *D-I-B. BID.* You mumble thanks knowing he won't reply. You have known him for a while now and have never heard the sound of his voice. What for, really? The transaction already took place earlier, using your credit card online. There's no need to speak; he knows it and so do you. And yet you feel nostalgic for the sound of a voice. You're not interested in the message itself but in the means of communication, which is increasingly rare. You most certainly are from another century.

The red carpet is stained — every kind of fluid spilled in sticky intimacy. The elevator is ancient, the metal rusted and the glass cracked in two; still, it glides upward in silence. It is how you imagine the ascension to heaven: broken bits of the world in conversation with the perfection of infinity. Slowly, the world is left behind and the elevator stops. The door opens, and, your steps suddenly light, you approach the heart of harmony.

You used to frequent these sorts of places when you were young. It was impossible to hear an echo of any kind there: every sound was devoured by the continuous murmur of laughter, clinking glasses, loud music, drunks arguing. At the back, behind a curtain made of wooden rods, the rooms were lined up, the beds creaking in frantic arrhythmia. For a few pesos you were happy, at least for a few minutes — always quick, always fleeting.

Carla opens the door for you, her skin white, incongruous dark circles under her eyes, wearing a yellow sweatshirt with an enormous white *C* on it, a blue miniskirt, and running shoes: she is dressed as a University of California cheerleader. She lets you in. "Good evening, darling, good evening." Her short blond hair, her full lips, her smile so wide it is threatening, the soft, experienced curve of her breasts, the miniskirt revealing her thighs. She has perfected the requirements of your none-too-original fantasy of a California girl. The ruined beauty of her face, her red eyes, and the intense blue veins on her pale cheeks contrast with the apparent image of health and vigor that her body projects. Some things cannot be hidden.

You sit on the round bed and let yourself be reflected in the mirror on the ceiling. The room is dark, making the furniture look faded in the ash-colored light. At last, a few minutes for you to relax. Will you be able to? You look at Carla again and tremble. If her hair were brown and she were to wear it like Flavia, they could be sisters. Perhaps the resemblance is in her lips. You try to banish the thought from your mind. Your daughter has the sweetest face, not yet marked by excesses.

You close your eyes.

You open them again. When she's not smiling, Carla's similarity to Flavia becomes indisputable. It's her age, you tell yourself; it's because you love your daughter so much that you see her everywhere you go.

You had the same feeling the first time you saw Carla. It was lunchtime and you were leaving McDonald's with a bag of French fries in your hand. Sitting at a table near the door, her elbows resting on a plastic tray full of napkins and what was left of a hamburger, she looked at you through teary eyes. She was wearing a red dress with a mustard stain on it, hoop earrings, and a necklace made of brilliant green stones. Something made you stop. You asked if you could help her. "My parents just kicked me out," she replied, sniffing and pointing to a bag of clothes on the floor. You had to get back to work, but she was almost the same age as Flavia, and there was something about her face that awakened your paternal instinct. "If you want to help, you could pay for a night in a hotel," she said, her tone firm all of a sudden. "I have ways of thanking you."

On the walls are two somber lithographs by someone who digitally combined Klimt and Schiele. The gold-framed mirrors, the Jacuzzi that has been broken for a month now, the blood-red bedspread, the television mounted in a corner of the room. The El Dorado tries to go unnoticed and not publicize what business it's in, but one look at any of the rooms is enough to tell you that it's an hourly-rate motel. Even though your relationship with Carla is now stable and you could meet elsewhere, you use the El Dorado so she can pay off her debt to the owners. They have helped her out of more than one difficult situation. Carla has room 492 every day from five until ten o'clock; you try to use at least two of those hours. You have never asked her if she sees other men after that; you would rather not know.

"You seem pensive, darling."

"I am."

You remember the message you received that morning. *Murderer, your hands are stained with blood.* What murderer? What hands? What blood? Who could have sent it to you? How had they managed to get into the Black Chamber's secret communication network? You couldn't evaluate how important that message was and had decided to ignore it. You don't know whether you did the right thing. Nor do you care. You are tired of your boss and his paranoia about security.

Carla hands you a glass of whiskey and sits down next to you. Hastened by her determined look, by the eloquent expression of desire on her face, you put a hand on her left thigh, pliant and speckled with red blemishes. She places her lips on yours; her warm, inquisitive tongue skillfully parts them. Frightened and trembling, you let yourself be led. That's how it happened the first time. You took her to a hotel, paid for her room, and helped her to get settled. You were about to leave when you were surprised by the urgency of her kiss, when she pulled you onto the bed, her hands hurriedly undressing you. Only afterward, when she told you to meet her the next day at the El Dorado, did you realize how she made her living and begin to understand her parents a little. But it was too late.

"Is this how you like it? You're so tense, darling."

Your time with Carla is your great escape to a way of being that has led you to see a psychologist on more than one occasion. Still, it's only a partial escape. Carla may caress and make love to you dressed as one of your wildest fantasies, but your mind is still elsewhere. You should let yourself go, let your mind take part in the experience as much as your body, but you can't be something you're not. In photos, you are always to one side, looking down at the floor, trying not to be noticed, never looking into the lens of the camera.

"If you don't want our time to slip away, you should stop thinking about your wife."

Your: the unbearable lightness of an *r* pronounced by a California girl, at least in that word. She is taking the imitation very seriously.

"I haven't thought about her in years."

It's strange but true. You have been meeting Carla on a regular basis for two months now, and you don't feel like you're being unfaithful to Ruth. Devoid of desire, your marriage has become a quiet friendship. She lives her life and you live yours. You have stimulating conversations, the product of an affinity for the same topics, but sleeping together has ceased to be an adventure and is instead a tolerable inconvenience.

The way Carla unbuttons your shirt or plays with the zipper on your pants is evidence of her skill. Your socks fall to the floor in the shape of an *x*. You are naked and your reflection in the mirror on the ceiling is deformed. Those can't be your chubby legs, nor that disproportionate torso. And all those wrinkles on that face . . . The years take their toll.

She is about to slip off her miniskirt when you stop her.

"The idea is for you to leave your clothes on. That's why I asked you to dress that way."

Her gaze is vacant. There are three moles on her left cheek, and the way she speaks is slightly annoying. *Darling* this and *darling* that. Fucking *darling*. She crouches on the bed and begins to play with you. Nibbling, her tongue slippery. You are going to surprise her by lasting a long time, because while she does her work you will distract yourself by thinking about the man who deciphered Purple, about Bacon's anagrams in Shakespeare's work. As Carla goes about her business, you focus your mind. If the letter *a* is added to the last two lines of the epilogue of *The Tempest*—"As you from crimes would pardon'd be / Let your indulgence set me free"—the following anagram can be formed: "'Tempest' of Francis Bacon, Lord Verulam / Do ye ne'er divulge me ye words."

Have you fallen in love, or is it need that brings you to her? You don't know. What you do know is that in your office in the archives you began to miss your time with Carla, long to be reunited with her body. You took money out of your savings account to pay for her lodging, to buy her clothes, so that she doesn't have to see other men (but you suspect you don't have enough money to buy her exclusivity). Once, without Ruth's knowledge, you let her sleep in the Toyota. Your visits to the El Dorado after work are now daily; you had to find excuses to explain your late arrivals to Ruth. And you didn't leave Carla even after you found marks on her right forearm one afternoon: the smiling prostitute did drugs. How naive you were not to have realized that from the beginning. No wonder her moods changed so quickly, her eyes were so vacant, her jaw sometimes trembled faintly.

You asked her. Kneeling in front of you, she stayed perfectly still and seemed to vacillate between whether to tell you the truth or not. All of a sudden she began to cry. In between sobs, she told you that a friend had got her addicted to heroin. She had done everything she could to stop, including a methadone treatment program. She was now hooked on methadone and worked as a prostitute to pay her debts.

"Please, help me," Carla had implored. Only ghostly similarities with your daughter remained. You stroked her tear-stained cheeks. You wondered exactly what methadone was, what its effects were. You now knew where the majority of the money you gave her went. The marks on her forearm were in the shape of a cross; you weren't religious, but you knew to pay attention to the world when it spoke to you. You held her, pitied her. You would help her, you wouldn't abandon her.

Your Ericsson rings. You are tempted not to answer. You are even more tempted to answer. Carla continues to devote herself to your member, her expression becoming annoyed when you interrupt her. You see the number on the screen — a call from your house — and turn off your phone.

chapter 8

FLAVIA AND HER MOM are eating dinner in faint, flickering candlelight. Dad, who is always late these days, says he has to work overtime. Obviously the rules can be changed when it suits him. There had been times when she wanted to take her dinner to her room, but Dad had forbidden it. The only rule that had to be respected at home was the one regarding dinner—everyone had to be together and the abundant wires that connected them to the world had to be disconnected.

Ruth spills her glass of red wine on the white tablecloth. She watches the dark stain spread, making no effort to stop it. On the rug at Flavia's feet, Clancy lifts his head, startled, then goes back to sleep.

"Are you OK?" Flavia asks, taking a sip of her guarana juice, trailing her fork through her pasta from side to side.

"I had a bad day. Don't ever teach. Learn everything you possibly can, but don't teach it to anyone. Ingrates. It just gets worse and worse. What a waste of time."

"You're right. I don't know how our teachers put up with us."

Flavia knows that her mom's problems are not just today's. Her laughter has been absent for a long while now, laughter that used to cause glass to rattle (she recalls a scene from the frantic movie *Run Lola Run,* one of her favorites). And she is drinking more and more, behind everyone's back. The maid has shown Flavia the empty vodka bottles in the garage—that clear alcohol, which lets Miguel think she is drinking water. How can Flavia tell her mom that she might understand, that she's willing to listen if her mom feels comfortable confiding in her? She can't. It's impossible to break down those barriers. The same with Dad. Adults live in another world, where things are done differently. Would that be her fate too? Would she one day cross the border separating that strange land from her own? Would she become just another adult, unable to understand adolescents?

"I keep getting nosebleeds," Ruth says. "At first it didn't worry me, but it's happened several times. I went to the doctor today for a checkup. They did a few tests, an endoscopy. They think it's a vein in my nose that's giving me problems. I'll have the results soon."

"Does Dad know?" Flavia's tone is unworried. She should pretend to be a little more interested, knowing what a hypochondriac her mom is.

"He doesn't have a clue what's going on around here. I don't think he cares."

"That's not true."

"Right. You're his darling daughter. It started to bleed after an incident in class today. It happens when I'm stressed. Frustrated. Which is most of the time lately."

"You're frustrated?"

"Don't ever teach."

She lights a cigarette and gives Flavia permission to leave the table. Flavia stands up. Mom smokes a lot, a pack a day – it might be that. She'd better not mention it . . . or she'll get that into her head. Black tobacco. The pungent odor adheres to clothes, the curtains, the furniture. It took possession of the house a long time ago, will never leave. It's in the pictures in the living room, in the family photos on the walls, on the lamps in the rooms that for months have been at half light to save energy: you have no idea what's going to happen with the electricity bill, whether it will continue to rise exorbitantly or whether the government will freeze rates.

Clancy has woken up and follows her to her room, his nails clicking loudly on the parquet floor; they need to be cut. Without turning the light on, Flavia walks barefoot past her desk with its two humming computers, the walls covered in posters of Japanese movies, pink sheets on the bed, and shelves overflowing with her collection of board games (Life, Clue, Risk, Monopoly—intolerable memories of a childhood and early adolescence lived far away from any type of monitor; it seems impossible to her, but there was such a time).

A hacker would laugh at her tidy room, at the childish, feminine touches. At one time she considered herself a hacker, when she was fourteen. She had just discovered the power of computers and enjoyed having fun at the expense of her few friends who had them. She would access their Compaqs and Macs and make the mouse move strangely or turn the screen on and off—harmless things like that. Then the next day in class her friends would tell her that it was as if their computers had been possessed by some strange force, and Flavia would laugh to herself at their innocence and jokingly offer to perform black magic to break the spell.

She helps Clancy up onto the bed. She'd better not let Mom see. She complains about the smell he leaves on the blankets.

In the darkness, the menacing shapes of trees and neighboring houses are silhouetted clearly against the window. She is a shadow looking out at other shadows. All the houses are the same, symmetrical, lined up facing one another; all the walls are painted the same cream color, the shingles an intense red, the balcony with its gothic metal railing, the fake chimney. The neatly cut grass along the sidewalk, the carnations, the hibiscus, the rubber trees. It makes her uneasy.

She looks out at the windows illuminated in other houses, portals to other worlds, so similar to and different from her own. Someone is watching a soccer game on TV, logging on to Playground, printing porn photos from sexo.com, visiting Subcommander Marcos's Web site, reading in bed, hacking a virtual casino, calling her boyfriend on her cell phone, writing a poem on a laptop, burning a CD, looking sadly at a postcard from New York where the Twin Towers can be seen in the distance, listening to a concert on rollingstone.com.

Someone, with no lights on in the room, is trying to forget the world outside and create a quiet space for introspection.

But the world keeps intruding. Flavia pictures herself getting off the bus and that guy approaching her. Rafael's thick eyebrows are hard to forget, and his cell phone is yellow, even though the image in her mind is blurry and in black and white. The way he spoke was curious, as if he wanted to say something without actually voicing it.

She thinks he must be connected to the Resistance and realizes that everything is linked to her obsession.

She goes to her desk and sits in front of her computers. She opens e-mail, reads the latest news. A group of hackers has taken control of various government and private company sites (GlobaLux being one of them). They have also sent a virus to the computer networks at several federal organizations. An e-mail from a cracker friend warned her two days ago that this would happen. The Ministry of the Interior has declared a state of emergency because of "this concerted attack." Flavia reads the information. Even though she tries to maintain her journalistic objectivity, she is dying to know whether the Resistance is a local group. For four years now she has been refining her knowledge of cyber outlaws; she has approximately three thousand files on hackers, from neophytes to big names, most of them Latin American. Her computers search and file their conversations in chatrooms, on IRC (Internet Relay Chat), and in Playground. The information has given her files a sophisticated depth. Even though they don't like to admit it, the media and the intelligence service are some of AllHacker's most loyal surfers. Few in Río Fugitivo know as much as she does.

She reviews her files and prepares a series of Identikits on those who are in the Resistance. They are speculative, since in truth she is unsure of the group's makeup. She isn't even sure if the hackers who wound up dead were part of the Resistance. In fact, she doesn't even know whether Vivas and Padilla were hackers; the information she was given could have been false.

She would like to get her hands on a photo of Kandinsky to put on her site. With a scoop like that, her reputation would be bumped up another few notches. No one knows who he is or what he looks like. Although she would get into trouble if she did publish it. Hadn't her meeting with Rafael been a warning? Two years ago, when she helped the Black Chamber catch a couple of hackers, she had received death threats and her site had suffered several DoS attacks ("denial of service": a computer is instructed, for example, to bombard a certain address with e-mail, and the flood of traffic hangs the system). Since then she had promised herself that she would be more neutral on the topic, that she would spend her time informing above all. She has a love-hate relationship with hackers. They say they prefer secrecy and anonymity, but they also like to let their pseudonyms be known when they manage to do something that they believe is worthy of admiration. As long as they see that she is independent, they will leave her alone.

Flavia has a hunch: Rafael belongs to Kandinsky's inner circle. He was trusted enough to be in charge of contacting her, to abandon the virtual world in order to send a message to the real world. He may even be Kandinsky himself. It would be incredible if it were true, but why not?

She needs to create a false identity and go into chatrooms and IRC channels, or some of the neighborhoods in Playground, to find out the latest. Hackers live in the shadows, but they can't keep quiet. Sooner or later they need to tell someone about their exploits. Hackers are marvelous storytellers.

She decides to log on to Playground. A little more than a year ago, three recent graduates from San Ignacio High School had borrowed money from their parents in order to acquire the rights to the Playground franchise for Bolivia. Created by a Finnish corporation, Playground was both a virtual game and an online community. There, for a modest monthly fee — twenty dollars, which could grow to much more, depending on the time you spent — anyone could create an avatar or use one of those that Playground put up for sale. The game takes place in the year 2019. Participants try to live in an apocalyptic land governed by the strong arm of a corporation. Playground's success in other countries was replicated in Bolivia. It started out with the young middle class in the country's largest cities and slowly spread to outlying areas, other generations. Flavia spends several hours a day there. She has spent all of her own money and is now in debt to her dad. Time and again she has promised him that she will limit her visits. She has tried, but she lacks willpower. Sociologists refer to the financial problems resulting from abuse of the game as "the Playground effect."

In the upper left-hand corner of her screen, Flavia sees the number of hours she has left for the rest of the month. Not many. Oh well, it doesn't matter. If she runs out, she'll buy more time. But where will she get the money? When Albert was in charge of the Black Chamber, he would contract certain jobs to her, allowing her to earn a few pesos. She doesn't have that source of income any longer, and AllHacker doesn't bring in anything either, since she does it purely as a hobby. Somehow she needs to make her abilities profitable.

She lied to Rafael: of course she has several recurring identities on the Web and creates others as she needs them. She assumes the identity of Erin, a hacker searching for someone to guide her, a mentor, a father figure.

Jeans, boots, a black jacket, and Ray-Bans: Erin walks through the streets of Boulevard, Playground's downtown. The neon lights of bars and nightclubs, the art deco style of the businesses: the screen is supersaturated with loud colors; the noise of cars and motorcycles, voices and music vibrates from the street. A couple of weeks ago at the Golden Strip she had felt she was being watched by a stranger drinking a martini at the bar. Dark, handsome, wearing a long black trench coat. Was that one of the identities of the man who called himself Rafael?

She heads to the Golden Strip.

There is a street fight. Two men are surrounded by a jeering crowd; one has a knife in his hand and the other is wielding a broken beer bottle. The neighborhood around the Golden Strip is dangerous. The police have abandoned it to the drug traffickers and whores. Erin likes the sensation that anything can happen. Last time she wound up in a sleazy hotel room with a mocha-skinned Thai girl with a scar on her cheek.

She doesn't stop to watch the outcome of the fight. Beside the Golden Strip shines the sign from another bar, Mandala. Rafael had used that word. She decides to go in. She heads to the bar but is accosted by a blonde with enormous breasts who asks if she'd like a little action. *Yeah, but not with you.* She orders a shot of tequila.

A while later the dark-skinned man sits down next to her. Even though he isn't wearing the trench coat, she recognizes him: it's the same guy as last time.

RIDLEY: i thought ud never come back
ERIN: u gotta have faith specially when street encounters r hard 2 forget

Flavia would never be able to say something like that in person.

RIDLEY: what street encounter
ERIN: 1 in a galaxy not 2 far from here
RIDLEY: ur confused my name is ridley
ERIN: kandinsky
RIDLEY: ridley

Erin looks at him closely, trying to discern Rafael in his features.

RIDLEY: my face looks like lotsa others were not very imaginative we all choose the same tall dark handsome avatars w/ sunglasses and trench coats theres also the question of technology being notoriously behind when it comes to facial details itll get there 1 day

Flavia thinks that if the police don't intervene, Playground's private security agents will. The person calling himself Ridley has just committed a mortal sin: references to a character's digital nature are prohibited in Playground. Early on that type of conversation had been frequent, but a movement had fought valiantly to prohibit it and managed to impose its vision of the digital world. The cardinal rule of that world was not to shatter the illusion of reality, to suspend belief so that a person's avatar could be seen as real. When she is in Playground, Flavia tries very hard not to mention the world that awaits her the moment she turns off her computer. That doesn't mean it sometimes doesn't just slip out, like her reference to the "street encounter in a galaxy not too far from here"— a second-degree infraction: no reference was made to the digital nature of persons, but one was made to the reality outside.

Two armed men appear on screen wearing the navy blue uniforms of Playground security agents. They read Ridley his rights. Ridley says goodbye to Erin, shakes her hand, turns around, and lets himself be escorted by the guards. When they reach the door, he surprises one of them with a blow to the neck and runs out. The guard falls to the floor, writhing, while his partner chases Ridley.

On screen, Flavia can see the panoramic view from a security helicopter flying over Playground. The powerful searchlight glides over the streets in the Boulevard until it focuses on Ridley. Immediately there is submachine gun fire from the helicopter. Ridley gets hit in the arm but manages to escape, losing himself down a narrow, garbage-strewn street.

There is a knock on her door. Flavia has just enough time to put a screen saver of Dennis Moran, Jr., over the image of Mandala.

"How are you, princess?" It's her dad, his smile forced. "I'm sorry I didn't make it home for dinner. Work is crazy. And to top it all off, there's an emergency."

She gets up and gives him a kiss, smelling the whiskey on his breath. Whom is he trying to fool?

chapter 9

Ramírez-Graham enters the interception room accompanied by Baez and Santana. Baez had worked with the administrators of Playground for a while, specializing in tracing hackers who tried to penetrate its security systems; Santana was an expert in the new, lethal generation of viruses with which malicious programmers infected computers on the Internet. Ramírez-Graham, having embarked on his project to revive the Black Chamber, had stopped hiring the linguists and professionals in the humanities that Albert had surrounded himself with and instead filled the main positions with computer analysts. It was true that certain areas of modern linguistics and computer programming languages had much in common; in fact, he had known many linguists at the NSA who had been recycled as experts in various computer languages. Still, it was a question of emphasis. If the priority was cybercrime, he preferred to have people trained in computer science who also knew something of linguistics and not vice versa.

Already seated at the table are the other members of the Central Committee. The pale, late-afternoon light filtering in through the windows whitens their faces. An enormous photo of Albert dominates the room. Folders are scattered on the table; a map of Río Fugitivo posted on a whiteboard is dotted with several red *x*'s that have no apparent order. Each one represents the location of a computer that sent the virus to government offices. The entire city is the scene of the crime. The entire fucking city.

"Any news?" Ramírez-Graham asks, sitting down. "Sin pérdida de tiempo. I'm tired of this game."

When he is upset, his American accent becomes more pronounced and he forgets his almost perfect Spanish syntax. It is disconcerting: it's as if a foreigner holds one of the government's highest positions. Well, Ramírez-Graham is a foreigner.

"The computers that sent the virus are in private homes and Internet cafés, research centers, and public offices."

The voice is Marisa Ivanovic's. She is the first woman to form part of the Central Committee. Ramírez-Graham has seen her working in her office until late, playing distractedly with her necklace while reviewing data on the screen. She always looks disheveled; locks of brown hair fall over her eyes, and he wonders how well she can see. In a way he admires her. He knows how difficult it is for women to break into this field, to stay in it, and to find their voice.

"Which means that . . ."

"Those computers were used via telnet to launch the attack. The owners are innocent. We're tracing the virus's steps—its fingerprints, so to speak. But we probably won't find the source, the mother computer. Just like before. The Resistance tends to be very careful."

Ramírez-Graham detects a note of admiration in Marisa's voice. That is one of his problems: his employees are seduced by the romantic notion of hackers that has been spread by the media. The myth of Kandinsky: a local hacker who was able to infiltrate the Pentagon's security system. There is no proof, but that is what legend says, and legend does not need to be founded on truth in order to become established as truth. Kandinsky has easily paralyzed the government whenever he has felt like it, and those who defend the law cannot compete with the glamorous hacker counterculture.

"Have you investigated the code that was used to create the virus?"

"It's still too soon," Santana says. "Right now the only concrete thing we have is that it bears the Resistance's signature. It's a delicate piece of work, probably written by Kandinsky or one of his closest collaborators — nothing to do with script kiddies. I'd hazard a guess that it's a new version of Simile.D."

Santana knew a great deal about the worms the Resistance used: Code Red, Nimda, Klez.H, and Simile.D. Simile.D was a "conceptual virus," a lab sample that its programmers had made public for others to see. By being able to change its features on the fly, it could fool antivirus programs that trace a code's fingerprints (which, for example, was how Klez.H was stopped). In this case, all that antivirus programs could do was trace behavior that looked like a virus, find ways to replicate the structures that were programmed in an encrypted routine modeled to hide a virus, or study the virus code itself. It wasn't hard to do, but it did take time, which is why Santana had recommended other ways of maintaining system security: accepting codes that had digital signatures from reliable sources and maintaining a database with all of the accepted codes. To do so, Ramírez-Graham needed a budget that he simply did not have.

"There's no visible structure," Baez says. "No figures are formed on the map of the city, faces don't appear in the binary code . . . Kandinsky isn't as obvious as Red Scharlach. His labyrinth has no order."

Ah, Baez's literary allusions. Of all the members of the Central Committee, he is the one who seems interested not only in his work but also in what surrounds him — the political situation, the economic crisis. Ramírez-Graham has even discovered that Baez is quite the literature buff. He does have to laugh at the way Baez dresses, though; he tries to be elegant, but the details escape him — white socks with a dark suit or a loud tie. He had been the same, just another unkempt programmer, until he met Svetlana.

"So," he says, "perhaps his chaos is a type of order — "

"Like in fractal geometry," Baez interrupts.

"Please," Ramírez-Graham continues, "put all of the coordinates on the map into an algorithm of progressions. Maybe that will give us the next point in the continuum. Maybe the location of the next attack. Or maybe the source of it."

"I've already done that," says Marisa. "You're going to be surprised at the result — it gives me the Twenty-First-Century Towers, the building where you live. The computers weren't chosen at random. They were chosen expecting that we'd do what you just suggested."

"So they're jokers on top of it all. They're making fun of us, and we can't stop them. But make no mistake, this time heads will roll if we don't dismantle the so-called Resistance. There's discontent in the upper echelons."

"Well, imagine that," Baez says. "Maybe it's time to tell them that they can't expect miracles of us. We can intercept a ton of information and efficiently decode everything that's encrypted by low-tech means — which luckily for us is the norm in this country — but if we're faced with people who really know how to program, there's not much we can do. And this is only the beginning."

"If we take your argument further, then we're no longer needed," Ramírez-Graham retorts. "Instead of reorganizing the Black Chamber, we should simply close it."

"Maybe we haven't been needed for a long time," Baez replies. "You've got to admit that we can't stand up to your average hacker. We can't even easily read e-mails that have been encrypted with a good piece of software, the kind you can buy on the street — unless each one of us spends three months trying to break the code."

Bacz pauses, looking at the faces around him as if confirming that they are waiting for him to continue. His only defect, thinks Ramírez-Graham, is that he's always trying to steal the show.

"The cards we've been dealt have been to work in Río Fugitivo," Baez continues. "So we entertain ourselves by intercepting and deciphering homegrown codes, but when something real comes along, then, then . . ."

An atmosphere of pessimism invades the room. After months of being defeated by the Resistance, Baez, Marisa, and Santana have been made to feel impotent, to mistrust the usefulness of their own work. Ramírez-Graham had chosen each of them after a long and careful search, had trusted them because he thought that they were among the best computer programmers and analysts in the country, and he was angry that they felt defeated so soon. Even worse was the fact that perhaps they were right. He had gone through a similar crisis during his last few months at the NSA. That was why he was here. But by the looks of it, the problem could not be solved by a change of geographical location; it had become inherent to the profession. It was programmed into the code of today's cryptanalyst.

He would like to tell them that they are right, but he is the boss, and as such he has to set an example.

"It's not the time for existential questions." He pauses, taking a drink of his Coke. "Let's get Kandinsky, and I promise you that, out of my own pocket, I'll pay for a month of psychoanalysis for each of you. It's time to get creative. Let's hear your opinions. Estoy abierto a sugerencias."

I'm open to suggestions... At times he can't help translating from English: after all, it's the language he thinks in.

"We've already done a couple of things," Marisa says. "The virus was programmed so the infected computers would launch a DoS attack at a certain time, aimed at all the computers that until then had been safe. This would have crashed the entire system. We've blocked the address of the ISP where the attack originated. At first we thought about just changing the addresses of the Presidential Palace and other government buildings, GlobaLux and the Black Chamber, but the attack would've continued and debilitated the entire network structure even further. Still, we did that too."

"Well done. But that's defense, and what I'm interested in now is offense."

"If I may," Marisa says, "I've spoken with Baez about this. It might be time to try to get information through unorthodox methods."

"So we're back to the same thing," Santana says. "Why are we here?"

"Not necessarily," Baez says. "Albert also had paid informants. Sometimes it's necessary. How many codes were really deciphered during the cold war? Most of them were obtained thanks to the work of spies, saving both time and money. If you'll allow me, and I hope you won't take this as a criticism, but you have a very purist view of what we're doing. As if intelligence were sufficient for dismantling codes. Sometimes it's not."

Ramírez-Graham does not like to be criticized, but he tries not to show it. He needs to play fair with them. After all, he encouraged them to make suggestions that depart from the norm. Thinking outside the box is good, thinking outside the box is good . . .

"All right," he says. "Do you have someone particular in mind?"

"There are plenty of Rats," Baez suggests. "Any one of them could help us."

"Rats are corrupt," Santana replies, "and they often sell false information. Ask our colleagues in the intelligence service. They've gotten rid of a few innocent people by blindly following information they got from Rats."

"I think I know who could help us," Marisa asserts. "In fact, I know that Albert turned to her during his last few months here. She's young, likely still in high school. Her name is Flavia, and she maintains the most up-to-date site on Latin American hackers. Sometimes — I don't know how she does it — she manages to get exclusive interviews with them."

"Is she from here?" Ramírez-Graham asks. "From Río Fugitivo?"

"Uh-huh," Baez says. "She's all right, but she's not as good as Marisa makes her out to be."

"She's Turing's daughter," Marisa says, smiling. "And I'm sorry, Baez, but your prejudices are showing. Flavia's not only good, she's very good."

"Our Turing's daughter?" Ramírez-Graham asks, suspecting that they are making fun of him.

"Is there another Turing alive?" Marisa says, making the final thrust.

Our Turing? No fucking way!

chapter 10

THE CLOUDS SHINE BRIGHTER than a carnival. The new moon has wrapped itself around a mast. Every afternoon is a port. And I remember . . . Because I don't know what else to do. I hold a dark passionflower in my hand. My taciturn face is extraordinarily remote . . . My slender, leather-braider's fingers. I remember my voice . . . That I can no longer hear. Slow. Resentful. Nasal. Every now and then sibilant.

I am an electric ant . . . And tired . . . I am fed through tubes. They're waiting for my resurrection any time now . . . Neither one nor the other. I won't die.

I'm tired . . . Shadow after shadow visits my room. Who would have imagined. I arrived here many years ago. Which is nothing from my perspective. And I stayed.

My former colleagues come. They sit down. Look at the clock. The minutes pass. They're in a hurry. The day is ending. But Turing could spend the whole afternoon. He's waiting for the oracle . . . The phrase he'll decipher . . . The one that will allow him to go on with the week . . . The month . . . The year.

Poor Turing. He doesn't know how to be happy. He hasn't changed since I met him. When he was Miguel Sáenz and didn't even know that Turing had existed. One sultry day . . . A slate-colored storm curtaining the sky. The trees were flailing wildly. He came alone. Looking for work. For him and his wife . . . They had been recommended. I had been told that they were talented. They could be useful to us. They could be useful to Montenegro. They could be useful to me . . .

It was my idea. Like in Bletchley Park . . . Linguists. Mathematicians. Crossword puzzle experts. Chess players . . . People who would use their intellect. Who knew about logic. Like Turing . . . Who would have imagined. He looked like he was the brightest. He ended up being the brightest. And the most useful . . . He had a good memory. And. That's all that interested him. He wanted to be a human computer. Pure logic . . . Or at least that's what it seemed like to me . . .

I remember the cigarette in the hard visage. His gray overcoat. Against the now limitless storm cloud in that park. But I didn't know how prodigious his memory might be, and even that was nothing compared to me. Who was Memory itself. Of cryptanalysis. Of cryptography. Or are they the same?

At that time I was studying Latin . . . I studied during my free time. Between interviews. He was impressed by the books in my briefcase. Lhomond's *De Viris Illustribus* . . . Quicherat's *Thesaurus.* Julius Caesar's commentaries. That great cryptographer . . . An odd-numbered volume of Pliny's *Naturalis Historia.*

He was more impressed by my anecdotes about the profession for which I wanted to recruit him . . . Running through centuries as if they were afternoons . . . Speaking of details as if I had been there. As if I were immortal . . .

What's certain is that he didn't know. Maybe deep down inside we all know that we're immortal . . . Sooner or later. Every man will do everything there is to do and know everything there is to know.

Nothing impressed him as much as my tale of 1586. Of my participation in Walsingham's trap for Mary Queen of Scots . . . At that time I was Thomas Phelippes. In the midst of the storm . . . Both absorbed. I told the future Turing about Phelippes. As if Phelippes were someone else . . . But Turing could sense that I knew Phelippes too well. He could sense Phelippes. Would have liked to have been Phelippes . . . I told him. What I wouldn't give to have been him. To participate. Somehow. In history . . .

Electric ant. Having come to Río Fugitivo who knows why. *Tempus fugit . . .*

Mary had been accused of conspiring against her cousin Elizabeth. Queen of England . . . Mary wanted the throne of England for herself. She had escaped from Scotland . . . She was a Catholic queen and the Protestant nobles had organized a revolt against her. They put her in jail. Forced her to abdicate . . . A year later Mary escaped from prison. She wanted to regain the throne, but the troops loyal to her were defeated at Langside. Near Glasgow . . .

Facts and more facts. Dates and more dates. Names and more names. Everything can be ciphered in a code. History can be ciphered . . . Perhaps our lives are no more than a message in code awaiting its decoder . . . It's one way to understand such loss.

The guard has left the window open. Or maybe it was the nurse. A warm breeze blows into the room . . . Caressing me. The birds are singing in the trees . . . Like they used to sing in the green valley. The one I remember.

What valley? What period in my life? The medieval towers. A hummingbird suspended in the air. Seconds. That seem like minutes. Time doesn't pass . . . It passes. But it doesn't.

The weather is about to change. It'll rain soon. That's how it's been every day lately.

Mary found refuge in England. Elizabeth was Protestant and afraid of Mary . . . The Catholic English saw Mary as their queen. Not Elizabeth. So Elizabeth decided to keep her under house arrest for twenty years. Poor Mary. They say she was very beautiful . . . Intelligent . . . Unlucky . . . I remember the black velvet dress she wore the day she was executed. The charm of her accent. Her gentle manners. She was no longer the same. Her skin had aged. Her continual illnesses . . . Religion and its wars. The loss of the throne . . .

The future Turing listened to me with his mouth agape. Hanging on my every word in the persistent rain . . . Perhaps he was seduced by the surface layer. Perhaps he was searching for the messages that were hidden behind the story . . . Those who take up codes never stop searching. They are alert to the messages that others wish to send. They are alert to the world. Alert to their own messages . . . Messages that someone inside might be sending without their knowledge. Suspecting themselves . . . No one ever said that this profession attracted balanced individuals. The unhealthy pathology of the cryptanalyst. The paranoid pathology of the cryptanalyst.

He who lives by the code dies by the code.

Once twenty years of house arrest had passed. Sir Francis Walsingham. Elizabeth's minister . . . Who had created a secret police force with fifty-three agents across the European continent. Machiavellian . . . If the word weren't so overused. But time marches on and everything becomes overused . . . Infiltrated Mary's inner circle. He placed one of his men as Mary's messenger.

One of Mary's followers. Babington. Just twenty-four years of age. Conceived of an ambitious plan. To free her . . . Then murder Elizabeth so that a rebellion by Catholic Englishmen would put Mary on the throne of England. Mary sent coded messages to her followers . . . The messenger . . . Before delivering the letters. Copied them and gave them to Walsingham. Sir Francis had an experienced cryptologist in his employ. Phelippes. Sir Francis knew that kingdoms are not won or lost by weapons alone. You also have to know how to read secret messages.

Decipher them . . . Decode them . . . Dismantle them . . .

You have to know how to read the words hidden behind the words. That's what I want for you. Future Turing . . . To help me keep this government in power. With so many conspirators around. We need the military and the paramilitary. People trained to kill . . . But we also need cryptologists . . . People trained to think. Or to decipher the thinking of others . . . The ideas hidden in the mist of words . . . It was raining. I could see that my speech was convincing. I could see that the future Turing would never leave my side.

I spit up blood. I sleep with my eyes open. I shake during the night. My body is rebelling . . . Can immortals die? Did I come to Río Fugitivo to die?

I must have done something terrible to have been sent to this country. After having been in the great centers of civilization . . .

Deciding the fate of the planet. I wind up on the periphery of the periphery . . . But you don't argue. You do what you have to do. And I did it well . . . I did it well . . . I can continue on my way in peace. This country has an admirable secret service . . . There is democracy today. But whoever wants to could try to remain in power . . . The infrastructure is solid. Whoever wants to tell secrets behind the government's back. Has his days numbered . . .

And meanwhile. I spit up blood.

I'd like to know how it was that I thought what I thought. How it was that I decided what I decided. It's very hard to imagine how you thought.

You chase your own tail.

The letters between Babington and Mary were ciphered using an index that consisted of twenty-one symbols corresponding to the letters of the alphabet . . . Except for *j*, *v*, and *w*. And thirty-six more symbols that represented words or phrases. *And. For. With. Your Name. Send. Myne.* Et cetera. Unfortunately for them . . . Walsingham believed in the importance of cryptanalysis. Ever since he came across a book by Girolamo Cardano . . . That great mathematician and cryptographer . . . Author of the first book on the theory of probabilities. Creator of a steganographic device and of the first autokey system . . .

Walsingham had a school for code decipherers in London. Any self-respecting government should have had one at their disposal . . . Phelippes was his cipher secretary. This I told the future Turing . . . I was his cipher secretary. He was short. Bearded. His face pocked by measles . . . His vision poor. He was about thirty years old. A linguist. He knew French. Italian. Spanish. German . . . He was already a famous cryptanalyst in Europe. Phelippes. I told the future Turing as the storm rained down . . . It was difficult for me to speak in the third person. But that's the way my life was. That's the way my life is. First and third person at the same time. Always.

The messages between Babington and Mary could be deciphered using a simple analysis of frequencies . . . Babington and Mary. Confident that they were using a secure system of communication. Spoke with increasing frankness about their plans to assassinate Elizabeth . . . The message on July 17, 1586, sealed Mary's fate. It spoke of the *design* . . . She was worried about being freed before or at the same time that Elizabeth was killed. She was afraid that her captors would kill her. Walsingham had what he wanted. But he wanted more . . . To tear the conspiracy out by its roots . . . He asked Phelippes. He asked me . . . To forge Mary's handwriting and ask Babington to give her the names of the other conspirators . . .

Phelippes was a great forger. He could forge anyone's handwriting. I was a great forger. I could forge anyone's handwriting . . . So I did. That's how they fell. Poor Babington and Mary . . . If they had communicated without codes. They would have been more discreet . . . But they lived at a time when cryptanalysis was advancing more quickly than cryptography . . . A magic time in which decipherers surpassed encrypters. My kingdom for an analysis of frequencies.

On February 8, 1587. Mary. Queen of Scots . . . Was executed. Decapitated. In the great hall of Fotheringhay Castle . . . All of this I told the future Turing in the midst of the storm . . . The city shrouded in mist. Like the messages. We wound up drenched . . . Huge raindrops running down our faces. Our pants were soaked. Our shoes were waterlogged. It didn't matter . . . The future Turing saw himself as a Phelippes.

He saw himself as I saw myself. As I have always seen myself . . . I, who have no beginning and do not know if I will have an end. He saw himself helping to disarm a conspiracy . . . Forming part of history. The secret possessor of secrets . . . He saw that he could be more than he was. He saw that deciphering codes was not a game . . . Lives were at stake. The destinies of countries. Of kingdoms. A correct deciphering would abolish chance . . .

He's been with me ever since. Never abandoning me. Electric ant . . . Connected to tubes that keep it alive. Connected to tubes that keep me alive. Or would my heart continue to beat even if there were no tubes?

chapter 11

YOU WALK into the living room, a glass of whiskey in your hand, the ice rattling in the amber liquid. You sit down on the green velvet sofa and turn on the television, anxious to delay your encounter with Ruth in the bedroom. It's a strange game without any winners. She does the same thing, closeting herself in the study preparing for classes, correcting exams, reading the biographies of scientists and spies. There are nights when the bedroom remains empty until the early morning. Sometimes you sleep on the sofa, cursing Ruth out loud, insults that you will have forgotten by morning, while she, plagued by insomnia, her body immune to sleeping pills, invents work to fill the time.

The whiskey no longer burns your throat but slides down naturally, as tends to happen as the evening wears on, after the first few glasses. You become lost in thought, counting the vertical brown stripes on the sofa.

The announcer with a trimmed beard on the main news channel is announcing the attack that was perpetrated by the Resistance and turns the story over to a reporter at the entrance to the Presidential Palace. The virus has swept through government computers, and none of its Web sites have been left untouched (nor was GlobaLux safe from the attack). Images of the graffiti on the sites are broadcast: photos of Montenegro with a noose around his neck, insults about the technocrats who are governing the country without understanding it. The secretary of state has declared a state of emergency. The Workers' Union and well-known civic and indigenous leaders have expressed their solidarity with the hackers. The Coalition is continuing its preparations for the blockade of Río Fugitivo tomorrow. You can picture the young cryptanalysts and software code experts at the Black Chamber, high on adrenaline, in search of the clues that will lead them to the perpetrators. They will call soon, and you will have to go back to the office. They need your experience to trace the history of the evasive Resistance, to find coincidences in the encrypted code, the sometimes invisible signature that the murderer leaves behind on the body, the fingerprints left at the scene of the crime. They need the memory of the archives, which is not entirely artificial yet but soon will be. Ramírez-Graham has ordered that all documents be scanned and digitized — drawer after drawer of papers. In the end, all of the papers stored in the basement will be transferred to the hard drive of some minuscule computer.

Ruth appears in the doorway wearing a cream-colored flowered robe, a cigarette in her hand. She seems nervous. You turn off the television.

"Have you heard the news?"

"Yes, unfortunately. I'll probably have to go back to the office."

"Flavia's in Playground, as usual. We really have to limit her time. The bill last month was far too high."

"Yes, something will have to be done. Just be patient — it's her last month of classes."

"Oh, I'll speak to her. She's got you wrapped around her little finger. You start out fine, raising your voice, sounding firm, until she looks straight at you and you melt."

"There's nothing wrong with being kind."

"And what exactly do you win by being kind? It's as if she's living in a hotel. She comes out of her room only to eat. To speak to her, you practically have to e-mail her. Or phone her. I read somewhere that it's not good to let your children have computers in their room. Who knows what they can access."

You wish you were with Carla, letting her rest her head on your chest and fall asleep in your arms. The unmistakable expertise of her tongue can't compete with the vulnerability that hides behind the aggressive façade. You picture the marks on her forearm, fascinated. You've tried to help her, even paying for her to check into rehab; she didn't last long, just three days. The first night she got out, a silly argument pushed her over the edge and soon she was throwing glasses and cans of Cuba Libre at the wall, insulting you as if she didn't know you. You would like to do more than you already have, but you know that addiction, any kind of addiction, winds up capturing whoever dares approach it.

"I was at the doctor's today. I've been getting nosebleeds, all the time."

"Really? I wonder why."

"Worry, maybe. Anxiety. Or something worse. My mom died of cancer. Well, she killed herself before the cancer could. I guess that's what worries me."

"You think a few drops of blood mean you have cancer? Let's not overdo it . . ."

Her face has aged. When you first met, her complexion was so smooth that a geisha in her prime would have envied her. Now her skin is losing its elasticity; it is a mask that no longer fits her skull. So many years have passed since the day you were introduced, in the cafeteria at the university. If you hadn't come in out of the rain that afternoon, into that smoke-filled room, and if you hadn't run into a friend who was chatting with Ruth . . .

"What're you thinking about?"

There she is, sitting next to you on the sofa, the woman who had shared her passion for cryptography. That woman who snored as if she had the hiccups, whose skin smelled of moisturizers, was the person responsible for the course your life had taken. And to think that when you met her, you were studying biology . . .

"Someone found a way into my private e-mail account this morning. They sent me an easily decipherable code. I spent the whole day worrying about the message, when I really should have been worrying about how they accessed my account. Who? And why?"

"Maybe they chose you for a particular reason. What did the message say?"

"That I'm a murderer. That my hands are stained with blood."

"Aren't they?"

"They aren't."

"Then you've nothing to worry about."

That tone of voice . . . When Montenegro returned to power in 1997, Ruth asked you to resign. Despite the fact that he returned by democratic means, she had only seen Montenegro as he had once been: a pathetic dictator. She had never been able to separate, as you had, the work from the ends that had been achieved by means of it: the defense of governments with doubtful morals. So scrupulous, so attuned to ethical questions, she had threatened to leave you more than once if you didn't resign. And yet she was weak; you didn't do what she asked and she is still with you.

"I'm not worried," you say, somewhat agitated. "I've never shot anyone. I've never even touched anyone. I never left my office."

"The same old argument. Only the one who pulls the trigger is guilty."

She stands up, stubs out her cigarette in the ashtray, and leaves the living room. She's angry. Should you have been more sensitive when she mentioned her nosebleeds? She is such a hypochondriac that you don't know what to take seriously anymore. If she has a headache, it's a fatal tumor. If she cuts her leg, it'll become infected and she'll lose it to gangrene. Ruth has become rigid over the years, has lost her soft edges. What a contrast to those endless nights spent at her house when she would tell you, passionately, about the code that had saved Greece from being conquered by Xerxes; when she taught you, using pads of tracing paper that quickly ran out, to decipher monoalphabetic and polyalphabetic substitution codes, to understand them using ADFGVX, Mayfair, and Purple. To others, you were a couple of bores; to the both of you, those were the nights when magic happened, when you fell in love.

One hundred sixty-nine brown vertical stripes. Had they chosen that number intentionally?

You need to go to the bathroom. Damn bladder rules your life! You have to get up at least three times during the night. Ruth always thought it was strange that you could function during the day after such a fitful night. But you have never needed much sleep. She used to; there was a time when her sleep was so deep that you could go in and out of the room, turn the light on, root through drawers, and she wouldn't even stir. Now her frequent insomnia gives her nothing but grief, puts her in a bad mood during the day.

Those nights when you were young, when you would visit her at her house, not only had you fallen in love with her, but you had realized that you wanted to be a cryptanalyst. Ruth had discovered cryptanalysis when she was a child; she and her father would send secret messages in crossword puzzles that they wrote themselves. One day a question about the origin of what they were doing led her to an encyclopedia, then to the public library, and, later, to become obsessed with the topic. She had mastered the history and theory of cryptology, she could even decipher complex codes (although it might take her hours), but she lacked the intuition that, combined with technique, was needed to find the key that would unlock the secret message. You had an abundance of intuition, at least in this area. You even gave yourself over wholeheartedly to mathematics, a science for which you had a certain ability but that didn't necessarily attract you. This much is certain—you never wanted to become a cryptanalyst of algorithms sitting in front of a computer. It didn't take you long to become the student who surpassed the teacher. Still, there were no territorial jealousies. Ruth preferred theory to practice, the colorful anecdotes that allowed her to build arguments as solid as they were unusual regarding the course of world history. *The laboratory for you,* she would say, *and someday I'll write the book.*

But where could a cryptanalyst find work in the country in which you were unlucky enough to have been born? Emigrate to the United States? Send your résumé to the NSA? You continued studying biology, looking at codes simply as a sophisticated hobby. At times you would play with them and ask yourself whether an expert geneticist was not, in a way, also a cryptanalyst; there were secret messages in DNA too, and deciphering them would perhaps lead you to the primitive nucleus of life. But no, you preferred to work with words. You began to develop your own secret codes, irritating your friends with letters they could read but not understand.

Everything changed as a result of the political instability. The university was closed. Montenegro was dictator, and the military was fighting a bloody battle to eradicate communism, whose revolutionary flags were sparking unrest in middle-class students, politicians, and workers. The two of you found yourselves at a loss for what to do. A cousin of Ruth's in the military, knowing your skills, offered you both work at the Dirección de Orden Político (DOP, the Office of Political Stability), which was later renamed the Servicio de Inteligencia de la Nación, the National Intelligence Service, or SIN. Albert, an American consultant from the CIA, was organizing an agency that would report to the DOP; its exclusive mission would be to intercept and decode messages from opposition parties. Ruth's cousin could arrange an interview with Albert. "You'll be providing a great service to the country," he said, twirling his long mustache. "We're surrounded by conspirators with foreign backing. We need trained people in order to face them on equal terms. We need to excise this cancer from our organization."

You swirl your glass of whiskey — concentric circles forming on the surface — and remember that key moment in your life. Ruth had squinted her eyes and looked at you, unsure. Work for the military? For a dictatorship? It was you who convinced her: it was a job to survive, there was no need to be so righteous. "It can never be just a job to survive," she had said. "It's better to die of hunger than to work for the wrong cause." "Easy to say, but it's not a luxury we can afford right now." Ruth's next words, spoken softly, were as sharp as a knife: "Don't you believe in anything with conviction, Miguel? Do you at least believe in God?" "There's order behind chaos," was his well-thought-out reply. "There's purpose behind chance. Our mission is to search for order and purpose. If both of those words are synonymous with God, then I believe in him. That is, I believe in the possibility that one day I might find him. But don't ask me to look for him in a church."

You asked her at least to let you meet with Albert — you wouldn't lose anything by it. Oh, how you returned from that meeting in the plaza: transformed, seduced by that handsome, blue-eyed man with long brown hair and graying beard, who was so cultured and spoke proper Spanish, his accent indefinable, somewhere between

German and American. You finally convinced Ruth, and you both started to work for Montenegro's government. She didn't last long. You did. You have been working for the government ever since. You have served, without favoritism, spineless dictators and cruel ones, democratic presidents who respected the law and others quite open to breaking, by any means possible, the backbone of the unions and the opposition. To do so, you concentrated obsessively on your work without wondering about the consequences. In your eyes, the government is a great abstraction, an enormous, faceless machine. You follow orders without questioning them; your principles are those of the current administration. And this is how they have repaid your loyalty: promoting you, but in reality distancing you from the action.

You finish your glass of whiskey, get up off the couch, and take the stairs to your room, thinking about Carla, about Flavia, about the message you received. On the wall is a wood-framed, yellowing, somewhat faded picture of all the personnel who started the Black Chamber. The photo had been Ruth's idea: all eighty of you were lined up in two rows on the stairs at the entrance. Some were looking at the camera, others to one side. Groups of five people formed one letter of a bilateral cipher code that was written by Francis Bacon in *De Augmentis Scientiarum*. According to that code, the combination of two letters was enough to represent all the letters in the alphabet. Thus, *a* was represented by *aaaaa, b* by *aaaab, c* by *aaaba,* and so on. In the photo, those who were looking at the camera stood for the letter *a* and those who were looking to one side the letter *b*. The first five in the first row, from left to right: front, side, front, front, side—the letter *k*. Thus, the eighty of you spelled out the phrase *knowledge is power*.

To the left, also in a wood frame, is a black-and-white photograph of Alan Turing; behind him is the bombe—the enormous machine he invented to defeat Enigma and that was a precursor to the computer. You stop. A little black ant is walking on the glass that covers the photo, just on Turing's cheek. You take out your handkerchief and squash it.

You look at the ant carefully. His decapitated body is still moving. Nothing happens by chance; there is a reason for every action, even though most often that reason is hidden. What does the ant on Turing's photo mean? The impotence, the desperation at being faced with the continuous proliferation of messages around you, slides down your throat like bile. Sooner or later you will take out a knife and cleave it into the heart of the world, so that it will reveal its secrets once and for all. But no, violence is not for you. It's more likely that you'll wind up vanquishing or being vanquished by your attempts to understand the stubborn, continuous whispering of the universe.

You put your handkerchief in your pocket and continue up the stairs.

Thanks to Ruth, you already knew about Turing when you met Albert. You were honored when, three months after starting work at the Black Chamber, Albert decided that all of his advisers should have nicknames and he named you Turing. By that time your exceptional ability to decipher messages had made you Albert's top adviser.

Your cell phone rings for the second time that night: they need you at the Black Chamber.

chapter 12

RUTH SÁENZ KNEW the ritual by heart. She would walk into classrooms where chalk particles floated in the morning light filtering in through the windows; she would set her Argentine brown leather briefcase—survivor of taxi abandonments and sudden downpours—on the table; ignoring the handful of sleepy adolescents who were supposedly her students and who would look at her indolently, she would write the day's topics on the dark green chalkboard; she would turn around and after a few minutes of announcements, a couple of comments to lighten the mood, to make her students feel that there was nothing to fear, that they were all in it together, begin her well-practiced routine. The clicking of her heels crossing the room from left to right, her voice that started out doubtful but gained confidence, her restless hand that took every opportunity to write cryptic signs on the board.

It has been twenty years already. She can still remember the days when not even a freckled, green-eyed student's frenzied asthma attack had derailed her. Now all it takes is for her to spy the outrageous color scheme of a student's clothing or, yesterday, the inopportune ringing of a cell phone for the next few lines of her mental paragraph to be covered by a black spot, blotting them out, erasing them.

That day had been like so many others. She had put up with a student who was applying lipstick while she spoke of the impact that decoding the Zimmermann telegram had had on the course of World War I. With her brightest smile, she had endured the student she discovered e-mailing his girlfriend. She had ignored, to the best of her ability, the dark-haired girl who was surreptitiously doing a crossword. But now that class was coming to an end, the hallway was becoming noisy, the seats in the first row were creaking, restless, and she felt the approach of something that all her colleagues had faced but to which she had naively thought she was immune.

"Prof, you have chalk on your back."

"Well, that's good. It means you're at least paying attention to something."

But she was the one who wasn't paying as much attention as usual. Class would be over at nine; just a few hours later she would be meeting with Judge Cardona. When they first spoke and she told him she was willing to tell him everything she knew, she hadn't been entirely sure. Slowly, she convinced herself that it was inevitable. The night before had been Miguel's last chance to accept his share of responsibility. Everything would have been different if he had. At least they would have had time to find a solution that would ease their consciences. Her conscience, she should say: all those years, giving Miguel one more chance. What had he said last night? *I'm not worried. I've never shot anyone. I've never even touched anyone. I never left my office.*

It was time for her to accept that he was at peace with the past. She wasn't—thus the need to speak with Cardona, despite her anxieties and hesitations. She didn't know what it would lead to, but she was certain that she had run out of excuses. How did that quote from Dante go that she had recently read in a history book? *The hottest places of hell are reserved for those who in times of moral crisis maintain their neutrality.* Or something like that. Indeed.

Ruth walked toward the window. She had asked a rhetorical question—without first-rate cryptanalysts, would the Allies have won both world wars?—and decided not to fill the silence with her own easy answers. Let them make something up, dare to explore the obvious. She brushed chalk off her purple blouse, which went well with her new black pants. Out in the patio, around the immense pepper tree that had survived more than one fire, students were patting one another on the back and making plans for the rave that weekend, exchanging telephone numbers and chatroom nicknames, maybe even passing OxyContin and Ritalin between the pages of their notebooks. Such complacency; it made one feel guilty for bothering to try to teach them anything. Didn't they know that the university would be closing at noon to avoid the blockades and protests that were being announced for that afternoon? Río Fugitivo was falling to pieces, and it was as if they hadn't heard. What had happened to the university as a place where one questioned the system and oneself? Perhaps it was different at the state university.

She moved away from the window. Maybe she should have done what many of her colleagues had: accept that her work didn't interest anyone else, simply devote herself to her research and make teaching secondary, a foggy, obligatory footnote. Twenty years, and all she had to show was an occasional thank-you postcard from a student who, passing through Helsinki or Aruba, for some obscure reason remembered some phrase of hers, some class, some chat during office hours.

One of her students held up her hand. It was Elka, tall and thin, dark-haired, her features slightly Indian.

"Without first-class cryptanalysts, the Allies would never have been able to defeat the Germans," she said. "But that supposition is just as valid as this other: with better cryptographers, the Germans would never have been defeated. There are so many factors that decide the course of a war—it's impossible for just one of them to be the deciding factor. Or one might be, just not the one we expect."

Elka was intelligent, even though she wasn't terribly interested in showing it. She hardly ever participated in discussions, didn't try her hardest on exams. Ruth was surprised to find her voice screeching, unpleasant. Maybe that was what inhibited her? At one time Ruth had been traumatized by her crooked teeth and thin lips, as if drawn with a fine brush. Ah, the difficulties and embarrassments of the genetic code.

"My whole class," Ruth said, walking nearer, adopting the most persuasive tone in her arsenal, "is aimed at convincing you that there *is* one reason that's more important than all the others. If Enigma hadn't been decoded during World War II, the war would have gone on for at least another couple of years and the outcome would have been uncertain."

"That's easy for you to say," Elka went on, looking nervously at the tile floor speckled with gum. "Every professor thinks that his or her science has the definitive answer to a problem. They don't realize that the limits of their own discipline blind them and prevent them from seeing the forest for the trees."

Why so aggressive? As Ruth walked toward Elka, out of the corner of her right eye she saw something that took her a moment to process. Once she finally had, the force of the impact surprised her. Gustavo, her best student — dimpled cheeks and James Dean sideburns — was oblivious of the discussion and, protected by a barrier of books on a chair, was typing industriously on his cell phone. Probably playing solitaire.

The lyrics from a song Ruth had once sung at a karaoke came to mind: "All your yesterdays've gone to waste, All your yesterdays are tomorrow's memory of loss." She turned around, grabbed her briefcase off the table, and left the classroom, slamming the door. Her heels echoed in the hallway. She walked quickly to her office.

A glass of water. The desire to break down in tears. She shouldn't be so impulsive. She usually wasn't. But she had been for two days in a row already. What was wrong with her? She wanted the ballet dancers that surrounded her on the walls, attentive Degas prints, to impart some of their peace to her. That's why they were there, after all. One, two, three . . . The books on the shelves, the announcements for that month's concerts at the university, the blurry photo that one of her students had e-mailed from Moscow. Four, five, six . . . In a metallic frame, a four-year-old Flavia playing in the garden with a toy rake, her smile wide, her expression bright — long, long before she withdrew into the shell in which she lived now. Ruth's favorite photo. Seven, eight . . . Miguel in black and white, his hand over his mouth, unable to look directly at the camera. Why that irritating habit? Nine . . . Yellow leaves in the plant pots; they needed watering. Ten. Her manuscript in the bottom right-hand drawer of her desk. The black book of Montenegro's dictatorship, nearly three hundred pages written in different codes.

She took off her shoes. Degas's dancers. Maybe that should have been her world.

A knock at the door. She wanted to shout, "No one's here!" Her good manners got the better of her.

It was Gustavo.

"Professor, I'm so sorry." His hands behind his back, as if hiding a knife. "It wasn't my inten — "

"I should have thrown it on the floor."

"It's nothing personal. Your classes are the most bearable, by far. It's the semester. By this point, all we can think about is summer holidays."

"At least you're honest."

"You know I love your class." His gaze was remorseful. "The topic is incredible — it's made me look at world history differently."

"What was on your cell phone that couldn't wait a few more minutes?"

"Battleship with my girlfriend in her statistics class."

"At least I'm not the only one."

"It has to do with your class. The German ships are sunk because the Allies have found the code. How do you keep the Germans from finding out that the Allies know, or might know, all their secrets? Knowing too much can be counterproductive."

"It usually is. Don't do it. Don't do it again. Please." Ruth shook her head in a gesture of defeat or exhaustion.

She prayed she would feel more optimistic when she saw Judge Cardona. She had to be able to maintain the conviction of her principles, latent for so many decades; her words had to be able to obey her ideas and wishes. All she wanted was to live up to the image she had once had of herself.

chapter 13

THE WOMAN HAS JUST LEFT. Her high heels still echo in the hallway, harbingers of bad luck. In the dark room, seated on the wicker chair from which he conducted their conversation, Judge Cardona believes he has achieved an important victory. He scratches his right cheek, as if his nails might be able to make the spots disappear. He lights a cigarette and smokes it indolently, letting the ash fall onto the red paisley carpet. He is drinking a beer out of the bottle. Some of it drips onto his shirt. In his hands is the tape recorder. Victory? Pathetic moments, really, when the world becomes heavier. Pathetic as it is, it's a victory all the same. The vigil is embellished by sudden fury. He looks for the BMP in his briefcase. For months now he has been addicted to Bolivian marching powder. What a name. The world has always been devoid of sensation, is unable to stimulate him on its own. He needs chemicals to feel alive. He has tried other drugs—cocaine, heroin—but nothing has produced the euphoria that BMP does. When he first discovered it, he was drowning in indolence; not even the memory of his cousin meant much. A friend who was an LAB flight engineer passed him a couple of tablets at a party. He threw up in the elevator, but then his easily tired eyelids stayed open until the soft morning light; he wound up asleep in a bar at eight o'clock in the morning, his face in what was left of his fricassee. A powerful ex-minister of justice for Montenegro and all. What would the papers have said if a photographer had captured a moment like that? He hasn't given up BMP since then. He crushes two tablets, rubs the powder on his gums, and lies down on the bed.

The television is on. The Coalition's blockade was sporadic throughout the morning. It is now two-thirty on a Thursday afternoon, people are heading to the plaza, and neighborhood committees are beginning to protest. Soldiers are posted at strategic bridges and gas stations. He changes the channel, muting the volume: images of a bomb exploding at a nightclub in Bogotá. The news — as abusive as the excess of scandalous news is — works well, but his best BMP experiences have been while watching cartoons, especially Road Runner; the coyote's complete lack of common sense and his relentless persistence are ideal for the drug. This time, however, he would rather turn off the television. He rewinds the cassette. The agitated voice of the woman, whom he had known just how to steer to the best fishing grounds, would go well with BMP. Information that reveals broad tracts of his past is there, captured on tape. He can amplify that voice or turn it down; the tape is elastic and, with its continuous hiss, is willing to help bring what happened back to life. Perhaps now a small step can start him on the path to rebuilding his life.

"Everyone has a price. There's a price for everyone." That's what Iriarte, a university classmate, used to say when they would discuss corruption in the judicial system. "What's yours?" "None," Cardona would reply with conviction. Iriarte was now in jail for having accepted a bribe to free a well-known drug trafficker in the early nineties. Cardona had visited him a few times, had been moved by his skeletal frame, his sunken eyes. Iriarte wanted to die. "When I said that everyone had a price, deep down I thought I was immune. I repeated it as a way of banishing temptation. Like when someone says that we're all mortal, but inside they believe they're immortal and behave that way. Not me, I used to say to myself."

Cardona approaches the half-open window, pulls back the curtains, and looks out at the leaden sky threatening the city. His gaze rests on the military posts on the corner. The plaza is empty, but an explosion of voices, shouts, antigovernment slogans, can be heard from neighboring streets. Will the blockade complicate his plans? Ah, Iriarte, what would you have to say about me now? Pompous conviction that one is superior to everyone else, living with one's nose in the air, far from the masses . . .

When had it all started? It was impossible to say. He remembers that when Mirtha was murdered, he promised himself he would find the killers one day. Years later the dictatorship fell, and he celebrated it as a personal victory. It was time to be rid of that little man who had promised the country "order, peace, and work" but had not said anything about the cost of achieving them. Then Cardona became a lawyer and, albeit timidly, entered local politics. He was a right-winger, but the parties on the right were weak and fragmented. In the mid-eighties, Montenegro returned to public life and founded a political party that quickly became a real alternative. It was ironic; his party's ideology was eerily close to Cardona's beliefs. Cardona's friends invited him to join many times, but he could never bring himself to do it. He attacked Montenegro repeatedly, not because he did not agree with his ideas; mostly, it was because he felt that a dictator had to be tried and sent to prison, as in other South American countries. It was in pure defense of the rule of law, which said that those guilty of crimes, those responsible for abusing power, had to be punished.

The years went by, and in 1997 Montenegro became a democratically elected president. Cardona felt he had to accept the country's verdict. The wounds had been healed, there was no use being bitter about the past, it was better to look toward the future. He continued to attack Montenegro during his first years in office, especially when he used force to suppress protests—"dictators never cease being dictators"—but his convictions waned.

He was in his office late one afternoon, reviewing files on a criminal case, when his secretary knocked on the door and told him there was a call from the president's office. He was more than surprised. Why would Montenegro want to talk to him? Cardona answered. Montenegro's personal assistant told him that he had an appointment with the president the next day at five in the afternoon, and then hung up. He remembers how he left his desk, both nervous and elated, and approached his secretary to ask her immediately to book him on a flight to La Paz the following day.

He recalls Montenegro's office, a hand-embroidered coat of arms framed on the wall, the gold in brilliant contrast to the red and green. Without leaving his chair, Montenegro looked up and held out his hand. Cardona sat down, unexpectedly humble before the power of that short man with a commanding voice.

"It's a pleasure to meet you, general."

He was a lap dog; all that was missing was for him to bow.

"I've heard very good things about you, judge. We need someone of your stature to become part of our project."

"I'm honored that you thought of me."

"Tell me, can you see yourself as minister of justice?"

"I see myself however you'd like to see me, general." At that moment he remembered his hatred, his promises of vengeance for what had happened to Mirtha. What would she say if she could hear him now? What could she say? She would probably understand that something that had taken place more than twenty years ago would not control his decisions now. What's the use in holding on to old resentments? One had to go on with life; that was that. He couldn't reject the offer. He's a *different* Montenegro, he's *democratic; this* Montenegro would never have his thugs kill Mirtha.

There were mirrors on all the walls. On the desk was a newspaper with a half-solved crossword puzzle and photos from Montenegro's days as a dictator, as if to say to everyone *Times have changed, but I'm not ashamed of my past.*

"Judge, my government is going to begin a sweeping campaign against corruption. At all levels. We simply cannot be ranked as one of the most corrupt governments in the world. In South America, only Paraguay is ranked higher." His voice was resonant and thick, his hands waved nervously in the air, his arms crossed and uncrossed.

"I wholeheartedly agree, general."

"So then, I can count on you?"

If there had been even the slightest doubt, a hesitation. But no, the yes came so easily, the hands that reached out, the firm grip, the eyes that locked — if he only knew, or perhaps he did and was delighting in the ease with which the tempted fall into the sticky web of power. They might hate him, but they couldn't say no; the possibility of issuing orders, of meeting with Montenegro in the magnolia-filled gardens of the presidential residence, of trying to make their mark on the country's twisted destiny, was stronger.

"You can count on me, general."

The receptions at the home of the Peruvian consul, the parties at the American embassy.

"I'm very glad to hear it. You've spoken poorly of my government on several occasions. Not to mention of me personally. There are attentive ears everywhere." To use a cane and hat, to feel, all of a sudden, at the center of the action. "But I knew you would accept, despite our differences. You're a patriot, and you know that the nation comes before all else."

"Thank you for your confidence, general. And thank you for accepting that I have had small differences of opinion with you from time to time."

Montenegro is a good person deep down, and he confides in me. He says he hasn't made a mistake with me.

Cardona feels the room sway. He sees himself sitting down, smoking a cigar while he converses with Montenegro; lying on a bed with a tape recorder in his hand; wandering through the room rubbing at the spots on his face; drinking a few glasses of whiskey in order to find the courage to present Montenegro with his resignation, because the government is not what he thought it was. Or better yet, working for the government, he is not who he thought he was. He had believed, for example, that it would be easy to say no to the friend who asked for his help in getting in touch with the minister of the interior regarding bulletproof vests that he had for sale. He had believed that he could ask his friend to leave his office when he said that Cardona's take would be twenty dollars per vest and that he would take forty dollars. Twenty thousand vests were sold. The original price per vest was two hundred and fifty dollars; with all the surcharges — all the money going to people in the government so they would approve the deal — each vest cost the government seven hundred dollars. Cardona didn't have to do anything; he simply had to pretend he hadn't seen anything. And yet, and yet . . .

Cardona now remembers that one day, in the garden of the presidential residence in San Jorge, at a reception to honor Montenegro's birthday, he saw two deputy ministers wearing British cashmere and Italian loafers, speaking to each other about a deal they had just concluded, and it reminded him of the vests. But later, when he left the residence, he was no longer thinking about them. He was remembering Mirtha, asking himself why he had ever agreed to work for such a despicable man.

He sees himself walking into the Presidential Palace, being led to Montenegro's office. He would like to yell at his former self, block his path, tell him not to make that mistake.

He turns on the tape recorder. He doesn't hear the woman's words or his own, which angrily take possession of the room. The last thing he sees before falling fast asleep is an image of the hand-embroidered coat of arms in Montenegro's office.

The words on the tape recorder, not knowing what else to do, speak to one another.

"Let's begin with your name."

"Ruth Sáenz."

"And you are . . ."

"A historian. Professor at the Private Central University of Río Fugitivo."

"Louder, please. If you'd like, you can move a little closer to the table. You were saying. A specialist in . . ."

"World history of cryptanalysis."

"Rather pretentious, one might say."

"It's my father's fault. He was fanatical about secret messages and passed on his interest when I was a child."

"Married."

"Wife of Miguel Sáenz. Currently head of the archives at the Black Chamber."

"You worked there as well."

"A long time ago. During Montenegro's first government."

"During the dictatorship."

"There was a gringo adviser they called Albert, although I'm not sure that was his real name. Albert had persuaded military leaders that a national service needed to be created for intercepting and decoding messages. That it was the only way to strengthen the dictatorship. Marxist movements in hiding were slowly regrouping. The government had to stay one step ahead of them, intercept their messages, decipher them, and take action. A cousin of mine in the military offered to put us in touch with Albert so we could join the service."

"And you accepted."

"It was a very good offer."

"But you didn't stay long."

"The information we deciphered was used so that groups of paramilitaries could arrest young leftists and send them into exile or kill them. It was difficult for me to do my work impartially, to wash my hands of the end that was brought about by our means."

"Your husband stayed on."

"He's one of those rare apolitical beings. He could distance himself from what was going on around us. Simply concentrate on his work, obey orders."

"You didn't object to his continuing to work for the service."

"I did. Weakly. I justified it by saying that it was sufficient that I didn't dirty my own hands. That he did was another thing. And I used him as a source of information."

"Explain what you mean."

"I told myself that one day I would write a book that would justify my actions. In it I would reveal everything I knew about the dictatorship. So I started to take notes, patiently, of all the cases in which Miguel had taken part. When they began, when they ended. What specifically Miguel's job had been. What the final outcome was. The dates, names of those arrested, those murdered, those who disappeared. In many cases, concrete proof. In others, merely conjecture."

"A sort of black book on the dictatorship. Or rather than a book, a chapter. Could you give it to me? To use as evidence."

"Yes. So many years have passed. I can't lie to myself any longer."

"There will be very serious consequences. For your husband, perhaps even for you. You may regret it."

"Perhaps. But that comes later, and right now I'm only concerned with the present."

chapter 14

RUTH SÁENZ'S HEELS echo on the pavement. She walks with a cigarette between her fingers, glancing left and right every now and then, making sure that no one is following her. She has done so ever since she left the hotel. The military and a vociferous group of young protesters brandishing signs insulting the government and GlobaLux were arriving just as she was leaving. She had been lucky—a few minutes later and she would not have been able to leave the plaza. She holds on tightly to her purse, which contains tranquilizers that have no effect on her, a cell phone that rings but that she never answers, a worn photo of Flavia, tubes of lipstick, and pens.

She has no idea where she is headed. Her path has been erratic, determined by which streets are still open. Río Fugitivo is a city under siege; the blockade called for by the Coalition has begun. Stones, chairs, and corrugated iron have been piled on streets and avenues to cut off traffic, which has begun to back up. It is still moving freely on very few roads. Armored jeeps and army trucks patrol the streets, and military police are on the bridges, camouflaged and in combat position. Those behind the barricades heatedly chant protests and insult the soldiers, who are avoiding direct confrontation—at least for now. Tension in the city is rising, and everywhere the whir of helicopter blades can be heard overhead.

Ruth is sure of one thing: she does not want to go home. After leaving her voice on the tape recorder, she felt empty; she had no desire to see Miguel again, to act as if everything were continuing as usual. Miguel would soon hear about her conversation; she is sure that the government knows of Cardona's plans to bring Montenegro to justice. Cardona told her that he had not spoken of the matter with anyone, but this is a small country, and plots and insurrections come to light sooner rather than later. Truth is fabricated in whispers, late at night and early in the morning in the persistent drizzle.

She has left downtown, is walking along a street stained by the resin from pepper trees. Like the spots on Cardona's cheeks.

"Let's talk specifics." Cardona's irritable voice, at last getting down to what really interests him. "September of 1976, for example. The Tarapacá plot, young officers who wanted to overthrow Montenegro. Do you remember?"

"I'm a historian. It's my job to remember dates."

"After the dictatorship intensified in 1974, a group of officers planned to surprise Montenegro on one of his frequent visits to Santa Cruz. It was a plan that had taken many months to organize, down to the last detail—perhaps the one that came closest to overthrowing Montenegro. Days before it was to be put into place, in the most mysterious manner, chilling in its effectiveness, all of the conspirators who had anything to do with the plan, both military and civilian, were eliminated."

"I know the details."

"Was your husband involved in any way?"

"So many things happened during that decade. Why does that one in particular interest you?"

"There may be both ethical and personal reasons at once. So you won't talk?"

Walking under the pepper trees, Ruth remembers that instant, which already seems remote to her. Her last opportunity to keep quiet and burn her manuscript. You don't talk one day, don't talk another, and soon months and years have gone by without talking, and silence is no longer an option, becoming instead the dark side of your personality. Habit is often stronger than conviction.

"And will everyone know of your personal reasons?" she asks, trying to gain time. "Doesn't that discredit you? Aren't you the least appropriate person to carry out an impartial trial? Perhaps the Argentine judge who's interested in extraditing Montenegro is the right person for the job."

"I would also be discredited for having been a minister of Montenegro's," Cardona says, continuing to look at her fixedly, as if to intimidate her, to prevent his prey from escaping at the last moment. "The way things are, or better yet, the way things are here, there's no one better to see this through. Everyone, one way or another, is discredited. If we wait for that impartial person, history will hand down its judgment long after we're gone. And Montenegro should pay for his crimes in life, he should be judged by his peers."

"You'd better hurry. Rumors say that his lung cancer is in its final stages."

"Let them not say we were cowards who let him do whatever he wanted. Let them not say we were afraid and forgetful, and that as a prize we democratically elected him president. Well, let them say that, but not only that. Cancer. I didn't know. Other rumors say he's senile."

"The fact of the matter is that he's sick and won't be with us for long."

"Which would be a shame. That is, if he dies of natural causes before we can accuse him."

"Aren't you afraid?"

"I'm afraid." His voice quavers. "Very afraid. Of everything. Of the dark and the light of day. Of my enemies and my friends. Of big gatherings and empty rooms. Of busy streets and quiet ones. I'm even afraid of myself. I've always lived with fear. I was afraid of spiders and bees when I was young. I'm afraid of being afraid. I've been afraid since long before I met Montenegro. I've been much more afraid ever since I met him. I simply want to do one thing in my life that is free of fear. One thing will be enough."

Ruth contemplates that aging face in the semidarkness of the room and for the first time thinks of Judge Cardona as a person. She knows what circumstances brought her to this grave moment, but what led him here? What events? He had been Montenegro's minister of justice. Had he come to know him so well that he had discovered the truth in what they said about him? What the hell had the man done to make Cardona so eager for vengeance? She has her suspicions, but the truth is evasive. Ruth puts her hands together, interlacing her fingers — adorned by nothing more than her wedding ring — feeling the sweat on her palms. She observes the gray day through the white, partially opened curtains. The sky is weighed down by heavy, threatening clouds — it will start to rain at any moment.

Perhaps something unites them after all. Perhaps both of them want to redeem an entire life of lies in a single act. Perhaps both of them think that redemption is possible, that one act can erase the past.

She throws her cigarette on the ground. Her left breast aches. Or is it her lungs? Should she go back and speak to the doctor? Or is it just a trick of her imagination? Her friend's brother, who was not yet fifty years old and led a healthy lifestyle, had complained of aches all over his body and had gone to the doctor. They could not find anything and advised him to go to Chile for a general checkup. In Santiago, they diagnosed him with leukemia and gave him three months to live. His blood had been contaminated by radioactive elements. It was a mystery how and when that had happened. But that was fate, that was life. You could start on the road to death when you least expected it.

It was so easy for Miguel and Flavia to dismiss her as a hypochondriac. They weren't trapped by fear; they didn't have a mother and other relatives who had died of cancer. Lately it had become worse. Maybe her body knew something that her mind didn't. Or perhaps they were right and she was a hypochondriac. If they cared about her at all, then the question they should have asked themselves was, what did it all mean? Was it something other than fear? She didn't know.

Three blocks farther on, a group of individuals is stacking logs and boulders on the pavement. The protesters are of all ages. Twelve-year-old kids taking up arms for the first time, young people who were born in democracy and are tired of accepting its imperfections, older professional agitators who know how to harness the people's fury. The blockades are primarily to stop traffic, but in some cases stubborn protesters don't even want to let pedestrians pass; at others, they ask for a "contribution" in order to be let through. Cars have been stranded on the streets, their owners having locked and abandoned them to danger. A car alarm shrieks obstinately.

She does not feel like confronting anyone, getting into an angry discussion. They will ask her why she isn't obeying the blockade. *The only way to make the government back down is to unite the people.* Oh, if only they knew. But the truth of the matter is that the Coalition has managed to unite the most diverse groups by standing up to the government. The poor who complain about the lack of electricity in their neighborhoods, middle- and upper-class women who rant about the rate hikes. Unionists of the old guard, young hackers espousing a principled, anti-globalization discourse. Montenegro hadn't calculated how much opposition there was in Río Fugitivo when he transferred control of the electricity to foreign hands. He thought the people were so desperate for an efficient power company that they would be willing to accept the cost of privatization. And after a decade of continually privatizing almost all sectors of the economy, he knew that people would complain, just not loud enough to be heard. The government allowed the protests to begin, failed to provide a quick solution to the problem, thinking that things would die down. Because it underestimated the power of the Coalition, little by little the matter of privatizing the electricity in Río Fugitivo had become a referendum on whether or not Montenegro should stay in power and whether or not the country should continue with its neoliberal policies. The government had shown itself to be weak, vulnerable, and its problems had multiplied.

"Miguel's boss," she says at last. "Albert. One of the people in charge of intercepting messages pointed out to Albert that ads for a nonexistent bookstore had been published in one of Río Fugitivo's newspapers, *Tiempos Modernos,* as it was called at the time. The ad was very small, practically unnoticeable in the lower right-hand corner of one of the inside pages."

"You remember all the details."

"I dream about them every night. Underneath the name of the bookstore was a famous phrase from one Bolivian author or another. The ad came out on several consecutive days in early August and then ceased. Albert, almost as a routine matter, passed the file of ads on to Miguel. And Miguel, who at that time was nearly invincible, discovered that each of the ads contained a ciphered message: the day on which the coup would take place, the names of contacts in the city, the time, et cetera. All of the information regarding the coup was being blatantly transmitted in the city's best-known newspaper. People tend to be overconfident and make those kinds of mistakes when they think their code is extremely secure."

"So . . . so it's true. Albert and Turing were responsible for preventing the coup."

"You could say that. What at that time was considered to be the government's most important triumph — the dictatorship against opposition movements — was the work of Albert and Miguel. Well, Miguel above all."

"And how did he feel?" Cardona asks, scratching the spots on his right cheek. "Did he receive any sort of honors from the government?"

"Because of the nature of his work, the government couldn't publicly give him an award. No one could even know that Albert or Miguel existed. Miguel Sáenz was a bureaucrat lost in a branch of the civil service and had nothing to do with Turing. Montenegro couldn't ask him to the palace, but he did send a brief note of congratulations with one of his aides. Anyhow, it didn't matter. Miguel did his work and that's it — it didn't matter to him that Montenegro was his boss. He distanced himself from everything that went beyond what Albert put on his desk. He wasn't interested in honors, wasn't bothered by anonymity."

"And how did you feel?"

"I didn't find out for some time," she says. "Putting two and two together, I came to the conclusion that Miguel's long nights of work had everything to do with dismantling the planned coup. Miguel told me so when I asked him a few weeks later. He responded without any emotion whatsoever. It made me sick. But I had become so used to being sickened by him that it became something I could live with."

Ruth does not want to face the protesters. The fervor in their eyes, their fists raised high, their loud chants. She has to admit that the Coalition leaders, recycled from union movements and politicians on the farthest left, have done an admirable job. She can't stand them—demagogues able to harness civil fury at so many unmet demands but incapable of proposing any viable alternatives to overcome the concrete problem of the supply of electricity in Río Fugitivo. "Now globalization is the cause of all our problems. But we have to look back. Before that word entered our vocabularies, we were backward, dependent, exploited neocolonies struggling for a freedom that would never be ours. The discourse has to change so that everything can remain the same."

She has to change direction again. What if she just goes home? No, she doesn't want to see Miguel. She has to admit that there were times when she loved him as she thought one should love. That there were times when he was everything to her. In the beginning, Ruth had dreamed that they would both go to the United States or Europe to get their master's degrees and then not return; they would have a bright future in the strange field of work they had chosen. But Miguel was obsessed, not ambitious. He didn't want to leave Río Fugitivo, not even to move to La Paz. He had a good job—what more could he want? Without dreams to unite them, their intimacy quickly faded. Love had not entirely run its course when insidious routine took hold. Then, something worse: deception, at least on her part. Their ethical, moral differences.

Why hadn't she divorced him? It would have cost less than so many years of self-deception. Maybe she thought that suddenly everything would change. They were both getting caught up in their work, perhaps as a way to avoid the hellish silence that resulted when they were together. When he wanted to have children, she found excuses to postpone it: she couldn't bring a child into a home without love. As the years went by, Miguel stopped insisting. And yet, owing to a miscalculation, one day she found she was pregnant. That is how Flavia was born. A tepid hope that everything would change. A hope that was soon dispelled.

She stops all of a sudden. She has just realized that if the government militarizes the city, tanks will be posted at the university entrances and they will be closed indefinitely. Soldiers will search offices for proof of conspiracies by professors and students. Her manuscript is in a locked drawer in her office.

"So," Cardona says quietly, "Albert and Turing."

"It's as if you're more interested in them than you are in Montenegro."

"Not exactly. But you have to start somewhere."

She had better go to the university immediately, before it's too late.

chapter 15

THE FIRST FEW MONTHS after leaving home, Kandinsky lived with Phiber Outkast in his disorganized room. A sleeping bag on the tile floor. Notebooks and loose pages covered in scribbles, computer program diskettes and manuals, empty Coke cans and pens on the desk and a chest of drawers, a profusion of cables snaking along the floor, dirty clothes piled in a corner. On the walls, posters of rock groups: Sepultura, Korn. Kurt Cobain and KILL MICROSOFT stickers on the windows. The house is noisy. Phiber Outkast has three teenage sisters who are discovering the chaos of hormones, and their parents never seem to stop shouting and cajoling. There is leftover food in all the rooms; forks and knives are never returned to their rightful place and stubbornly remain on furniture buried in dust.

At times he misses the mood, the atmosphere of his house. He used to live in an Italian neorealist film; now he is in the middle of a frenetic cartoon, more anime than Disney. But Phiber's computers make up for it all: PCs with enough memory and speed to make Phiber the envy of his friends. He assembled them himself, having stolen the pieces bit by bit from a computer repair shop where he worked for a few years. Both of them take their lunch and dinner to the room, close the door, and, trying to isolate themselves from the surrounding noise with headphones, sit in front of their monitors until the morning light shines in through the windows. They sleep fitfully throughout the morning.

They are chatroom fanatics, constantly changing identities.

Names pile up in their wake. At times they wind up so lost in their own labyrinth that they find themselves chatting to each other without realizing it—one pretending to be Ze Roberto, a retired firefighter in Curitiba, the other Tiffany Teets, a fifteen-year-old in search of kinky sex. In between, there is always time for online games, above all MUDs, or multiple user domains, where they assume roles in laborious medieval or futuristic fantasies.

Their activity takes on a more serious tone in the middle of the night. They begin to look for victims to hack. Their targets are common citizens: Phiber thinks that is the best way to practice until the time comes for more ambitious attacks. Kandinsky has gone along with him but no longer entirely agrees. A hacker's ethic is that governments and large corporations are fair game but that civilians should be left alone. Still, he says nothing, feeling uncomfortable, and does what his colleague tells him to do.

During their long nights together it becomes clear to Kandinsky that Phiber will never be anything more than a script kiddie. Faithfully following the instructions for programs downloaded from sites like attrition.org, he is like any adolescent orchestrating a DoS attack against the mayor's office. It is small-potatoes hacking, and cheesy. Kandinsky, in contrast, uses the programs he finds as a starting point. Reworking their basic code, adding and extending, he makes them more malleable, efficient, powerful.

Phiber watches Kandinsky work with a mixture of pride, envy, and jealousy. He feels as if he is back in kindergarten at the Centro Boliviano Americano, where from the sidelines, his fists clenched, he would watch the other children easily absorb the rules of the game the teacher had prepared or start to stammer out their numbers and colors. All of a sudden he would run up behind one of them and start punching, as if trying to steal the secret ease with which that child could name the world. It is difficult for him to live with someone who makes him feel inferior. Right now he needs Kandinsky, but he knows that separation is inevitable.

Their first big triumph: accessing the Citibank database in Buenos Aires and leaving with several credit card numbers and their respective passwords. On IRC, Phiber Outkast contacts a Russian hacker to whom he sells the credit card numbers. The money is paid by means of a transfer to the Western Union branch in Santa Cruz. Phiber Outkast travels there by bus and uses a fake ID to collect the money. It is practically impossible for anyone to suspect them, since for the Citibank assault first they took over a computer at the University of Mendoza, and from there they telnetted to a computer in Río de Janeiro, then another in Miami, finally arriving in Buenos Aires. Nevertheless, Interpol is on the trail and they need to minimize risks.

Other triumphs will follow. An insurance company in Lima. A Calvin Klein store in Santiago. A car dealership in La Paz. It is not a lot of money each time, but it is adding up, a mountain of earth piled high by diligent ants. Early one Sunday morning, after hours of work, Kandinsky accesses the server of a Canadian virtual casino and for ninety minutes manages to make every roll of the dice in crap come up pairs and every pull of the virtual slots produce three cherries. During that time, no one in the casino loses. Kandinsky wins $110,000. An investigation by CryptoLogic, the company in charge of the casino's software, establishes that a hacker was behind the uninterrupted wins but is unable to establish his identity. The casino pays all the winners.

With his money, Phiber Outkast decides to open a company dedicated to computer system security. "What better façade?" he says enthusiastically. "They'll think we're protecting them when really we're doing the opposite." Kandinsky consents. He is still thrilled by his entry into the casino. For the first time he is proud of his accomplishments and is overcome by the power he possesses. Only now does he recognize his self-worth. His talent is so natural that he has had little time to reflect on it, to realize the magnitude of his gift. In religion classes at school, the priest would tirelessly recite the parable regarding talents: each one of us would be judged for the way in which we had allowed what we had been given to flourish. Kandinsky thinks he can live with that kind of final judgment hanging over his head.

Up until now, he has agreed with all of Phiber's plans. He owes him: Phiber has fed and housed him during a difficult time. But he feels ever more distant from him. Phiber's only objective seems to be monetary. Kandinsky is drawn to fooling the security systems of large corporations and the government, but he does not think that the end should be solely financial. He wants to do something else with his life, but the question remains: what?

The name of the company is FireWall. They have rented office space on the seventh floor of the Twenty-First-Century Towers. Their logo is at the entrance: a hand shielding a computer from a large blaze. Kandinsky and Phiber offer their services to the Chamber of Industry and Commerce. Not many are interested. In some cases the excuse is the recession; in most other cases the reason is that few companies in Bolivia have realized the importance of having a secure computer network. A company's bank account numbers, its commercial strategies, the information on its sales plans, its profits and losses: all of it is on hard disk drives protected by passwords that an average hacker could easily crack.

Kandinsky is disheartened. At one time he thought that this might be a legal job he could like. Phiber Outkast asks him not to forget the goals they have set. This is only a façade.

"What goals?" Kandinsky asks. "To get rich?"

"Having cash will give us the freedom to do whatever we want."

Phiber tries to calm him down; it is not in his best interests to lose Kandinsky now. Kandinsky washes his hands of the whole affair and goes to an Internet café to play online games. At the entrance is a sign announcing the imminent arrival of Global Playground in Bolivia (*Live a parallel life for a modest monthly sum!*). Kandinsky wonders what the hell that might be.

All the while, Kandinsky entertains himself by studying the bodies of Phiber Outkast's sisters. Laura is fifteen and has brown hair that falls over her forehead; her breasts are round and firm. Daniela is fourteen and has blond hair cut very short; her long legs and agility have made her a fearsome beach volleyball player. Gisela, her twin sister, has black hair with bangs cut by epileptic scissors; she discovered makeup a few months ago and plasters her eyelids as if it were her patriotic duty to do so. The family is from Sucre and the three girls spend summer vacations there, where they are known as "the grapes of Sucre" because of their different hair colors. Kandinsky does not like speaking to them; they are haughty, and he is afraid of rejection. And so he imagines: Laura thinks that kissing means using her tongue as if it were a snake on the attack and exchanging saliva by the gallon; Daniela strokes Kandinsky's member, laughing mischievously, like a little girl carrying out some naughty plan that she has been hatching for a long while; Gisela lets him touch her in exchange for a blood friendship pact at sunset.

Kandinsky buys the latest Nokia, silver keys on a shiny black background. One afternoon he approaches his parents' house and watches from the sidewalk outside. His dad is on the patio, fixing a bicycle.

Kandinsky approaches with determined steps and, before his dad can process what has happened, hands him an envelope of money and disappears.

Walking back to Phiber Outkast's house, he finds himself looking at the jagged mountains on the horizon, the diffuse violet light of sunset. He is searching for a cause that will allow him to better himself, one that will allow him to transcend. In 1999, his attention had been held by the enormous protests by anti-globalization groups against the WTO in Seattle. Young people from the West were protesting against the new world order in which capitalism was the only option. If there was discontent in industrialized nations, the situation was even worse in Latin America. The recession had taken hold of the country. Montenegro continued to privatize companies that were strategic for national development; he had announced, for example, the bid for the power company in Río Fugitivo. Bolivia had followed the neoliberal model for about fifteen years and had done nothing other than make the economic inequality more pronounced. A straight line connected the closing of the mines and his dad's forced relocation with the protests against globalization.

Perhaps that is the cause he is looking for.

He feels bad for having bought the Nokia and throws it in the garbage.

When he arrives and goes into the room he shares with Phiber, he realizes how stupid that was. Despite the fact that the computers sitting on the desk were assembled locally, were they not also a product of the same corporations he wanted to fight?

He needs to act intelligently, to beat the enemy at its own game. After all, wasn't that the message of someone like Subcommander Marcos? The Zapatistas have a Web site and disseminate their proclamations via the Internet. Their flexibility at adapting the enemy's weapons allows them to thrive.

Being a purist will lead him only to a monastery, and that is not the path he wants to take. Two hours later, he returns in search of the Nokia. He finds it.

Kandinsky meets women in the recently inaugurated Playground. It is a fascinating virtual world: not a medieval fantasy but a modern city, like the one he knows, though slightly futuristic and decadent. Armed with some of his avatars, he walks through its virtual streets. He hates the Boulevard because of the excessive advertising on its neon signs: Nike, Calvin Klein, Tommy Hilfiger. He prefers the dangerous neighborhoods, because he knows that there he will find women who are more open to adventure. There is never a shortage, even though the women who attract him most do not live in Río Fugitivo. They surreptitiously agree to meet later in cafés or bars, using already-established codes because the rules of Playground prohibit mentioning the real world. Sometimes the meeting is disappointing: the avatar with knee-high boots and a suggestive miniskirt belongs to an overweight secretary or an overly madeup gay who exhales cigarette smoke in his face. At times the avatar is similar to reality and there is a second date and, if he's lucky, a few hours in a motel. Within a few days, Kandinsky grows tired of the women and again takes up the chase in Playground.

One night he meets an avatar named Iris. Somewhat androgynous, with military boots and a square jaw. He invites her to have a drink in a bar on the Boulevard. She accepts, on the condition that she pay her own way. She does not want to owe anyone anything. *A guy can't even be gallant with virtual women,* Kandinsky thinks. He wants to say this to her but doesn't, because he knows he would be committing an offense.

At the Electric Sheep, after Iris introduces herself, an exchange comes out of nowhere:

IRIS: globalization is the cancer thats eating away @ the world even Playground is a symptom of this cancer the new opiate of the masses a virtual screen where people amuse themselvés w/o realizing its all a setup by big corporations we have 2 get away from this go live in a cyberstate

KANDINSKY: we have 2 create a lot of seattles

IRIS: thats not the answer the empire allows protests in order 2 have more control

KANDINSKY: if u dont like Playground then y do u come here

IRIS: scouting trip its always good 2 know enemy terrain

The conversation comes to an end: the Playground police appear, read Iris her rights, and suspend her for ten days. Iris disappears from the screen as she screams about the need for isolation.

Kandinsky thinks about what she said. It struck a chord deep inside him.

He runs into Iris again ten days later. They agree to meet outside of Playground, in a private chatroom on the Internet.

KANDINSKY: thx 4 coming back i thought a lot about what u said

IRIS: i dont go often i cant stand Playground ads everywhere

KANDINSKY: thats the way it is on the net

IRIS: not everywhere that wasnt the original idea y it was created there r pirate utopian cyberstates temporal autonomous worlds

KANDINSKY: pirate utopian

IRIS: like the privateers from the 18th C a series of remote islands where ships restocked n loot was bartered 4 provisions n other things communities that live outside the law outside the state even 4 a short while islands on the net

KANDINSKY: these days its not possible 2 live outside the law outside the state

IRIS: in cyberspace it is thx 2 encryption programs like public-key cryptography PGP anonymous email

there r autonomous political communities defining
a space where the nation-state cant reach w/ its laws
thats cryptoanarchy i live in 1 u should visit fredonia

KANDINSKY: law will arrive sooner or later

IRIS: in these pirate utopias there r virtual laws virtual
judges virtual punishments institutions that
respect the moral autonomy of the individual
theyre just egalitarian not like institutions in the real
world whats important is that they exist even 4 a
short time then reappear in another place on the
net autonomous temporal worlds no permanent
government structures thats what we want

KANDINSKY: u dont get anywhere w/ anarchy

IRIS: anarchy isnt about blowing up banks or stores its
not ignoring authority its asking that authority b
able to justify its authority if it cant then it should
disappear its about giving more responsibility back
2 the individual thx 2 new technologies its possible 2
undermine the power of the nation-state remember
the net we need 2 go back 2 it take control of virtual
space the way is cryptoanarchy

Kandinsky will visit Fredonia, and the social organization of this MOO will excite him. (MOO is an object-oriented MUD: participants in MOOs have more freedom to create and modify the virtual universe as they go.) He will discover that there are over 350 MOOs on the Web, each one with different forms of government and social organization. He will live in Fredonia for a month and a half. He will not meet Iris in person, but during that time he will fall in love with her; they will share a virtual home and will even, in the ecstasy of passion, talk about having a family.

One morning he will wake up saying to himself that it has all been a magnificent dream but a dream after all. He will say goodbye to Iris and thank her for having shown him the way. Now he too has a pirate utopia. It was true, people had to take back what belonged to them; Playground had to be attacked until it came to its knees; people had to reclaim virtual space, and not only that but real space as well. There was a government, there were corporations to fight against. It was no use hiding on an island on the Internet.

One Sunday, Laura will take him by surprise in the bathroom. After a quivering encounter — the sound of pigeons on the roof — she will slip out of his arms and disappear in silence.

A little while later, his skin still tingling with excitement, Kandinsky will go back into the Citibank site. This time he won't steal credit card numbers; he will destroy the homepage and replace it with a photo of Karl Marx and graffiti proclaiming the need for resistance.

It is the birth of Kandinsky's cyberhacktivism.

PART II

chapter 16

YOU HURRY INTO the Black Chamber, the building silhouetted against the immense, brusque night like a lighthouse in high seas. The ritual of the ID card in the slot. The police officers at the entrance barely acknowledge you this time, a slight nod of the head, their faces tense, or perhaps they are tired, trying not to yawn. It has been a long night, and there are still a few hours left to go.

Outside darkness reigns, but inside the building you are bathed in white light, intrusive in its intensity. You walk down the hallways as so often before, anxious, excited, when you knew that destinies depended on you, when with a snap of your fingers you could abolish chance. Counting silently, reviewing the frequencies of letters in any phrase that came to mind—*a cat hidden with its tail sticking out is more hidden than a tail with a cat sticking out*—you would head to the Decoding Room, where Albert, a cigarette between his lips under a NO SMOKING sign, his unbrushed hair on end, would be waiting with the file of intransigent messages for you to attempt to break. *Un-sol-va-bles,* he would say, exaggerating the pronunciation, giving each syllable a breath of independence. *Can you?* Opening the crypt to find someone alive inside, heart beating, breathing labored. *Un-sol-va-bles.* You were the first to try, or at times the last, when all the other cryptanalysts in the building had thrown their hands in the air. Albert trusted you, and his question was rhetorical: he knew you could. You would take the file without looking him in the eye—such waste in the exchange of messages—and would already be pondering the solution, even before facing the problem. Clearing away the undergrowth, leaving a clean slate for your mental algorithms, as if your life depended on each attempt. Ah, stubborn intellect constantly trying to outdo itself!

But you do not head to the Decoding Room now. You have not headed there for a long time, ever since Ramírez-Graham arrived. It hurts when you recall the day you did and were denied entrance. You no longer belonged to the inner circle. You returned to your office, only to find that it was not yours anymore. Your books and files, photos of Ruth and Flavia, as well as a clock that had stopped working long ago, all lay in a cardboard box. You had been reassigned; you were now head of the archives. A promotion, they said, congratulations, but you felt as if it were a demotion. Otherwise, why the closed door? The metaphor became literal the first time you descended to your new office, in the basement.

The atmosphere in the Bletchley Room is frenzied. The computers are on, the screens glowing like aquariums; people are coming and going. You miss that hustle and bustle. Romero Flores, a cryptanalyst with a perpetual tic in his right eye, approaches. He acts as if he is your friend, but you hate the way he stares at the photo of Flavia on your desk and tells you that you have a verrrrrry beautiful daughter.

"You're late. The boss was looking for you."

"Just what I need. Whenever they say it's urgent, it's never anything important."

"It is this time. They need your memory, Turing."

"The memory of the archives, you mean."

The red diagonal stripes on his tie ... What did the red and blue mean? Was he trying to say that Turing was going to be reprimanded by Ramírez-Graham?

Once again the elevator ride, the descent into that infinite well of information, that well of infinite information. Otis, green walls, maximum six passengers, 1000 pounds, last inspected nine months ago. Could it launch you into the abyss without haste? Yes, according to a calculation of probabilities. How many seconds have you spent in this elevator? All together they added up to minutes and hours, even days: a worthy sum of life.

You take your glasses off; the bent frame makes your eyes hurt. You put them back on. A spearmint Chiclet in your mouth. Less than a minute later, you throw it into the garbage. You check the news. Slowly, the government's communication services are beginning to work again. The electronic graffiti that was posted by the hackers has been mostly erased. You should have stayed at home.

Your first trip to the basement had been six months after you started work at the Black Chamber. That afternoon you had gone into Albert's office to discuss the week's news. You had already become his protégé. He assigned you the lion's share of the work and were his salvation when a ciphered message resisted interpretation by others. Your coworkers were jealous of that preference. It didn't matter to you. Nothing mattered as long as you could be near Albert, do what he told you to do.

That afternoon Albert came out of his office and asked you to accompany him. You walked down the narrow hallways toward the elevator. He continued speaking in his captivating voice with his strange accent, Spanish at times inflected by foreign syllables and intonations. Where was he really from? He spoke of how much there was to be done in Río Fugitivo. Once you were in the elevator, he said, "The government has given me carte blanche, but there's no money. With more money, I'd perform miracles." "You should take it with a grain of salt, boss. You've already done plenty." "Our enemies never sleep, Turing." The door opened. You did not know where you were. Stumbling in the darkness, you followed him. "I'm going to turn this floor into the general archives. So much paper accumulates. We have to begin to organize it, file it all." Albert stopped and turned around, bringing his face close to yours. You felt an anxious tremor in your lips. You looked down at the floor. "Turing, look at me. There's no reason to be ashamed." You lifted your gaze. His lips drew closer to yours. You tried to dissociate yourself, become detached from the moment, see yourself from afar as if someone else were in the basement with Albert, but you discovered that you did not want to distance yourself entirely. You wanted to please Albert. You wanted your boss to be happy. He deserved nothing less.

His mouth stopped before touching yours. Was he testing you? Did he want to see the extent of your submission? What you were capable of? He already knew: you were capable of anything. No more proof was required; there was no need to kiss you. He turned back around and continued speaking of his plans to install an archive in the basement. Nothing had happened.

There were other incidents similar to the one in the basement, but Albert never actually touched you. You told yourself that unlike the real Alan Turing, you were not attracted to men, although you did have to admit that you felt slighted when nothing happened. You were extremely disappointed when you found out that there were other men and women in Albert's life, but you did nothing to tell him of your feelings. In time you discovered that his interest in you was purely intellectual and you quietly accepted your role. Something was better than nothing. The threats of physical contact became fewer as the years passed but never disappeared entirely.

"Wake up, Mr. Sáenz."

Baez is in the room, Santana next to him. Ramírez-Graham's acolytes. You detest them. They think that everything begins and ends with a computer; without one, they couldn't add up a simple sum. With such mediocrity in charge, how did the government expect to combat the signals that crossed in the air, the electronic pulses that smelled of treason, that oozed conspiracy?

"Mr. Sáenz, you're late."

You hate that Baez doesn't call you Turing. Is that his way of saying you are beneath him, that you are just an old civil servant who hasn't been fired solely because of compassion? No, not only that, it's the secrets that you keep, the files you've seen, the orders that have been given or the fury that has been unleashed as a result of your work. Arrogant upstart had barely learned his first incoherent words when you were writing—better yet, deciphering—your years of glory. And to top it all off, now they call you a criminal, a murderer, and without even showing their faces. Cowards.

"I had to drive carefully. The power is out in some areas of the city."

"All right, OK," Baez said, "but you really must leave a little earlier in order to arrive on time. Punctuality is key. There's no time to waste. All right? OK?"

"We haven't had much luck with the virus," Santana interjects. "But we do have the source code for the software that posted the graffiti on the government sites, and we've found certain suggestive indications."

Source code? Software? Sites? Santana's Spanglish is a joke . . . He should save himself the trouble and simply speak in English.

"It's a lucky break," Baez says, "but we all need it. Like the boss says, a criminal's fingerprints can be found even in software."

Not always, you think. Hopefully not this time. So you want to see Ramírez-Graham defeated? That would imply that the government would be defeated. You'd better erase those thoughts from your mind. But it's impossible to confront thought, to prevent it from taking whatever route it chooses. Albert had been on to something in his search for the algorithm that allowed thought to think. Behind the disordered associations of ideas was an order that had to be found, the narrative trigger that was the source of supposed mental chaos. Just like machines, like computers, the human brain had certain logical processes that led thought from one point to another.

"We need," Santana says, "to compare what we have with other graffiti that has similar code. All codes from other attacks were stored on a computer that was infected, but luckily they had all been printed and filed. You must know where they're stored."

You remove your crooked glasses. It is rumored that Ramírez-Graham is in danger of losing his job. He has been unable to catch the men—young men, adolescents, children?—in the Resistance. Ever since they came on the scene, they have played an offensive game of chess against Ramírez-Graham, destroying his pawns, maiming his bishops, and now they are about to take his queen and checkmate his king. Ramírez-Graham walks through the hallways carrying the files of information he has managed to amass, puzzles that are invariably missing a piece and cannot be completed. That's the price of such arrogance. You admit it: in this case, and only this time, you are on the side of the creators and not the decipherers of code.

"Can I see what you have?"

"Whatever you need," says Santana. "Just hurry. Did you know that the boss has decided to turn to your daughter? They say she's very good."

"No, I didn't know. And yes, she is. She has helped us before. During Albert's time — oh, not more than two years ago. Thanks to her, we caught a couple of hackers."

"Crackers, you mean."

If they think that mentioning Flavia will bother you, they are wrong. On the contrary, you are filled with pride: she is your flesh and blood. Albert was the first to realize how talented she was. Ruth and you thought her dexterity with computers was just a sophisticated teenage hobby. Flavia would go places, and you with her.

Baez hands you a black file. Why black, you ask yourself, and not yellow, as always, or blue, or red? You shouldn't read too much into the colors. You open it: pages of binary code, zeros and ones in rigorous formation, capable in their repetitive simplicity of hiding the complete works of Vargas Llosa or the detailed figures from the latest census. The zeros and ones, are they forming any kind of figure? Nothing obvious. You can think of several cases where the creators of code left messages in them, signatures, distinctive signs, mocking or disdainful phrases. They think they're so smart and can't help one final gesture of superiority. What would your work be without these small weaknesses of passion? It is impossible to tame desire completely.

You look up the map of the archives on your computer. To those who were in charge of this floor before you, filing meant simply accumulating information in a disorganized manner. And just as it is easy to lose a book in a library, it is also easy to lose information in an archive. The map on the blinking screen is quite incomplete—black spots on the skin of the tiger. You know, and sigh sadly because of it, that a good deal of information has been lost forever.

One section contains different source codes that have been found on hacked computers. You type *graffiti* and *Resistance.* Just in case, you type *Kandinsky.* Box 239, top shelf, row H. Your memory is the computer's memory. With nary a gesture to betray your sense of triumph, so that Baez can suffer a little bit more, you open the door to the archives, turn on the light, and lose yourself in its narrow aisles.

The arthritic wood creaks, and the poorly ventilated enclosure smells musty. On the shelves are boxes containing papers, diskettes, Zip disks, CDs, videos, DVDs, cassettes. Like museum artifacts, collected you have no idea how, there are also eighteen-inch acetate disks, precursors to vinyl disks that were used during World War II and that can be listened to only on a machine called a Memovox (there is one at the National Archives Building in Washington). Diskettes that can no longer be read because they were written using programs such as Lotus, comprehensible only to those who studied computer science in the seventies. Optical disks that were in fashion in the eighties and have disappeared from the market. The information age produces so much information that it winds up suffocating itself and becoming obsolete. The speed with which technology changes results in new equipment that quickly replaces what came before. Thanks to digital technology, more and more data are being accumulated in less space; what is gained in quantity is lost in the fragility of the new media, in their inability to persist. Today information is being stored as never before in the history of man; today information is being lost as never before in the history of man. At times you wander through the aisles without noticing it. Other times you feel every drop—bit, pixel—of information, what is lost and what still exists, and you feel close to a mystical ecstasy, to the rapture that a mischievous god has in store for you.

You come to the stand you were looking for. You open a few boxes and take out several files, hold them in your hands. They aren't heavy, but you feel them push you to the floor. You kneel down, pressing the files to your chest, look left and right and up —box after box in the process of decay.

You touch your old skin, lined with wrinkles. You too are information that is decomposing irreversibly. You feel that there, up above, someone wants to speak to you. You have no idea what that someone wants to say. Perhaps it doesn't matter.

chapter 17

FLAVIA OPENS THE REFRIGERATOR and takes out an already bitten apple. She lies on the sofa and turns on the television. She watches the news: nothing about the hackers who were killed; no news about the Resistance; an interview with the Aymara leader of the coca growers, who announces the formation of a political party and declares himself "future president of the country." She switches to a channel with Japanese cartoons—*Haruki*, about a frog or a toad that survived a nuclear attack. How were the Japanese able to universalize their pop culture so easily? Soon there would be Haruki backpacks, Haruki pajamas, Haruki sandals . . . She mutes the volume on the television and turns on the stereo: the Chemical Brothers, "Come with Us." Techno goes better with the images.

The pictures that surround her in the living room have a single theme, stormy nights in the impressionist style. Who would have imagined: the French spent thirty years painting flowers and trees and created a style that still persists today. Her parents' old-fashioned taste is incongruent with the world of anime and the Chemical Brothers. She would rather have something else on the walls. Lichtenstein, for example. But even that's not enough; something closer to her taste would be digital art, pictures that can't stay still.

She reads her e-mail on her silver Nokia. The guidance counselor at school has written, asking where she is: *It's 9:15 A.M. and you're not in class.* Oh, the miseries of technology, which connects her to the world and prevents her from completely escaping it (unless technology is used for that very purpose).

The house is empty. The closed curtains block out the morning light. More than once she has thought she was alone, only to discover Mom locked in her room. Maybe she's home now? She should go up and check. She eats her apple with great relish.

Flavia understands her parents less and less. They seem so distant from the beauty of the world. Dad . . . he's been different for a long time now. Or maybe he was always like that and she is only just realizing it. Mom has imprisoned herself in an exhausting straitjacket. The two of them used to do things together; they would find any excuse to go to the supermarket or the mall and between purchases would tell each other their secrets, as if they were friends. As far as Flavia was concerned, her mom *was* her best friend; she had never managed to relate that well to girls her own age. But the intimacy and trust had ended. Maybe it had simply been a phase between the ages of ten and thirteen, when a girl was reaching puberty, her body and mind transforming, and she needed, as never before, the support of someone older to stave off her fears and reaffirm her confidence.

She eats the core of the apple and goes up to her room. It smells of pears, her favorite fragrance. She opens the curtains, letting the daylight burst in. Her computers are in sleep mode, an image of Duanne 2019 on the screen saver.

Flavia logs on to her Web site. Instead of the homepage there is the symbol of the Resistance and a message: her site has just been hacked. She feels like punching the screen, destroying that arrogant symbol.

She reads the message. It is a friendly attack. One, in order to tell her that she needs a better security system. And two, that she should stop attacking the Resistance by means of unfounded rumors, because that will only get her into trouble. In fact, they need her for their fight. She should join them; she thinks the way they do, she is like them. Big corporations are oppressing Latin American countries. They make the rules that suit them and then call the game they play globalization.

She does not know how to respond. The Resistance's struggle seems idealistic, utopian to her. Yes, she does understand the threat that big corporations represent to a small country, but from that to defeating them is a stretch. An unbridgeable chasm. She wonders what the Resistance's next step will be. The government communication system on the Internet has been successfully hacked; they managed to paralyze the flow of information for over a day, but everything has gone back to relative normality. Surely the government's new firewalls will be much more difficult to penetrate. If the purpose was simply to send a message, to show Montenegro that it would not be easy for him to give in to large corporations, then they had achieved their objective. If the purpose was to try, together with the Coalition, to get the government to rescind its contract with GlobaLux, she thought it would be much more difficult. The company would create a lot of jobs, and the power company had been inefficient when it was in the hands of the government. And she was not entirely opposed to GlobaLux. True, nearly all government companies had been sold, with the result that Bolivians were poorer than ever and, to top it all off, living in a mortgaged country. But that didn't necessarily mean that all types of private control should be rejected. *If that's the way it's going to be,* Flavia thought, *we'd better just close the country's borders.*

She would have liked to ask the sender what the Resistance had to do with the deaths of Vivas and Padilla, but it was clear that this was not a two-way conversation. Was this message the work of Rafael? Was Rafael Kandinsky? Hard to say. The leader himself wouldn't be likely to follow or threaten her in person; others would do that for him.

She logs on to Playground using the identity of Erin and heads to the Wharf, an area populated by those who deal in drugs and information, by paid adventurers and prostitutes. Erin goes to Faustine, a casino with a dubious reputation. She is searching for Ridley and thinks he might be there, if he's still in Playground at all. Cameras set up in strategic places monitor her steps, groups of soldiers patrol the streets, and a helicopter flies above her in the metallic blue sky.

Faustine is full of avatars at the blackjack and crap tables. Their conversations melt into a murmur that must compete with the electronic music blasting from a jukebox. Erin makes her way through the crowd. A redhead offers her services; a white powder with gold sparkles covers her face, makeup that has become the fashion for announcing sexual availability. Her rough hands rest on Erin's shoulders, who is not interested and declines, but not before whispering that she likes her supersaturated red blouse with its dizzying neckline.

She sits down at a blackjack table and orders an amaretto with Irish Cream and a splash of grenadine. Next to her is a bald man with a gaff in his right hand and a dog at his feet and a woman who is high and slurs her words when she speaks.

The cards are dealt: an ace and a king of hearts. Blackjack. It will be the first and last time; she will lose her next hands to the house, represented by a man in a black suit, his features somewhat feminine, his thin lips pursed in a disdainful sneer.

Someone touches her shoulder. Flavia sees him before Erin does and becomes excited for both Erin and herself. It is Ridley—the link, she hopes, that will lead her from the virtual labyrinth of Playground to Rafael's hideout in Río Fugitivo.

Erin loses once again and stands up from the table. Ridley's right arm is in a sling. His left cheek is bruised, a shade somewhere between blue and purple. They go out into the street and walk toward an esplanade lined with lime trees. Flavia wonders if they are fragrant; Playground's reality lacks the sense of smell.

ERIN: theyre still after u

RIDLEY: they caught me beat me put me in jail 4 a nite the police dont forgive they have a surveillance system thats more effective plus they use good informants 2 hide it im talking 2 u but u might be 1 of them

ERIN: dont even joke

RIDLEY: i know otherwise i wouldnt b here still its dangerous come w/ me 2 my hotel its nearby

Erin decides to follow him. The hotel is two blocks away, in a decrepit area that borders the port. Flavia admires the realism of the building, the way the Playground designers keep improving the details of the city. There is no elevator, so Erin and Ridley walk up the stairs, the wood creaking loudly. The walls are dirty and covered in pornographic graffiti. They pass by two men who are in the midst of what appears to be a drug deal and arrive at the room. Ridley keeps the curtains closed and turns on the light.

RIDLEY: its harder 4 them 2 intercept r conversations here

Erin takes off her boots and lies down on the bed. Ridley lies down next to her and kisses her neck; Erin lets him. With his good hand, Ridley unbuttons her shirt, freeing her breasts. He kisses them hurriedly, as if he doesn't want to waste time on them in order to get to what he really wants. When he starts to unbuckle her belt, Erin stops him.

ERIN: u could at least start w/ a kiss on the lips men ur all the same

Ridley kisses her on the lips while continuing to unbuckle her belt. Erin can sense his anxiety. Her hands slide down his muscular body, finding his erect penis. Soon they are both naked.

ERIN: must b uncomfortable w/ your hand like that
RIDLEY: id forgotten all about it

Flavia touches herself with the fingers on her right hand. Erin closes her eyes and feels the pleasure of having Ridley inside her. The tremors and panting take her deep into the moment.

When it is all over, Erin crawls under the sheets and lies next to Ridley. When it is all over, Flavia closes her eyes, wanting to lie down on her bed and sleep.

RIDLEY: im not gonna ask u 2 come w/ me i just want u 2 listen i have a secret and need 2 tell some1 if something happens 2 me find my parents the address is on this paper i cant contact them myself find them and tell them that their son disappeared 4 a just cause
ERIN: ur starting 2 scare me
RIDLEY: im scared 2 but willing 2 carry on til the end
ERIN: til the end of what

RIDLEY: i belong 2 a group we have a plan 2 rebel against the government of Playground free rselves from this dictatorship theyve subjugated us based on pleasure its the worst kind of dictatorship they control all r movements tricking us by telling us were free

ERIN: u wont achieve what u hope 2

RIDLEY: better 2 disappear trying than continue 2 b part of this

ERIN: do u have anything 2 do with kandinsky

Ridley hands her a folded piece of paper. Erin opens it and reads an address. Flavia copies it down, suspecting that this may lead her to Rafael.

The silence in the hotel is broken by the urgent pounding of feet on the stairs. Ridley gets out of bed and quickly puts on his pants. Without saying goodbye to Erin, he opens the window and jumps onto the neighboring roof. Erin watches him disappear. Just then, two military police officers break down the door and aim their guns at her.

MP 235: dont move dont move stay right where u r

Flavia thinks it won't hurt to tell the truth. Erin follows Ridley out onto the neighboring roof.

ERIN: he went that way

chapter 18

RUTH DISCOVERS that her suspicions were correct: all the gates leading into the university have been closed. The patios are deserted and a couple of armored cars are at the main entrance, along with riot police in bulletproof vests and helmets, carrying rifles. Fifty yards away, a group of university students is hurling insults at them. Another group of students is confronting soldiers who are guarding the McDonald's half a block from the main entrance. All its windows have been smashed. Ruth has eaten at the fast-food restaurant often since it opened at the start of the semester; sometimes she even held her office hours in that bright space, with its polished floors and clean bathrooms where there is always toilet paper.

Her feet hurt. Such a lot of walking today; she shouldn't have worn high heels. Should she give up? She lights a cigarette: black tobacco, like her parents used to smoke.

She tries to calm herself. Even if they find her manuscript, they won't be able to decipher what she has written, her long accusation against the government. Each chapter is written in a different code, and so they would also need the notebook — out of reach in a safety deposit box at the Central Bank — that contains the key to the codes. Each of the codes is used only once, like the one-time pads favored by the Nazi Enigma operators. Well, she did use one code twice and knows that repetition is careless, an open door through which other cryptanalysts can enter. The Nazis had been careless too, perhaps because they were overconfident about the infallibility of Enigma, perhaps out of exhaustion.

She will take a look around. She may have better luck at one of the side entrances; at the very least she will move away from the confrontation. She finishes her cigarette and tosses the butt on the ground. Along the way she pictures the shaken faces of the university students, some of whom are in her classes. She had no idea that those even-tempered faces contained an energy about to explode, discontent that needed only the proper excuse to spill over. Perhaps the calmness and sinister conformity that they usually exhibited were an exaggerated form of superficial resignation: not accepting that it is impossible to change the state of things but still searching for the shape the outburst will take. Like terminally ill patients who seemingly accept their condition with clarity and little resentment, when in reality they are silently preparing for the inconsolable wail of desperation that will emerge in the predawn hours, or perhaps in the middle of the day, when the curtains in the room tremble before the power of the sun.

It is strange to see the vacant patios, the enormous, solitary pepper tree, no students resting in its shade. The windows of the four-story building let light stream into the deserted classrooms and offices. Perhaps a bench has been knocked over, texts and notebooks are on the floor, a chalkboard bears insults aimed at a professor, a coffeepot is still on in the cafeteria, exhaling clouds of steam. Once again the universities have shut their doors. Will the floor soon be littered with manure from the soldiers' horses, as it was during Montenegro's dictatorship? What bitter memories do the locks on the gates bring back? How many generations have been left with their studies unfinished? Back in the seventies, in the early eighties . . . Those in the nineties were luckier. The wheel of life continues to turn, and some things move forward while others are forced back again.

Ruth wasn't able to complete her course of study because Montenegro closed the universities. She never got her official degree as a historian. Thanks to her work in the field, she managed to obtain a counterfeit degree. Perhaps that was the reason she hated

Montenegro. Perhaps it had nothing to do with principles: she had been forced to live with the fear of being discovered at any moment, of being exposed as a fraud. She would be fired from her job, the target of public scorn.

Three soldiers stand at the side entrance leading onto the Calle de los Limoneros. Ruth gathers her courage and approaches, her face as contrite as she can make it. She is about to enter when one of them, his voice surly, stops her: "Entrance is prohibited, ma'am."

"I work here," she says, displaying her university identification. "I'm a professor. I haven't come to cause any trouble—I just need to get into my office for a minute. It's urgent."

"Sorry. Orders are orders."

Ruth knows that orders are never really orders: they can always be violated. It is simply a matter of settling on the right price and the precise moment in which to offer it.

"Officer, please. Try to understand. The university might be closed for weeks, and if I don't get in now, I won't ever get in. Pretend the order hasn't been issued yet, that you get it as soon as I leave. If you do me this great favor, I will value it as only something like this can be valued."

Her logic is irrefutable: let me in because the door has just been closed. As if in the first five minutes after closing, it might still be open.

The soldier looks at her, confused. His jaw is sharp, belligerent. His uniform jacket is unbuttoned over his stomach.

"Well, I suppose I could go with you. And I'm not an officer, ma'am. Thanks for the promotion, but I'm just a soldier."

Now there will be an opportunity for bills to exchange hands without uncomfortable witnesses.

"I'm very proud," says Ruth flatteringly, "that you soldiers are keeping the peace at such a critical time for our country."

The soldier looks at his companions, as if asking them for permission to defy an order, insinuating that they will get their share. They agree by imperceptibly nodding their heads, as if the nod were not a nod at all, giving them an excuse, a subterfuge that would exempt them from the law that had been broken. It was a matter of keeping up appearances.

The soldier opens the door. Ruth enters with hesitant steps; she cannot believe that her appeal worked. As she walks next to him on their way to the main block of buildings, she lifts up her head, discovers strength within herself. She wonders how much money she has in her purse.

They cross the basketball and futsal courts diagonally. Oh, the intolerable things that Miguel makes her do. She has to admit that there have been tender moments between them. She remembers one night in particular, when he came home from work and said excitedly that he had a big secret to tell her. Did she want to hear it immediately or wait until they were in bed? She had said she'd rather wait, delay the surprise as long as possible. Once under the covers and with the lights turned out, Miguel told her about a complex code that he had just deciphered. His happiness moved her so much that she embraced him with an intensity of love she had never felt before. Were all those decades worth a few epiphanies? Perhaps. Had it not been in vain after all? Perhaps not. But she had crossed a line, and there was no going back. Ruth couldn't always find salvation in another human being; sometimes she had to do it alone, gritting her teeth and closing her eyes. Or opening them, as her mother had done seconds before she shot herself in front of Ruth, preferring death at her own hands to the irreversible, painful decay of flesh.

She feels a warm liquid running from her nostrils and brings her hand up to her lips. She touches the liquid, tastes it. Blood. Is that why she thought of her mother right then? Had her body known before she did that her nose was bleeding? It was telling her it was afraid because it had just realized that there, deep within her, some of her cells had begun to host a cancer. She was a hypochondriac, paranoid, but not this time. How many of her relatives had died of cancer? Her mom, Grandpa Fernando, several aunts and uncles, a few cousins. Genetic mutations were part of her worrisome heritage.

"Is anything wrong?" the soldier asks, stopping.

She takes a handkerchief out of her purse. She will call the doctor from her office. You don't make calls like that from a cell phone. You have to be sitting down.

"It's nothing, officer," she says, trying to stay calm. "I just realized what it is I'm going to die of."

She starts to walk again, her high heels resounding, her gaze proud. The soldier watches her walk away, not knowing what to do. Then he follows her.

chapter 19

THE MORNING ENDS. The afternoon ends. The night ends. The day ends.

My life does not. I persist despite myself. It's my blessing. And my curse. I am an electric ant . . . Soon there will be a new reincarnation . . . I've been in this country longer than I should have. In a medicinal-smelling room. Awaiting another. More stimulating. Battlefront. I've done everything here that I had to do . . . They don't need me. I don't need them. Despite the fact that they're keeping me as a talisman. Or a prisoner . . .

Perhaps the government wants to make me disappear. I know a great deal. But I can't speak . . . No one can interrogate me.

Words are composed and decomposed in my brain . . . They can't be pronounced . . . And I want to catch myself thinking. Trap thought in the act of thinking . . . And decipher it . . . See what there is behind every association of ideas. Perhaps another association of ideas . . . A winding course, like a river. But logical in the end.

I am an electric ant . . . That wants to die and can't.

I wanted to stay. Or someone inside who knows more than I wanted me to stay . . . I write and am written. I am. Luckily. Other interesting things . . .

I am Edgar Allan Poe . . . I was born in 1809. Even though I don't remember my childhood . . . They say I invented the modern short story. And the detective novel. And also horror stories . . . I tried to explain the composition of a poem rationally. I had great faith in reason . . . And yet my narrative was filled with the irrational . . . I was an alcoholic. Delirious. Perhaps thought is nothing more than another form of delirium . . . Perhaps reason is the greatest delirium of them all.

In a country of delirious beings. Reason is king . . . It's delirious to connect ideas logically. Among so many hurried ramifications . . . Pursuing the correct one . . .

My favorite hobby was cryptology. In 1839 I wrote about the importance of solving puzzles . . . Above all, secret texts. I invited my readers of *Alexander's Weekly Messenger.* In Philadelphia . . . To send me texts ciphered in monoalphabetic codes of their invention . . . Many arrived . . . I solved almost all of them . . . It took me less time to decipher them than my readers had taken to encode them.

I followed my intuition. Perhaps intuition is the most sophisticated face of reason . . .

Thought is capable of thinking things that we don't think it thinks . . . It's even capable of thinking the unthinkable . . .

When I used my intuition . . . I was reasoning without knowing it . . . That's why it's good to give in to delirium.

Turing didn't read a lot of literature . . . Once I invited him to my house. He was surprised by my vast library. My books in Latin and Greek . . . In German and French . . . He looked at me with his startled eyes. I told him that I found inspiration in literature . . . How to say the most obvious things using the most obscure words . . . How to hide meaning in a forest of phrases . . . Literature is the code of all codes. I told him. Sitting in my chair. My back to the window. The rain pattering . . . That it's one way of looking at the world. Of confronting the world. Of becoming immersed in the daily battle . . . Trying to see what's hidden. Covered by a layer of reality . . . Trying to reach the core . . .

He kept staring at me. Admiring and incredulous . . . Standing next to a bookcase . . . I got up and looked on a shelf. I gave him a book with a bound cover . . . The complete works of Poe . . . I told him he would learn much by reading it . . . I told him to read "The Gold-Bug" . . .

I moved as if to kiss him. I liked to play that game with him ... To see whether he wanted to kiss me. Whether he could.

Poor man ... When he left. He was still somewhat stunned.

I am an electric ant ... Capable of spitting up blood ... And of keeping my eyes open without seeing a thing ... Not even Turing ... Sitting, awaiting my words. Poor man. He has never broken the spell ... Meeting me was the best thing that ever happened to him. And also the worst ... I taught him to do his job ... And not to ask questions. Not investigate. That was for others to do. Obedience is the rule ... One can converse with authority. But not question its orders ... I treated him as an equal. As a friend. So that. When it came down to it ... He would be a good subordinate ... And he was ... And he is ... He can't cope on his own. He still relies on me. He wants me to help him find his way ... Like I used to. He still doesn't suspect. That in reality I helped him not to see the way ... To concentrate only on what was in front of him. On his desk.

In order for a government to survive ... Civil servants like Turing are necessary.

Markets. Ruins of fortifications. A river. A very green valley.

Turing was fascinated by Poe's short story. Turing was fascinated by my short story.

He came to discuss it with me in my office the next morning ... As he did. I remembered the foggy morning when I created the monoalphabetic code for "The Gold-Bug" ... Legrand has to decipher it in order to discover where Captain Kidd ... Who died a century and a half ago ... Hid his treasure. The code is simple:

53##+305))6*;4826)4#.)4#);806*;48+8@60))85;]8*:#*8+83(88)
5*+;46(;88*96*?;8)*#(;485);5*+2:*#(;4956*2(5* — 4)8@8*;406
9285);)6+8)4##;1(#9;48081,8:8#1;48+85;4)485+528806*81(#9
;48(88;4(#?34;48)4#;161;:188;#?;

They were different times. When the art of keeping secrets still hadn't been mechanized ... A code had to be confronted using pencil and paper. It helped to know some cryptological methods ... For example. Knowing the frequency with which each letter in the alphabet appears. I had begun with pure intuition. Then I learned. By reading an article in an encyclopedia... That my style was a rudimentary form of frequency analysis. By the time I wrote the story... I had completely mastered the method.

Legrand knew that the most frequent letter in English is *e.* When he discovers that 8 occurs thirty-three times in the code... He supposes that 8 equals *e.* The article *the* also occurs frequently ... And if the combination ;48 occurs seven times in the code... Legrand decides that this equals *the.* A general look at the code will reveal an area that is apt for the attack... Thirty-two symbols before the end. Now *thet(eeth* can be read. The letter behind *(* has to be uncovered... There is no word in English that is the equivalent of t*(eeth*... So Legrand thinks... I make Legrand think... That the *th* at the end belongs to another word... And he is left with *t(ee.*

Trying each letter of the alphabet... The only word that makes sense is *tree*... So we have *the tree thr---hthe*... For the three spaces... Legrand decides on *oug*... Three more symbols have been uncovered. #. ?. 3. And so on. Until the text is deciphered... Which reads. *A good glass in the bishop's hostel in the devil's seat forty-one degrees and thirteen minutes northeast and by north main branch seventh limb east side shoot from the left eye of the death's-head a bee-line from the tree through the shot fifty feet out.*

Still mysterious... But now the problem is for Legrand. Not for cryptology. To solve.

I'm exhausted. It's raining. Out the windows. My throat is dry. I would like to go outside... To disconnect myself from these tubes. My mission here is done...

Turing never felt comfortable working with computers... He learned a great deal. At least he tried to. But he was nostalgic for the days of pencil and paper... When cryptograms were like crosswords... When one faced a problem. Armed with intuition and deductive reasoning... He reread Poe's story over and over again. It was his favorite. It struck the deepest chord in him. And made him realize that he was an old-fashioned man... Someone who would've been happy in any era. Prior to the one in which he had been born . . .

Seeing him wandering through the hallways of the Black Chamber moved me.

Maybe he would've been happy if he'd been immortal.

Maybe not. You never know . . . I know that I'm immortal. And I'm not happy.

chapter 20

RAMÍREZ-GRAHAM IS SHOWERING when his cell phone rings. He reaches out with his wet hand to grab the Nokia, covering it in soap; he watches it slip onto the floor. Fuck.

"Hello? Boss?" It is Baez. "What was that?"

"I dropped the phone. I'm in the shower."

"Oh, I see, I thought it was static. I just spoke with Sáenz's daughter. She'll call tomorrow to tell us whether or not she's interested. She didn't seem too sure. I gather she's been intimidated by hackers. They trust her as long as she remains neutral and uses her site only to inform — they won't like it if she collaborates with the government again. She's been threatened before, when she worked for Albert."

Ramírez-Graham asks him to insist, not to let her get away, and hangs up.

He gets out of the shower, cursing his work once again. Even if he does succeed now, his pride will be bruised, because he will owe his success to a teenager. Kandinsky's fall will be his salvation: he will hand him over, gagged, to the vice president, and that very same day he will buy his return ticket to Washington.

He dries himself with a monogrammed towel and changes in front of the full-length mirror in his room. His wet feet leave damp footprints on the parquet. Supersonic comes toward him, wagging his tail and looking up at him with his bright eyes. Maybe his sensors are telling him that his owner won't play with him again tonight? Ramírez-Graham smiles at him and pats his metallic head, his alert ears. He read in the Sony manual that the interactive model he bought would acquire different characteristics depending on the kind of relationship it had with its owners. The first few days, as tends to happen with every electronic gadget he acquires, Ramírez-Graham read the manual into the early morning hours and taught Supersonic several tricks: how to fetch the tennis ball when they played in the park, how to wag his tail when he got home from work. Supersonic was a happy dog that slept at the foot of the bed, issuing a faint whistle of satisfaction. Then, owing to the urgency of his work, Ramírez-Graham forgot him. The dog languished before his eyes, fading almost imperceptibly. His future as basement junk was already assured, just as soon as his batteries ran out.

In the kitchen, Ramírez-Graham serves himself a glass of Old Parr on the rocks and pours Cheerios into a bowl. On Saturday mornings he goes to a supermarket that specializes in American products and fills his cupboards with Doritos, M&Ms, and Pringles.

He turns on the Toshiba flat-screen TV in the living room. The pain in his stomach is returning; he heads to the bathroom in search of his pills. Maybe he has lost the mucous membrane that covers and protects the stomach? Intestinal flora, that's what it is called. Or is he lacking the gastric juices that help digestion?

He returns to the living room and finds a news channel. If successful, the indefinite blockade called for by the Coalition could turn Kandinsky into a symbol of the anti-globalization movement. Ramírez-Graham has to admit that he is living in a strange country. In the United States, a hacker would never dream of joining forces with union members. Fucking weird. The puzzle he's been given to solve is written in a language he doesn't recognize. He misses his office at Crypto City.

Crypto City, the Black Chamber . . . Since he had come from such humble origins, who would have thought he would have gotten this far? He was devoted to mathematics thanks to his mother. Exhausted after a long day at the public school where she worked, she still had time to sit down with him at the kitchen table and teach him the theory of numbers, using games she took from *The Man Who Counted.* He learned almost without noticing. Beremiz Samir, the man who counted, found poetry in numbers. He could distribute thirty-five camels between three Arab brothers and have the brothers be satisfied that the division was just. With four number fours he could form any number (zero = 44 − 44; one = 44/44; two = 4/4 + 4/4; three = 4+4+4/4; four = 4+(4 − 4)/4 . . .). He preferred the number 496 to 499, since 496 was a perfect number (one equal to the sum of all its factors, excluding itself). He could explain how it was possible that a Muslim judge could give three sisters different numbers of apples (50 for one, 30 for another, and 10 for the third), ask them to sell the apples for the same price, and still manage to have them all earn the same amount of money.

Almost without noticing, Ramírez-Graham went from playing those games to creating his own. He was interested in cryptology, an arcane branch of mathematics, because of the multiple applications it contained for the theory of numbers. When a copy of the software program called Mathematica fell into his hands, he began to program cryptographic systems on his own. He could not understand how mathematicians had survived before the computer was invented. For those who worked with enormous numbers, like cryptologists, the speed of the computer was an ally without par. A century had passed before it was discovered that one of Fermat's numbers was not a prime number, as his celebrated theory suggested, and two and a half centuries before it was discovered that another number was not prime; with a program like Mathematica on the computer, those centuries became less than two seconds. Fermat thought that the number $2^{32} + 1$ was prime; using Mathematica, you only had to type the command FactorInteger and then $[2^{32} + 1]$ to discover almost instantly that Fermat was wrong.

Even though his grades in high school were not very good, he was accepted into the University of Chicago because of affirmative action, which had done so much for Latinos. But he outdid himself in Chicago: he had a job offer from the NSA two years before he graduated. Even though years of solid work in Crypto City did not make him a star, it did make him a presence who was well trusted by his superiors. He had to remember all of that before giving up on Kandinsky.

He sits down in one of the chairs with the files he brought from the Black Chamber. The light from a lamp illuminates his profile, leaving the other half in shadow. Supersonic lies down at his feet and wags his tail, vainly attempting to attract his attention. Electronic dogs are just as annoying and needy as real dogs, but at least they don't shit everywhere.

The files are classified documents, found in a special section of the archives — the Archive of Archives — inaccessible to all but the director of the Black Chamber. They tell the story of how the chamber was founded in early 1975 and of its first few years of operation. They explain the reasons that gave rise to the building, how the original mission was established, what the directors were looking for when they hired personnel.

He would like to find out more about Albert. The entire building is under his spell. Whenever Ramírez-Graham goes into his office, he can't help but remember that Albert used to work there. At times he feels a ghostly silhouette is watching him work, controlling his steps and his words. That silhouette is attached by a rusting chain to the Enigma machine, like a grandfather in *One Hundred Years of Solitude.* He had liked that novel but had also laughed at how his schoolmates believed it was the extravagant and exotic reality of Latin America. Sure, they do things differently down there, he would tell them, but it isn't exotic. At least, that was not the Cochabamba of his vacations. There were parties and drugs and television and a great deal of beer, just like in Chicago. No grandfather chained to a tree, no beautiful adolescent ascending to heaven. But now that he lived here, fuck, his imagination was betraying him. Maybe García Márquez had been right.

He has thought about visiting Albert at the house where he lies secluded and dying, but before disturbing him he needs to have a sense of the Black Chamber and clarify the legend. These documents will help him to do that. And they will help him to forget about Kandinsky for a while.

He ponders his empty bowl of Cheerios, disinclined to rouse

himself for more. If only Supersonic were a robot—now that would be something. If he could buy a robot that he could send to the kitchen to bring him more Cheerios, and while we're at it, the bottle of Old Parr . . . The monthly salary for a maid in this country was not even one hundred dollars. At times he was tempted to hire one, but he couldn't bring himself to do so. It would be far too strange having someone live in his apartment, serving him from six in the morning until ten at night, maybe rifling through his drawers when he was out. Once when he was on vacation in Cochabamba he had gone out with a girl whose father watched television without ever leaving his chair. Since he did not have a remote control, he used the maid to change channels. As he sat watching his favorite programs in the living room, the maid had to stand in the doorway the entire time, attentive to his slightest gesture. Ramírez-Graham would never forget that sight.

As he reviews the documents, he thinks about Svetlana. He would give anything for her to be here in this very living room, he sitting in the chair and she sprawled on the floor, working on her laptop as she had in Georgetown, preparing a report for the insurance company where she works.

But now he can't think of her without thinking about their son. He can picture him crawling on the rug, pulling Supersonic's tail, the dog patiently taking it—his software recognizing children and having been programmed not to react to their provocations. Ramírez-Graham looks down at his feet. Now he sees him, now he doesn't.

The documents in the file he is holding tell of Operation Turing. He read the first few pages without paying much attention; Albert, after all, was obsessed with Turing and before giving that name to Sáenz had also used it to name a room in the chamber and a couple of secret operations. Ramírez-Graham soon discovers that this operation refers to the Turing he knows, to the head of the archives—a man he views as someone like his grandfather, useless but refusing to retire.

He finishes his glass of Old Parr. Supersonic growls at the wind that buffets the windows. Reading on, Ramírez-Graham gradually learns that between 1975 and 1977, certain intercepted messages came into Albert's hands and were sent directly to Turing. The argument: they were particularly difficult, and Albert did not want to waste time having other analysts try to solve them. Turing had quickly become his right-hand man, and Albert believed him to be nothing less than infallible.

The light of the lamp flickers, the images on the TV blur: another GlobaLux blackout. Ramírez-Graham closes the file and tries to resign himself. Patience, patience. No wonder everyone here is so religious.

It's impossible—he'll never get used to so many annoyances. He just wants to do his work and not worry about whether or not the infrastructure is falling to pieces.

Ten minutes later, the lamp and the television come back to life. He opens the file again. Something doesn't seem quite right. For a secret message to be considered difficult, first you have to try to solve it. Or was Albert capable of deciding at a glance how difficult a message was? And as far as he knew, Turing was not terribly fond of computers. He tried to decipher messages using pencil and paper, as if the real Turing had never existed, as if cryptanalysis hadn't been mechanized a century and a half ago. A truly difficult message needed to be attacked with the brute force of a Cray. An analyst came on the scene only after the computer had identified certain weak spots in the message. Even using that approach, a great number of messages went unsolved. And yet Turing had deciphered everything that Albert had put on his desk. Either the people encrypting messages in Bolivia in the seventies used extremely rudimentary methods, which was possible, or Turing was a natural, one of the most brilliant cryptanalysts in the history of cryptanalysis.

Something does not add up. He tells himself that he'd better keep reading.

The lamp and television go dark. He gets out of his chair, feels around for his cell phone. He doesn't know whom to call, what to do.

In the darkness of his apartment, Ramírez-Graham pictures Turing twenty-five years ago, young, at the height of his power at the Black Chamber. He pictures him in an office full of papers, receiving the files that Albert hands him, immediately setting to work, not willing to let down the person who holds him in such high regard.

For the first time he feels compassion for that tired old man he has relegated to the basement, whom he thinks of firing at any moment.

chapter 21

JUDGE CARDONA LEAVES the hotel with his black briefcase in hand and comes upon a hostile, cloudy sky, the sense that drizzle is imminent. It had been brighter in the hotel room. He does not remember Río Fugitivo being like this, a city of weak sunshine and gray clouds about to pour rain. Nostalgia has gotten the better of him, and the sunny days from his childhood and adolescence, which perhaps were few, have eclipsed all others. It happens to the best of us. We are restless creatures, governed by an incurable desire for paradise. But paradise is not what we have been given, so we invent it in our memories, based on a few furtive weeks when we were happy, perhaps in the beginning or somewhere along the way where the road forked and life took us. The tricks of fate, which can also bring happiness.

There are police in the plaza and the neighboring streets are deserted, with sticks, nails, and stones scattered on the pavement and sidewalks and debris swirling in the wind. It is Friday afternoon. Yesterday, after the woman left, Judge Cardona overindulged in BMP and passed out on the white tile bathroom floor after vomiting violently. He woke up today at noon, a bitter taste in his throat and mouth, his palate extremely dry. "History was being made as I slept," Cardona, stroking his beard, says to the doorman.

The doorman tells him that he was right to have stayed in his room. The evidence of yesterday afternoon's and this morning's confrontations is all over the streets. Everything is blockaded. Yesterday a group of demonstrators took the plaza and then the police took it back. Today they plan to reach the mayor's and the prefect's offices; the police have cordoned off the plaza. "If I were you, I'd stay in my room. This is going to get ugly. The demonstrators will be back with renewed force, and the police will use tear gas. I've seen it a thousand times. You learn a lot working in the main plaza." He blinks as if he has no control over the muscles in his eyelids.

"Unfortunately," Cardona says, scratching his right cheek, "I have urgent business."

Every time he comes to Río Fugitivo, something strange happens. Existing in multiple historical temporalities, its inhabitants dream of the modern convenience of cable TV but are anchored to the premodern past of strikes and street protests. It's no different from the rest of the country. Many Internet cafés do not progress make. Many supermarkets and shopping centers either.

Cardona had better walk. Avenida de las Acacias is relatively close by, only about ten blocks away. He touches his briefcase and feels protected — from the future, the past, himself. His legs are tingling and exhaustingly heavy; the effects of BMP are still coursing through his body. Dry throat, nausea. Perhaps he should wait a while, until his mind clears, until the fog lifts. No, no, no. He has waited long enough. Neither lucidity nor a lack thereof will change the radical cruelty of the facts. There are such things as avenging angels, whose only purpose in coming to earth is to exterminate. Oh, to whom do you entrust your soul? Perhaps he should go to the cathedral on the other side of the plaza, behind the scrawny palm trees, as a prologue to what cannot then be undone. Perhaps the wine-colored spots, scattered over his body like an archipelago in entropy, will disappear from his skin, and with them any sensation of fulfilling a pact, any reminder of an obligation. But no. Someone has to be responsible for the cousin who is dead. Someone has to be responsible for Mirtha. Someone, however feverish he might be, has to atone for his own sins. All the questions he has about the hell of a dictatorship can be reduced to just one, or several grouped under the same theme: who is ultimately responsible when a life is taken? Who, conscious of his actions or not, assumed this celestial right? Infamy should not remain in an abstraction called "the dictatorship," it should be personalized in a body that breathes, in a face with eyes that avoid or meet your gaze.

Cardona walks through a group of policemen. A sergeant with thick hands and a white mustache stops talking on his walkie-talkie and looks at Cardona as if he knows him from somewhere. The spots are easily recognizable; perhaps the beard has thrown him off. He asks Cardona for his ID card, his tone slightly annoyed; Cardona shows it to him. The sergeant is surprised to discover a well-known name. He looks at Cardona as if making sure that the person in front of him is in fact someone who was once minister of justice. His tone changes: This is no time to be out on the street. The demonstrators are just two blocks away. Cardona replies that he has an urgent business meeting to attend and, since the sergeant is so worried about his security, asks him please to assign two officers to escort him.

The sergeant calls over two of his men. "Mamani. Quiroz. Accompany the judge to the barricade and return immediately." Mamani and Quiroz, with their sleepy, fearful eyes, station themselves on either side of him. *They could be my children,* he thinks. But he has never had children. It had been difficult for him to find a stable relationship, to make plans for the future.

Back when he was fifteen, he had put his obsessive interest in soccer and friends to one side and begun to focus on women, strange beings who actually scared him a little. Perhaps he was afraid because he went to San Ignacio, an all-boys school; by not having women around, by spending his time closed up in that masculine world of obscenities and masturbatory fantasies, he did not know how to treat them. Then Mirtha became his obsession, but she had disappeared as quickly as she had entered. Nothing had been the same with women since.

Two fighter jets thunderously cross the sky, leaving a cottony slipstream in their wake. He snaps out of deep thought. Will it rain? Most likely. Seventy yards from the barricade he can see the fury on the demonstrators' faces: they are throwing cans and bottles and have started a fire in the middle of the street, using cardboard boxes and newspaper. "This is our mission—it's time for the Coalition!" The demonstrators' refrain is vague, out of sync.

"This is insistence, it's time for resistance! An end, an end to this globalizing trend!"

He is approaching the barricade when a rock hits him above his right eye. He lets his briefcase fall and brings his hands to his face. One of the officers escorting him has also been hit; he is on the ground and bleeding from his left temple. The demonstrators cross the barrier and are held back by a police squad. Cardona hears shots in the air, and dry pops; he realizes it is tear gas. There are shouts, the sound of metal on metal. "Fucking pigs!" The phrase rises above all the other noise, taking over. "Pigs go home!" There is blood on Cardona's hands: his right eyebrow has been cut. He feels sharp, hot stabs of pain above his eye. He can barely open it, and the pain makes him dizzy. Should he go to a hospital? He picks up his briefcase; he had better keep going. Haltingly, he reaches the corner and turns left. He begins to run down a seemingly never-ending street as he feels a stinging in his eyes and a bitter smell fills the air. *Tear gas,* he hears someone shout, *tear gas.* The doorman had been right.

Cardona tries to keep moving with his eyes half closed. Adrenaline is suffocating his lungs. This is how Mirtha must have felt when she was facing the police and military at demonstrations. He had missed all of that. All he had wanted was for the university to reopen so that he could begin his studies. If it did not open soon, he would go to Brazil or Mexico. He had wanted to start a career, was worried about his future, not very interested in what was going on around him. One day he told this to Mirtha, who had come into his room while his sister prepared tea. She had asked him what he thought about the political situation and then told him she was surprised by his egotism, his ignorance of what was happening in their country. She was ashamed of him. *I can imagine what's going on. I'm not dumb, but I'm not brave; I'm not a hero,* he told her. *It's not about that,* she said, shaking her pigtails, *it's about keeping our dignity.* Then she had gone out into the living room. It was the last time he had seen her alive.

He stops four blocks farther on, as he is leaving the Enclave. He passes by the building that at one time housed the telegraph company, Doric columns and two naked neoclassical goddesses flanking the entrance. He walks past a seven-story building; there is no sign to indicate what it is, but it must be important, because it is being guarded by several policemen. He can still hear shots being fired in the air. Television cameras arrive on the scene. A reporter shoves a microphone in his face and asks a few questions. Cardona keeps walking, his eyes burning. "Wait . . . aren't you . . . ?" Luckily, behind him several others are anxious to be interviewed. He does not want to have anything to do with cameras. He has not been around them for a long time now. And to think that at one time he had wanted to be in the limelight, to be in the best photos with Montenegro. *We're about to announce the new criminal code.* His office full of papers and requests for interviews. Weekends at the country homes of one ally of the regime or another, drinking Cuba Libres next to a pool, chatting with Montenegro's obese wife. It was rumored that she was behind the corruption in customs. Montenegro's godson, the ex-mayor of La Paz, white beard, affable smile, a glass of whiskey in his hand, approaching and remarking that Cardona must be hot, that he should take off his jacket. "In a while, thank you," Cardona had said, thinking about the file in his office with the concrete proof of bribes the godson had taken to accept a bid. The opposition was pressuring him to take the godson to court. He wasn't sure what to do, which he now thinks said a lot about him. Everything became clearer after Montenegro approached him beside that very pool and told him, in the same calm yet imposing tone his father had used with him when he was a child, to make that file disappear. It was not a suggestion; it was an order. "Certainly, general," he had said. "Of course, general." He also had photocopies of the invoice for a Beechcraft airplane for the presidency, $3 million, with Montenegro's signature authorizing the purchase. And he had a study by a consulting firm indicating that no more than $1.4 million should have been paid for that plane. So where did the money go? How could he ask the general? Time and again he had wondered whether he had the stomach for what passed as politics. He learned that he certainly did have the stomach for it. Next to the pool, the owner of the house — wearing a coquettish, incongruous white hat that covered her balding head — asked everyone to gather together to toast

Montenegro's wife on her birthday, *Happy birthday to you, happy birthday to you.* Montenegro looking sullen, beside him whispering, *Forget about that plane, judge, you're either with us or against us. Trust me, general. I simply need to have my answers prepared; reporters, the opposition, will soon be asking questions.* The water in the pool sparkling in the sunlight. *Answers for everyone's questions except my own.* The godson patting him on the back. *If you don't have the answers, you'd better leave.* Better late than never. Leave, hide from the cameras, from power, not be the one to show your face in such a shameful manner. *Going for a swim, judge? It's a little too late, I think, general. It's never too late for anything, take my word for it.*

His eyes itch. He opens and closes them, again and again. The pain is throbbing. Even though his legs still feel stiff, the effects of the BMP have finally worn off. The violence in the street has forced him to wake up.

It's never too late? Judge, know thyself. Can he understand himself? For years he thought he did. Everything was clear to him: the objectives, the motives, the reasons, the intuition. Now all is blurred, and his pride has prevented him from asking for help. Well, yes, he once did. He went to a psychiatrist six months ago, after a week of insomnia. Sitting on a black leather sofa in front of that young woman with glasses too big for her face and an Argentine accent, he couldn't think about anything but how his friends would laugh if they knew. Men solved their problems on their own; shrinks were for sissies, and to top it all off they were ridiculously expensive and never offered concrete solutions. He told the woman about Mirtha, about his year of working for Montenegro. He said he had betrayed his cousin and felt the need to avenge her death, to kill those responsible. He told her he wanted to assassinate Montenegro, but he knew this was impossible. And if not him, then those responsible for Mirtha's death. At the end of the hour, the psychiatrist concluded that his concern for Mirtha, his need to avenge her death, was genuine. But, she asked, would he have felt the need if he hadn't destroyed his own self-image that year he spent working alongside Montenegro? She asked him to ponder that question and come back with an answer for his next visit, in a week. She called a couple of days later, to check on him. She was concerned that he was entering into a dangerous phase—all that talk of revenge and killing. Cardona listened to her and later asked what she meant by "dangerous phase." "Just that," she said. He remembered how uncomfortable he had felt on the black sofa, thanked her, and hung up. He never went back to see her.

Four blocks away is the house where Albert is being kept. He can see it at the end of his visual field, unobtrusive, unnoticed by neighbors and passersby. Jacarandas along the avenue. It is the house where someone who for a time moved the strings of Bolivian history is taking refuge. He should leave everything that is past behind and worry only about looking forward. He should walk with steady steps to that house. Ruth had gone to get the concrete proof that accused Albert and her husband, naming them responsible for several deaths, including Mirtha's. But Cardona, once he had received confirmation of his suspicions from Ruth's mouth, does not need proof. All he needs is to maintain his conviction, to stay strong. There should be no doubt. Maybe the force of his actions will be enough to bring him peace, to make living with himself bearable once again. For the rest, all he needs is the target and the polished metal in the briefcase that he is holding on to so tightly—or that is holding on so tightly to him.

chapter 22

KANDINSKY LIKES TO WALK in the downtown area, known as the Enclave. He enjoys the motley collection of street vendors and the pervasive aroma of skewers of *anticuchos* and *chola* sandwiches being sold on street corners; the decaying façades of buildings; retirees and the country's old heroes sitting on benches in the plaza, reading newspapers; and the massive cathedral, its steps now the protectorate of beggars. Years ago, during one of the fleeting bursts of economic prosperity that have marked the history of Río Fugitivo, the Civic Committee worriedly watched how new construction was popping up at will all over the city. These buildings altered the urban landscape, and while they did give Río Fugitivo a more modern, progressive face, it was not worth losing its image as a traditional city, a quiet refuge. Colonial churches and nineteenth-century mansions were being destroyed; the quiet enchantment of old, of that which stood as testimony to the passing of time and by its mere presence battled the empire of what is ephemeral, was being lost. Could the downtown not be an enclave of tradition in the midst of so much modernity? The Civic Committee mobilized its forces to try to prevent any new construction in the old quarter. They were successful, but the battle continues. Today the new city is laying siege to and suffocating the old, flanking it on all sides, waiting for a single mistake in order to achieve victory once and for all. The Enclave is sufficient proof that what is old in and of itself is not enough to bear witness to history and grandeur. Buildings dating from the late nineteenth century—the National Telegraph Company, the local railway headquarters—and from the mid-twentieth century—the Departmental Theater—stand empty and are dying a slow death. Other buildings persist in defiance, like the mansion that today houses the Palace Hotel and the one that was once the headquarters of *Tiempos Modernos* and is now the computer institute where Kandinsky studied.

Kandinsky would like all of Río Fugitivo to be like the Enclave—a place frozen in time, its back to the hypermarket that the planet has become. There are many others who think like him, even in the same empire. He has not forgotten the Seattle protests in November 1999; they made him realize that he is not alone, that there is generalized discontent with the new world order. If young people in more prosperous countries are capable of erupting as they did in Seattle, it is possible that an even more devastating explosion could occur in a region as poor and with as many contrasts as Latin America. Río Fugitivo should become the Seattle of Bolivia and the whole continent. The work of Kandinsky and a few other activists is designed to ensure that the winds of discontent will be felt.

The first thing you need to begin a revolution, Kandinsky thought, his hands behind his head, is to recruit people. He was lying in his sleeping bag while Phiber, having gone to bed late, was snoring. Kandinsky's fingers ached and were still moving as if he were typing on the keyboard, a habit he had picked up over the past few weeks. What words was he writing in the air? What software code was he improvising in front of an invisible monitor? In the early morning a cold draft still permeated the room, but the first rays of sunlight were peeking in through the curtains. Outside the window, the red neon light on the sidewalk across the street was starting to lose some of its brightness. The city was waking up; the streets were filling with the screeching of buses and the high-pitched voices of newspaper vendors.

Kandinsky had not been able to fall asleep. It happened sometimes, when his head continued to spin. He couldn't stop thinking, couldn't disconnect. Thought thinks and drags you along with it, to fertile or not-so-fertile lands. The important thing was to unite thought with desire, intuition, feelings. When the rational and irrational were in tune, sparks flew.

Sometimes he imagined himself with Laura, who had ignored him ever since their encounter in the bathroom. Who did she think she was?

The first thing he had to do was leave Phiber's house. With all the money they had earned, he could get an apartment. It was absurd to have a well-stocked bank account and sleep on the floor in a sleeping bag each night. Phiber said they shouldn't call attention to themselves with a lot of sudden purchases, that the police would become suspicious. The office they had set up was enough. "There's no rush."

But there is, Kandinsky thought. He had decided to claim his part of the money and move that very week. The revolution couldn't wait. He needed to find partners and followers like himself, discontented with the way things were and willing to do something about it. He pictured an army of young people taking back the proposals for utopia and social change from previous generations, shaking off their apathy, and unleashing their fury against a government bought by multinational corporations, against the new world order. Discontent was in the air, and it was simply a matter of harnessing it. It wouldn't be easy, but as a mural on one of the walls at San Ignacio said, nothing is impossible for those who are capable.

Kandinsky yawned. Perhaps sleep was finally on its way. He realized that this would be a different revolution. There would be the usual street demonstrations, emotional speeches from a balcony in the main plaza, but at least some of it would be carried out from a distance, by means of computers. It might not even be necessary to meet his comrades-in-arms in person.

Geometric figures floated on the screen saver, eyes that seemed to be spying on him.

Just as he suspected, Phiber did not take the news of his leaving well. In the afternoon, on their way home from an Internet café, shouting and recriminations occurred as they crossed Suicide Bridge. Phiber said he felt used: Kandinsky had taken advantage of his hospitality in order to earn his trust and then leave.

Kandinsky remained silent. "Maybe you're right," he said at last. He did not feel like arguing. He would accept all accusations in order to accelerate the breakup.

Phiber stopped and looked him in the eyes, imploringly. "Please, one more year. I just need another year."

"I've made up my mind," Kandinsky said, his tone unchanged.

He never thought to tell Phiber about his plans and invite him to participate. Phiber was made of a different metal.

Phiber did not say another word the whole way back. When they reached the house, he told Kandinsky that he couldn't come in; Phiber would bring all of his belongings to the door.

"We have to divide the money," Kandinsky said.

"Don't even think about it. As I see it, you're leaving the partnership. The money will be there, waiting for you, when you decide to come back."

Kandinsky would not accept the bait. He knew it would be easy to obtain as much money as he had with Phiber, or more.

He turned around and left, listening to Phiber's insults. The only thing he regretted was not having been able to say goodbye to Laura.

Kandinsky slept in a small square a block from his parents' house and San Ignacio. In the mornings, sitting on a bench across the street, he would watch the activity at San Ignacio, long pauses of quiet during classes punctuated by brief bursts of euphoria during breaks. He also watched what went on at his house. His dad got up early to work on the patio; nothing had changed. His brother had grown and become a stocky young man. His mom left early, probably to look after someone's baby or clean houses.

At times he wanted to play the role of the prodigal son, to show up at the door, tell his parents that he was back, and be swept up in their embrace. It had been a prank that had gone on too long, and he wanted to help them, be with them in their old age. But he knew that returning was impossible. Once a path had been chosen, any path, the only choice was to continue down it, even when returning home. Objects and people moved as much as you did; they did not stand still for anyone.

During that time Kandinsky went to Portal to Reality, an Internet café in the Bohemia district. He was waited on by a young woman with a metallic right arm. From afar, Kandinsky watched her delicately hold a glass, flip through the pages of her agenda, type on the keyboard. The arm was controlled by her brain, learned to move intuitively, recognized the shape and texture of objects and adapted to them. The young woman had a round, dull face and flat chest, but Kandinsky was drawn to her, or perhaps to the relationship she had with her arm. It was the kind of relationship he would have liked to have with his computer — intuitive: to program codes without needing a keyboard. He asked her out, but she turned him down. *Maybe she's shy,* he thought. He would have to try again.

The café was frequented by youths with bulging wallets and a knack for underestimating everyone else. It was easy for Kandinsky to bet with them in online war games — Lineage, taking place in feudal Japan, was in vogue — and fill his pockets. Soon he would go back to hacking a few personal accounts and would transfer the money to an account he created for himself. Once the money had been withdrawn, he would close the account and disappear. He would rent a little apartment on the outskirts of the city, on the way to the hilltop where the Ciudadela, or Government Citadel, was, and he would buy a computer, an IBM clone.

Everything was now ready for him to put his plan into action.

Kandinsky spent hours in Playground with the intention of recruiting people. There was an anarchist neighborhood where avatars who were discontent with the politics of Playground met in the plaza and cafés. Kandinsky suspected that their dissatisfaction corresponded to dissatisfaction on the part of their creators in the real world. Of course, that was not always the case. Sometimes an anarchist avatar belonged to a docile yuppie and that of a revolutionary was controlled by someone who worked for the presidency. But he had to start somewhere.

Then it occurred to him that it was better not to mix the two worlds, at least not initially. Why not recruit those avatars for an insurrection against the government of Playground? The virtual world would be an opportunity to carry out a test before moving on to the real world.

In a plaza made up of orange and purple pixels, next to a fountain spouting yellow water, Kandinsky's avatar, which he called BoVe in honor of the French farmer who attacked a McDonald's as an anti-globalization protest, recruited two avatars, one androgynous and the other a digital being with the head of a unicorn and the body of a tiger. (Digital beings combine the head of a mythical animal or a famous person with the body of another animal or person: a gargoyle with Ronaldo's body, a hydra with Britney Spears's body. The creator of digital beings was a graphic designer who had disappeared mysteriously; because of the proliferation of pirated digital beings, his sister patented his invention and looked for the most probable applications. One of these had been to sell the possibility of their use to the corporation in charge of Playground.)

One night the avatars painted revolutionary slogans in various places in Playground where ads for Sony, Nokia, Benetton, Coca-Cola, and Nike were prominent. In all the attacks they left the signature of the Restoration, the name Kandinsky had given to the group: a capital *R* with the @ sign instead of the letter *a*. Chased by the police, they escaped down the streets of the anarchist neighborhood and managed to hide in a professor's home. One of the avatars was caught as he jumped over a fence and fell into the yard next door; security forces took him to the Tower, the infamous building where the avatars that were most disruptive to the regime were held.

Radio Freedom, one of the few clandestine media that the government of Playground had not yet managed to silence, spread the news of the attack. Gossip and rumors magnified the Restoration's attack, and so began the legend of BoVe in Playground.

In the solitude of his apartment—a desk with a computer, a black-and-white television, a stereo, and a mattress on the floor—Kandinsky began to think about his next move. He read in the newspaper that Montenegro's government had granted the contract for the provision of electricity in Río Fugitivo to GloBaLux, an Italian-American consortium.

chapter 23

YOU EAT LUNCH at the Black Chamber's cafeteria, much to your disgust. The soups taste like paste — or what you think paste would taste like if you tried it — there are usually grease spots on the cutlery, and the meat is tough, full of intricate labyrinths of nerves. You have told yourself time and again that you will not eat there and just before lunch, almost as if it were a ritual, murmur that you will go home as you used to, to eat with Ruth and Flavia, watch the news on TV for a while, and take a half-hour nap with a handkerchief covering your eyes (the extravagant routine of domestic life). But then you find some excuse to postpone going home at least until that night. And so you send an e-mail to Flavia — perhaps a digital photo or a thirty-second video clip of you clowning around in the hallways of the archives — as insufficient compensation.

You are alone at a table in the farthest corner of the cafeteria, reviewing another coded message that you received this morning, when Baez and Santana approach, plastic lunch trays in hand.

"May we join you?" Baez asks.

You try to detect any mocking or sarcasm in his voice. Upset and worried, you would have liked to say no. You are about to finish deciphering the message, and all indications are that you have been insulted again: *criminal, murderer, your hands are stained with blood.* Your good manners prevent you from refusing.

You close the file that contains the message. You observe the two of them, one blond, the other dark — opposite sides of the same coin. Black pants, white shirts, and ties. Albert had encouraged individuality and let people dress however they wanted; Ramírez-Graham thinks he is the head of a boarding school and has imposed a strict dress code at work. You could pick them out just by their clothes. Under Albert's reign those with the most talent, like himself, flourished in Río Fugitivo; Ramírez-Graham's mantra is that one person's victory is everyone's — influenced by his reading of *The Three Musketeers,* Turing muses — and there is no way for anyone to stand out from the rest.

"The boss is fuming," Baez says, taking a bite of his hamburger.

"No wonder," Santana replies. "The Resistance humiliated the government."

"And Montenegro's looking for someone to blame. Or his government is, same thing. Because at this point, Montenegro is a puppet whose strings are being pulled by his inner circle. His family. His wife. If he dies, they'd probably keep him artificially alive until the end of his term."

"Sure, and we pay for it."

"They think we're magicians."

"We're supposed to intercept all communications in the country."

"And decipher them."

"I always say that maybe the old methods might have better results — go looking for compromising papers in garbage dumps."

"Fucking Resistance. The computers those kids have are more powerful than ours. Maybe we're irrelevant?"

"Maybe the next president will get rid of us just like that. If it's the leader of the coca growers, there's no doubt about it."

"That's why we envy you, Mr. Sáenz."

"Sincere envy."

Their speech is disjointed and loud, their mouths full. They are disturbing your peace. They both rose rapidly thanks to their blatant courting of Ramírez-Graham. Better yet, they didn't even have to rise, they started at the top. Albert wouldn't even have hired them.

"We would've loved to have lived during your time," Baez continues, lowering his voice. His expression seems sincere.

"A golden age," suggests Santana, his tone admiring.

"And we'd like to listen to you." Back to the loud tone, the words spoken emphatically. "Have you tell us what you've seen."

"You're part of history. We're not."

"Unless a miracle happens."

"And we take part in nabbing Kandinsky."

"That son of a bitch."

"They say he's not even twenty years old."

"No one has a clue. He could be anyone."

"He could even be working here."

"He could be our boss."

"He'd kill you if he heard you say that."

"He'd applaud if he heard me. Isn't that his rule? Be paranoid — distrust even ourselves."

"Yeah. I can't even read e-mails from my girlfriend without wondering whether she's sending me secret messages, telling me that she really hates me."

"I can't even read my own notes without wondering if I'm trying to send myself a secret message while doing everything possible not to be deciphered by myself."

There is something pathetic about the exuberance of their speech and gestures. You might be irrelevant, but at least you are a museum piece. They are the worst kind of irrelevant, born at the wrong time for their profession. Both of them see you as the archives, and you, who fought so hard against it and cursed your obsolescence so much, begin to believe that maybe accepting your new state is not so negative after all.

"There's not much to tell," you say. You will not give them the satisfaction. The first thing you have to learn in this profession is to keep a secret, even from your own colleagues.

"Of course there is. Don't be so humble."

"The one who has a story to tell is Albert," you say. "He knows everything about everyone."

"But he can't talk anymore."

"Which isn't a bad end for people like us," you say.

"Well, at least tell us something about him. Was he as smart as they say?"

"Is it true he was a Nazi fugitive? A good friend of Klaus Barbie's?"

"Two Nazis in charge of secret operations when Montenegro was dictator, one in charge of the paramilitary and the other in charge of gathering intelligence."

"I've worked at the Black Chamber since its inception," you say, your voice firm. "And I can swear that Albert did not know Barbie. Barbie came on the scene in the eighties, with García Meza's government. He was a DOP adviser, but he had nothing to do with the Black Chamber."

"Makes you wonder," Baez says. "Barbie came to Bolivia in the early fifties. You can't tell me that he spent thirty years here doing nothing. How can you be so sure that he wasn't a secret adviser to other military governments before the eighties? Maybe he felt secure enough during García Meza's time that he came into the limelight, but remember that as a Nazi fugitive, it was in his best interests to keep quiet. His big mistake was to have had the nerve to come out into public life."

"Please excuse me."

You stand up suddenly and look for the door. You appear to be upset.

"Is something wrong?" Baez says, trying to stop you. Both seem surprised. They are used to the calm demeanor with which you usually accept everything, the way the muscles of your face do not show emotion when they seem to be making fun of you. But that is one thing. It is another, altogether different thing to make fun of Albert.

"I'm not going to tolerate you two offending Albert."

"I apologize," Baez says. "Honestly."

"Me too," Santana says. "We were just talking. No offense."

You accept their apologies with a faint smile and leave. Far too talkative, both of them; they won't last long in this profession.

You still have quite a while before you have to go back to work, so you decide to visit Albert. It is your monthly visit, pushed forward by a couple of days. Perhaps he will be able to help you decipher the enigma of the messages you have been receiving. Perhaps, as in other times, a few phrases from his delirium will illuminate certain things for you.

Albert lives on the second floor of a modest house on Avenida de las Acacias that has a garden of dried roses and a scrawny rubber plant. The walls are painted blue and covered in a listless creeper. The first floor is vacant; an exterior staircase leads directly up to the second floor. A policeman guards the entrance, allowing in only those who have been authorized by the government.

It takes you a while to get there. The avenue is blocked; they won't let you through, so you have to park your Toyota at an intersection and then pay them a few pesos. A young man hurls insults at you after he takes your money. "And don't you dare say that you gave us a handout!" You do not reply. You are looking at the face of the Liberator on the bill. He is staring at you fixedly, wanting to tell you something. What? What, for God's sake, what? "Think about what you're doing, and next time stay at home! The city has been shut down and you're incapable of joining a widespread civil movement!"

You are thinking about the indestructible face on that bill and have to force yourself to come back to the here and now. You continue on your way without responding to the young man; you hate confrontation. And anyhow, you aren't really even sure what they're protesting. The capitalization of the power company? The increase in the monthly electricity rates? With as many strikes and protests as there are, it is hard to differentiate the relevant from the irrelevant. Everything would run more efficiently if there were more respect for authority, if time and money weren't wasted arguing about it and not recognizing it. You are living in difficult times.

The police officer stops reading *Alarma* and greets you with a slight nod. His eyebrows are white and his skin a discolored pinkish. A genetic defect, a poorly written code. He knows you but still asks to see your ID card. You hand it to him respectfully. You stand staring down at the front page of *Alarma*. "Strangled His Son While Sleeping." Who was sleeping, the son or the murderer? You picture a sleepwalking killer, his body moving even though he is absent, incapable of taking responsibility for his own actions. You picture his mind working amid dreams, thoughts jamming together of their own accord, far from the rational being who is capable of controlling them. *Perhaps we're all sleepwalkers,* you think, *our acts, ideas, and feelings guided by something or someone outside ourselves, or someone who is inside us.* The effect is the same. "Strangled His Son While Sleeping." That something or someone inside or outside us who controls us tells you that within those words is a message that could help you to understand the meaning of the world. You will wear yourself out looking for the code that will unravel the phrase, that will return order to a little piece of the universe arranged by some First Cause.

"It must've been hard to get here," the guard says, looking at your identification. "They're not letting anyone through. The army should intervene—tear-gas them. That'd make them as quiet as church mice."

You nod. At one time you wondered where your respect for authority came from. You had had a privileged childhood. Your dad was an engineer with a good job at the national petroleum company. He was tall and heavyset, his voice firm, intimidating; he was always organizing his colleagues and subordinates in an attempt to obtain better working conditions. His mistake, if you can call it that, was to join a hunger strike by the regular workers. The other engineers decided not to back the strike, because they said it had nothing to do with their demands. Your dad was the type to be easily moved and could not do the same. A lot of his workers were his friends. The administration gave him several opportunities to reconsider his position, but he stood firm on his principles. In the end, they fired him. He could have forgotten about the matter and looked for work in the private sector, but he did not want to; he decided to appeal his dismissal to the very end. Lawyers' fees ate up Dad's savings, and your family slowly lost its privileges. The company's management, backed by the government, would not concede, and your dad was defeated, became a resentful man. You can remember him mumbling insults as he watered the lawn. Wandering through the house at night, unable to sleep, his lips trembling. Perhaps that is when your respect, your fear of authority, began.

Or perhaps there was something innate that made you learn that lesson from that experience, because another temperament might have learned the opposite lesson.

"Go ahead," says the police officer, going back to his newspaper. "But please don't stay too long."

The room smells of eucalyptus leaves and medicine. Albert is lying on his bed, the covers pulled up to his chin. His eyes are open, but you know that he is sleeping. Several tubes connect his body to a cream-colored machine on one side; the tremulous geometry of his vital signs blinks on the screen. You still feel humble and insignificant before that reverential, once so powerful figure. The first few times you came, fooled by his eyes, you thought he was awake and tried to strike up a conversation, to no avail. Now what you do is tell him, without stopping, everything that has happened at the Black Chamber since the last time you saw him. And that face scored by wrinkles, that body closer to death than to life, lets you talk just as it used to, even though you never take full advantage of the opportunity. Sometimes, all of a sudden, his lips will make an effort, and a few words or phrases issue forth. At first they seemed incoherent to you, but visit after visit, you've discovered that, like an oracle, they tell you something illuminating about your current situation. A sort of personal *I Ching*, your own private sibyl. Albert had been interested in discovering how thought thought; he wanted to find the algorithm, the logical steps that led from one idea to another by way of predictable nervous ramifications. *We would save so much time,* he said, *if we could control the noise of the world; it would be so much easier to learn of our enemies' plans.* It is logical, then, that there is some coherence to his delirium. It is logical, then, that his delirium be interpreted as a code that is aware of the world.

You sit down on a chair next to the door. The walls seem barer than usual. A few photos, three or four, have been taken down. Someone from the Black Chamber had assembled a biography of Albert in Bolivia on those walls. Albert in his office, the ever-present cigarette in his mouth. Albert shaking the hand of a young, ambitious Montenegro. Albert with the Enigma machine that he had put in his office for inspiration. There was even a photo with you and other colleagues from the early days. Which pictures were missing? Your memory will soon tell you.

The first time Albert became delirious was two years ago. You were in his office, talking about Montenegro's vice president, who had met with Albert to tell him that they had approved his plans to reorganize the Black Chamber. Albert did not like the vice president—too Americanized. But he trusted Montenegro: after all, Albert had stayed in Bolivia thanks to him. And the Black Chamber existed thanks to Montenegro. All of a sudden, you heard him mumble a string of incomprehensible words. He said that he was called Demaratus, that he was Greek and he lived in Susa. He had invented stenography. He said he was called Histiaeus, ruler of Miletus. He said he was Girolamo Cardano, creator of a steganographic device and the first autokey system. He said he was immortal. He could not stop talking. You gathered your courage and threw a glass of water in his face. He reacted. He apologized. But it was too late; two days later the same thing happened, only this time in the Vigenère Room, in front of a group of cryptanalysts. After several minutes of a disjointed lecture, they realized that something strange was happening to him. Somebody approached Albert to ask him to take a seat, to calm down, but Albert reacted with fury and tried to hit him. He threw folders and pens to the floor, tried to kick anyone who was in his way. Three cryptanalysts wrestled Albert to the ground and held him down until an ambulance came. They took him away in a straitjacket. He lost consciousness, and when he awoke, he was no longer the same. His eyes were vacant and he could not talk, except, every now and then, wandering phrases that you tried to understand. Ever since then he has been secluded in the second floor of this house on Avenida de las Acacias.

You cross your hands and begin to speak. You tell him that you miss his presence, symbol of security and confidence for everyone at the Black Chamber. And you tell him about the latest happenings. About Kandinsky and the Resistance. About Ramírez-Graham and his disrespectful changes to the rules instituted by Albert. About the inexplicable codes you are receiving. Insulting, unjust phrases. All those years of service to the country don't deserve such a reward. You ask him to help you. If he were by your side, you would feel stronger and could easily dismiss any insults.

From the street you can hear the sounds of the few cars still in circulation. Through the window you can see the mountains on the horizon, which always surprises you. You wait. There is no response. For a moment you wonder if Albert has ceased to exist. Then you see a slight movement under the blankets, the exhausted stirring of breath in his body.

"Kaufbeuren," Albert says out of nowhere, startling you.

"Kauf . . . ?"

"Kaufbeuren. Rosenheim."

"Ros . . . Ros . . . ?"

"Kaufbeuren. Rosenheim. Huettenhain."

He is quiet. You memorize his words, or what you understood of them. Kaufburen. Rosenheim. Wettenhein. You would like to stay a little longer; perhaps Albert will say something else. But you can't; you have to get back to work. You will leave wondering what those words mean.

At least, in the silence, you will remember which images on the walls are missing. And you will discover that deep down there had been a motive for your visit today, something your unconscious knew before you did: you wanted to confirm or deny what Baez and Santana had said.

One of the black-and-white photos on the wall is of a group of men. You have never paid much attention to it; the faces are somewhat blurry. There are nine men in two rows, five wearing army uniforms and the other four in shirts and ties. One of them, on the far left, is Albert. The person next to him, you suspect, you sense, is Klaus Barbie.

chapter 24

FLAVIA STEPS into Portal to Reality. The first floor is glowing with red and yellow lights; trance music by Paul Oakenfold is blaring from the speakers. School and college students face the monitors of Gateway computers that are lined up in three rows. On the walls are posters of *The Matrix,* Penélope Cruz in a scene from *Abre los ojos* and another from *Vanilla Sky,* and various covers of *Wired.* An ad in orange letters proclaims *Now we rent cell phones!* At the counter, Flavia asks for a computer in one of the private cubicles on the second floor, if possible. A redhead with a safety pin in her lip informs her that they cost double what the computers on the first floor cost and hands her a number without taking her eyes off her monitor. She is playing Lineage. The first time Flavia came to this café, the girl who waited on her made her nervous; she had a metallic arm and used it as if it were nothing. It was the strangest thing. She was born that way, she had said, that arm was normal to her, and what seemed strange was to have two arms like Flavia. Flavia wound up staring at her own arms as if they were some rare beast for a whole week, touching them, even biting them.

The atmosphere seems pretentious to her, out of place in Bohemia. But she has to admit that Bohemia isn't like it used to be, and what once would have been out of place here is now part of the norm. The neighborhood has become popular as a result of the cafés that surround a plaza with a statue of Bob Dylan in the middle. University students and backpackers were the first customers in those places with an alternative air to them, where the Aymara worldview, new Mexican cinema, and Björk's music were all topics of conversation. Then the clubs with their techno music had come on the scene, and Daddy's little girls in the latest fashions—high-heeled platform boots, plastic miniskirts, and tops that were more like lingerie—and the rich kids who frequented Playground, armed with their cell phones imported from Japan. Gaining notoriety was the easiest way to lose originality.

She walks up the stairs. From what she could make out on the paper that Ridley gave Erin, Rafael should be in one of the cubicles on the second floor. But she can't picture him in a place like this. He is like her, someone who prefers the empty Internet cafés in the Enclave. If her suspicions are right, Rafael has something to do with the Resistance, and a place like Portal to Reality would be anathema to hackers who are part of that group.

The atmosphere on the second floor is completely different from that on the first. There are no glowing lights, no posters. Twelve cubicles, most of them empty. Flavia's steps waver. She surreptitiously looks inside cubicles where the door is ajar. Nothing here, nothing there. She will go down to the last cubicle, just get it out of her system, and then go home.

Behind her, she hears someone whisper her name. She stops and turns around; a door to a cubicle has just opened. She approaches; a few dreadlocks fall over her forehead. Sitting on a black leather chair is Rafael, who with an imperious gesture motions her to hurry. Flavia enters the cubicle and Rafael closes the door. There are black circles under his eyes, and his pupils dart anxiously from side to side. Flavia notes that this Rafael is very different from the calm, self-confident one she met a few days ago on the bus.

"Smarter than I thought," Rafael says. "You found me. At times I didn't think you would, that the message from Ridley to Erin was too cryptic, that you wouldn't realize it was really a message for you, et cetera."

"If you know as much about me as you think you do, then

you should have a little more faith in me," Flavia replies, now sure that one of the things she finds most attractive about Rafael is his sonorous, masculine voice. She could never fall in love with him just in Playground, but maybe soon you won't have to type to communicate there, you'll be able to chat out loud, like talking on your cell phone. So many technological breakthroughs, and yet we write more and more; it's a bit old-fashioned if you think about it.

"There's no time to waste. If you got here, that means they could read the message and find us too."

"Who are they?"

"The Resistance."

"You could've arranged to meet in a less obvious place."

"I picked a place like this precisely because it is obvious."

"What does the Resistance have against you? And what does the Resistance have to do with the Restoration?"

Rafael takes a deep breath. The chair squeaks.

"The Resistance and the Restoration are the same thing. The Restoration was a virtual group that came together to stage resistance in Playground. The people who controlled the avatars were hackers, who then formed the Resistance, to make the leap from virtual space to reality."

Flavia furrows her brow, trying to understand. Steps can be heard outside the cubicle. Rafael puts his right index finger up to his lips. The steps fade away.

"Man, you're paranoid," Flavia says.

"I know them well—I was one of them. For me, it all started out as a game. Maybe it never stopped being one, and that's my problem. It's just the way I am. It's hard for me to take things seriously. Even if it's a matter of life and death. That's why I spent hours and hours in Playground. Because in a sense, everything on screen becomes a game. And because I could get information there. You know I'm a Rat, right, or if you didn't, you suspected. A good Rat, the honest kind."

"You're not a hacker?"

"A means to an end. I do it to get information, as a last resort."

Rafael looks at her as if he has neither the time nor the patience to explain everything in detail. Flavia wonders what she can do to help him. She also realizes that this feeling is new, touching a man's hands and not being overcome by hostility. When she was fifteen she tried dating, went to the movies and parties with a few different boys, but she hadn't been able to go too far. As soon as they touched her, she felt repelled as if by a negative force.

"It all started out as a game," Rafael continues, "until I let myself be charmed by BoVe. And I became part of the Restoration."

"In Playground."

"Exactly. It was sort of a test, to attack the government of Playground, develop a model of resistance that would later be put into practice in the real world. Sure, it wasn't easy to figure out the model—there's no direct correspondence between one world and the other—but at least we tried. I became part of Kandinsky's inner circle in the Resistance. Because, as I'm sure you figured out, BoVe was Kandinsky's avatar in Playground. I was the one who could get things in Playground that would later be sold on the black market to finance our activities. Don't ask me how I did it. Let's just say it's one advantage of being a Rat.

"Our bad reputation is well deserved. One of the things we do is extort from people who work at the company in charge of running Playground, get them to tell us how to obtain valuable objects like extra lives, magic cards."

Rafael stands up and places his hands against the wall behind him. Flavia can sense the exhaustion in his gestures. She is trying to understand, but something about his explanation does not quite fit.

"So that's how it goes," Rafael continues. "The truth is that later, when the Resistance began to operate in the real world, I wanted to meet Kandinsky in person. I couldn't. I realized that not one of the main hackers—the inner circle, if you will—had met him in person. It was a justified tactic to avoid being turned in, and, of course, so that the myth could grow. No one knew the great hacker but everyone had a story about him. So the myth that started in Playground about the avatar named BoVe made its way into the real world about the person known as Kandinsky, who was in charge of the avatar BoVe. Sound complicated? It isn't."

"And what's my role in all this?"

Rafael sits back down. Restless, he bounces his legs. He rubs his chin.

"The media, even the most critical ones, have surrounded Kandinsky with this aura. Here's someone from the third world who has managed to bring big corporations to their knees. He's the most vivid expression of resistance against a government that has savage neoliberal policies. And yes, Kandinsky is all of that. But he is not a god." He pauses, clearing his throat.

"He's just as fallible as the rest of us," he continues, his voice booming even though he's speaking quietly. "He got to the top not only because he's able to manipulate technology or because of his charisma but also because he's ruthless, crushing any dissent in the organization. The Resistance doesn't tolerate internal resistance. The power behind his struggle against the government and corporations is based on a fundamentalist approach that doesn't allow internal debate. Through my avatar, Ridley, I began to suspect something in Playground. It all became clear to me when a couple of members of the Restoration turned up dead and they wanted us to believe the government was responsible. But it was way too much of a coincidence that it was exactly the two people who had opposed BoVe at an earlier meeting."

He is speaking quickly, as if he has only a few minutes to make his case.

"Something similar happened in the real world a little while ago. Two hackers wound up dead."

"Vivas and Padilla."

"Right. Both of them belonged to the Resistance. And, not being ready to accuse Kandinsky, I decided that you were the person to make the accusation public. Your site is about hackers, so I decided to tell you everything I knew. Of course, I had to pretend that I was warning you about the danger you were in if you continued investigating Kandinsky's identity. They were watching, and one wrong step could mean the end of me."

"So then it was you . . ."

"Yep. And I was impressed by your courage, publishing everything. Well, almost everything. You didn't mention that it was Kandinsky . . ."

"I needed more concrete proof. I insinuated that it was. A word to the wise . . ."

"I'm not reproaching you at all. I felt bad, like a coward, because I had put your life in danger. That's why I was following you. I felt responsible for you and wanted to protect you."

Flavia looks at him with astonished eyes. She doesn't know what to say.

"Ridley contacted Erin in Playground," Rafael says, "because he was afraid for her life. I'm doing the same thing with you right now. Maybe they'll get rid of me, but at least you know the story and you'll take care of making it public."

"There's not much I can do if I don't know who Kandinsky is."

"Not even we Rats can help you with that."

Rafael kissed her on the lips. It was a kiss that began sweetly, then turned passionate. Flavia put on a surprised expression; what really surprised her was how long it had taken. She had thought their meeting would be a purely romantic one; she hadn't suspected the complicated plot that would unfold in her presence.

"I'll stay in touch, either here or in Playground," Rafael said. "You leave first. Don't turn around for any reason. As soon as you're on the street, I'll leave the cubicle."

They kissed again. Flavia left the cubicle, walked quickly down the stairs, and went up to the counter. She gave the number back to the redhead, saying that she hadn't used the computer. The girl looked at her strangely and checked her screen to verify that fact.

As Flavia left, she saw two men in dark glasses get out of a dilapidated red Honda Accord. It seemed strange to her that the Honda remained next to the sidewalk in front of the café with the motor running. By the time she realized what was happening, it was too late. She turned back into the café just as shots were being fired. Rafael, who had started down the stairs, fell face down and rolled until his body was stopped by the metal handrail. As the men in dark glasses ran out of the café and disappeared in the car, Flavia, immune to the panic around her—students screaming under tables, clamoring in search of nonexistent emergency exits—ran to where the body lay, the blood soaking his white shirt, his heart beating, beating, no longer beating.

chapter 25

RUTH STOPS IN FRONT of the door to her office, on which there is a photo of Bletchley Park and Mafalda and *The Far Side* comic strips. Her feet hurt; her high heels have become intolerable. She takes them off and leaves them in the hallway next to a garbage can. The soldier looks at her curiously, expectantly. He has buttoned his jacket, making him appear more formal. Ruth feels that she is a little calmer. Her nose has stopped bleeding. Can veins burst like a stream when it floods during the rainy season? And can they then return to their course just as unexpectedly? What geological faults are opening up day after day in her aging body? What will her tired cells reveal in future endoscopies, colposcopies, laparascopies?

She takes out her keys. Whatever might be happening inside her, she will try not to be overcome by panic. She will not be like her mother, who in the face of the inexorable deterioration of her body decided to end her life in the blink of an eye, imposing the horror of the spectacle on Ruth.

She hands a few peso notes to the soldier. He seems dissatisfied, holding the bills up to the light as if to confirm that they are real. In the soldier's suspicious gaze and coppery complexion, in his defiant stance, legs spread apart, body leaning forward, Ruth perceives the social distance that separates them. But what can she do? It's not her fault; she will not fall into that trap. She has fallen into it many times before—when she saw the varicose veins on her maid Rosa's legs and made her go to the doctor, paying for the treatment, or when Rosa told her that she was saving to buy a television and Ruth helped her with a few extra pesos, only to find out later that Rosa had given the money to her ex-husband. She has learned that no well-intentioned action will fix the unfixable. Everything she does simply clears her conscience for a few minutes, an afternoon, at best a whole day.

Ruth hands him another few pesos and goes into her office. The soldier remains outside, watching her out of the corner of his eye through the half-open door, his hand to his cap in a frozen gesture, as if posing for a photograph.

The office smells of jasmine and black tobacco. She lights a cigarette, looks absently at the papers on her desk—lecture notes, others for an article on the role of the NSA in the Falklands War (the NSA had managed to decipher the Argentine army's codes; it contributed 98 percent of the information that the English had at their disposal during the war); the books on the shelves—histories of cryptanalysis by Kahn, Singh, Kippenham; videos of movies relating to cryptanalysis for her class next semester—*U-571, Windtalkers, A Beautiful Mind, Enigma;* the Degas prints on the wall.

She unlocks the bottom right-hand drawer of her desk and takes out the manuscript. She used so many different codes in it. The one she is proudest of is a polyalphabetic substitution code she herself created based on Vigenère, which had not been deciphered for centuries. Even the title and her name on the cover page are in code. People might say hers was a sick obsession. That was normal; it was the only way of relating to the codes. At least she had turned her dedication into an inoffensive curiosity. At least she had had the necessary integrity to realize where her work at the Black Chamber was heading and to resign in time.

"May I make a phone call? To my doctor. You can dial if you like."

"Go ahead. Just hurry."

Ruth dials the number. The secretary tells her that the doctor hasn't come in because of the blockades. Ruth asks for her test results. The secretary replies that the lab is closed, so please call again tomorrow.

She leaves the office pressing the manuscript against her chest. She and the soldier walk through the deserted patio on their way to the main entrance. They can hear shouts and explosions; the soldier, however, walks as if he is in no hurry. Ruth matches his stride. At last, she thinks: She will hand the manuscript over to Cardona, and that will be the end of Miguel. She will go home to pack her bags and tell him that her lawyer will soon be filing for divorce. She will take a taxi to her dad's house in the northern part of the city. Perhaps she will look for an apartment or, better yet, decide to leap into the abyss, resign from her job and move to La Paz. She is worried about Flavia. Will she go with Ruth or stay with Miguel? Perhaps neither of those two options. She is so independent.

"What's in those papers that's so urgent?" the soldier asks without looking at her.

"It's part of some research I'm doing. I'm a historian. I didn't want to be without it in case this goes on for a while. Now at least I can work at home."

"Me, it'll be a long time before I get back home. We're confined to barracks when there's a state of emergency."

"Where do you live?"

"In Tarata. Uh, that's where I'm stationed. But I'm not complaining. They gave me a new rifle. I didn't even have a revolver before."

"What happened to yours?"

"It was stolen a month ago."

"And they didn't give you another one?"

"They have to take it out of my paycheck. They only give me a new one when it's paid off. But that can take months. And thieves don't wait. Luckily, nothing happens in Tarata. Sometimes drunks get into fights — that's about it. And you can earn a bit in tips from the tourists who visit President Melgarejo's house. It's really ugly and small. They used this horrible cement during the restoration. Students who come always feel let down."

Such a normal conversation is out of place amid the shouts and explosions that are increasingly closer, flames and columns of smoke rising up from the McDonald's. Maybe there is nothing normal about that conversation. After all, when would she have another opportunity to converse with a soldier?

"It's not an easy job," he says. "When they send us to remove the blockades, sometimes I see people I know on the other side. They insult me and call me a traitor. Uh, maybe they're right. But unless they can get me another job, a decent one that I like, I'll stick with this. It's all I've got. What am I gonna do? We all do what we like. Or what we can."

They reach the entrance. The other soldiers haven't moved, and five more have come as reinforcements, along with two German shepherds straining at their chains as if trying to break them. Ruth stops, uncertain. She does not know what to do, where to go, what route to take. To the left are the main door and the McDonald's that is on fire; to the right, blockaded streets and a group of demonstrators marching, chanting a chorus of antigovernment slogans. *An end, an end to this globalizing trend* . . . Two police cars with their sirens screeching block the way. She stands looking at one of the German shepherds, his shiny black coat, the saliva dripping from his vicious canines. Perhaps it had been a bad idea to come to the university. Perhaps she should have gone home.

A couple of video messages are waiting on her cell phone. One from Miguel, another from Flavia. She doesn't open them. She is tired of getting messages from Miguel, who, bored in the archives, calls without anything to say, just to waste time. As for Flavia, nothing she does seems urgent. For years now Ruth hasn't cared much about her. Perhaps ever since she found herself competing with Flavia for Miguel's meager time, for his diminishing affection, and soon discovered that she was losing.

A big-bellied sergeant holding a cap in his right hand approaches the soldier that accompanies Ruth. He asks him what the hell this woman is doing standing in the doorway.

"Can't you see that it's dangerous?" he shouts. "Didn't I tell you to evacuate all civilians? I don't want a single soul in the university."

"We did evacuate everyone, sir," the soldier replies, his tone frightened. "This lady came later. She's a professor. She wanted to go to her office to get a manuscript."

"And so what did you do, huh? Don't tell me you went with her."

"It's just that . . . sir."

"It's just that nothing. Did you go with her?"

"She told me it was urgent. She needed to work at home."

"And since when did they hire you as secretary? Or office boy? If it's all right with you, then damn it, why not let everyone line up here to go in and get their papers? And let the world fall to pieces in the meantime. The only reason I don't lock you up right now is because we need people. But you'll hear from me later."

"Yes, sir." The soldier stands at attention.

The sergeant approaches Ruth. In ceremonious tones, he says to her, "Pardon me, ma'am. May I see what you're holding?"

"Nothing that would interest you, officer."

"Sergeant, please. And begging your pardon, I'll decide whether it interests me or not."

Ruth shows him the manuscript without letting go of it. The sergeant looks at the title page.

"And what are these hieroglyphics?"

"It's a book I'm writing. About coded messages in Bolivia's history. I'm a historian."

The sergeant's eyes sparkle, the muscles in his face stretch as he grins: it is as if he has just discovered that his shrewdness has stood him in good stead once again. A book about secret messages can only be a secret message itself.

"Allow me," he says, and before Ruth can reply he has the manuscript in his hands. He opens it at random, reviews a few pages. Line after line of letters that do not form comprehensible words, that do not make up a coherent paragraph, a chapter that makes any sense.

"You'll have to excuse me, ma'am," he says emphatically, "but I'm going to have to hold on to your book. I'm going to have to review it calmly, just to be on the safe side."

"Sergeant, this is an affront!" Ruth shouts, reaching out for her manuscript with one hand. "I haven't got a minute to waste. I need to get to work immediately."

"I understand, I do. But you do see that the situation —"

“I have nothing to do with what’s going on. What, do you think they’re secret messages from the Coalition? A secret plan to get rid of GlobaLux? The addresses for members of the Resistance?”

“Calm down, ma’am. I’m the one who doesn’t have a minute to waste. Don’t make me arrest you. There’s nothing to be afraid of if you’ve nothing to hide.”

The sergeant turns his back on her. Ruth throws herself at and pushes him. He takes two steps forward, loses his balance, but manages not to fall. He turns around and orders his men to arrest her.

Ruth’s nose begins to bleed again. Several explosions can be heard.

chapter 26

I'M TIRED. SO TIRED. And the light still shines in my eyes.

There's nothing I can do . . . But wait . . . I will be reincarnated in a young body. There will be a period of hope. Of energy . . . Of plans that can be brought to fruition. A young body. But never very young. I will be a parasite on another body. That has already been comfortably installed in life . . . And I will help it to explore the multiple possibilities for its talents . . .

It has always been thus. I have no childhood. I never have. Some say it's the best time of life. I don't think so. But I really can't say . . .

Sometimes images of a playful child come to me. I don't know who he is . . . I don't know where he came from. He's running through pastures on the outskirts of a town . . . He's taking apart and putting back together a typewriter that he found in a garbage dump. He's writing on it . . . Words that make no sense. Secret codes.

I'd like to have a childhood. At least once in my life.

Tired body . . . Sore stomach. Neck. Eyes that don't want to close. Phlegm in my throat . . . The inevitable flowing of blood . . .

The machine that counts my heartbeats is still working.

I'd like . . . At some point . . . To die . . . And not wake up. Perhaps it's too much to ask. Perhaps the being that is responsible for me . . . The one that has given me this miracle and this misfortune. Will take pity on me and give me a definitive end. Meanwhile. I will continue to be many men.

I was Charles Babbage. Professor at Cambridge. Known for many things . . . The most important of which was to announce. Circa 1820. The principles that would serve as the basis for computers . . . I was obsessed with the idea of using machines to do mathematical calculations . . . I dreamed about building an analytical engine and a differential engine . . . I even resigned from my professorship at Cambridge for seven years. I died at the age of seventy-eight without having realized my plans. However. My ideas remained. Other men after me . . . Made it possible for the logical structure of my analytical engine . . . To serve as the basis for computers.

I was drawn to cryptology because of my interest in statistics . . . I liked to count the frequency with which a letter was repeated in a text. That was the reason . . . That I was one of the first to use mathematical formulas to solve problems of cryptanalysis. I was one of the first to use algebra . . . It surprises me that there weren't many others before me.

One small step. At the time . . . That would later have enormous consequences.

Like everything of mine.

Unfortunately. I didn't continue my research. The notes I'd been taking were left incomplete . . . I became involved in other things. I became distracted . . . What could I do? That's how I was.

The rain beats against my window. On the roof. It mists my view of the mountains of Río Fugitivo. Their outlines blur. A diffuse, somber light takes hold of the day.

I've always liked the rain. Saying *always* is no hyperbole here. My personality is more akin to twilight than to bright, sunny days. So radiant. The sunlight in this city. I had to create my own semidarkness. And hide myself away in it.

There's noise outside my room. I have a visitor. Is it Turing . . . Or is it someone else . . .

I don't want to see anyone. I don't want anything. I'm just waiting. For an end to this cruel cosmic joke . . . That keeps me here. On the periphery of the periphery. While elsewhere battles are being fought . . . The heart of an empire is being attacked and defended using secret messages . . . People will say it's my fault . . . That I chose to stay in this place. It's true. At that time. What I was doing seemed important . . . My presence was needed here. It's true. It was my fault.

Electric ant . . .

But I wasn't the one to decide all of my steps. I write my destiny. While someone writes me.

I was José Martí. I was José Martí. Martí José was I. José was I Martí. Was. Martí. I. José. I dreamed of a free Cuba . . . And dedicated all of my efforts to the struggle for freedom. I lived in New York for many years. Meeting with patriots who thought like me. And who wanted our island to be free from the Spanish yoke . . .

In 1894. I planned an uprising. Together with José María Rodríguez. And Enrique Collazo . . . We coordinated it with the movement of Fernandina . . . To avoid dangerous indiscretions. That could shatter our plan. We decided to encrypt it. I used a polyalphabetic substitution code . . . When I contacted Juan Alberto Gómez. One of our main contacts . . . I used four alphabets. The code word was HABANA. Six letters. But one letter repeated three times . . . Resulting in four different letters. It wasn't necessary to note anything down. You just had to memorize the rhythm . . . Which was 9-2-3-2-16-2. This meant that . . . When it was alphabet 9. *A* corresponded to 9. *B* to 10. *C* to 11. And so on . . . When it was alphabet 2. *A* corresponded to 2. *B* to 3. And so on . . . In order to decipher. The rhythm was placed below the code. Let's say that we wrote

9-6-30-6-28-2-14-8-32-15-13-29

And underneath it the rhythm:

3-2-16-2-9-2-3-2-16-2-9-2

That meant that first you had to see which letter corresponds to the number 9 in alphabet 3 . . . The *g* . . . And then what corresponds to 6 in alphabet 2 . . . The *e* . . . The resulting phrase: GENERALGOMEZ. Not difficult . . . Once you have the key. In my letters to Enrique Collazo. I also used four alphabets . . . But the code word was MARIA.

Medieval towers. Ruins of fortifications.

A special envoy was to take the letter to General Gómez . . . In the plan for the uprising . . . We wrote that a cable would be sent "that will indicate you are able and free to work on the island" . . . Then there would be a final cable indicating "that outside what needs to be done is done" . . . And which would say "hold off lifting personal security until ten days after receipt of the cable" . . . The instructions indicated that they were to "assure the benevolence or indecision of the Spaniards rooted on the island" . . . That they were not to take any "purely nationalistic or terrorist measures" . . . But they were to "use the full force of weapons against any Spaniard who is armed" . . .

The plan failed. Because one of our own. Committed treason against us . . . And warned of the shipment of arms that we planned to send to Cuba. From the United States. The shipment was seized. So you can see that to win a revolution. It isn't enough to encrypt a message. People like to talk more than they should . . . They don't want. To become. A Universal. Turing. Machine.

Which is a pity.

I'm tired. There's noise outside my room. A lot of noise.

Only the rain will make me at all happy this afternoon. Which is on its way to piling up. With so many. Other. Afternoons.

Kaufbeuren. Rosenheim. Huettenhain.

chapter 27

RAMÍREZ-GRAHAM HAS JUST received a message from Baez: Sáenz's daughter is willing to cooperate. A squad car has gone to pick her up and bring her to the Black Chamber immediately. Ramírez-Graham turns off his cell phone and sets it down on a pile of files on the desk in his office. He stares at the slow, unpredictable movement of the angelfish in the crystal-clear water of the aquarium. The way they elude the galleon sunk in the depths. The treasure spilling out of the chest. The floating diver on a rescue mission.

He is still not entirely convinced of the merits of the idea, but it is to his advantage not to reject any option. *Thinking outside the box... Thinking outside the box...* He would rather catch Kandinsky using conventional methods, keep the confrontation as a clash of intellects in which one encrypts codes or takes advantage of a system's weaknesses in order to penetrate it, and the other deciphers the codes or finds the fingerprints left by the criminal when he hacked into the system. But his fear of possible failure is stronger. He has not been trained for it, has never experienced it, does not know how to cope with it.

He pours himself a cup of coffee and leans back in his swivel chair, facing the luminous windows that, together with his paintings, add color to this building of bare walls and oppressive ceilings. The liquid burns his tongue. He is drinking it not because he likes the taste but to calm his nerves. How many cups today? Four, despite the fact that he has enough trouble sleeping as it is. His nausea has come back; perhaps an ulcer is developing.

The pile of files belongs to Operation Turing. He would have liked to have finished reading them but has not been able to get very far since he arrived at his office; the struggle against the Resistance demanded his urgent attention. Still, he has already reviewed most of the files and does not think he will find the incriminating document that will solve the mystery, the phrases that will point in an unmistakable direction. Instead, he thinks he already has the most important information and now all that is missing is some intellectual effort in order to get to the bottom of the matter. Or perhaps a stroke of luck, devastating intuition, will be enough.

He has learned a great deal and continues to feel sorry for Turing's bad fortune, his destiny.

He should have stayed with Svetlana. He left when she needed him most. She will never forgive him. But it was too much for him. Those days, the only thing he wanted was to escape that mournful place, where hearing the shouts of children playing in a nearby yard or seeing a baby in a supermarket caused a pain that seemed to lacerate his skin. Their future child had been fifteen weeks old when he perished in Svetlana's belly. How stupid he had been, the way he had refused to accept fatherhood and with his words provoked a series of events that concluded in the accident.

He feels like calling Svetlana and asking her to forgive his behavior. He picks up the telephone and dials the number he knows by heart.

Svetlana's voice sounds rigid and yet vulnerable on the answering machine. He is about to leave her a message, but in the end does not. What for? Instead he will surprise her one morning at the entrance to her building. He will beg her forgiveness and ask for a second chance. She is very proud and he is unsure of his success. But it doesn't matter. Her answer is secondary. What he needs to do is to make amends for his mistakes and behave decently, even if it is too late.

Yeah, right. Of course I care about the answer.

He closes his eyes. When there is a knock at the door, he has no idea how much time has passed. He looks at his watch: 10 A.M. It is Baez, standing next to a teenager with messy brown hair and a far-off gaze. *A Rasta wannabe, I know the type.* He has seen many like her at the cafés in Georgetown. She doesn't look at all like her father, he decides. He stands up, asks them in, offers them a seat.

"Thank you so much for responding so quickly," he says, taking a sip of his cold coffee. "We need more people like you. Otherwise, as I'm sure you've seen these past few days, there is chaos."

"I didn't come here out of some abstract sense of patriotism," she replies, crossing and uncrossing her hands. "And don't treat me like a child, with that paternalistic tone. I think the Coalition is a bunch of idiots who only know how to say no to everything and have no alternatives to offer. But I wouldn't lose sleep at night if one of these mornings Montenegro was found hanging from a streetlamp."

Well, well, well: this girl is opinionated. She's not like her father in that respect either.

"Then why did you come, if I may ask?"

"Because Kandinsky is responsible for killing Rafael, a hacker I truly respected. As well as for killing two other hackers this month."

"We didn't know that," Baez interjects. "Rafael who?"

"I don't know. He was killed outside an Internet café in Bohemia. I was with him minutes before. I'm surprised you didn't already know."

"Baez," says Ramírez-Graham, "please find out what information we have in that regard. We must know something."

"And the other two hackers . . . ," Baez says, staring straight at her. "Vivas and Padilla. I read what you posted on your site. From what we've found out, they were just two petty hackers. There's nothing that links them to the Resistance. Even less so their deaths."

"There won't be anything to link them," Flavia retorts. "You'd have to sift through mountains of deleted chat conversations on IRC channels, find their pseudonyms, stuff like that. Just trust me."

Baez looks at her with a mocking expression on his face.

Ramírez-Graham wishes that Baez were a little more professional. He sometimes intimidates those who could help them. And yet Ramírez-Graham recognizes that he has not been the ideal role model for Baez. Maybe instead of coming to the Black Chamber he should have stayed working in the solitude of an office, confronting elusive algorithms and taking his fury out on them (pencils that snapped, notebooks and calculators that flew through the air, computer monitors that received repeated blows).

"People like Kandinsky ruin the reputation of hackers," Flavia continues. "There will be more deaths if we don't stop him. He's a megalomaniac who deserves to go to jail."

"I'm surprised," says Ramírez-Graham. "You're the first person to speak poorly of him."

"Besides," Baez interjects, "the reasons for his struggle are all wrong."

"The reasons are good," Flavia contradicts him. "It's his methods that are wrong. Kandinsky doesn't allow different opinions or any hesitations. He takes them as a personal affront. That's not part of a hacker's ethics."

"Excuse me, but those who operate outside the law have no ethics."

"Hackers are in favor of the free flow of information. They hack into systems in order to open up what never should have been closed and then share the information with everyone. A building like this, by its very nature, is their enemy. And people like you are the opposite of what they represent. You'll never understand them."

The expression on Baez's face becomes uncertain — his lips turn downward, the muscles on his cheeks tense — as if he is ridiculing Flavia's reply but at the same time admiring her courage for voicing an indiscreet opinion.

"What do you need to do your work?" Ramírez-Graham asks. "We can put our best computers at your disposal. The office of your choice. I don't know what you were paid before, but I can assure you it will be better now."

"Just pay me. I'd rather work at home. What I need are all the files you have on Kandinsky."

“We’ll give you everything we have on the Resistance,” says Baez. “But I assume that you already have information on the subject.”

“Even more information,” adds Ramírez-Graham. “So you’re sure that Kandinsky was behind those killings? Young lady, you seem to know more than we do.”

“I wouldn’t be surprised,” she says, her tone biting.

In that quick, confident reply, Ramírez-Graham thinks he can see a bit of Svetlana in Flavia.

chapter 28

In the pouring rain, Judge Cardona passes through the open gate that leads to Albert's house. He crosses the yard and goes up the stairs, reaching out to touch the creeper on the wall; dried leaves fall onto the steps. The door to the second floor is locked. He knocks loudly. He presses his handkerchief against his right eye; it is still bleeding but not as heavily as before. His vision has become blurred, and the pain tells him that the cut is serious. He will do what he needs to do and then there will be time for everything else, even a trip to the hospital. The rain sets off the cowlicks in his hair and runs down his cheeks.

The guard opens the door; his face is elongated, and the white of his eyebrows and the pale pink of his skin make Cardona think that he is an albino. He had an albino classmate when he was in school; he and his friends would make fun of the boy until he cried. They said he was the color of pink toilet paper. They told him that God had taken him out of the oven too soon. If Cardona had known that one day his skin would be covered in spots and that kids would stare at him in the street, he never would have teased that boy. You provoke early on, but the mortifying revenge doesn't come until later. The passing of time most certainly stores up an occasion or two when we'll be spat on in the face.

The guard lets Cardona pass, watching warily how the soles of his shoes leave wet marks on the floor. He seems about to ask Cardona to take his shoes off, but says nothing and goes back to his seat behind a table that rocks on one uneven leg. Cardona looks at the cracked walls, on which hang last year's calendar and cheap watercolors of the landscape around Río Fugitivo — the bridges and the river and the ocher-colored mountains. Cardona never would've imagined Albert choosing those paintings. Someone probably decorated it all for him — maybe the owner, the one who rented him the apartment. Albert had arrived here unconscious, in a straitjacket, his brain beaten to a pulp after all those years of working with codes, the neurons confused, the power of the synapses weakened by the sheer number of encrypted, dangerous messages.

"Ay-ay-ay, you're cut," the guard says. "You better get that looked at. You might need a few stitches."

There is a notebook and a small black-and-white television on the table. Cardona, briefcase in hand, looks at the screen with its live images of the confrontations between police and demonstrators in the plaza. It is a strange, phantasmagoric sensation to be watching a scene he had been part of a few minutes earlier. He wonders whether he might appear on the screen at any moment, his briefcase in hand, being escorted by the police as he tries to leave the plaza.

"Is he expecting you?"

Cardona shakes his head in reply. What an absurd question — like a butler keeping up appearances when an invitation to a party arrives while his master lies dying in the other room, the butler parsimoniously replying that his master will be unable to attend. Or perhaps the question is to see whether Cardona has permission to visit Albert. The guard's eyes are sleepy. His boots have been shined, and his olive-green uniform looks freshly ironed. He is wearing a green cap. From time to time he looks down, making sure that Cardona doesn't notice, as if to find out whether his recently polished floor has been stained with blood, whether the water running down Cardona's body has left a puddle. He's probably from the countryside, Cardona muses. No doubt the villagers had looked at him as if he were some sort of strange beast, thought that the birth of an albino was punishment from God on the whole town. They would have asked the priest to perform an exorcism or sacrificed a llama to calm the evil spirits.

The guard asks to see Cardona's ID card. He hands it over with a wet hand. "A cut and caught in the rain," the guard says.

"Uh-huh. Seems like nothing's going right this afternoon. I should have stayed in my hotel room."

"Would you like to hang up your coat?"

"No, that's all right. I won't be long."

"If you're lucky, the rain will be over soon."

The weather: obligatory topic of trivial conversations between strangers in elevators and taxis. Meteorological changes save us from our panic at empty spaces, required moments of silence. The untimely fury of our words, desperate to fill the void. The guard notes down Cardona's name and asks him to sign.

"I'll hold on to your identification."

"No problem."

Everything is much easier when the objective is clear. Cardona is not interested in hiding his name. It will all come to light, sooner rather than later. They will be surprised by his cold-heartedness; they will speak of a man who went insane when he was fired from the ministry. Or had he resigned? A bit of both: he was forced to resign. He did everything they asked him to, enthusiastically at first, then reluctantly. They had come to realize his lack of goodwill. Well, it wasn't exactly that. Everybody has a right to doubt, and that he did. The problem was, he wanted to swim in the river and stay dry. He felt remorse at losing his most cherished convictions, but at the same time he loved wandering the halls of the Presidential Palace, feeling that so many people depended on his decisions. The gall they had — they made him realize his worth and then they turned around and closed the palace doors on him. He regrets not having given a farewell speech before resigning. In front of the photographers' cameras, he could have pointed his finger in a magnificent, dramatic display at the regime's corruption, from the president on down. Montenegro was no longer a dictator, but he was still corrupt. There were no more deaths under his administration, but it was still a dirty regime. He was privatizing the country, or rather capitalizing it, to use the euphemism of the day, though not even to the highest bidder, for the good of the country, but to the one most willing to be bribed, the one best at bribing.

Farewell speech? He was very good at speaking the truth in front of mirrors, but he wasn't able to talk when he had to. Around Montenegro, he always behaved as if he had no tongue. He had lost his chance. Even now, he has to accept that he is afraid of confronting Montenegro. He needs to take his revenge on other people. Should he have continued to see the shrink? He distrusted her; she was making quick money off him, diagnosing platitudes. She wouldn't tell him anything about himself that he didn't already know.

Montenegro hadn't given him the opportunity for a glorious finale. Cardona had left the government through the back door, one afternoon when pinkish clouds lay on the horizon outside his window, when three soldiers from the military police had come to his office and asked him to accompany them. He feared the worst. They drove him home in a Jeep, left him at his door, and told him not to go back to the ministry. They took his office keys and asked him, with a courtesy that hid the violent repercussions if he did not comply, to refrain from making statements to the press. Was that any way to treat him?

His cold-heartedness, however, comes from having nothing to lose, nothing to live for, once the necessary acts he has been preparing for have been carried out. And in the face of being able to plan something in minute detail, to perfection, his biggest surprise derives from the lack of surprise. He will do this without hiding his identity, in the light of day, blessed by the luck of having the military and police forces distracted by the unrest all over the city. In any event, he would have done this even if there had been no commotion at all. He heads down the hallway to Albert's room.

"Just a minute," the guard says. "You can't go in with that briefcase."

Cardona knew it couldn't be that easy. What would Turing's wife say when she found out? Poor naive thing had gone to get the documents that corroborated her story, the proof of the crimes that Turing and Albert had committed. Her words had been enough to condemn the two men. Cardona sets his briefcase on the table. The rain falling on the roof becomes heavier.

"Can I take a gift I brought for him?"

The guard nods his permission while looking distractedly at the television screen. The manager of GlobaLux, a man from La Paz who pronounces his *r*'s and *s*'s as if his life depends on them, is making a statement before the cameras. The local face of a global project, Cardona muses. Very smart. The manager has a thin mustache and continues to speak, threatening lawsuits, millions in compensation. Cardona stops listening and suddenly remembers the title of a movie: *Albino Alligator.* He takes out a silver revolver with a silencer, which he purchased from one of his bodyguards when he was minister, and in one quick movement extends his arm and shoots the guard twice. The guard's hat falls off and there is surprise in his sleepy eyes; his body collapses heavily. The olive-green uniform is stained a dark red.

It is the first time Cardona has ever done anything like this. He was a timid child who did whatever it took to distance himself from violence. As a boy, he was sickened by the sight of dogs or cats that had been hit by cars, their entrails hanging out, dead or on the verge of death. And he hated going to his grandparents' country estate, because his cousins would laugh at him if he didn't go out to hunt sparrows and hummingbirds with pellet guns. They called him Mary Magdalene, and he would look up at Mirtha out of the corner of his eye, hoping in vain that at least she would stop the attack. He can still remember those humiliating lunches when his cousins and his sister would sing *Mary Magdalene, that's you, Mary Magdalene, that's you,* until he would get up, run to his grandparents' room, and slam the door.

At times he thought that with a personality like his, he had been born in the wrong country. That's why he had hidden behind his legal studies; they were the desperate anchor, the rationality of law that would counteract the chaotic violence of the world. All in vain. In the country that held the world record for number of coup d'états, the law was a puppet that was burned at the stake with shocking frequency.

He looks at the guard slumped on the floor. He has fallen on his side, the bullets having gone in through his chest and abdomen. Cardona would have liked to have known his name. Just as some remembered him as the "spotted man," he would remember the guard as the "albino." He feels compassion for the guard's unjust death, for the family that will mourn him. It is they, the innocent ones, who always pay the price. Even when it's a matter of avenging an innocent death. He had wanted to defend them from his position as magistrate. At least he had in the beginning, before he discovered how sordid the system was, how corrupt the scales of justice were. He had been so naive, so idealistic. What would his cousins say if they saw him now? What would Mirtha say? From the looks of it, people are capable of doing things that life has not destined them for, at least not on its polished surface.

He walks into Albert's room. It is austere, with carnations on a table and photos on the walls, photos that tell the tale of victory. Albert, who had arrived in Bolivia as one more CIA agent sent to advise the dictatorship on intelligence operations and had quickly become indispensable to Montenegro. Albert, who did not want to go back to the United States, resigned from the CIA — or was he really a Nazi fugitive? — and achieved the miracle of organizing an efficient institution in this country, in charge of internal security, of monitoring the opposition, listening to their conversations, intercepting their secret messages, and decoding them. An institution so efficient that Mirtha and her comrades had not been able to elude it. Turing had deciphered the message that indicated where her group would hold a clandestine meeting and had given it to Albert, who had passed it on to the DOP so that they could take things from there.

The rain slides down the windows. Judge Cardona shivers. His clothes are wet. Albert is lying between the sheets in bed, surrounded by the smell of eucalyptus, old age, and decaying flesh. His body, or what remains of it, is connected to wires leading from a machine on one side of his bed. His heartbeats pulse in the graphics on the screen; perhaps they are artificially sustained by it. Cardona approaches the edge of the bed. Albert's eyes are open, the only sign of life in that skeleton covered by skin that has lost all elasticity. Even if he does nothing, this man is not long for this world. Cardona is the judge in charge of delivering the final verdict. The red-hot stabs of pain in his eyebrow do not let up. He had better hurry. He aims at Albert's chest, and the man continues to stare with wide-open eyes at a place that may not even be in this room. "Kaufbeuren," he says, out of nowhere. He's delirious, Cardona tells himself. "For my cousin," he announces out loud, solemnly, emphatically, in the booming voice that had left him long ago. "Mirtha. She could have given so much to this country. She could have done so much for this country. And for me. For me." He fires once, twice, three times.

chapter 29

ON YOUR WAY BACK to the Black Chamber, you find that the police have been able to clear some of the streets. Chewing a spearmint Chiclet, at several intersections you can see tires and wood burning in flickering flames, a landscape of confrontations that has been familiar since childhood, in a country where your fellow citizens will not accept the dictates from on high. At times the years pass by languidly, lazily, with no sign of movement on the earth's crust, but that peace is nothing more than a pause between shakeups, and it is simply a matter of waiting patiently for a new tremor to come. The epicenter varies: the mines, state universities, the tropics of Cochabamba, the highlands of La Paz, the cities. The motives vary: protests against a coup d'état, the minimum wage, hikes in the cost of gasoline and basic necessities, military repression, plans to eradicate coca crops, dependence on the United States, the recession, globalization. What remains invariable is a nerve center of discord. You know this because as hard as you try, it is impossible to isolate yourself completely, dedicate yourself to your work, and forget about the situation. Not completely, not here in this place. But you have to try. Being impervious to what surrounds you is the only way to survive, not to be dragged along by the gale of the present.

Lana Nova is reporting the latest news on your cell phone. The protesters had tried to take the mayor's and the prefect's offices, with a death toll of seven. Ah, Lana, how do you keep your facial muscles so calm in the face of such stabbing reality? Your creators endowed you with a few gestures, you are capable of insinuating emotions, but you still have a long way to go before you can fool us. If you were a replica trying to pass as one of us, we would have caught on to you long ago.

The city's prefect, a private businessman who missed the tranquility of his car dealership, had accepted responsibility for the protesters' deaths and had resigned with a speech that was almost prophetic: *There will be no GlobaLux, but neither will there be an adequate provision of electricity over the next fifty years. Our children and our children's children will continue to live with blackouts. A Pyrrhic victory, the kind we are used to.* A large group of demonstrators had laid siege to the GlobaLux offices and threatened to set them on fire; the manager in charge of the consortium shrieked that if order were not restored soon, his bosses would break their contract and demand millions in compensation from the government. The Resistance had claimed responsibility for spreading a new virus that was quickly propagating in government computers, destroying files along its way. The chairman of the Civic Committee and members of the church were trying to negotiate with the Coalition. The government had announced the deployment of troops, the militarization of Río Fugitivo, and an urgent meeting of ministers at the negotiating table. The news continued: protests and blockades in Chapare and disturbances in the Aymara communities around Lake Titicaca . . .

You turn off your cell phone: too much information for your own good. You are going to have to block it out, stop it from capturing your unconscious, taking over your imagination. Otherwise you will soon be having nightmares of soldiers firing on civilians and white hands that are not so white, hands that are stained with blood.

There are more police officers at the entrance to the Black Chamber than usual. They submit you to questioning, as if it were your first day on the job. They study your ID card, compare your scanned fingerprint with the one on your identification. It's not their fault; the order must have come from Ramírez-Graham, so exaggerated. As if this building were being targeted by protesters. As if the Black Chamber did not derive its power from its anonymity, on the edge of the Enclave, near the telecommunications building and the Museum of Anthropology. A familiar site, an amorphous neighborhood friend. Albert was a genius. If the Black Chamber had been established in La Paz, as Montenegro had wanted, it would have been the target of everyone's hatred. In Río Fugitivo, the Black Chamber goes unnoticed and calmly weaves its web of intrigue.

You throw your gum into the garbage can, put another piece into your mouth.

One of the police officers has a metal pin in his lapel with a red-and-white shield on it. What does it mean? This is the question you always ask yourself, the inevitable search for the lair in which meaning is hidden. Because you assume that nothing you rest your eyes on is what it seems to be; everything is a symbol, a metaphor, or a code for something else. The nervous way the police officer gesticulates, his arms outstretched, moving his fingers as if he were using an incomprehensible language to speak to the deaf; the way his leather belt has skipped one of the loops on his pants . . . All answers must lead to a single one. If the program that runs the universe were mathematical, there would be a primary algorithm from which the rest would be derived. If the program were computational, there would be three or four lines of code that could explain both the tides and the leopard's spots and the wide variety of languages and the movements of your right hand and the way houseflies fly and the birth of the galaxies and Leonardo da Vinci and Borges and Flavia's damp hair and the shadow thrown by willow trees and Alan Turing. At times you are tired of the incessant artillery of your brain, incapable of rest even in sleep, and you ponder the question and ask yourself, *What is the meaning of wondering about meaning?*

Perhaps you are condemned to be an enigma to yourself. And perhaps it is worth applying that lesson to your attempts to trap meaning in the maelstrom of codes that surround and overwhelm you. Perhaps everything, deep down, is nothing more than an enigma.

The police apologize for the delay and let you pass. The hallways are bustling. Santana informs you that they have checked all the computers in the Black Chamber; some of them have been attacked by the new virus, others were spared. Like last time, there does not seem to be a clear motive to indicate why the virus chose some computers over others. The ones in the archives are working perfectly. He asks you to be careful when opening your e-mail and to notify him immediately if anything unusual happens. You would like to tell him that something unusual has been happening for days now: someone has penetrated your secret account and is sending you threatening messages. You say nothing.

You feel the need to urinate. Urgent jabs of pain in your bladder, incontinence reflected in your furrowed brow. You take off your glasses, clean the lenses with a dirty handkerchief.

Kaufburen. Rosenheim. Wettenhein. They must have something to do with cryptology. Perhaps they are lesser cryptanalysts that you haven't heard of before? More of Albert's delirious reincarnations? Pathetic and comical, believing yourself to be immortal.

Ruth is the historian; she could give you the answer in seconds. You'll ask her.

As you ride down in the elevator, you realize that you could open the door and Napoleon could be there on his horse, something unexpected and fantastical that will distance you from reality. O ye of little faith, perhaps it's time to go back to church. You haven't been for a long time — not since you were a teenager, when you used to go with your parents. And perhaps what you've been feeling lately is reminders of your mortality. Perhaps the secret writing you're searching for is the writing of God.

A video message from Carla is on your phone. She has removed her makeup from the night before, and her skin looks old. Her resemblance to your daughter always surprises you. A Flavia of another color and a different hairstyle, a Flavia whom life is aging rapidly. She asks you to meet her today, she'll be waiting for you at six. It's urgent, she says, she needs your help. She has no one else to turn to. Her parents have turned their backs on her again.

You don't want to be moved, to fall into that trap, but you find yourself thinking that Flavia could have been Carla if she hadn't had your counsel and protection. No one is immune to anything.

Then you turn the logic around: Carla is one possible version of Flavia. Your paternal instincts won't allow you to abandon her. You will go see her. You turn off the video message.

You walk down the aisles of the archives to do something that has been on your mind since you left Albert's house. Various boxes of classified material in the archives contain the history of the origins of the Black Chamber. You do not have permission to read those papers, but who's going to know?

Perhaps there you will find the trail that will lead you to Albert's real identity.

chapter 30

KANDINSKY WILL NEVER really know how the Restoration survived those first few months when Playground's police forces were suppressing it. He cannot even argue that they had underestimated his group, because in fact the government did everything it could to annihilate them. Lying on the parquet floor of his apartment, listening to electronic music through his earphones, sometimes he thought that their technical prowess was what had fooled the government's machinery, as functional as it was uncreative. At other times he suspected that their guerrilla warfare tactics had achieved the flexibility of movement that renders a large army impotent. He has even wondered whether the government of Playground intentionally allowed the Restoration to survive as generous proof that it was not as totalitarian as its critics might suggest. In this way of thinking, the Restoration unwittingly becomes the government's accomplice, since by fighting the government it allows the government to entrench itself even deeper in power.

He has had various theories, none of which are entirely convincing. In the end, he has wound up believing that what happened was one of those coincidences in which history specializes. Any number of things could have failed at any point, and yet they did not. Once the group had managed to survive the difficult battle of those first few months, everything became easier. His legend was being disseminated across Playground and attracted individuals who felt marginalized by the system, people with a great talent for manipulating Playground's technical rules and anxious to attack, at least symbolically, the structures of power that sustained it in the real world.

His fingers drum on the parquet floor to the beat of a song by Air, a French group he has been listening to lately. The bones in his hand ache. Maybe he has carpal tunnel syndrome? He has read about the symptoms on the Internet: fingers, hands, and wrists falling asleep, tingling, and aching — all symptoms he has. It should be easy to fix the problem, but he doesn't want to go for a checkup. He doesn't think there are specialists in Río for a syndrome that is caused by overuse of a keyboard. Or perhaps it is the panic that he associates with clinics and hospitals: he is afraid of losing control, has dreamed that they anesthetize him and he never wakes up. Or it might be just one more step in his progressive abandonment of all physical contact with other human beings.

He sometimes has panic attacks: he will become paralyzed, unable to type a single letter for the rest of his life. And all before he even turns twenty-one.

He sighs, his face lit up in the night by the blue light of the computer monitor. Violent winds pound the windows. He is wearing an alpaca sweater but still feels cold. He has come a very long way in a short time. Now he has to turn down volunteers who want to form part of the Restoration. He does it all online, by means of avatars, and has no interest whatsoever in meeting the people who control them offline. It becomes continually more complicated and requires a good nose and extreme paranoia, since there is no shortage of security agents who want to infiltrate the group. It is alarmingly easy to invent identities in Playground. That same ease provides him with a defense: he uses over fifteen identities to constantly review both candidates for the Restoration and those who are already in it. His suspicious inner circle — his few trusted avatars — do the same. There have been a few infiltrators, but he has been able to eliminate them in time. He sleeps little, less and less every day, but he knows that the only way to preserve the integrity of the Restoration is by means of microscopic attention to detail.

Only leaders who are willing to take nothing for granted survive. A little paranoia — or a lot of it — never hurts.

He takes off his earphones and stands up, stretching muscles that are in need of exercise; his joints crack like the sound of a broom handle breaking. Feeling his way in the darkness, he heads to the refrigerator to look for food: hot-and-sour soup in a take-out container. He empties it into a bowl and puts it in the microwave. He has not been out of the apartment for days. His scraggly beard and long bangs are both in need of a trim.

He looks out the windows at the vague outline of the Government Citadel on the hilltop. The local offices of the ministry of information. If only they knew that his computer stores as much information about the government as all of the computers in all of the buildings in the Government Citadel.

On a table are file folders containing all the information he has downloaded from the Internet regarding the bid for the power plant in Río Fugitivo. The company that will be in charge, GlobaLux, is an Italian-American consortium. To Kandinsky, this is the most vulgar symbol of Montenegro's neoliberal policies. In a desperate race toward total privatization, the government has carried on the work of its predecessors and relinquished control of sectors that are strategic to the national economy. Not many are left. The railway has been passed into Chilean hands; the telephone company is held by the Spanish; the national airline was owned by Brazilians for a while but fell back into the hands of a local group — backed, rumors say, by an Argentine holding company. The Americans are looking covetously at the natural gas and petroleum and now, together with the Italians, will have control of the electricity in Río Fugitivo. This final blow, in Kandinsky's opinion, is an indication of the government's complete abdication in the face of the forces of globalization. When there is nothing left to sell, the Restoration will reach out from the virtual world of Playground into the world that sustains reality.

It is time to go out and initiate the Resistance.

"Go out" is just a metaphor. It is time to go online and initiate the Resistance.

• • •

Ever since his time with Phiber Outkast, Kandinsky has done everything possible to erase his prints from the world. He does not even go out with women now. Even though he misses spending time with them, and though he is sure that by shying away from them he has lost something very important, he is convinced that the mission he has set for himself makes any kind of contact dangerous. Anonymity, he reminds himself when he feels like wandering through the streets of Playground in search of avatars that will lead him to women. He is a twenty-first-century monk, his apartment a monastery, the computer an instrument that allows him to isolate himself without isolation. He should shave his head, put on a tunic, and turn his movement into a cult.

It helps that no one knows him. The mystery of BoVe in Playground is due in part to the fact that no one knows who controls him. But how can he mount an attack against GlobaLux and the government without knowing the hackers who will form part of the Resistance in real life? Can he simply trust those who control the Restoration avatars in Playground? Impossible. There are some whose real identity is not at all like their behavior in Playground. Playground is a fantasy world, a universe where one can try on multiple identities, wear them as if taking part in a huge street carnival, and take them off when the party is over.

Late at night he walks through the rainy streets of the semi-deserted city. He arrives at his parents' and approaches the house. There is a silhouette against the window: his brother. He finally confirms what his intuition told him before: he has embarked on a road of no return. They have grown apart, and there is no way he can one day play the role of the prodigal son, as he has hoped for so long.

And yet he is fighting for them. Fighting to give his parents' jobs dignity and worth. Fighting to give his brother a future. One day they will understand.

When he returns to his apartment, he will have decided that it is not yet time to show his face. After hours of hacking into the files of those who are in charge of the Restoration's avatars, he will come to the conclusion that he can trust four of them. One is Rafael Corso, a Rat who works in the vicinity of a shopping center in

Bohemia. Another is Peter Baez, a computer student who works for Playground. The other two are Nelson Vivas and Freddy Padilla; both earn their living working for the online edition of *El Posmo.*

That same night he sends them an encrypted e-mail message asking them to meet him in a secret IRC chatroom in Playground. There he tells them of his plans. All of them accept without Kandinsky's needing to insist.

The group that Kandinsky has named the Resistance begins to operate a few weeks later. The first attacks are aimed at large corporations: a virus in Coca-Cola's accounting system in Buenos Aires, a DoS attack on AOL-Brazil and Federal Express in Santa Cruz. Lana Nova, who has just been given an upgrade and now has twice the number of her original facial expressions, reports that the only concrete thing the police know is that the attacks originate in Río Fugitivo. Some editorials proudly point out that in terms of technical ability, "our youth have no need to envy those in the so-called First World."

Months go by. GlobaLux takes control of the electricity in Río and immediately decrees an average rate hike of 80 percent (some companies have their rates hiked by 200 percent). The government pays no attention to the first signs of civil unrest, violent demonstrations outside the GlobaLux offices. Soon after, it is announced on the news that a Coalition Party has been formed in Río Fugitivo, a heterogeneous group of political parties, unions, industrial workers, and campesinos that is willing to confront the government.

Kandinsky, who has decided to unite the Resistance's fight with the Coalition's, laughs to find himself in such strange company. Ideologically, he thinks that his fight goes beyond the joint struggle with the Coalition. However, the truth is that teenage hackers unable to face reality except from behind a computer monitor are marching side by side with weathered unionists holding dynamite in their hands at street protests. Unknowingly, old and new ways of fighting join forces against the same enemy.

• • •

Sitting in front of his computer, Kandinsky plans his next move. The fingers on his left hand ache. He should rest for a few days, but he won't; he believes he is capable of overcoming physical pain. He feels powerful, illuminated by a divine mission. Nothing can stop him. He will do what needs to be done, whatever it costs, whoever falls.

PART III

three

chapter 31

GRAY CLOUDS WHIZ PAST. Thunder can be heard in the distance. Lightning illuminates the sky for an instant. Immobile . . . Between these stinking sheets. Pissing myself . . . Saliva dripping from my half-open mouth. I have to appear as if death is near . . .

It won't arrive. It won't ever arrive.

I am an electric ant . . .

I've been in this situation many times. A knife sliced through my stomach five centuries ago. A bullet exploded in my head in the nineteenth century. I persist . . . I don't know what else to do . . .

Turing left quite a while ago . . . Luckily . . . He will spend hours mulling over my words. As if they made sense. Maybe they do . . . I can't see it. My memory is failing. Which is strange. When it's my own memories . . . And not something else. Such as. A parasitic memory of one of the other beings that I was . . . That I am.

I'm left with no one but myself. As usual. Exhausted by my own ideas. Incapable of being surprised by my own feelings . . .

I am many . . . But I am only one . . .

Historians always focus on those who led wars. They think that the ones who ordered the movements of troops are the ones most responsible . . . For the course of events . . . They also focus on the soldiers. The fate of a nation can be found in their bravery or cowardice. They're not very interested in cryptologists . . . Those who cipher and those who decipher. Office work isn't terribly exciting . . . All that math . . . Too much logic . . .

And yet they have determined the course that wars have taken.

This was never as true as in World War I. During the day ferocious battles were fought . . . Five hundred thousand Germans killed. If we include Verdun and the Somme. Three hundred thousand French . . . One hundred and seventy thousand British . . .

But the real battle was fought by cryptographers and cryptanalysts . . . The radio had been invented. The military was fascinated . . . By the possibility of communication between two points without the need for wires . . . That meant there were more messages. It also meant they could all be intercepted . . . The French were the best. We French were the best. We intercepted a million of the Germans' words over the course of the war. A code was created . . . And deciphered . . . Another was created . . . And deciphered . . . And so on. A war without cryptographic discoveries goes down in history. All good intentions . . . That ended in failure. Handing over all of their secrets.

During the war I was the Frenchman Georges Painvin . . . I worked for the Bureau du Chiffre in Paris . . . My job was to look for weak points in the Germans' codes. One of the most important was ADFGX . . . They began to use it in March 1918. A little before their big offensive that same month. It was an intricate mixture of substitution and transposition procedures . . . Since the code was transmitted in Morse. The letters ADFGX were keys. You see, they didn't resemble one another at all in Morse code. So there was no possibility of confusion.

In March 1918, Paris was about to fall. The Germans had come to within sixty-five miles. They were preparing for the final attack . . . All that was left for us Allies was the possibility of penetrating the ADFGX code . . . And thereby learning where they would concentrate their attack.

And I . . . Georges Painvin . . . Dedicated all my efforts to just that. I lost weight. Two pounds. Five pounds. Twenty pounds. Thirty-five pounds . . . Until the night of June 2, when I managed to decipher a message written in that code . . . Which then allowed other messages to be deciphered.

One of them urgently requested munitions . . . The message

had been sent from a location fifty miles from Paris . . . Between Montdidier and Compiègne. If the Germans needed munitions there . . . It was because they would attack from that area. Our reconnaissance planes confirmed it. Allied soldiers were sent to reinforce that section of the front . . . The Germans had lost the element of surprise. And then they lost the battle.

My throat is filled with phlegm . . . It's . . . Hard . . . To breathe . . . All of my passages are narrowing. Even someone who is immortal. Feels pain . . . And the unmistakable sensation of imminent death.

I am an electric ant . . . Connected to these tubes. I'd like to escape. Jump through the window to freedom . . . As I once did.

This waiting for another body exhausts me . . . Who will I be incarnated as this time? In whom will the spirit of Cryptanalysis live on?

Perhaps an adolescent, by himself in a recreation room. With a crossword puzzle . . . Acrostics . . . Anagrams . . . Or doing calculations on a computer. Trying to create his own algorithms . . . An algorithm that will get to the root of his thoughts. There's something artificial about our intelligence . . . Or perhaps the artificial intelligence of machines is what allows us to understand our own . . . It's the prism through which we see ourselves.

I think I just heard the sound of a gun being fired with a silencer . . . But I can't do anything. The guard who was at the door has shot someone. Or maybe they shot him . . . Maybe they're coming for me. I wouldn't be surprised. Nothing surprises me . . . Except the long wait . . . How long the wait is . . .

I don't know where I was a child. I don't know if I was a child.

I worked at Kaufbeuren.

It's raining. And thundering. Perhaps the shot I heard was thunder. But no. They're impossible to confuse.

But what Painvin did. What I did. Wasn't as important for the course of events . . . As what happened with the Zimmermann telegram. You could, in fact, say that this particular deciphering altered the outcome of the war. And no one would argue . . . Not even historians who know nothing of cryptography. Or perhaps they would.

It happened in 1917 . . . The Germans had come to one conclusion. The only way to defeat England was to stop provisions from reaching the island . . . The plan was to use submarines to sink any ship that attempted to reach its shores. Even neutral ships . . . Even American ships . . . But there was the fear that the Americans would react to the attacks . . . And decide to join the war. This had to be prevented . . . So German strategists hatched an absurd plan. But it was approved . . .

They knew that there was tension between the Americans and the Mexicans. The idea was to get Mexico to declare war on the United States . . . Such an attack would keep the U.S. occupied . . . Defending their own territory would prevent them from focusing on Europe . . . There was also the possibility that Japan would take advantage of the war and land troops in California . . . Back then . . . Mexico had a good relationship with Japan. Which made the Americans nervous.

Steps are drawing closer. They're coming toward me. A shadow silhouetted in the doorway. I open my eyes. My gaze is vacant. As if my eyes weren't open.

I don't know him. He has spots on his cheeks. Wine-colored spots.

The decision to cordon off the British Isles using submarine warfare was made at Pless Castle . . . In Silesia . . . Where the German high command was located. Chancellor Hollweg was against the plan . . . But Hindenburg and Ludendorff were the ones who decided how the war was fought . . . And they were able to convince the kaiser.

The man stops next to me . . . He has a gun in his hands. With a silencer . . . He doesn't need to use it. He could just disconnect the tubes that allow me to breathe. The ones that turn me . . . Into . . .

An electric ant . . .

Six weeks after the decision was made. A newly appointed minister of foreign affairs . . . Arthur Zimmermann . . . Arrived on the scene . . . He sent a telegram to Heinrich von Eckardt. German ambassador in Mexico.

In essence . . . The telegram read . . . *We plan to initiate unre-*

stricted submarine warfare February 1. However we will try to keep United States neutral. If this does not work we propose an alliance with Mexico under the following conditions. Fight the war together. Declare peace together. Our total support and agreement for Mexico to recover territory lost previously. Texas. New Mexico. Arizona.

A shot fired into my chest.

The telegram was sent by telegraph. There were no radio stations in Mexico capable of receiving the telegram from Berlin.

The bullet slices through my skin . . .

So it was sent to the German embassy in Washington. Thanks to an agreement with Woodrow Wilson . . . The Germans used American wires to send their coded messages between Berlin and Washington. So there was nothing suspicious about this.

Blood seeping into my pajamas.

What the Germans didn't know was that the messages between Berlin and Washington. Passed through England.

A puddle extending outward . . . Life seeping away . . .

Or more precisely. Through Room 40. The prestigious cryptology division of Naval Intelligence. In the Admiralty Old Building. Eight hundred radio operators. Eight cryptologists.

A puddle that stops. But doesn't stop.

The man with the spotted cheeks leaves the room. Albert closes his eyes. He's dead . . . I'm dead . . . About time. Time to look for another body.

I was arrested in Rosenheim. Markets. Ruins. Medieval towers. A valley. A boy.

At that time radio operators encrypted codes following sequences in codebooks . . . It was a rudimentary, dangerous method. When an enemy ship was sunk . . . The first thing they tried to find was the codebooks. Toward the end of 1914 . . . A German destroyer was sunk. They found several books and documents . . . In an aluminum box. The men of Room 40 discovered that one of the codebooks was the *Verkehrsbuch.* Which was used . . . Among other things . . . For the exchange of messages between Berlin and its naval attachés . . . In their various embassies abroad . . .

When the Zimmermann telegram arrived in Room 40 . . . Two

cryptologists . . . the Reverend Montgomery and Nigel de Grey. Read the first line.

130. 13042. 13401. 8501. 115. 3528. 416. 17214. 6491. 11310.

The first line generally contained the number of the codebook that was used to cipher the message . . . The number 13042 reminded them of another number . . . 13040 . . . Which belonged to a German codebook that Room 40 possessed . . . They also had a book containing variations of this code. So it was easy. For me. Montgomery . . . And for me . . . de Grey . . . to decipher at least the main parts of the message.

I'm dead. Another body.

When they used codebooks. The Germans tended to cipher their messages twice . . . As a precaution . . . However . . . They hadn't with the Zimmermann telegram. In February 1917 . . . President Wilson was advised of the telegram. In March . . . Surprisingly . . . Zimmermann admitted to the authenticity of the telegram. On April 6 . . . The United States declared war on Germany.

I. Am. Dead.

No I'm not.

Another body. The same body.

Electric ant.

chapter 32

FLAVIA SITS DOWN in front of the computer. Her parents are out and the house is silent; all she can hear is the meowing of the neighbor's Siamese cat, which is in heat and is not letting anyone in the neighborhood sleep much lately. The morning breeze blows in through the partially open window, a breath of air rustling the branches of the trees and caressing her back.

She won't leave the house until her mission is complete. Rafael deserves that much. She doesn't know how things would have unfolded with him, but she is sure that she will never meet anyone so like herself.

Flavia had never seen death up close. It will be impossible to forget Rafael's bloodied chest at the bottom of the stairs in the Internet café; his eyes were wide open, but he was already dead. When the police came, they asked her whether she had seen anything. She was afraid of getting involved. Sobbing, all she said was that she had just met him on the bus. She didn't know anything. They let her go, told her they would contact her later. Once alone, Flavia thought it over and decided to contact them first. She said that she would talk, but only to people at the Black Chamber. She had information that might be of interest to them.

Flavia had given herself to Rafael when she was Erin and he was Ridley. Did that count? Were those avatars extensions of themselves, or were they completely independent? Just as we may be nothing more than the means by which our genes perpetuate, maybe we are simply the instruments that bring our avatars to life on a screen. Flavia was someone's avatar and she controlled avatars that lived in Playground, which in turn controlled others that lived inside computers in Playground . . .

One of her most successful tactics when searching for hackers had been to create a "best friend." Since all hackers on the Internet have nicknames, it is easy for Flavia, or anyone, to hide her identity. Flavia tends to disguise herself as an online friend of the hacker she wants to contact. To do so she uses some of the identities she has already created and consolidated both in Playground and on IRC, or she creates a new one, depending on the situation. She has "best friends" for some of the most dangerous hackers. Her avatars talk about technicalities, discuss sites to be hacked, and tell hacker jokes; they share a hatred of authority, and sometimes she reveals personal details about her life. Once trust has been established, the hackers do the same with her. At one time she tried to create female best friends, but she didn't get very far: the world of hackers is almost exclusively male. Women have to resign themselves to not being taken seriously or to being hacked relentlessly until, as often happened, they are pressured to stop. Flavia was accepted because she was there as a reporter in charge of AllHacker and not as a hacker.

She reviews all the information about Kandinsky that is stored on her hard drive. It isn't much. At one time he was associated with a hacker named Phiber Outkast, who stopped circulating a while ago; he has something against San Ignacio High School; and his tactics for attacking the government are similar to those of a group in Playground called the Restoration. She obtained this information surreptitiously on IRCs and chatrooms in Playground. While the world of hackers seems to be impenetrable at first glance, the truth is that they need to communicate with one another and sometimes do so on open channels. They think they are safe because the words they type in chatrooms disappear within minutes; Flavia's computers, acting in unison, sift through chatrooms and 15,000 IRC channels preferred by hackers searching for key words, and file much of what they find.

Kandinsky is more careful than your average hacker, but he

has still left enough information for Flavia to begin her search. People — even those in the Black Chamber — mistakenly think that most hackers can be defeated when you discover their technical approach or fingerprints on their codes. In the great, computerized world of the twenty-first century, Flavia uses deductive methods that nineteenth-century masters such as August Dupin and Sherlock Holmes would applaud. Her motto is something that John Vranesevich, the world's foremost expert on hackers, said: "I don't want to be an expert in the gun; I want to be an expert in the people who pull the trigger."

Her first step is to connect with some past or present partner of Kandinsky's. She searches "Phiber Outkast" in her database. The computer provides her with the names of seven hackers who have used that pseudonym at some time. Four of them seem interesting. Flavia decides to use the name Wolfram for herself. First she sets up a monitoring system on the computers that belong to those four hackers. By the end of the morning she has narrowed it down to one, who now calls himself PhatalWorm. Her files indicate that he is in his twenties and works at an Internet security company in the Twenty-First-Century Towers.

That afternoon Flavia has Wolfram send PhatalWorm a message about the inherent weaknesses in antihacker security systems. PhatalWorm is not surprised by the message — hackers are used to strangers trying to strike up conversations in chatrooms — and replies with a long diatribe in which he says that the only system that hasn't been fooled in all of Bolivia is FireWall. They chat about security systems for two hours. Wolfram says he knows a few secrets about FireWall.

PHATALWORM: like

Flavia will take a chance. Hackers write the letter *f* as *ph*. It looks better in English, Flavia thinks, but she adopts this style whenever she chats with hackers, just in case.

WOLFRAM: i was a phriend of K a long time ago he told me he was phurious about phirewall he knew everything

PhatalWorm is in a difficult position. If he admits that he knew Kandinsky and was his partner back when he called himself Phiber Outkast, he will be admitting that he is a hacker who sells antihacker systems. He disappears from the chatroom.

He returns at midnight. The temptation to announce his friendship with Kandinsky is irresistible.

PHATALWORM: that big activist with a conscience hypocritical PHUCK
WOLFRAM: u used 2 b phriends
PHATALWORM: a long time ago it doesnt matter

It is evident, however, that it does matter. Having known Kandinsky in person, having been his partner, lends PhatalWorm a certain amount of prestige by association. It is a secret that rises to the surface in all its glory without Wolfram's having to prod. Like a reformed alcoholic nostalgically recalling his days as an irredeemable drunk, PhatalWorm tells Wolfram that Kandinsky is who he is thanks to him and proceeds to tell stories about Kandinsky's humble origins. Flavia reads, saves, records, and ends the conversation with some concrete information: Kandinsky used to live in a rundown house near San Ignacio High School.

The next morning Flavia passes this information along to Ramírez-Graham. He tells her that he will keep her apprised of their investigation.

Flavia stands up and goes into her parents' room. The bed is made: her mom didn't come home last night. Nor does she find the blanket her dad uses when he sleeps on the living room sofa, where Clancy is now sprawled. She asks Rosa. Rosa hasn't seen either of them; they haven't come down for breakfast. Strange—they're usually so predictable, so routine. Maybe they got caught by the blockade. But they would've called.

She finally goes to bed but cannot sleep. She has not done enough.

chapter 33

THE CELL IS CRAMPED and foul-smelling, with seven women crowded into the tiny space. Two of them are carrying babies, one of whom is crying disconsolately. His face is dirty, with soot marks on his cheeks. *He's hungry,* Ruth says to herself, the anger palpable on her trembling lips. *Hungry, and they're not going to do anything about it.*

She approaches the bars of the cell and shouts to a police officer who is leaning in the doorway that leads out onto the patio. Tall, mustached, with a chain in his hands, the officer approaches.

"Go ahead and punish us," she says, "but the babies too? He's not going to stop crying until he gets milk."

"Oh, he'll stop. I've proven that more than once. They get so tired that they fall fast asleep."

"That's no way to treat people."

"No one told you to get into trouble. You go out into the street to stir up a commotion and think that because you're women we won't do anything. Well, this time you're screwed."

"Not even animals deserve to be treated this way."

"What do you know about what they deserve? Get used to it."

He turns around and disappears. Ruth mumbles insults. She is barefoot, and the soles of her feet hurt. They confiscated her manuscript, and without it she feels helpless. They also took her purse and her cell phone. It was a mistake to have gone to the university on such a day. What was her rush? She should have waited until the blockades were over, until the city was demilitarized.

She heads to a corner of the cell and sits down on the floor, her back against the wall. She brings her hands up to her face and strokes the bridge of her nose. Her nostrils hurt. Perhaps tiny ribbons of blood are pooling there, about to let go. She mustn't forget to call the doctor again tomorrow morning, first thing.

She tries to calm herself. These drops of blood that fall from her nose are nothing to worry about. She has just been tense these past few weeks. All the rest is simply rampant hypochondria, with a meaning so clear and simple that she couldn't see it: the blood was her body's way of rejecting Miguel and her own way of life. The truth was staring at her the whole time.

True, the same thing had happened to her mom. But she hadn't paid attention to what was occurring inside her body, couldn't imagine that her cells were degenerating so rapidly, even though they were. At least Ruth has gone to the doctor, and now she just has to wait for the test results. She shouldn't get carried away until she gets in touch with the doctor. Cancer might be hereditary, but that does not mean it is her fate.

Her last violent visit with her mother is still as vivid as if it had happened yesterday. How could it be otherwise? Her mom was in her room, leaning up against two pillows in bed. Her robe was stained with phlegm. In the semidarkness, Ruth was surprised by her mother's baldness, the sudden way the taut skin on her cheeks had contracted and was wrinkled like an empty wineskin. In less than two months she had gone from living an active retirement to unimaginable suffering. She was crying, and Ruth approached to comfort her. "Don't touch me," her mother said angrily. "Don't look at me . . . I'm ashamed to let you see me like this." Ruth had tried to joke. "Oh, Mom, you're still so vain." "I want you to leave . . . You, your brothers, your dad . . . Leave me alone!" Her hands were shaking, and it was difficult for her to breathe. Ruth wanted to console her. Perhaps she had come at the wrong time, but there had never been a good time in the last two months, ever since the night her mom had complained about a pain in her chest. The next day the doctor who saw her at the hospital sent her to see a specialist, but not before telling her that he feared the worst. By the end of that day the oncologist had confirmed their suspicions and was categorical in his diagnosis: the cancer was so far advanced in her liver and lungs that he gave her less than six months to live. "But I hardly smoke at all," her mom shrieked in the hospital hallway. That was a lie: she smoked two packs a day. Ruth sat down on the edge of the bed. She watched her mom search for something behind the pillows; suddenly she was brandishing a gun. "Put that down, Mom! Where did you get it?" It was the gun with the pearl handle that her dad had bought back when there was a rash of burglaries in the neighborhood. "Go on, sweetheart . . . I can't take it anymore." Ruth tried to take the gun away from her mom, who aimed it at her own chest and fired.

A woman sitting next to her jumps up and holds Ruth's hands in hers. Her face is round, her eyes red and very wide.

"Oh, please," she says, "you have to try and help us when you get outta here."

"You may get out before I do."

"How? Why, just look at your clothes. You'll be leaving here in no time. Just like that."

"What did they pick you up for?"

"We were blocking the avenue to the airport. The soldiers came and chased us with chains, grabbing us and our husbands too. But we had to protest! The power bill has gone up so much that we can't pay, and they've got no right. We're tired of them sticking it to us."

"You're absolutely right. It's the same all over the city."

"If you get out, don't forget about us. I'm Eulalia Vázquez." She points to the woman next to her. "And she's Juanita Siles."

"If you get out first, remember me. Ruth Sáenz."

They shake hands. Ruth closes her eyes, overcome by exhaustion. She should be at home, relaxing in the tub, up to her neck in hot water. All those times she had to fight for the bathroom with Flavia, who spent hours in there. What can a person be doing in a bathroom that takes so long? And Miguel didn't let Ruth assert her authority but defended Flavia and let her get away with everything.

The baby continues to cry. She wants to shut him up, to have the cries and shouts of her cellmates disappear. She understands, knows what they are going through, but it is hard to remain calm with so much desperation around. More than anything, she wants to keep a cool head.

Ruth realizes that the blame for the strange course her life has taken can be laid at Miguel's feet. The man for whom her first attraction had taken her by surprise. She liked the long periods of silence in which he would get lost, his evasive glances, his humble gestures that tried not to attract attention. Introspective and intelligent, he was everything that Ruth looked for in a man. She had hated the ones she had dated as a teenager and young adult: loud, clumsy, aggressive in their masculinity. Miguel also understood her passion for the art of codes, which others had found boring and, in the end, *out of place* in a country like theirs. As a boyfriend of hers had once said, "We have a duty to pursue passions that are more useful to the nation." She had responded that the nation was an arbitrary limit for passions, that the only confine that would suffice was the universe. Years later, when she told Miguel this story, he had applauded her response. Ah, Turing: he had wanted her to teach him and had wound up knowing more than the teacher. Not only that, he had given himself over to cryptanalysis as if nothing else existed. Sure, it was important to try to transcend context in your activities, but that did not mean losing sight of it entirely.

She argues with Miguel in silence. She has done this so often before that she knows the exchange of opinions by heart, the veiled accusations and the surprising firmness of the replies. Over the past few months she has had the courage to tell him to his face, but maybe she waited too long, until the intense grumbling of unspoken phrases had already resulted in irrevocable damage. Today's gesture is not enough to counteract the accumulated anger and bitterness or to put their lives on course again, propped up as they are, heading steadily into the abyss.

Exhausted, she sleeps. It will be a fitful night: she will be woken several times because of the children or her cellmates crying. Fatigue will help her to fall back asleep quickly. She will have nightmares—the bloody waters of the Fugitivo River carrying her manuscript away, or she will want to read a book, only to discover that it has been written in a code incomprehensible to her.

The next day, in the afternoon, the mustached officer approaches the cell door and calls her name. She stands up, surprised. The other women bang on the bars, begging to be let free. The police officer opens the door and tells Ruth to follow him.

She crosses the threshold. The pale light filtering in through a window hurts her eyes. Only then does she realize that her cell had been in utter darkness and that she had had to strain to make out the faces and silhouettes of her cellmates.

She looks at the rain outside the window, trying to find beauty in the falling raindrops that cut the day into parallel lines.

"Hurry up," the officer says, grumbling. "The chief needs to speak with you."

chapter 34

RAMÍREZ-GRAHAM IS DRINKING a cup of black coffee in his office. He has finished reading the files that he took out of the archives. He learned little about Albert but much about Turing. What he knows saddens him. He had better leave politics as soon as possible and get back to his algorithms. He has to escape from the Black Chamber.

Baez calls him. "Boss, I need you to come to the Security Room right away." Ramírez-Graham does not feel like moving. Baez thinks everything is urgent.

"Anything to do with Turing's daughter?"

He spoke with her a few hours ago. Then he had spoken with Moreiras, the head of the SIN in Río Fugitivo. A few minutes ago Moreiras had called him with information. There were only a few houses like the one they were looking for near San Ignacio — it was basically an upper-middle-class neighborhood. However, he had good news: they had discovered that the family in one of those houses, which was also a mechanic's shop, didn't know where to find their oldest son, a young man of about twenty. Could it be that the circle was finally closing?

"No, but everything to do with our Turing," Baez replies.

Ramírez-Graham stands up angrily. It is impossible to have a minute's rest at the Black Chamber. He had been able to relax more in his office at the NSA, even though he had more work. Perhaps that had something to do with the fact that he was not the boss at the NSA and could shirk his responsibilities for a few minutes. Perhaps it was another cultural difference: in Río Fugitivo no one seemed capable of making a decision. Ramírez-Graham even had to sign the orders for the monthly allotment of toilet paper for the building. While Baez was one of his most capable and independent subordinates, Ramírez-Graham now thinks that he should actually have reprimanded him at the beginning for not consulting him when the matter of the Resistance first exploded. Baez had wanted to take care of Kandinsky himself, as if he were a minor problem, and had failed to highlight the seriousness of the situation until two weeks after the first attack on the government sites, when he was left no choice. Still, that frustrated act of independence had won him points in Ramírez-Graham's eyes and turned Baez into one of his most trusted men. It had caused rumblings in the hallways: Baez had been at the Black Chamber only a little over three months when he was promoted to the Central Committee.

The Security Room houses the monitors for the closed-circuit system that surveils the building and surrounding areas. Baez is leaning over the shoulder of one of the guards. Ramírez-Graham takes a Starburst out of his pants pocket and approaches them. His gaze rests on what they are watching: Turing, yes, Turing, searching through the files in what Ramírez-Graham calls the Archive of Archives, the small area to which only he has authorized access. It must be frustrating for someone in charge of the archives to have an inaccessible island within reach in the midst of that enormous ocean of documentation. What a temptation, as well, to see what is hidden there, to discover the beginning, the creation myth of the Black Chamber.

The creation myth: Ramírez-Graham had better speak with Turing. He had better reveal the real Albert, the real Black Chamber to him. It would hurt, but someone had to do it. Such daring in that insidious plan. Truly impressive. And it was true: as a professor of his used to say, if your ideas aren't daring, then why have them? But it should not therefore be concluded that daring justifies sacrificing the truth.

"Boss," Baez says anxiously, "are you going to fire him?"

"If I fired him, I'd have to fire everyone."

"I don't get it."

"I'm not sure whether I get it myself," he says, turning around, chewing his Starburst. "Tell Mr. Sáenz I'll be waiting for him in my office, please."

Turing enters Ramírez-Graham's office, looking down at the floor as if trying to pass unnoticed. Ramírez-Graham cannot help but feel sorry for him, a ghost with glasses. But no, a ghost has more presence.

"Sit down, please. Coffee? Candy?" he asks, offering him the package of Starbursts.

"No, thank you."

"You're doing me a favor. These were hard to find. I was told you could buy them at a store that sells imported products, but no. An old woman sells them in a kiosk in Bohemia."

Ramírez-Graham stands up and walks to the window. He sits back down again. Should he tell him everything? He has no choice.

"Mr. Sáenz, I don't know whether you know this, but there are hidden cameras in every office and corner of this building. The cameras have caught you doing strange things in the archives on several occasions. Not terribly hygienic, in truth."

Turing shifts in his seat.

"The McDonald's cup. The Road Runner."

"Ah . . . I can explain. I have a problem. Incontinence. I'll bring you a doctor's certificate."

"I let it go because, well, you weren't bothering anyone." Ramírez-Graham picks up his coffee cup, holding it in the air as if forgetting about it. Svetlana always used to laugh at that gesture, telling him that it was as if he were posing, motionless, waiting for the photographer's flash. "But a few minutes ago the cameras caught you in the section of the archives that's off-limits. Yes, I know, we should have separated it from the rest of the room, put on a door and several locks. It was too tempting there, so handy. It's one of the many problems I found when I arrived, but there's not enough time to deal with everything. However good our intentions might be."

"I wasn't doing anything wrong. I was just curious."

"You wanted to know about Albert. About your creator."

"Someone here insulted him. I wanted to make sure that what he said wasn't true."

"You didn't find the documents. You didn't find them because I have them. I was curious too. Albert is an enigma to us all. But tell me, what was the insult?"

"That Albert . . . was a Nazi fugitive."

"Yes, yes, I've heard the rumors. I'm sorry to say that I don't know how much truth there is to them, but I don't think there's much. No creo que son ciertos. Sean ciertos, I mean. They would have extradited him like they did Klaus Barbie when democracy returned."

"That's true. They didn't do anything. After 1982 he was technically no longer the boss, but he stayed on as an adviser, and everyone knew that in reality he was in charge."

"He was lucky. What goes on in the chamber is so secret that it took a long time before most people realized what his role was during the dictatorships. Well. I don't know what to say. I can tell you, though, other things that are important."

Turing makes some guttural noises, as if he is clearing his throat.

"The last time I went to see him," he says, "Albert spoke three words. Kaufbeuren. Rosenheim. Wettenhein. I found out that the first two are the names of cities in Germany. I didn't really hear them too well, but by searching I found out how they were spelled. Kaufbeuren, Rosenheim. I have no idea about the third, but maybe I didn't hear it right. My wife would know, but I don't know where she is. I've called her several times, but she must have turned off her cell phone."

"And the German cities make you think that Albert wasn't a CIA agent but a Nazi. Who knows? Maybe he was a CIA agent who worked in Germany during the cold war. But I don't want to talk about that. I have something more important to tell you."

He did not have definitive proof, but he was sure that he was right. Ramírez-Graham came from a culture where things were said up front. It would be very painful for Turing, but in the long run he would be doing him a favor. It would help him stop . . . stop living a lie.

"Mr. Sáenz," he says. "You are one of the Black Chamber's great heroes. That's why it hurts me to say what I'm about to say. Do you remember your first few years here? When you acquired your fame as being infallible? Able to decipher everything that Albert put on your desk? I'm going to tell you how you were able to do that."

Ramírez-Graham clears his throat.

"You were able to do that because those messages were meant to be deciphered."

"I don't understand."

"It's quite simple and complicated at the same time. Let me start at the beginning, with Albert. According to the confidential documents I read, toward the end of 1974, during the third year of Montenegro's dictatorship, Albert, who was in Bolivia as a consultant with the CIA, requested an audience with the minister of the interior. He told him, in so many words, that at the end of the year he would be assigned to another country but that he was willing to leave the CIA and stay in Bolivia if he was offered a job. Albert told the minister that a government like Montenegro's needed a specialized intelligence service and that he could put his experience with the CIA at Montenegro's disposal and take charge of organizing such a service. The minister told him, in so many words—what I read wasn't tape transcripts, you see, but the report that the minister sent to the president—that the government already had an intelligence service."

Ramírez-Graham walks up to the aquarium and taps the glass a few times, as if trying to get the angelfish's attention. He then remembers that he hasn't yet fed them and does so as he continues speaking.

"Albert replied that the government didn't have anything like the NSA, an agency whose only responsibility was to intercept electronic signals and coded information of all kinds and to decipher them in order to keep the government apprised of the opposition's plans. The times ahead made establishing such an agency an urgent matter. The Communist infiltration of South America, the

Soviet and Cuban financing of political parties and Marxist guerrilla groups, had to be fought using all of the weapons at the government's disposal. The minister answered that Albert had never worked for the NSA. Albert replied by saying that he had been the liaison between the CIA and the NSA for a time and that he knew of what he spoke. In the minister's opinion, something about Albert didn't add up. His accent, for example, was not at all that of an American speaking Spanish. It was — how shall I say? — as confusing as if a German had learned English and then Spanish. Even so, he found Albert fascinating."

"I know all of that already," Turing said, impatient.

"Wait. Just wait a moment. I don't have conclusive proof of what I'm about to tell you. There are a lot of things in the documentation that are hinted at, written between the lines. But I'll put my job on the line for what I'm about to tell you. So, as I was saying, the minister got one of those ideas that gave him his reputation as the smartest man in his graduating class at military college. He would accept Albert's idea and radicalize it."

He pauses, takes a drink of his coffee.

"Sometimes it was necessary to eliminate someone in the opposition, and a few scrupulous military men opposed this, saying that the prestige of the army was not to be tampered with. Those soldiers had formed a group called Dignity. They were asking, among other things, for clarification of the definition of 'political crime,' which the government used to justify having a member of the opposition arrested, exiled, or anything else they decided to do. Dignity didn't want anyone to be detained without concrete proof, but sometimes, as you know, there was no proof."

He touches the glass case that covers the Enigma machine. What must it have been like to use one of them? How had it even been possible to program cryptographic systems without software?

"The minister thought that it was better to err on the side of acts rather than omissions, as the governments in Chile and Argentina had. Better to make a mistake on bad faith than to leave a single possible Communist agitator alive. There are no white gloves in a dirty war. The soldiers who formed Dignity found that argument insufficient. But perhaps they could accept the need to eliminate certain persons if there was convincing proof that they were involved in conspiracies. The minister could use Albert."

"Use?" Turing asks incredulously.

"They could plant intercepted messages and use them as need be. He told Albert to come back, that he would consult with the president. A week later they had approved the plan to set up the Black Chamber in secret, an organization that would be a branch of the SIN and that would be managed, at first unofficially, by Albert."

"That's a lie. Albert was never used by anyone. He was too intelligent for that."

"For the first few months of 1975, the hard line of Montenegro's government did use Albert. However, by the end of 1975 he became part of the conspiracy, once he realized that he was being used. At first he said nothing. Then he revealed that he knew what was going on but was willing to continue his work. Perhaps he had no other choice. He knew too much—he would be eliminated if he resigned."

There is confusion in Turing's eyes. Ramírez-Graham notes the grief on his face but must not stop. He finishes his coffee.

"By that time a certain amount of sophistication had been achieved in terms of planting information that was supposedly intercepted. For example, they published notices containing secret messages in newspapers, then they discovered those messages and accused some opposition group of having published them. That's how, for example, the military and civilians who were involved in the Tarapacá plot that planned to overthrow the government were eliminated. The government didn't have overwhelming proof to get rid of them, so it invented secret messages about the conspiracy in order to justify its actions to Dignity."

"And what was my role in all of this?"

Ramírez-Graham pauses.

"In order to avoid suspicion inside the Black Chamber, Albert suggested that planted information should be given to the fewest cryptanalysts possible—the majority of them would work on analyzing real messages. Albert had a favorite cryptanalyst to whom he gave all the planted information. He chose him because he was immune to political shifts, was incapable of thinking about the consequences of his work or feeling remorse because of it. A man who lived as if he were not part of history."

For the first time in the whole conversation, Turing lifts his eyes and looks straight at Ramírez-Graham.

"I'm sorry, Mr. Sáenz. Albert took all of the messages that you deciphered from a manual on the history of cryptanalysis. It wouldn't be hard to prove. Chapter one, a monoalphabetic substitution code. Chapter two, a polyalphabetic substitution code . . . In reality, neither you nor this building had any more reason for being than to hide how sinister Montenegro's dictatorship could be when it realized who its enemies were. Inertia is what allowed you to keep your job and this building to continue functioning once the reasons that gave rise to it were no longer valid. Believe me, Mr. Sáenz, I understand how difficult this must be for you. Understand how difficult it is for me too. After discovering all of this, do you think it's easy for me to be here still?"

chapter 35

UNDER THE GLOW of a red neon light, the El Dorado receptionist is logged on to Playground. His avatar is in a brothel where the women are modeled after some of the most famous porn stars. He has just closed a deal with a tall redhead wearing knee-high boots. She takes his avatar by the hand and leads him through silk curtains to a red-painted hallway, a row of rooms one next to the other on both sides. You ask him who she is. You want to have a normal conversation, something that will bring you back to the everyday world. You know that it's not going to be easy. A person shouldn't find out things he isn't prepared to know.

"Briana Banks23." It is the first time you have heard his voice, as weak as if his vocal cords could not tighten enough to produce a resonant sound. "Whoever has the trademark must be making more money online than the real Briana Banks. There are over seventy replicas in Playground alone."

He presses the pause button and the image of Playground freezes. You admire Briana, her firm thighs sheathed in silver shorts, her long, long legs. With those enormous breasts and that tiny waist, she is an excessive digital creation, the work of some fevered graphic designer who spent the night going through pinup magazines and decided to improve on his models.

The receptionist hands you the gold-colored key to room 492. "So, Carla again tonight," he says, grinning complicitly. "There's nothing better for business than a happy customer." You look down at the floor as you feel the blood rush to your face, and then you slip away, heading with tentative steps toward the elevator.

One. Two. Three. Four. Five. Six. You look carefully at the white numbers in the middle of the black buttons. Before pressing the 4, you ask yourself whether such a simple progression could hide a secret message. Never take anything for granted; even the most innocuous places are capable of hiding some writing, a signature. And few things hold as much sway over you as an undeciphered message. As if the miracle of the world would gain power simply by being hidden.

You would like to stay for hours in that noisy metal box, in that mirrored crypt, for your ascension to continue. You would then open the door and come out into an unknown world, where there would be none of the anxiety that you feel right now. Because nothing is what it seems, and the translucent waters of the river have turned murky. The women of your fantasies have their arms mapped by the cartography of drugs. The legend of your work has become an anecdote as memorable as it is obsolete. The actions of your entire life—your uninterrupted service to the nation—are for some the consummate fingerprints of a criminal career. It doesn't help to have discovered today that they might be right, and that to top it all off, most of your life has been a lie.

You come out of the elevator into a familiar space. Whom will you find behind the door you are heading toward? The California cheerleader or the real Carla? And what does she have to do with the mixed-up rest of your life? Is it that everything leads back to a plan that you can barely decipher between the lines? Is it that some secret plot conjures up the footprints your path takes and at the same time conjures you?

You miss Albert. He would have told you that paranoia is healthy. Admirable man, your discoverer. Still, not even he could have prepared you for what you discovered today. That insolent Ramírez-Graham. And the worst of it is that you think he might be right. It would be difficult, very difficult, to live with that certainty.

The years you spent in Albert's presence were unique. You were excited simply by the fact that he was in the same building, that you could walk a few yards and find yourself in his office, in his overwhelming presence, with his booming voice, his outrageous intelligence. You worked better, applied yourself to the task, felt that you were fighting for an objective that transcended your triviality as a man. You dedicated your entire life to that foreigner. You lived to hunt down secrets, knew that everyone had enemies, and yet you thought that he did not. Yes, you suspected that he treated you differently, that he hid things from you. But hiding the purpose of your work at the Black Chamber? No amount of cryptography would have been sufficient to encode so many lies.

Oh, Albert. He was very cruel to you. Worse still is that you were willing to forgive him, at least to try to understand him. Who were you, after all, to put yourself on his level, to dare to question him, to search for the ultimate reasons behind his motives? You always asked yourself the why behind the why, but when it came to Albert you entered sacred territory.

Carla opens the door and sees you standing immobile halfway between the elevator and her room. She is barefoot and wearing a purple baby doll that you find incongruous right now. It's the one she was wearing the afternoon you remember most clearly in your relationship, when she had one of her many outbursts. You were in bed watching television, having just made love; you were smoking, and she was drinking a can of rum and Coke. Out of nowhere, Carla made a joke about your member. She said it reminded her of her customer's, someone she had seen last week. Her comment hurt; you suspected that she still had other customers but preferred not to broach the subject. You expected her to do the same.

You picked up a folder containing the newest rules that Ramírez-Graham had instituted at work and began to read it. Ten minutes passed. She turned off the television and apologized; you did not respond. She tore the file out of your hands, ripped the pages one by one, and threw them onto the floor. You got up and got dressed, your socks inside out, your tie hanging loose. You told her that you would be back once she had calmed down, when she felt better. "Which might be never," you said without looking at her. She shouted: What did you know about her life? What did you know about her problems? You tried to help her, but it was all superficial. You didn't understand how difficult it was to struggle against addiction. "Son of a bitch," she shouted at you. "Bastard. Egotist. You don't know what real pain is." She threw the can of rum and Coke at you as you were walking out the door. It hit the wall and splattered on your coat. You were so angry that you took the stairs. You arrived at your car wanting to disappear from Carla's life, but you could not make yourself leave; you stayed sitting in your Toyota, brooding over your remorse. You went back up to room 492. If you didn't help her, who would?

"What's wrong? Here I am waiting and now I find you in the hallway. I called downstairs and they told me that you'd come up, but you never arrived."

How can you answer her question? How can you tell her that you have just discovered that the past twenty-five years of your life have been a ruse? How can you tell her that it is true, that your hands are stained with blood? And, worst, the blood of innocent people.

You approach and collapse into her arms.

chapter 36

JUDGE CARDONA finds a pharmacy on a corner two blocks from Albert's house. It is closed. He rings the bell, and a short while later a woman with small eyes and a hawkish nose appears at a window on one side. She opens the door.

"Come in, come in," she says, turning her back on him and rummaging through drawers in search of alcohol and gauze. Cardona sets his briefcase on the floor. Water is running off his clothes and onto the carpet.

"I'm sorry, I'm making a mess."

"Don't worry."

Cardona's arms and legs are cold; he feels the uncomfortable wetness of clothes sticking to his body. He would like to be back at the hotel already, sitting next to a radiator or a heater, getting warm.

"Have a seat," the woman says, pointing to a chair on which a Siamese cat is lying. "You're drenched. And that cut has to be taken care of right away, before it gets infected. What happened?"

"Thank you, ma'am," Cardona replies without moving, clinging to his briefcase. "I was in the wrong place at the wrong time. I came across the demonstration in the plaza."

"Oh, I'm so sorry. But if you ask me, I completely agree with what's happening. Did you see the electricity bill last month? They come here to a poor country to get rich. Please, sit down."

Cardona walks over to the chair and pets the cat, which has no intention of leaving its place. It smells of urine and is losing its fur; bits of skin are visible along its back. The woman pounds the counter with her hand, and the cat jumps up and runs into the back of the pharmacy. Cardona sits down. He remembers a conversation he had with Valdivia, the minister of finance, in the hallway of the Presidential Palace. They had just left a cabinet meeting where they had been discussing the problem of grassroots movements that were opposed to the privatization of national resources to foreign companies. Valdivia looked worried.

"My dear judge, our people want the economy to recover, but when investors come from outside, they shout to high heaven. They don't understand that capitalist companies are not charitable organizations — they invest in Bolivia because they want to earn a profit. It's a never-ending problem, and I don't know how we'll ever change it."

"I don't think we ever will," Cardona said. "A poor country isn't used to success. We're not used to people earning beyond what they need to provide for their family. That's where the phrase 'to earn a living' comes from. Honest work means earning a living. And if someone earns money, amasses wealth for himself, he's selfish, corrupt, or both."

"You're right. We yearn for modernity, progress, but we're also afraid of losing our traditions. We want both, and that's just not possible. The neoliberal model is condemned to fail here, if it hasn't already."

Cardona would have liked to have said that the problem wasn't the model but how it was being applied. Instead he asked, "But do you think that people will reach the point where they'd rather put investors on the run? If so, we should just close our borders right now."

"Oh, they'll put them on the run, all right, and the next day they'll wake up with nothing. It will be a victory with no winners — just the kind of victory we like."

The woman looks closely at Cardona's wound. "You're going to need stitches," she pronounces.

"With no anesthetic?"

"Stay calm."

"Will it hurt?"

"It won't take a minute."

He closes his eyes and lets her do what she needs to do. He wonders whether he will have enough strength to reach Turing's house. He has to; he has to finish what he started.

He leaves the pharmacy under a drizzly sky. His cut was deep and required three stitches. It still burns, but the pain is subsiding. Turing's house is located in a gated community on the outskirts of the city. Will he make it? He knows how to get there, he has studied the names of the streets; Río Fugitivo has avenues that run the length of the city, and it is difficult to get lost. It will take about forty-five minutes to get there on foot. The blockades are the problem. With the way the city is, full of demonstrations and police, there will be risks. It could start to pour again at any moment, and he would have to take shelter somewhere. He is exhausted; his clothes are wet and stained with blood. So, what then? Go back to the hotel and take a shower? Lie down on the bed and let the drugs wash over him? Leave it all until tomorrow? No. Tomorrow Ruth will find out about Albert's death, put two and two together, and suspect Cardona. She will know that the trial was a ruse, a necessary lie to hide the merciless truth. Because the law is of no use in this country, mere subterfuge so that those in power can dictate the course of events at will. Cardona always knew it, just didn't want to believe it. Perhaps he thought that his word, his convictions could triumph. Vanity of all vanities, if that was the case. But no. Deep down all he wanted was to be one of them. And the only way he can exonerate himself is by taking the law into his own hands. By acting as judge and jury. Defeating the law will be his victory. And the only way to escape his own grave is by shooting his way out. He wipes his face with a dirty handkerchief, the purplish spots on his cheeks glowing.

Cardona decides to continue on his way, far from the upheavals of collective will but at the same time paradoxically sure that what he has done and what he is about to do are an essential part of that will. A historic afternoon, and here he is, helping to create history as it is being destroyed. He comes upon streets and intersections littered with stones, broken bottles, and sticks; cars that defied the blockade and wound up with their tires slashed; stubborn fires devouring broken chairs, garbage, and newspaper; desperate firefighters trying to put out the flames with hoses that lack water pressure; groups of young people who have come in from rural areas, heading downtown; military troops on lookouts and police battalions clearing the streets of stones and running after demonstrators with tear gas; journalists with microphones and cameramen with cameras that never stop rolling, capturing the violent abandon and showing live images of the country, recording these scenes for online and television news broadcasts, for the summary of the week's events on Sunday, for historical archives. No one recognizes Cardona, nor does he do anything to be recognized. He walks on roads that run parallel to the main avenues, avoiding direct confrontation with the protesters. It's better this way. He is happy to have retired from the government in time, not to be part of the collapse. Ah, as if that were the whole truth. Frantic caravans of words obscure reality. Had he retired, or had he been forced to retire? They had made him tender his resignation. Perhaps they had realized that he wasn't one of them. Or they hadn't realized that he wanted to be one of them.

While he walks, Cardona plays with a verse from Rubén Darío. *Celeste fue la triste historia de mi corazón* and unused to getting lost in the face of such obsequiousness. That's what being a minister does to you. What would Mirtha say if she knew that from time to time he missed the lunches and dinners at the presidential residence? Would she accept the tangled way in which he is apologizing? Would she be offended that he had to drag her memory into his own conflict? *Blue was my heart*, he mumbles. *Blue my heart is still.*

Every now and then Cardona stops, exhausted, and wonders how it will all end. Will Montenegro fall? It is by no means a certainty: the government has been rattled before and has always found a way to sustain itself. The opposition forces have the necessary will to shake the government's foundation but not to give the final push that will precipitate its fall. Perhaps there is the fear of waking the ghosts of coup d'états, which fill the country's past. No one is happy with the way things are now, but the effort that it took to reestablish democracy two decades ago still weighs heavy.

In the face of such hesitation and uncertainty, someone should do to Montenegro what Cardona just did to Albert: approach and shoot him point-blank in the chest. End of story. The demise of one baroque structure, which would likely give way to a new structure no less baroque. But that was for others to take care of, those who were up and coming. And yet who was capable of doing it? Who would not hesitate when listening to Montenegro's sometimes strange way of speaking? He would put a cigar in his mouth, bite down on it, and begin to talk. The words would tumble off his lips as if he were drunk. Cardona had had to pay close attention in order to understand him. Montenegro exercised his power in the smallest of details, obliging people like Cardona to concentrate as hard as they could in order to understand what he said, making them see that, just like the cigar, he had them between his teeth and could destroy them simply by biting down.

He lets out a sigh of relief as he turns a corner and sees, three blocks farther on, the gated community where Turing lives.

As he approaches, a question forms inside him, taking him by surprise: what has he done? He looks at his hands, dotted by wine-colored spots. Why kill the poor albino guard? He didn't have anything to do with it.

He continues on, thinking that even with Albert gone, he still misses the Presidential Palace. Cardona now knows he is no different from all those murderers he accused of sustaining Montenegro's dictatorship such a long time ago. *Blue was my heart.*

Everything has been an excuse. All of this has very little to do with Montenegro's culpability and everything to do with Cardona's. The state chewed him up, then spat him out. *Blue my heart is still.*

chapter 37

ONE NIGHT KANDINSKY decides to visit his parents. He waits for what seems like forever for the door to open. His mom's eyes light up at the sight of him; he melts into her embrace. She is thinner; he can feel the bones along her back.

"What a surprise! Come in, come in. You're so pale."

All of us, little by little, lose weight, begin to disintegrate. In the hallway he comes upon his dad's sullen face, grease-stained coveralls, and gray, threadbare T-shirt. He coldly shakes Kandinsky's hand.

"Thought you'd forgotten about us."

Everything seems small, dirty, and rotten to Kandinsky. Had he really lived here for more than fifteen years? How had he been able to stand it? He looks at the boxes piled high in the hallway, the flickering light of the lamp in the cramped living room with its color TV, the walls crumbling from the humidity, the poster of San José, and the effigy of the Virgin of Urkupiña with a lit candle at her feet in the kitchen. He misses the workshop, would like to see the bicycles — broken-down skeletons standing on their heads — that await his dad's deft hands, the tools strewn on a wooden table, the screws and chains on the dirt floor. When he was a boy, in Quillacollo, he could spend hours watching his dad work. It wasn't a stretch to go from that to tearing apart and putting back together anything he could get his hands on, radios and television sets found in garbage dumps.

He says nothing. He had suspected he would feel like a stranger; that this is indeed his feeling, however, hurts. He had held on to a faint hope: his parents' house was his house too. Perhaps returning was no longer possible. So now what?

He will not ask them for forgiveness; this visit is already an apology. He will not tell them what he does. He will give them a wad of cash and say goodbye, telling them that he has not let them down, that they can always count on him.

He goes into the room that he used to share with his brother, Esteban. The smell of dirty clothes and stagnant air assaults him. His bed is gone. Esteban is stretched out on his, smoking and reading by the light of a lamp. He is well built, taller than his older brother. Kandinsky extends his right hand. His brother does not acknowledge the greeting, tapping his cigarette into an ashtray on the bedside table.

"How are you, bro?" Kandinsky asks.

"Fucked, but still honest."

His tone does not invite further conversation. Kandinsky doesn't know what to say to him either, what to ask him. He notices the difference in the way they are dressed. He is wearing brand-new jeans and a black sweater. Esteban is wearing old brown pants and a faded red shirt.

"What're you reading?"

"Nothing that'd interest you," Esteban replies between gritted teeth, as if trying to contain the annoyance caused by Kandinsky's presence. "Just old Marx."

"What makes you think I wouldn't be interested?"

"You're not the type."

"You'd be surprised."

Fucked, but still honest. What was that supposed to mean? Suddenly he understands: it's because of that time when he came and gave his dad an envelope of cash. They have no idea how he earns a living and came to the conclusion that those bills could have been obtained only illegally. How else could he have gotten them? Such miracles didn't happen in this country. They are so honest and even prouder than he is. They could forgive him for disappearing, but not for possibly having done something illegal to escape poverty.

"You're not being fair to me."

"Whatever. You have no right to demand anything of us."

Kandinsky leaves the room. He walks past his dad without saying goodbye. He gives his mom a quick kiss and heads out the door. One day they will know the truth. One day they will understand.

He walks along the sidewalk that borders the main building at San Ignacio. His fingers twitch nervously. The tingling sensation comes back into his hands and wrists. At times the pain is unbearable.

A guard dog appears from among the pine trees behind the wrought-iron gate, his open mouth slobbering. He snaps at the fence, startling Kandinsky, who spits at the dog and begins to run.

In Playground, Kandinsky meets in a private chatroom with the four members of the Restoration whom he chose to accompany him in the next phase of his plan — Corso, Baez, Vivas, and Padilla. The chatroom has 128-bit encryption, one of the most secure on the market. Kandinsky, through his avatar BoVc, tells them that all their work against the government of Playground has been a preliminary step for what is to come.

KANDINSKY: were at war a new type of war b proud u were chosen 4 the most diphicult part
BAEZ: whos the enemy
KANDINSKY: security systems govt sites multinationals w/ investments in the country
CORSO: whatre the objectives
KANDINSKY: phinal V no more no less
CORSO: 2 much
KANDINSKY: its not 2 late 2 leave
PADILLA: were with u we just need speciphic objectives
KANDINSKY: globalux the rest is up 2 u use the whole arsenal virus DoS graphphiti
BAEZ: were part of the Coalition

KANDINSKY: were not part of anything but people think of us as the resistance well be the resistance we are the resistance

He asks each one of them to act on his own, to prevent the intelligence service from finding similar structures that might get them caught. They will report to him once a week, in a previously agreed-upon chatroom.

They sign off and meet up again in the anarchist neighborhood in Playground, this time together with the other members of the Restoration. They will speak as if their conversation in the private chatroom never took place.

The attacks signed by the Resistance begin at the same time as the Coalition's protests against the hike in electricity rates (there are street demonstrations of all kinds in the country's largest cities, but the center of events is Río Fugitivo). This coincidence will lead the country's main media analysts and advisers to the ministry of the interior to conclude that the groups are working in concert. Traditional uprisings, which were notably successful in the second half of the twentieth century, had managed to unite forces with a new kind of rebellion, one that used digital technology to send its message and to paralyze — sometimes for hours, sometimes for days — information systems belonging to the government and a few large corporations.

The media cover the huge national protests against the government. The leader of the coca growers, through his anti-neoliberal tirades and insults hurled at the *imperialist gringos*, is able to unite the forces of the left that had been dispersed and fragmented for the past fifteen years. The analysts do not consider him a possible candidate for the presidential election next year; they say that his support is limited to rural areas of the country and does not reach the departments in the tropics. The media give the same coverage to the coca leader as to the Resistance's movements. They are fascinated by the figure of Kandinsky and have quickly turned him into a cyberspatial combination of Don Quixote and Robin Hood. There are no photos of him or statements that reveal his identity, which leads to a series of speculations. Some say he must be a foreigner, because of his name and because such technological prowess could only come from abroad; others say that he is actually a local rebel and that even the government should be proud of his work. Hundreds of young people from different social classes appropriate what he represents—his anti-globalization stance, his decision to confront their submissive government—and there is no shortage of hacker apprentices, copycats by the dozen, who try to follow his lead and attack the Web sites of local mayors, a regional development company . . .

Lying on the mattress in his apartment, watching Lana Nova report the news on his cell phone as he lets his hands rest, Kandinsky loves the media coverage that surrounds his movement. He revels in his subordinates' successful attacks even more. The most creative is Baez, who has implemented an electronic version of what young Argentine and Chilean activists do when they discover where an official from the old dictatorship lives. They go to the official's home and cover the walls in phrases that allude to his past (quotes from victims of torture, resistance leaders), letting the neighborhood and the media know that someone who took part in the massacres lives there. This strategy of attack is known in those countries as *escrache.* Baez has a list of old civil servants from Montenegro's dictatorship and sends them e-mails containing a blunt message: *Murderer, your hands are stained with blood. Ciberescrache,* he calls it. He started out with a few of his colleagues at the Black Chamber. His next step will be to make the names known.

One weekend Nelson Vivas and Freddy Padilla are murdered, a day apart. Vivas is stabbed early Saturday morning as he leaves the *El Posmo* building, and on Sunday night Padilla is shot in the back of the head at the front door to his house. The media report these two deaths as if they were separate incidents; no one seems to know that both men were members of the Resistance.

Kandinsky's first thought is that the government intelligence service is breaking up his organization and that the same fate will soon befall the other members. He decides not to contact anyone for a few days. Nothing happens.

A few weeks pass. There is still no explanation for what happened to Vivas and Padilla. AllHacker, a site that Kandinsky often visits, has dared to speculate that the individuals who were killed were hackers belonging to the Resistance and that the person responsible for their deaths is Kandinsky. The reason: he is a megalomaniac who is more interested in maintaining his own power than in fighting the government. Delirious. Still, something worries him: how did the girl in charge of AllHacker know that Vivas and Padilla were members of the Resistance? Who is her informant? Someone in his inner circle? Or is she working for the government again?

He rules out Baez and Corso. He could not have made such a huge mistake. Still, he will watch them closely.

It has to be the government, which is on his trail and knows more than he thinks it does.

A hack into her Web site will convince him that the person responsible—a schoolgirl named Flavia Sáenz—does not know more than what she reported and is groping about in the dark, with no actual proof for her accusations. One of these days he will play a cruel joke on her and invite her to form part of the Resistance. She needs to be scared, be made to see that they are on her trail.

He meets with Corso and Baez in a private chatroom. He gives them free rein to reinitiate their attacks on Monday of the following week. They will be of a magnitude unsuspected by the government and will continue to increase throughout the week to coincide on Thursday with the Coalition's planned blockade of streets and highways. Corso seems uncertain.

On Wednesday of the following week, in the midst of the Resistance's unbridled attack on government and GlobaLux computers, Corso is shot dead at an Internet café in Bohemia.

Kandinsky feels trapped. He decides to turn off his computers and not leave his apartment until he finds out what's going on. He wonders how he will do that with his computers turned off.

chapter 38

MY DESTINY DOES NOT end in one man . . . My destiny continues in all men . . .

I speak these words on this terrible, mournful day. My body dead but unable to die . . . Looking out a window where the colors of evening alight after the rain. The lilac glow of sunset. The green of a tall pepper tree. Waving in the breeze. The washed-out blue of the sky.

The man who shot me has gone . . . My chest has been torn open by his lead bullets. My blood is flowing out from more than one hole . . . The sheets are being stained with yet another sticky substance. They are used to my dripping saliva . . . To the sweat from my pores. To my acidic urine. And now I'm swimming in a reddish pool . . .

The minutes tick by . . . I know that this is not how I will end. At most I will leave this life to return in another . . . Perhaps in New Zealand or Pakistan. I will be a cryptographer or a cryptanalyst . . . I will again obscure clarity by means of a code. Or reveal it by means of another . . .

I'm tired. I'm Albert. I was. I am so many more.

Huettenhain. I wasn't Huettenhain.

Approximately an hour passes and the next guard on duty. Dark-skinned and bucktoothed. Finds me . . . I hear panic in his voice as he calls his superiors. Asking for an ambulance . . . I'd like to tell him to calm down. To trust me. Or at least whoever created me. Whoever created us . . . Because the same Creator must have created us all. Or maybe not . . . Perhaps a mischievous demiurge created me. Perhaps that's how this cosmic joke can be explained . . . Knowing myself to be infinite in a finite body.

Immortal in a mortal body . . .

I breathe softly. As if my breath doesn't want to be noticed. As if it prefers calm to desperation . . . As if it also knows what awaits it. Or what does not.

Two paramedics move me onto a stretcher without a fuss . . . To them I'm simply another load. I leave my room. I will miss the window and nothing else . . . Not even the photos. Which will soon no longer be mine. They put me into an ambulance . . . It might be the last time I travel through the streets of Río Fugitivo. Its bridges hiding beggars and dead dogs underneath. And suicides. Those who committed suicide . . .

It's only right that this be my last means of transport. Ambulances are closely linked to my time here. Government security forces liked to use them . . . Its paramilitary was moved in them for more than one coup d'état . . . An innocent symbol for such a heinous crime.

And I was behind some of those coups. Decoding . . . Or inventing decoded messages. So that those who needed to fall fell.

I am an electric ant.

My spirit has no defined morals. Sometimes. Like now. I'm reincarnated in evil men . . . Other times in someone who fights evil. Or are they the same?

I was. For example. Marian Rejewski. The Polish cryptanalyst who helped to dismantle the intricate mechanism of Enigma . . . That powerful Nazi ciphering machine.

With Enigma . . . Pencil and paper were left behind. And technology became responsible for encryption . . . The ability to transmit secret messages was mechanized. Enigma looked like a portable typewriter . . . One typed a letter on the keyboard . . . The keys were connected by cables to rotating disks that mixed up the letters . . . Thus, one letter became another. One phrase became another . . . And from those disks ran other cables that led to a panel with dim lights . . . Each light represented a letter. The lights that lit up were the encrypted letters that made up the encrypted message . . .

But that wasn't all.

Every time a letter was encrypted. The rotating disk turned one twenty-sixth of a rotation. So that when that letter was typed again . . . It was encrypted with a different letter . . . And a different light lit up. Each Enigma consisted of three rotating disks. Twenty-six times twenty-six times twenty-six . . . Resulting in a total of 17,576 options. Not to mention the reflector . . . And the ring . . . Which complicated things even more.

It was invented by the German Arthur Scherbius in 1918 . . . They went into mass production in 1925. And were used by the German army the following year . . . The German army would eventually buy 30,000 Enigma machines. When World War II began. No country could compare with the security of the Germans' communications system . . . With Enigma. The Nazis had a great advantage over the Allies . . . They lost that advantage thanks to the work of many people. Above all Rejewski . . .

And the Englishman Alan Turing . . .

At one time I was both men. I helped to bring down the Nazis.

I was Rejewski. I was born in Bromberg . . . A city that after World War I belonged to Poland. And was called Bydgoszcz . . . I studied mathematics in Göttingen. I was shy. I wore thick glasses . . . I majored in statistics, because I wanted to work for an insurance company . . . In 1929 I received an offer to go as an assistant professor to the University of Poznan . . . Over sixty miles from Bydgoszcz. I found my true vocation there. I found myself there. The Polish government's Biuro Szyfrów had organized a course in cryptography, to which I was invited . . . They had chosen Poznan because it had belonged to Germany until 1918 . . . So the majority of mathematicians there spoke German. The biuro's intention was to prepare young mathematicians . . . In the intricate art of deciphering the German army's codes . . . Until that time it was assumed that the best cryptanalysts were those who worked with language. The arrival of Enigma changed everything. The biuro thought that mathematicians might do better . . . And they were right . . . At least about me.

The paramedics have given me up for dead. Like so many others on so many other occasions.

The ambulance advances and stops. Advances and stops . . . The driver has to get out and speak with those who are still blocking the streets . . . I hear bits of the negotiation. Please. Let us through . . . We've got an old man who's dying. They ask him for money . . . Sometimes they come and peer in through the rear window . . . See me lying on the stretcher. With my mouth open . . .

An electric ant that appears to be lifeless.

We continue on our way.

In order to tackle Enigma. The basis of my theory was the essential fact that the weakness of every cryptographic system is its repetitions . . . The basic repetition of Enigma was at the beginning. In the message key . . . Which consisted of three letters that were repeated twice for security purposes . . . This key determined the position of the rotating disks. Their sequence . . . The position of the rings . . . Et cetera . . . And the key was found in the armed forces cipher manual. The encoder thus indicated which key would be used. The one who received the message read the key and adjusted his machine for the signal that would come . . . So that the ciphered text was automatically deciphered.

A very simple idea came to me . . . If the first six letters of a message were the key . . . And if the key was the same group of letters repeated twice. Say, DMQAJT . . . Then the first and the fourth letters. The second and the fifth. The third and the sixth. Represented the same letters. They were just encoded using different permutations . . .

You could get a great deal of information about the first six permutations. If you received several Enigma messages each day . . . We had at our disposal at least a hundred messages a day. That's how we went about discovering the daily key . . . The signal key . . . It took us a year . . . Then the Germans' communication became clear to us. We spent the thirties struggling with Enigma's keys on a daily basis.

No one should underestimate what we did . . . No one should underestimate what I did.

We even built a machine. Called the bomba . . . Which could review all of Enigma's initial structure positions in under two hours . . . Until it found the daily key. All of this ended in December 1938 . . . When the Germans decided to make their machine more secure. And added two more rotating disks. That was enough to make decoding impossible. On September 1, 1939, Hitler invaded Poland . . . The war began. And I could do nothing. Just when I was needed most . . .

We stop again. The door opens. The light pierces my retinas . . . We've arrived at a hospital . . . The paramedics carry the stretcher. They go into the emergency room. I should tell them that this is no emergency . . . What has to happen will happen.

Maybe I'll go. Maybe I won't.

Deep down it doesn't matter . . .

Perhaps that's my punishment.

Kaufbeuren. Rosenheim. Names that come back.

The boy . . . Where was I a child? There are images of a valley. And of a boy. But I don't know whether that's my valley. Or whether I'm that boy.

I was Alan Mathison Turing. I was born in London in 1912. In 1926, I began to attend Sherborne. In Dorset. I was a shy teenager . . . Only interested in science. Until I met Christopher Morcom . . . He was also interested in science. We were friends for four years . . . Disaster struck in 1930. Christopher died of tuberculosis . . . He never knew how I felt about him. I never dared to tell him . . . He was. The only. Person. I have. Ever. Loved.

I decided to be a scientist. Christopher had won a scholarship to Cambridge . . . I wanted one as well. I wanted to do for him what he could not . . . I got the scholarship in 1931. I put a photo of him on my desk . . . And I concentrated on my studies. Four years later I got my degree . . . I went to Princeton for a few years. In 1937 I published my most important work on mathematical logic. *On Computable Numbers.* In it. I described an imaginary machine that would follow predetermined steps in order to multiply. Or add. Or subtract. Or divide. A Turing Machine for a particular function ... Then I thought of a Universal Turing Machine ... Capable of doing everything that each one of the Turing Machines could do ...

The first computers would be born from these ideas. Once there was sufficient technology.

It's no coincidence that I wanted to find the algorithms that allow our brain to function ... The logical steps by means of which thought allows itself to be thought ... The order that's hidden behind our disordered associations of ideas ...

Each one of us is. In his or her own way. A Universal Turing Machine. The world works like a Universal Turing Machine. There is an algorithm that controls all of the heartbeats in the universe ... Or perhaps it's a few lines of code ... All of the steps. From the simplest to the most complicated ... This will be proven. Once there is enough technology ... It could take years. Decades. Centuries. The only certainty is that I ... Who am bleeding in a tidy hospital room. Will be present.

In 1939 I was called by the Government Code and Cipher School to work as a cryptanalyst. Forty miles north of London. In an aristocratic mansion in Bletchley ... It was the headquarters for the government's efforts to intercept and read enemy messages ... Ten thousand people worked there. We were the inheritors of the prestigious Room 40 from World War I. During my first few months at Bletchley ... The work on Enigma ... Was based on Rejewski's discoveries ... But I had to find an alternative.

The war was quickly complicating the situation. Now Enigma consisted of eight rotating disks. And in May of 1940. The first six letters of the message disappeared ... The Germans had found another way to transmit the key. The bombes I built to tackle Enigma were much more complicated than Rejewski's bombas ... I finished the first design in early 1940. The first one arrived at Bletchley in March of that same year ... It was called Victoria ... And it was capable of scanning, quite quickly, the huge number of signals that were intercepted each day ... Searching for words that the military used frequently. Such as *Oberkommando* ... High Command ... Then the decoders went to work.

The basic idea was that Enigma ... Never encrypted a letter

using that same letter. So if the letter *o* appeared in the ciphered text . . . We were sure that the word *Oberkommando* didn't start there. These words that one assumed might exist in a message were necessary for the bombes to work . . . The bombe encoded them with the greatest possible number of options . . . If a combination of letters was discovered. Then the bombe could indicate the daily key used for that signal . . .

It was. In effect. The precursor to a computer.

In the beginning . . . It could take a week to find the key. The more advanced bombes might take less than an hour. In 1943 there were sixty bombes in operation . . . Thanks to them . . . In the first year of the war . . . England was already able to read the German army's secret messages . . . Thanks to this . . . Churchill learned of Hitler's intention to conquer England. And he prepared to defend it . . .

One of the main reasons for the Nazi defeat. Is. The defeat of Enigma early on.

There is the sound of voices in the room . . . I don't understand what they're saying about me. They've put an intravenous line in and soon the anesthesia will course through my body . . . The lights go out . . .

A blurry image comes to mind. That of Miguel Sáenz on his first day of work at the Black Chamber. Hunched over his desk.

He appeared to be so dedicated to his work. So unaffected by distractions . . . That he looked like a Universal Turing Machine . . . All logic. All input . . . All output . . . That's when I decided to call him Turing.

He always thought that the nickname was because of his talent for cryptanalysis.

The real reason was different.

chapter 39

CARLA HELPS YOU into the room. You lie down on the bed and she lies down beside you; you shelter your head between her breasts. The reddish glow of a lamp bathes you in the fading afternoon.

"I'm tired. So tired."

"I bet there's more to it than that."

"Anything I say would sound melodramatic and untrue."

You speak without looking at her, as usual. It is easier for you to speak words that veil your feelings, to express them indirectly.

"Try," she insists.

After a long silence punctuated by the sounds of cars in the street, you tell her — this time trying to get straight to the point.

"I've been living a life that's not mine."

"Come on . . . That doesn't help me understand anything."

You would like to fall asleep and wake up in another reality. At one time you had a heightened sense of reality; over the past few years it has become ordinary, and all of a sudden, in retrospect, it has become a lie. Albert, your admired boss, was a playwright filling your life with deceitful acts that had fatal consequences. All of your actions are irreversible; there is no way to bring back the victims of your talent for cryptanalysis. Oh, if only you had failed at least once. But Albert chose you because he knew you would not fail. Or perhaps the puzzles he gave you were not very difficult, were intentionally made to match your talents.

And you, who would have given your life for him. And you, who, admit it, are still capable of giving your life for him. How humiliating. How pleasantly, achingly humiliating.

You cling to Carla as if you are about to drown. Can she keep you afloat? That is asking far too much; all you have to do is stroke her arms to feel the infected wounds. With so much methadone in her system, she can't even take responsibility for herself. She has been the one clinging to you these past few months, the one who has made you, among other things, use your credit card — the numbers encrypted in each transaction, the presence of codes in the most insignificant gestures of daily life — to pay for her room at the boarding house, her debts at the El Dorado, her unsuccessful hours in rehab, and yes, don't fool yourself again, the methadone purchased behind your back. Did you really think you could pull her out of her abyss? Or is it that perhaps by being a Good Samaritan you were unconsciously atoning for the guilt that threatened to rise to the surface? Ruth was right after all. And those messages as well: your hands *are* stained with blood.

"Miguel, I can't understand what you're saying."

"I didn't say anything."

"I thought I heard you mumble something."

"Don't pay any attention to me. I must be delirious. Too much work. Too much stress."

"What the hell is wrong with you? Snap out of it. We need to talk."

"I'm listening."

"I'm all out of money, and I don't have anywhere to sleep tonight. They threw me out of the boarding house and kept my suitcase until I pay them."

Her voice is raised. No, please: you are not prepared for another angry outburst.

"I thought they were your friends."

"Even friends lose their patience."

"Didn't you have enough to get you through to the weekend?"

"You think a few pesos last an eternity. I'm tired, Miguel. We can't go on like this."

You know what she is referring to. Lulled by the pleasure of her skin, you said more than you should have. You told her that your relationship with Ruth had run its course and that only a lukewarm friendship remained of your love. You insinuated that if everything continued to go well between Carla and you, it wouldn't be hard to ask Ruth for a divorce. Oh, the things you said, the easy promises. Did you really think that there could be a future for the two of you? Was it one more of your indulgent self-deceptions? You picture yourself in a rented apartment, sitting in front of a computer reading the latest issue of *Cryptology* while Carla, sprawled on the bed, injects herself with a sharp, dirty needle, shouting at you to come help her hold the syringe steady. You feel a mixture of compassion and care for her, but not love. And admit it, you really don't enjoy the sex very much. After all that caged animal frenzy, you are left feeling empty.

"I'm not suggesting anything," she says, and you know that she is lying. "It's just that for a while now I've thought about moving to Santa Cruz. I stayed because you wanted me to stay. Now I see it's all been for nothing."

Her chest smells of one of those perfumes she is fond of, the kind that dulls your senses. Venomous plants or rotting flowers that triumph by demolishing their rival. Ruth is subtler with her perfumes, her selection of jasmine and soft almonds more refined. The sad thing is that you seem to have lost the art of understanding subtleties a long time ago. In the aseptic world of the Black Chamber, in the loneliness of the archives, you missed the smell of Carla and not Ruth.

"I don't know if it's the right time to talk about this."

"Then when? I'm warning you, if we don't make a decision, then this will be the last time we see each other."

There is a threatening tone to her voice. Only you could find yourself in a situation where a drug-addict prostitute feels she has the right to give you an ultimatum. Albert was wrong: you got here because your thoughts were incapable of thinking what they should have thought. There is no logic that imposes order on the world behind the associative paths that your thoughts take. And if there is meaning brave enough to be able to articulate the chaos of events — to cipher the uncipherable, if there is such a word — only a superior being could be at the center of that kind of conspiracy.

Carla strokes your cheeks, and you find yourself about to cry as you haven't cried since you were a child, when the world was young and your feelings were too. When had it become so hard to express yourself? Where had you acquired that shell that allowed you to escape your environment and its ambiguities? Over time you had become someone you never could have imagined when you were fifteen, when your dad would lock himself in his room with a bottle of whiskey and you would hear the muffled shouts that he never would have uttered in front of his children, the sobbing when he discovered that all those hours of work per week were not enough to support a family, and you mumbled to yourself that you wouldn't be like that, you wouldn't hide from yourself or from anyone.

You kiss Carla. There is, for a few moments, tenderness in the contact between your lips. As often happens, though, her tongue ruins everything as it thrusts into your mouth.

You close your eyes. You are exhausted, absolutely exhausted.

When you open your eyes, you are surprised by the light of day coming in through the windows. It is early morning; you fell asleep. Your bladder is about to burst. Carla stretches by your side.

"Good morning, sleepyhead. We owe a ton for this room, but I couldn't bring myself to wake you up."

"I want to go to church," you say out of nowhere, with a conviction that surprises you. Carla looks at you, confused. You head to the bathroom.

"Seriously," you continue. "I need to be alone for a few hours, but I promise I'll come back for you."

"Don't say it if you don't mean it," she says, sitting up on the bed, looking at you with bloodshot eyes.

Your mind has plotted your course as you slept next to Carla. You don't know whether you have a future with her, but you know that you don't have a future with Ruth. You will go to the chamber and hand your resignation to Ramírez-Graham. You will go to church to confess your sins, even knowing that you do not want any sort of atonement. You will go home and ask Ruth for a divorce. You will pack your bags and rent an apartment. You will take Carla to live with you. You will see if you can rebuild your life, bloodstained hands and all.

You give Carla some money to pay for her boarding house.

"I'll pay for the room on my way out," you say. "Then I'll see you here tonight at around six, seven o'clock."

You kiss her on the cheek and leave the room.

chapter 40

FLAVIA GETS OUT OF BED with sour morning breath; lines from the pillow mark her cheeks. She slept deeply for a couple of hours and had a strange dream in which she was incarnated as a digital being, logged on to Playground, and asked for asylum at an embassy—she did not want to go back to Río Fugitivo. They granted it to her, and she felt an enormous sense of relief.

She stumbles into the bathroom and looks in the mirror. It is as if a thousand veins have burst in her eyes and black circles ring them. She brushes her teeth.

As she rests her hands on the basin, out of nowhere reality comes flooding back, and all her efforts to appear strong disappear. Whom was she trying to fool?

She can't believe that Rafael is no longer here, that he is no more. He can't come back as another avatar, like when someone dies in Playground. His whole life had led up to that lackluster moment. So easy, to end a life that slips by, unconscious of itself, through the coordinates of space and time.

Flavia does not want to cry, not even a few hesitant tears. She wants someone to pay for what happened to Rafael. She is determined to return to the attack. Her work in regard to Kandinsky is not over: she has thought of a new way to get to him.

Clancy is sleeping in the kitchen. Rosa is moving quietly around the house. Outside, sparrows singing, the continuous hum of a lawn mower, a neighbor parking his car in his garage. The clouds have hidden the sun; it will rain soon. The campesinos will be happy: the drought that ruined their crops last year is over. If it has rained this much in November, what will it be like in January and February? She repeats what her dad used to say when she was little: *enero poco, febrero loco, enero loco, febrero poco.*

She pours herself a glass of orange juice, so acidic that it feels like it is cutting her tongue. A row of ants emerges from a hole near the fridge and attacks the sugar bowl. Flavia watches, lets them do what they will.

Her parents aren't home yet. Dad had left a message on the machine. He was at the Black Chamber; there were street protests, and he was going to wait until the situation calmed down. Flavia sits in front of the computer. Clancy has followed her and lies at her feet. She decides to put her plan into action. It won't be easy, but it's better than nothing.

In Playground, she logs on to the chatrooms most frequented by hackers. She discards Wolfram and creates Pestalozzi, a hacker from San Agustín who says he can't stand students from San Ignacio. She spends a few hours spreading his message of hate. Someone, she thinks, will take the bait.

By afternoon she has created Dream Weaver, a hacker from San Ignacio who argues with Pestalozzi and hurls insults at the Resistance. Flavia has to keep their conversation going, typing on two keyboards at once. It is no easy feat, but it isn't the first time she has done this. By the time evening falls, a few others have joined the conversation, but all left quickly. The subject does not seem to ignite the necessary intensity of emotions for a heated discussion.

She is about to take a break — her efforts have made her hands ache — when someone joins the chat, attacking Dream Weaver and defending Pestalozzi. He calls himself NSA2002. While keeping up a three-way conversation, Flavia tries to trace NSA's steps on one of her computers. Where did he log on to the Internet?

The answer surprises her: NSA2002 accessed the Net through a computer at the Black Chamber. It is possible that NSA2002 is telnetting from another computer and using the Black Chamber to confuse any possible pursuers. Still, it seems like too much of a coincidence that the computer being used is located there. And anyhow, what sense is there in telnetting for an innocuous chat about loving or hating San Ignacio?

The truth seems irrefutable to Flavia: NSA2002 is Kandinsky, the legendary hero of the Resistance, the man behind Rafael's death. Kandinsky works at the Black Chamber.

chapter 41

RUTH WALKS BEHIND the police officer. They go up a set of cement stairs so steep that she has to make an effort not to lose her balance. The hallways smell of urine. On one of the landings, a little shadow crosses swiftly between Ruth's feet; she imagines it must be a mouse.

"You're lucky," the officer says all of a sudden.

"Why? I haven't done anything wrong."

"Either everyone has done something wrong or no one has done anything wrong. And I think you've all done something wrong. But some are someone and the majority are no one."

"Are we playing some sort of guessing game?"

"Just shut up and follow me."

The police officer sneezes. Ruth follows him in silence. She repeats to herself, *Eulalia Vázquez, Eulalia Vázquez.* She has already forgotten the other woman's name. She can hear the rain drumming against the walls and on the roof. It will be good for her carnations in the garden.

The officer leads her into the office of the police chief, a fat, sweaty man around fifty years old. He is sitting behind a mahogany desk, talking on a silver Samsung. Behind him are the national coat of arms and a photo of President Montenegro; to his right, a poster of the River Boys soccer team and another of Jet Li. There are loose tiles on the floor, and flies are crawling on the windows and all over some folders lying on a low table.

"Good afternoon, good afternoon," he says, hanging up his

Samsung and standing. "We have just been advised that we have among us the wife of a respectable government civil servant. How can this be?"

"That's what I'd like—"

"It's just an expression, no need to answer. We know what happened. A mistake."

"Quite a mistake, I'd say. I've been here for over a day."

"I'm sure you understand that we are in a state of emergency and have to take cautionary, or precautionary, measures rather than regret our inaction. Although sometimes we do end up regretting our actions. It's complicated. In any event, I'm sure you understand. And if you don't, well, we still have no way of undoing this. Undoing what we wanted to do, that is. Perhaps we have made a mistake by preventing a mistake. Right. We offer our apology and will make sure that you are freed immediately."

"I suppose I must thank you, Mr. . . ."

"Felipe Cuevas, at your service."

"I would also like you to return what you confiscated from me."

"Ah, now that is another kettle of fish. Or rather, our kettle of fish. And exactly what we wanted to speak to you about. They tell us there has been a mistake—your manuscript was incinerated. I've been asked to extend our sincere apologies."

Ruth thought they would say something like that. There was no way the manuscript would be returned to her intact. It would be sent to the Black Chamber for analysis. There they would discover that it was a catalogue of all the political crimes that had been committed in the country thanks to the efficiency of the cryptanalysts at the Black Chamber.

She puts her hands together, raises her right index finger to her mouth, and bites on the nail until it breaks. *Vázquez, Vázquez.* What was her first name? She no longer remembers.

"Leaving without my manuscript," she says, practically shouting, "is the same as being made to stay. In fact, it would be better for me to stay locked up."

"You simply cannot stay. We need all the space we have. There have been many arrests—today has been absolute chaos. Worse than yesterday. Which was absolute chaos. Which makes today chaos squared. Or cubed. In any event, much worse than yesterday. And the word *chaos* doesn't even do justice to what has gone on out there."

Ruth remains quiet for a long while. She listens to the incessant pounding of the wind and rain on the windows.

"No," she says at last. "Nononononononono."

"That's what I thought. Captain, have her sign the papers and accompany her to the door."

Ruth's gaze scours the peeling walls, the cracked tiles on the floor, the cobwebbed ceiling. A fly lands on her hand; she lets it walk along her forearm. Then she turns and follows the captain. She mechanically does what the police tell her to do. She signs what she has to sign, walks down some narrow hallways, and arrives at the street. The captain hands her her purse and her cell phone, then turns back into the building without a word.

She walks barefoot, the breeze caressing her body. The sun has been obliterated by the lead-colored clouds; the rain has turned to drizzle.

The first thing she will do when she gets home is call the clinic and get her test results. Then she will wait for Miguel to come home. She needs to have a long talk with him. Or perhaps it will be short — perhaps there is no need for words.

Only then will she try to reach Judge Cardona. She doesn't know what she will say to him. Her steps gain confidence. Truthfully, she doesn't know what she will do when she gets home.

chapter 42

Ramírez-Graham is in the kitchen of his apartment preparing a sandwich when his cell phone rings. It is Flavia, her voice anxious. She tells him that Kandinsky is operating from inside the Black Chamber.

One of my guys? Is that possible? Yes, indeed. The suspect could be Ramírez-Graham himself. Why not? At the NSA they had taught him that you should be suspicious even of yourself.

"Are you sure this isn't a mistake?"

"There's always the chance, but I guess you asked me for my help for a reason, right? If we hurry, there might be time to catch him. I'm going to try to keep him chatting. There's a chance he might be telnetting, but, well, there's no harm in trying."

"Again, are you sure? I don't want to call the police if it's a false alarm."

"It'll be a false alarm if we keep talking. And no, I'm not sure of anything. I did what you asked me to, now you take care of the rest. Anyhow, a false alarm wouldn't be the end of the world. Just hurry."

Ramírez-Graham hangs up and calls Inspector Moreiras. He asks him to cordon off the Black Chamber and not let anyone leave.

"It's been a difficult day, and I don't think it's over yet. Do you realize what you're asking me?"

"It's important. Just do what I say, please. I'll explain it all later."

Moreiras mutters something and hangs up. Ramírez-Graham finishes making his fried egg sandwich. He arrived back at his apartment just half an hour ago; the protests in the plaza had spread throughout the Enclave, and he had not been able to leave the chamber until the police had cleared the neighboring streets. He only hoped that everything was coming to an end. He no longer cared that a teenager had given him the key to solving the problem. All he wanted now was to catch Kandinsky and go back to Georgetown.

Outside, he inhales the fresh air after the rain. He realizes that he might soon be taking part in a scene from a movie that he probably saw: the criminal trapped on one floor of a building while the chief of police shouts orders on his walkie-talkie and climbs the stairs with determination — or maybe takes the elevator — to the floor where the final confrontation will take place. He is finally about to see Kandinsky's face, if that Flavia is right. Yeah, right.

He speaks with Moreiras and Flavia again from his car. Moreiras tells him that the Black Chamber has been cordoned off and that they will see him there soon.

"We've asked everyone to come down to the Vigenère Room. Only one person hasn't — he's locked up in one of the offices on the top floor."

The Central Committee offices are there . . . Someone from his inner circle? Santana? Baez? Ivanovic? Could he have been duped that badly?

Flavia tells him that Kandinsky is still in the chatroom.

"Keep him there for fifteen more minutes," Ramírez-Graham asks.

"Something's bothering me, I don't know . . . The problem wasn't easy, but the solution was. Too easy."

"Some of the worst criminals make the stupidest mistakes."

"Still, it's a bit of a letdown."

The streets around the Black Chamber are darker than usual, as if the owners of the houses and buildings in the area are avoiding unnecessary electricity expenses or as if a sudden blackout by GlobaLux has plunged them into a night that is exceptionally dark. A group of soldiers is climbing a lookout. Ramírez-Graham hears on the radio that the government has reached an agreement with the Coalition and has ordered that the city be demilitarized.

Even with all the darkness, no house or building nearby matches the Black Chamber's ability to blend perfectly into the night, as if a black hole were located at its very apex and swallowing it whole. Ramírez-Graham enters the building and is blinded by the vibrant lights inside. Moreiras and three police officers are waiting for him underneath the Black Chamber's emblem, the man bent over a desk and the condor holding a ribbon in its claws bearing a motto in Morse code.

"My men are taking statements from everyone, except whoever stayed up on the top floor."

"Anyone in particular missing?"

"Several people. Some had already gone home by the time you called, so we don't know who's upstairs. Shall we go up? You know each floor, the layout of the rooms. We won't use the elevator, it's too risky."

Moreiras is husky and has a double chin, but there is something sweet about his face, a beatific expression that does not suit his position. Or perhaps, Ramírez-Graham thinks, it's because he looks so innocent that he can make the decisions he has to make.

"Does he know we're here?"

The man leaning over the desk in the Black Chamber's emblem reminds Ramírez-Graham of Miguel Sáenz. He had seen him that afternoon, when Sáenz came to his office to tender his resignation. Ramírez-Graham had accepted it; he had called him Turing for the first time when they said goodbye. He had patted him on the back, joked around with him, and walked him to the elevator. Turing had not been able to leave the building because of the disturbances; they had seen him wandering through the hallways, carrying a box with his personal effects. He would stop in front of a wall or a window and stand staring at it as if he were reading some secret message.

"He certainly does," Moreiras says. "Power to the top floor has been cut off. I have my men guarding the exits, but they can't do much in the dark."

"That can be fixed. We have a generator for emergencies. I'll have someone turn it on."

Ramírez-Graham is afraid of reaching the top floor only to be shot. He does not want any more twists of fate; he hopes to have the opportunity to see Svetlana again, to tell her how much he has missed her and to beg her forgiveness for having been so wrong. Even if his words and his gestures are received with indifference, he wants a chance to do what he has to do, even just once.

They go up the harshly lit stairs, yellow bulbs glaring down at them. Ramírez-Graham walks behind everyone else. He would have preferred to stay on the first floor and let those from SIN take care of this, but he is the head of the Black Chamber and has to set an example. And he wants to see the traitor's face. Can it really be someone from his inner circle?

They reach the top floor. The lights have been turned on. Moreiras asks the officers if they're ready. They reply with a slight nod, as if they aren't sure of their affirmation, as if they know that the question was rhetorical and that the truth is not required from them, just a rhetorical answer.

Moreiras kicks open the door and dives behind a desk on the right. The other officers follow him into the hallway; one joins Moreiras, the other two go to the left. *So this is it,* Ramírez-Graham tells himself. *The real thing.* He's not imagining it. And yet it still feels unreal. Better yet, it isn't unfolding as it does in the movies. Of course, if he were to get shot in the shoulder, he might change his opinion. Reality hurts.

A few minutes pass in silence. Moreiras shouts for whoever is there to surrender. No one replies.

He shouts again. There is only silence. He walks down the hallway, holding his gun in both hands, turning his body left and right. The officers follow him. Ramírez-Graham has not gone more than twenty yards when there is the sound of breaking glass and the thunder of shots being fired. He throws himself back into the stairwell, not knowing where the shots came from. When he gets up, he looks in from the doorway and sees a commotion in the hallway. Moreiras is lying on the floor, his face spattered with blood. One of the officers is trying to revive him while the other covers him and the third moves forward, firing his gun.

Suddenly Ramírez-Graham hears a scream, and another body collapses. He can't see who it is from where he is standing. The officer tells him that it is whoever shot Moreiras. Ramírez-Graham stands up and leaps into the hallway. The officer who was trying to revive Moreiras looks at him, helpless. "He's not breathing!" he exclaims, throwing himself over Moreiras's body again.

The officer who fired his gun signals the all-clear with his hand. Ramírez-Graham approaches, and together they move toward the body lying at the end of the hallway.

Ramírez-Graham does not need to see him to know that Kandinsky is Baez, that Baez is Kandinsky. Ramírez-Graham has come to the end of his career in Río Fugitivo.

Only now does he suspect that Flavia was right: the ending is a letdown. His only thought is that it had been easy to catch Kandinsky because Kandinsky had wanted to be caught.

chapter 43

JUDGE CARDONA WATCHES the guards in the metal booth at the entrance to the gated community, silhouetted behind the glass—glass that may be bulletproof. What was that line he liked? From that novel, in school. *I bet my heart on chance and I lost it to violence.* Something like that. It doesn't matter how it really goes; what matters is how it stays in our minds, how certain biological processes are able to shape our memories out of the ruins of reality. One of the guards is reading the paper; he lifts his head, and Cardona can see that he is cross-eyed. The other is watching the news on television. Cardona knows the routine: they will ask him for his ID card and will call the house to confirm that he is expected. There is no way to get past them. The best thing to do is to turn around and have a seat at the bus stop a few blocks away. There, in the humid breeze after all the rain, he will smoke a cigarette and the memory of his cousin will visit him, or perhaps his phantasmagoric ups and downs at the Presidential Palace.

There is no one on the bench at the bus stop. He sits down, resting his briefcase on his knees, and is suddenly overcome by exhaustion. The stitches above his right eye throb, and his legs feel heavy. He can no longer stand his wet shirt and pants, the squelching of his leather shoes. He touches the wine-colored spots on his cheeks. Have they grown? They are unpredictable but never fail in situations of nervous tension: little islands that are capable of growing into enormous archipelagos. He is desperate for Bolivian marching powder. Mirtha would not be proud of him. No one is, not even himself. It is his redemption, his dissolute mortal burden, his irrefutable error, his inherent corruption. He believed he was doing all of this just so that he would be able to look at himself in the mirror again. Now he knows that there's no way out, that nothing can save him, no matter whom he shoots. And yet he still shoots, already beyond himself, because if he has to choose between doing it and not doing it, it's just better to do it. He should lock himself up in an abandoned monastery; it would be better that way. He thinks he can hear the blood flowing in his veins. What sound does blood make as it circulates inside you? Is it like a rushing torrent of water? Or a quiet stream on a calm afternoon? On the surface he appears to be a stream, but deep down he's really more like the explosive rumble of a flood.

Sitting on the bench in the bus shelter, he momentarily convinces himself that the best thing would be to turn himself in to the guards, to confess what he has done. He realizes that in prison the memories, the words, would still be with him, lurking day and night, not letting him rest. It wouldn't work.

The bench is dilapidated; there is graffiti on the walls, cans and bottles are scattered on the floor. Cardona regrets the albino guard's death, not Albert's. Now that he is a criminal like Albert and Turing, what would he do with Turing?

He opens the briefcase and toys with the gun. Maybe he decided a long time ago that he could not live with himself anymore and that the only way to repent would be through his own sacrifice.

Yes, that's the word, sacrifice. But he would never be able to do it himself, just as he could not kill Montenegro with his own hands. Others had to die, and in the process, hopefully, mercifully, somebody would put a bullet in his brain. That's what the guards at Turing's community are for. Maybe they would be able to do their job better than the albino had done.

Cardona doesn't want to take chances. He opens the briefcase and removes the silencer from his gun.

He cannot sit still and heads to the guard booth. He has no idea what he will say, but something will come to him. The cross-eyed guard sees him approach and slides open the window; the other is still absorbed by the television.

"Good evening, how can I help you?"

"I'm looking for Ruth Sáenz. I'm Judge Gustavo Cardona. I have an interview with her."

"Can I see your identification?" The judge opens his wallet and hands over his ID card. The guard looks at the photo and then studies Cardona.

"You look familiar."

"I was minister of justice a few years ago."

"In the previous government?"

"In this one. I wasn't there for long. Not even a year. You know how things are, we're in and out like a revolving door."

"Sorry, I don't have the best memory for that sort of thing. I haven't seen Mrs. Sáenz since yesterday. It's been a couple of chaotic days, what with the blockades. But it looks like they've finally reached an agreement."

"You're telling me. These stitches are because of the damn blockades. When will we learn? As if the government ever listens to the people. And her husband?"

"Miguel Sáenz? I haven't seen him since yesterday either. He usually gets home around seven—we'll see what happens today. It's already seven, isn't it? Anyhow, I'll call. Have you heard the latest news? Some ministers have arrived to meet with GlobaLux. Looks like they're going to rescind their contract."

The guard lifts up the receiver and dials a number. Cardona looks left and right, shifts his feet, tries to conceal his nervousness. He concentrates on the images on the TV. A reporter is interviewing a group of young people near the main plaza. What do you think of the prefect's resignation? The storming of GlobaLux's installations? The decision by GlobaLux executives to leave the country and demand millions in compensation from the government? Their answers speak of how the people, led by the Coalition, have triumphed. So naive. Two days spent destroying the city, more than ten people dead. One step forward, twenty steps back. The people haven't won a thing; the people are still without electricity. But it is true that Montenegro is more fragile than ever and a mere puff could knock him down. It is simply a question of whether or not the vice president will do it. He won't; no one will. Misunderstood loyalty will result in Montenegro's finishing his term. And meanwhile the recession will deepen and the country will sink even further.

"Their daughter says to go ahead," the guard says. "Her parents aren't home, but she says you can wait for them there."

The guard lets him pass. Cardona nods his thanks, then stops.

"Do you need to check my briefcase?"

"No, that's OK. Second block, fourth house on the right."

Judge Cardona walks down the cobblestoned main street. The houses on his left and right are all the same, from the shape of the chimney on the roof to the brick walls and the winding driveway leading to the garage. The only details that change are the state of the plants in the garden and whether the gleam in the second-floor windows is yellow or blue. He trembles at the thought of going to the wrong house and being mistaken for a burglar. Second block. First, second, third, fourth . . . He stops and rings the bell. Ruth's daughter opens the door and lets him in. She is barefoot, wearing a gray sweatsuit with a yellow Berkeley logo. Who does she think she is with those dreadlocks, Bob Marley's daughter? She seems to be in a rush.

"Hi. Come on in. I have no idea where my mom is. My dad called and said he'd be a bit late. Make yourself at home. If you're thirsty, there's beer or lemonade in the fridge. Now, if you'll excuse me, I have to get back to my room."

"You're in an awful hurry," Cardona says. "What's so important, if I might ask?"

"Sorry, but you wouldn't believe me if I told you."

"Try me."

"It's secret."

"I promise I won't say a word. I'll never tell. None of us will."

Flavia rolls her eyes as if considering it, a proud look spreading across her face. *Just a kid,* Cardona says to himself. *Incapable of holding back. Dying to talk.* How disappointing. No one is ever any different from the stereotype. But Flavia turns around and goes up the stairs two at a time. Cardona is left alone, wondering whether the conversation he just had was real. He heads into the kitchen, opens the fridge, and gets himself a Paceña beer. It tastes bitter. He finishes it off and gets another. He sits down at the table, taking in the domesticity that surrounds him: bottles of spices lined up along the wall — garlic powder, oregano, cumin, mint — a can of olive oil, coffee stains on the tile floor, a cracked glass beside the blender. Turing, the same man who was capable of performing his work with such cold efficiency and who was responsible for countless deaths, also ate breakfast here, poured himself a cup of hot coffee, shook salt on his scrambled eggs on Sunday mornings. Oh, if only Cardona were capable of compassion: this would be the ideal moment to be overcome by it. He wonders who will get home first. He takes his gun out of his briefcase and puts it in the right-hand pocket of his jacket. He watches the slow tick of the clock that is hanging on the wall.

Less than half an hour later the front door opens and Miguel Sáenz hesitantly enters his own home. From the kitchen, Cardona observes someone who is uncomfortable wherever he might be. The thick-rimmed glasses, the wrinkled jacket, the black leather shoes: Cardona is in no position to judge the outward appearance of anyone right now, but he is still surprised by the pathetic, defeated air around Sáenz. Could *this* be the person who was indirectly responsible for the death of his cousin and so many others? He had been expecting someone more sure of himself, someone whose talent was obvious at first glance. Cardona stands up from the table and leans against the door frame that separates the kitchen from the front hall. Sáenz lifts his eyes and sees him there.

"Who . . . who are you?"

"I'm Judge Gustavo Cardona. Good evening, Turing."

"Ah, yes. You used to be a minister, right? What are you doing here? Who let you in?"

"Your daughter."

"Is she all right?"
"She's fine."
"Are you waiting for my wife?"
"I'm waiting for you. Just you."
"Is it important?"
"You have no idea how important."

chapter 44

IN THE END, you did not go home or to a church. Something, perhaps the force of habit, made you go to the Black Chamber. You went to tender your resignation, you told yourself, and yet you knew that it was just an excuse. You wanted to say goodbye to the building where you had spent half your life. You were forced to leave your car two blocks away; the blockade prevented you from driving any farther, and you were not prepared for confrontations. The protesters let you through on foot, but not before you paid a few pesos. You were surprised there were no soldiers; perhaps the main demonstrations were in the plaza and on the bridges, and there weren't enough troops to be on every corner. Even so, there was no excuse for the lack of protection near a place that was so strategic to national security. You should look for news on your cell phone, find out what was happening.

A wave of melancholy washes over you as you enter the Otis elevator that you have ridden in so often before. This is how everything ends: not with a bang but a pitiful sob. You go down to the ends of the earth, to the land of the dead. You are heading to the archives; you are already part of the archives.

You clean out your desk, putting all of your personal effects and papers into a cardboard box. You erase files from the computer, organize your e-mail. You walk through the aisles of the archives to say goodbye. On which shelf will they put your file? Or will they get rid of this entire floor, and all that you were, all that you did, will become nothing more than a few bits in the memory of some computer? It is your fate: code you were and code you will become.

You urinate a few drops in a corner of the room, no longer wanting to use the cup with Road Runner on it. Will they be filming you? It doesn't matter anymore.

You hand your resignation to Ramírez-Graham and think you can detect emotion in his voice. Perhaps he's not such a bad person after all. Perhaps his only problem is that Albert's job is too big for him.

The police do not allow you to leave. The captain tells you that all personnel have been ordered to stay in the building until further notice. The situation, which the military seemed to have under control on Thursday night, has worsened again. There are riots in the main plaza.

The news doesn't bother you. It is raining out and better to stay indoors until it passes. You trust that the authorities will impose order. Meanwhile, you have more time to say goodbye.

Your procession through the building, going to each room, saying goodbye to those walls that had witnessed so many historic moments and to those who worked there, took time. You knew that you were not leaving entirely. Something of your spirit would remain here.

The puddles in the streets are lit up by faint, intermittent sodium light bulbs. When you left the chamber, there was no light in the neighboring streets. You left your car where it was parked and walked for ten blocks before there was any electricity. You count the bulbs as you go, trying to see if their intervals might result in a coherent message in Morse code; you must always pay attention. The world speaks without ceasing, and it is your duty to listen and try to understand it. Now and then it even makes sense. Much more often the world vomits up delirious signals, phrases that lead nowhere, images without context.

Your cell phone rings. It is a video message from Santana announcing an emergency at the Black Chamber. He asks everyone in the building not to resist the SIN agents, to cooperate and convene in the Vigenère Room. You have no idea what could be happening—you left the building only forty-five minutes ago. You try to forget about it, reminding yourself that you no longer work there.

You discover a message from Ruth that you haven't noticed before: she needs to speak to you, it's urgent. There had been an emergency; she had spent last night and all day today in jail. They had let her out a while ago; she was wandering through the city and would be home late. You think, *Flavia spent the whole night alone.* You hope nothing has happened to her.

You call Ruth. Poor thing, she will be so surprised when you tell her that you are leaving. When you tell her you want to separate, even ask for a divorce. You promised Carla that you would ask for a divorce. But perhaps it would be best to separate for a few months, see how things go with Carla, and only then think about something as definitive as divorce. You have to admit that so many things tie you to Ruth. The years add up.

As soon as you hear her voice, you realize that certain things need to be said in person. You tell her that you are sorry about what happened to her and that you will be home soon. She tells you she is not there yet. You tell her that you resigned from the Black Chamber. Surprised, she asks you for details. Later, later.

"Actually," you say, "I want to ask you a favor. Since you know all about history, what do the cities Kaufbeuren and Rosenheim mean to you?"

"One of the Germans' most important intelligence centers was in Kaufbeuren during World War II. And Rosenheim . . . I'm pretty sure that was one of the cities where the Allies held German intelligence service prisoners, including several cryptanalysts. Why?"

Ah, Ruth, who has answers for everything: you will miss her. Bit by bit you are putting Albert's history together.

"Just one more question. Does Wettenhein mean anything to you?"

"Spell it for me."

You do.

"Erich Huettenhain," she says almost immediately. "With an *h* and two *t*'s. A lot of Nazi cryptanalysts were given new identities and offered work with the American and British governments. Huettenhain was one of them — one of the most important. He was involved in every single one of the Nazis' cryptanalytic successes. He was taken to the United States in secret and worked for the Americans during the cold war."

A war criminal working for the government . . . The Americans certainly were pragmatic. Could it be that . . . ?

"Do you think . . . that Albert could be Huettenhain?"

"He's not the right age. Could be his son. Oh, and you could have at least asked me how I am."

Ruth hangs up. You imagine a story. The story of Albert, a young Nazi cryptanalyst who operated out of Kaufbeuren and who, when the Allies arrived, was transferred to a detention center in Rosenheim. A brilliant cryptanalyst who had a mentor named Huettenhain. When Huettenhain was offered freedom in exchange for a new identity and collaboration with the American government, he accepted and asked that young Albert be offered the same deal. Albert was given a new identity; he made a career at the CIA during the cold war and was sent to Bolivia in the seventies. When he met you, he saw the possibility of duplicating the relationship he had had with Huettenhain . . .

So both rumors were true. Albert was a Nazi, but not a fugitive, and Albert was a CIA agent. Maybe it was no coincidence that when he was delirious, when he assumed the identities of the most important cryptographers and cryptanalysts of the century, he never mentioned anyone who worked between 1945 and 1974, the years that marked his clandestine entry into the United States and his arrival in Bolivia, the years when he worked for the CIA. Perhaps the German Albert, in order to do what he had to for the United States — an enemy country, after all — had to erase his life before 1945. But now that he was delirious and dying, what he obscured was his years of treason against the motherland. The Black Chamber had liberated him from his American fate.

It was possible. You will never know the whole story. But it is enough for you to feel like part of that great cryptanalytic continuum that went from Huettenhain to Albert and from Albert to you.

One of your neighbors pulls up in his Jeep, offering you a ride home. On the way you talk about how the government had failed to solve a trivial conflict in time and let it get out of control.

"I'm not so worried about the blockades," your neighbor says. "We're used to those—we don't even pay attention to them anymore. You know what worries me? The computer viruses, the Web site attacks. That never used to happen here, but now it has and we have to take it seriously. I work at the airport, and we're completely vulnerable to an attack of that nature. A virus would paralyze us just like that, in the blink of an eye."

"There's only a few people in the Resistance," you reply without looking at him. "And we still haven't reached a level of technology where cybercrime will be a problem."

You are minimizing the truth. The Resistance has made life impossible for the Black Chamber. And the attacks have been not only general but also individual. With the messages they sent to your secret e-mail address—because you are sure of it, it was the Resistance—they had achieved something that Ruth had tried in vain for years to do: make you feel guilty.

You are trying hard to rationalize your guilt. At times your thoughts go where you want them to, but deep down they continue on their merry way. You want to program your thoughts, but they program you.

"Still," your neighbor says, "as interconnected as computers are, there only needs to be a few of them. It's going to be a big problem. The government doesn't have the money to do what it should—create a special unit for these kinds of crimes."

Should you tell him about the Black Chamber?

"And the private sector," he continues, "as always, fine, thanks. I think this is just a taste and the serious stuff will come later, in a few years."

"It's not our nature to plan," you say, unwilling to continue this conversation. "We respond to things as they happen, on the fly."

You both drive on in silence.

You search for news on your cell phone. Lana Nova, her cheekbones glowing, announces that police repression has resulted in eleven deaths in Río Fugitivo, two in La Paz, and one in Chapare.

Three police officers have also been killed. The government, besieged on various fronts, has decided to give in to the Coalition's demands and promised to meet soon with the police that are on strike in La Paz, the coca growers in Chapare, the Aymaras in the provinces around Lake Titicaca, and businessmen in Santa Cruz. Montenegro has decided to survive his last few months by simply pushing the problems forward, so that the government that will assume power next August will be left holding the bag. The elections are in seven months; presidential campaigns will start in January, and already people like the leader of the coca growers and the photogenic but stupid ex-mayor of Cochabamba are declaring themselves as candidates. You cannot fathom Montenegro's weakness. If he does not impose his authority — and he knows this better than anyone — chaos and anarchy will reign, and any group of people willing to take its protests to the streets will feel that it has enough power to put the government into checkmate. In fact, they are already doing just that. You don't know much about politics and don't want to get into an analysis of the many sides of the conflict. What you do know is that the country has become what it is, has deteriorated, because of a shocking lack of respect for the principle of authority.

You turn off your Ericsson. Your last thought surprised you with the power of an epiphany. Deep down, if it was your job to decipher the secret codes of those in opposition to the government again, you would try to do it as you always had, efficiently, without regard for the consequences. Cause and effect are inextricably linked, trapping both the innocent and the guilty in their web. Everyone would be paralyzed if they dwelled on the ultimate reverberations of their actions. You could only be the best you could be at whatever you had been brought into this world to do. If Albert had used you, had he laughed at your good faith? That's not your problem; it's Albert's. You did what you had been entrusted to do; it wasn't your responsibility to know whether or not you were being deceived.

Your desire to visit a church was nothing more than a passing weakness. No repentance is possible. How many men, throughout the centuries, had naively worked in the service of despicable governments? Did that mean that their innocence was tarnished? Yes, perhaps, but it wasn't their fault. Otherwise, you would have to believe that history is a game for obedient children. That only those who worked for kind, impartial, and therefore utopian governments were saved. *Murderer, your hands are stained with blood* . . . Yes, they are, you have to admit it. Just like the hands of most everyone in the country during that decade, accomplices by their acts or omissions. You are sorry for the unjust deaths that resulted from the efficiency of your work. Very sorry. But beyond assuming responsibility for your actions, there is nothing you can do.

The car stops at the entrance to the gated community; one of the guards lifts up the yellow barrier. Your neighbor drops you off at your house.

In the hall you come upon a stranger. He is tall and robust, has spots on his cheeks, and it looks like he got caught in the rain. What is he doing in your house?

"Who . . . who are you?"

"I'm Judge Gustavo Cardona. Good evening, Turing."

"Ah, yes. You used to be a minister, right? What are you doing here? Who let you in?"

"Your daughter."

"Is she all right?"

"She's fine."

"Are you waiting for my wife?"

"I'm waiting for you. Just you."

"Is it important?"

"You have no idea how important."

"I'm not in the mood to play games. Tell me right now, before I call the police."

"I am the cousin of a woman who was murdered in 1976. She died thanks to the work that you and your boss, Albert, did."

"You're the one who's been sending those messages."

"I never sent any messages. I decided that someone had to stop the impunity. Other judges have taken care of the paramilitary, those who pulled the trigger. Some other ambitious judge will take care of Montenegro one day. And I will take care of the two of you."

"You're delirious."

"We all are. It's just that some people's delirium is less offensive than others.'"

Cardona pulls out his gun and shoots. A blow to the stomach leaves you breathless; blood splatters on your glasses, which fall to the floor and shatter. You grab hold of your stomach and collapse. Lying on the floor, you can just make out a shadow holding on to the handrail on the second floor. The shadow screams. It is your daughter, Flavia. Seconds later other shadows burst in through the door. You hear shots.

A guard kneels beside you, asks how you feel.

"The ambulance will be here soon — you'll be fine."

"Is he . . . dead?"

"Yes, he is."

You believe, because you do not know how to do anything but think, because thought only disconnects when you die, that everything makes sense now. Now you understand that your destiny was to attempt to decipher the codes that would lead you to discover the Code. It was not your destiny to decipher it but to search for how to decipher it. Your small victories were nothing compared with the opacity of the universe. But in that opacity you think you can detect the patient work of a higher being, someone who is beyond all the codes and can explain them. It even explains you, who are also code, as is the man who just shot you, and little Flavia, and Ruth, and Albert. You are all united in loss, codes in search of other codes in the labyrinth you inhabited for a few melancholy years.

Your last thought is that you have ceased to think, that in reality you never thought, you were always delirious, that the stranger was right, we're all delirious, you are a delirium, thought is a form of delirium, it's just that some deliriums are less offensive than others.

You wish that your delirium had been inoffensive. You know that it was not, and accept that. You are at peace, and close your eyes.

Epilogue

THERE IS A KNOCK at the door. Kandinsky does not know whether to open it. He has not been out of his apartment for several days. The police wouldn't knock so politely, he tells himself, and he asks who it is.

"Baez."

The response surprises him. Is this some kind of a trick?

"I don't know anyone by that name."

"You know who I am. Trust me. I've got nothing to do with the police."

Kandinsky timidly opens the door to discover a young man with a nervous gaze wearing a brown shirt hanging over the top of his jeans. He lets him in. Baez stops in the middle of the empty room.

"So you're . . ."

"So you're . . ."

They embrace cautiously. Despite the fact that they are the only survivors of the Resistance, Kandinsky finds the physical contact strange. It's new—he is used to talking with Baez's avatar in chatrooms or Playground. He doesn't know what to say, nor does he understand what is happening. He waits for Baez to speak.

"I didn't picture your apartment like this. I don't know. Just not so empty, so minimalist. Messier. The walls covered in posters."

"Of hackers I admire? There are none."

"Revolutionary emblems, something along those lines."

"The walls covered in graffiti? I don't need any of that here."

Baez walks over to the corner where the computer is. He touches the keyboard.

"I can't believe I'm in the presence of the great Kandinsky."

"How did you find me?"

"Easy. Anyone can, and someone else soon will. I knew the name of your avatar as head of the Restoration in Playground. Remember, I used to work for the company in charge of Playground before I went to the Black Chamber. I was responsible for the private files that contain the real identities of all the players. We were under strict orders not to reveal them, not even to our families. If we did, we'd be fired."

Kandinsky feels stabs of pain and clasps his hands.

"Do they hurt? You'd better take care of yourself—we need you. As I was saying, sometimes I would pass names to a friend of mine who's a Rat. I discovered a flaw in the system, a way that I could gain access from the outside without anyone's suspecting me. When I quit, I would still hack into the system to get a name or two and earn a few pesos when the Rat sold them. I went in to find out who was behind BoVe a long time ago. I found out where you lived but decided to keep it a mystery. I would come see you only when I had to. It was easy for me because I knew what I was looking for, but I guess someone in the police will think of it and put two and two together at some point."

Kandinsky gives a hint of a smile. He had been right to see Baez's potential as a meticulous hacker. The corporation in charge of Playground, a favorite target of hackers, has a nearly impenetrable security system that has managed to stop the majority of those who try to get past it.

"So why did you want to talk to me, if I might ask?"

"Because Ramírez-Graham, my boss at the Black Chamber, is after the Resistance, and he's getting closer and closer to finding you. He's being helped by that girl from AllHacker."

"She's just a stupid little girl. We shouldn't be afraid of her."

"I have a lot of respect for her. She knows all about us. And she's lethally efficient. Thanks to her, hackers have fallen in the past. Well-known hackers."

"You're talking about a woman."

"Indeed. They say there are no good women hackers. But there are exceptions to the rule, and she's one of them."

"Was it thanks to her that your boss had the other members of the Resistance killed?"

"No. I took care of that."

Kandinsky waits for some indication from Baez that he is joking, but is surprised by his seriousness.

"My boss . . . Ramírez-Graham was going to get to them sooner or later," Baez says. "He has excellent people around him. And they, under pressure, would have wound up talking. So I hired someone through my friend the Rat to take care of them. The last one, Rafael Corso, was eliminated just minutes after he met with Flavia. I don't know if he told her everything or not — I have no idea how much she knows. But extreme situations require extreme measures on our part. They had to be sacrificed for the greater good. And I'm willing to sacrifice myself for the cause — ours, the Restoration's, the Resistance's."

There is a fanaticism in Baez's voice that Kandinsky never expected to hear. Yes, he knew that Baez was one of the most dedicated activists, dating back to the anarchist neighborhood in Playground; he had been right to include him in the Resistance. But something about Baez scares him: his decision, perhaps, to see people as expendable cogs in the wheel. Baez said he was responsible for the deaths of three fellow hackers. There was no remorse; it was as if he were just another of those disturbed kids who spend hours in front of a monitor, so absorbed in Playground that in the end they can't distinguish between virtual deaths inside and real deaths outside it. That had never happened to Kandinsky; he was very clear about the separation between the two worlds. That one was more absurd and mundane than the other was another matter. With all of its defects and injustices, the real world was the objective of Kandinsky's struggle.

"You had them killed? Our comrades? Just like that?"

"It wasn't an easy decision to make. But I have a plan, and once you hear it, you'll agree that it was the best way to save the group. Are you OK?"

Kandinsky lets his arms fall limply by his sides. He can no longer feel his hands; it is as if they are asleep. Just his left hand used to be affected, so he had started typing only with his right. Now it is also in pain.

"Go on, go on. Don't worry about me."

"I was no one before I met you. I wasted my days going to and from work, with no direction. Working for the company in charge of Playground was a revelation. There I felt like I was using my talent for the enemy. I realized that a good job wasn't enough — I had to find a cause I could believe in passionately, one I could live for. And die for."

Baez paces as he talks, waving his arms, looking at Kandinsky with fervor in his eyes. Kandinsky is used to dominating situations and does not know how to take back the initiative.

"Then I found you and I found direction," Baez continues. "It all made sense all of a sudden. You taught me so much. With so many followers, you chose me. Even now, I can't believe I'm standing in front of you. You chose me, and I want to pay you back for what you did for me. I want you to let me be Kandinsky."

"You want to be me?"

"I'll assume your identity in Playground in order to confuse Flavia. My boss . . . Ramírez-Graham will set his people on my trail. They'll find me and believe they've found Kandinsky. They'll send me to jail, congratulate one another on their victory, and think they've solved the problem. Kandinsky will remain a hero, an icon of the rebellion against neoliberalism and globalization. You'll disappear for a few months and then reappear on the Net under another identity. Maybe you'll be a disciple of Kandinsky's, someone willing to continue the struggle. You'll recruit people, and the Resistance will rise up out of the ashes. With me in jail as Kandinsky, we'll keep the myth alive, and with you free, your technological prowess will still be at the service of the great cause . . ."

Baez pauses and clears his throat.

"You're looking at me as if I'm crazy. I'm not. Do you think I'm confusing the real world with the virtual world? Not at all. That's why I want to sacrifice myself. That's why I want you to stay alive."

Once Baez has finished talking, Kandinsky is convinced that the plan, as risky as it is improbable, is worthy of his admiration.

For the first time ever, he finds himself in front of someone who he feels is more intelligent and passionate than himself. And the ironic thing is that this person admires *him* and has just used his intelligence and passion to offer *him* an escape route. Kandinsky should really tell him that *he* is the one who should sacrifice himself to let Baez escape.

He does not. He approaches and embraces Baez.

"I hope you'll visit me in jail one day," Baez says. "Using a different identity, of course."

Kandinsky watches Baez's face. A shadow has fallen over it, and there is something tragic that does not match his joking tone of voice.

Two days later, Kandinsky learns of Baez's death during a shootout at the Black Chamber. The media splash color photos of an adolescent Baez and speak of the end of Kandinsky and the dismantling of the Resistance. Montenegro's only victory amid so many recent failures, they say.

Upon seeing the photos, Kandinsky understands what led an anonymous person to choose such a glorious death. He understands better why Baez did everything that he did. There had been a strange mix of arrogance and generosity in his plan. Baez had decided to leave the world by playing God, and while he was at it to create a heroic past, a mythology that would save him from obscurity. Kandinsky is alive, but he feels that his identity has been usurped. He hadn't thought of it like that when he accepted Baez's plan. Perhaps he should have just continued to be Kandinsky — whoever he was — until the end.

There is no time for lamentations. Kandinsky has to think about what to do next. His fingers drum painfully in the air. The first step: go see a specialist.

When he is discharged from a clinic in Santa Cruz with his hands bandaged, he at last feels free to go home to his parents' house. His brother watches him get out of a taxi and come inside with the taxi driver, who is carrying his suitcase. Esteban doesn't stop him; perhaps he has been caught off guard by the determination in Kandinsky's gestures, his decisive steps, his conviction at reclaiming a space that never entirely ceased being his.

Kandinsky will hug his parents and tell them that he has missed them. They will ask about his hands, and he will tell them that he fractured a couple of fingers during a fight. He will set himself up in what was once his room, asking his brother to forgive the intrusion, promising not to bother him. He will roll out his sleeping bag on the floor and take a long nap. When he awakes, he will prepare for more questions during dinner. He had better tell them the truth about his hands; after all, it isn't anything compromising. He will invent an identity like Baez's: he had been certified as a programmer, started to work for the company in charge of Playground, then quit because he felt he was working for the enemy. Poetic justice, after all.

He hopes to stay at his parents' for a few months, at least until he turns twenty-one. He will spend that entire time away from computers, letting his fingers rest. Then he will return to the attack. He has already thought of the name for his new group: KandinskyLives.

Acknowledgments

This novel is a corrected and improved version of the original in Spanish, thanks to the excellent suggestions made by Anton Mueller, my editor at Houghton Mifflin. The entire editorial team is first-rate and I am glad to be part of this publishing house. Lisa Carter worked so hard to achieve an impeccable translation that I will forever be indebted to her. My wife, Tammy, revised the manuscript with me and is my greatest support. Willie Schavelzon, my agent, has always believed in me and gently pushed me when necessary; I thank him and everyone who works with him at the agency for their constant efforts to spread my work.

Every novel needs many books behind it in order to provide texture. I will mention three about cryptanalysis that helped me when writing *Turing's Delirium*: *The Code Book: The Science of Secrecy from Ancient Egypt to Quantum Cryptography* by Simon Singh; *The Codebreakers: The Comprehensive History of Secret Communication from Ancient Times to the Internet* by David Kahn; and *Code Breaking* by Rudolf Kippenhahn.

Ithaca, January 2006